OVER THE EDGE

*To Robbin
aurfin new friend &
Greatest Ouids in Scotland.*

A NOVEL BY

Marc Paul Kaplan

*Marc Paul Kaplan
9/22/16*

KOMENAR
publishing

Disclaimer: This novel is a work of fiction. The places are real, as are the current events of the late Sixties, but the characters are pure invention. The stories and scenes are also fiction, despite any resemblances to Jackson Hole fables.

KOMENAR Publishing and Marc Paul Kaplan are grateful to:

"i sing of Olaf glad and big". Copyright 1931, © 1959, 1991 by the Trustees for the E. E. Cummings Trust. Copyright © 1979 by George James Firmage, from SELECTED POEMS by E. E. Cummings, Introduction & Commentary Richard S. Kennedy. Used by permission of Liveright Publishing Corporation.

Please note that permission to use the poem also states that E. E. Cummings' name will be used as shown here.

Grateful acknowledgement is made to reprint the following:
Bob Woodall for our glorious cover photograph, and Marilyn Kaplan for the photograph of our author.

Cover design by Sioban Bowyer

Interior design by BookMatters

Special book excerpts or customized printings can be created to fit specific needs.

For information, address KOMENAR Publishing, 1756 Lacassie Avenue, Suite 202, Walnut Creek, California 94596-7002.

Library of Congress Cataloging-in-Publication Data available

ISBN 978-0-9772081-6-6 (Trade Paperback)

First Edition

10 9 8 7 6 5 4 3 2 1

Printed in the United States of America

To the women in my life, especially my wife Marilyn,
my mother Bette, and my editor Charlotte, and to my son Matthew,
who, during the writing of this novel, matured into a young man as
impressive as any fictional character I could create.

Author's Notes

I would like to acknowledge and thank the following:

Charlotte and Richard Cook, who provided everything including inspiration, patience, editing, publishing and hand-holding.

Shelly Lowenkopf, book doctor supreme, and Noah benShea, dear friend and author, whose direction and experience were invaluable.

Dennis Marquet, who paid a high price in revisiting his own nightmares.

Ken and Sheri Jern of the Wildflower Inn in Jackson Hole for providing a home base, critical eyes and introductions to many of the area's unique characters.

Pepi Stiegler, Joe Royer and the many Jackson Hole locals whose insights and tall tales gave life to this novel.

The KOMENAR Publishing team of Sioban Bowyer, James Bucci, Anne Fox, Lisa Gallagher, John Randolph, Elisabeth Tuck, and Chelsea Wurms for their hard work and rapid response to problems and challenges.

Peter Handel, Julie Smith, and Cindy Neveu for their valuable support and contributions.

And one clarification: The Wort Hotel of 1969 has little resemblance to the luxurious, well-appointed Wort Hotel of today.

OVER THE EDGE

"Even when the White Dragon sleeps, shit happens."

—Teton proverb

January
1969

ONE

The Corvette rounded the long bluff crowding the highway a half hour from Reno, headed east. Wind ripped at the convertible's soft canvas top. Matthew scanned miles of flat brushland bordered by ranges of white-capped mountains. Vast vistas exposed gun-metal gray sky, supplied no cover for ambush, no traps, no mines. No kaleidoscope of flashing vibrant jungle greens, red earth, blue-to-dead black water. An involuntary release of air burst from Matthew's body, a body stretched far beyond taut.

The world opened wide. No speed limit. No cops. No rearview-mirror fixation. No decisions to make. Just haul ass straight ahead. Here only calming shades of brown and gray filled his head, size and space over-whelming. Peaceful. The word passed through him with an unfamiliar feeling. He rejoiced in the physical connection, the powerful rumble and vibration enhancing his one-hundred-mile-per-hour journey screaming down Route 40.

His hands remained tight around the wooden steering wheel. The great state of Nevada appreciated Man's basic needs. Matthew could focus on the promised, frozen land of Wyoming, so far away from the night-mares of Nam. And so close to what he craved most, to regain control of his life.

Minutes, then hours, passed with no surprises. Time traveled unno-ticed here on the empty wastelands. The impact of solid brown blended into shades—red-magenta earth, yellow-brown grasses, pink, copper, sand. He could almost bring himself to accept the unfamiliar comfort of security.

He rolled down the two windows in the tight cockpit of his Corvette.

Exhilarating, freezing air reinforced relief that had blossomed so suddenly that suspicion filtered its acceptance. No more crippling heat. But foul smells of the past still haunted him.

Matthew checked the gas gauge. Approaching empty, and he needed to pee. Could he make the seventy-five miles to Elko? The Corvette soaked fuel the way sand absorbed water. He'd planned to fill up in Battle Mountain, but the only station had been closed. Matthew twisted and flinched in the seat. Fingers explored scars on his forehead and cheek. He who was in charge would survive. Unknown variables of time and distance chipped away at his sense of control. His stomach tightened.

He descended from his flight across the high desert, dropping from a hundred miles per hour to a more fuel-efficient eighty. Control was the issue. Kicking in the TV screen in the Letterman lounge had cost him another two weeks in hospital hell, clarifying the price of losing control. Only the intercession of Dr. Nordman had gotten him released. Still, if he could survive the firefights of Asia, he could master fuel conservation.

Ten minutes later a break appeared in the patterns of brown. Empty space gave way to rusted clutter. Nothing moved in piles of ancient metal cars, trucks, appliances and so much more. Acres of rubbish in need of a fence. Where had all this crap come from? He picked out a railroad spur on the far side of the junkyard. The mess looked like the garbage of a third-world country. What a waste.

Then the skeleton of a tower for a once-proud Texaco star appeared leaning towards the remains of a two-pump gas station. A small, decaying dirt-beige adobe office squatted nearby. A large, newer sheet-metal-framed garage stood between gas station and junkyard. The only thing that indicated life was the surprising large OPEN sign in the filthy office window. Thanks for small miracles.

Matthew jammed on the brakes and pulled the silver-blue sports car into the space between the two antique pumps and the dying building. A surge of satisfaction. His discomfort dwindled. Gratitude overcame personal embarrassment.

Matthew eased himself out of the Corvette's deep contour seat. A chilling, steady wind slapped his face. The crumbling shack provided some shelter. He straightened up. Scar tissue stretched hot and searing, accompanied by the deep ache of abused muscle and damaged organs. Ever-present pain increased in sharp jolts.

Movement registered near the large garage. Two figures sauntered towards him. The skinny one had his hands in his pockets. Hidden hands stoked the familiar hot rush of aggressive alertness, adrenaline, and fear. Matthew's fingers jerked to his wounded forehead. At least the flow of energy muted the pain.

And these two men looked like evil cartoon characters, sleazy versions of Mutt and Jeff. All Matthew's alarms flashed. But he was in America. Nevada. Two guys to pump gas at a station where a customer was an event? Only took a heartbeat for his new-found control to be compromised.

Matthew worked around to the passenger's side and reached through the open window. The glove compartment sprung open at his touch. Paranoid. He was definitely paranoid. But that alertness had kept him alive, if not in one piece. He pulled out his loaded .38.

The very touch of the weapon wrenched him back in time, warning Matthew of the insanity he had to escape. What the hell was he doing? A gun? Here? Still he slipped the pistol into his parka pocket as he pressed his left side against the car. Frightening how comforting the weapon felt. If only he had a way to get to the .45 under the driver's seat.

"Fill it with premium. Please."

"Only got regular." The nasty nasal sounds came from the smaller, thinner one, hands still hidden in his pockets. "You sure that little piece of crap takes gas, or you want us to just wind it up?"

"Just fill it," Matthew said, this time omitting "please" from his answer.

The fat one grabbed the nozzle and reached for the gas cap. The other one spun a key in the face of the pump. Definitely a two-man job.

Matthew moved slow and steady to the edge of the adobe shack. His hand maintained a comforting grip on the pocketed pistol as he walked around to the back. He faced the wide-open barren expanse, unzipped his pants and peed. His hand shook only a little.

Ridges and small depressions filled the benign brown landscape. Possible cover for danger, for unpleasant surprises, for ambushes? He played out in his mind potential attacks from behind, the necessary responses. Maybe these wide-open spaces weren't the safe flatlands that had brought him comfort on the drive. Maybe things went to hell here as fast as they did in Nam.

He zipped up his pants and continued around the old building instead of retreating the way he had come. He stopped at the other corner. Fat Jeff leaned into the passenger-side window of his car. Skinny Mutt, ten feet in front of the Corvette, peered around the far corner waiting for Matthew to reappear. Suspicions substantiated. The bastards. At least the nozzle clicked off fuel.

A white flash flamed within him. Anger. Rage. Reflex action. The flight-or-fight response fused into an instant plan of attack.

Matthew ran to the car and kicked Jeff's fat ass as hard as he could. The man's oversized body jammed forward into the window opening, his legs flailing inches above the ground. Mutt, the thin one, wheeled into the barrel of Matthew's .38.

"It's loaded," Matthew snarled. "You don't get your hands out of your pockets, it'll soon be empty."

He was in combat mode, ready to kill, overprimed. Instinct said shoot first. But his heartbeat drummed out a call for reason. Please. Please don't go over the edge.

The thin one hesitated. Matthew fired. Something, probably the genesis of civilized reaction, jerked his aim to the side. Dirt exploded next to the thin man. Skinny Mutt's hands were in the air long before the dust settled. A surge of relief swept through Matthew at the man's reaction.

Then he grabbed the pants hanging from the fat man's wiggling ass and jerked him out of the car window. He slammed the man, face first, on the frozen ground, and drove his knee into the broad back. The crack of a breaking rib caught him by surprise. Too bad. He kept his pistol aimed at the thin man, now a statue, face as gray as the sky.

"Lie face down."

Matthew pointed to a spot next to the moaning fat man. The thin one jerked himself into movement and bellyflopped next to his buddy. Matthew frisked first the fat one, then the other, confused when he found only small jack-knives.

The white light within Matthew faded. He struggled for calm and waited for the gas pump to kick off. It did at $9.65. He dropped a ten-dollar bill on the fat man's back and the tension in his shoulders eased.

"Keep the change."

Matthew retreated to the driver's side, the gun aimed at the backs of the two prone men. He climbed in, adrenaline rush receding just enough to allow pain to resurface. He started the car and leaned over towards the passenger window. He couldn't see the bodies, but fired two shots into the adobe wall. The resulting positive rush jolted his body, rationalized as added persuasion to keep them from moving. But his schizoid mind registered the truth —he'd pulled the trigger for the hell of it.

*   *   *

What the fuck was he doing here?

Franky's wafer-thin kidskin loafers served as direct conduits for the chill surging up his legs. The camel-hair overcoat gave some protection. But the lightweight driving gloves were as worthless as his sheer wool Armani suit. They only allowed him to better grasp the .357 Magnum that tugged his right coat pocket down towards the ground.

None of this made sense. The freezing, garlic-laced air, the foul-smelling dumpster, the gun and the hulking man beside him, were his whole world. And everything was wrong.

Franky Fiorini wasn't trained for murder. Certainly neither college nor a goddamn M.B.A. had prepared him. Even inclusion within his father's organization fell far short of providing insight into why he crouched, crammed behind the metal garbage container with the massive goon Anthony.

And Anthony just stood there, immobile. Towering over Franky. Impervious to the brutality of this Manhattan winter. Crowding Franky in this cramped, squalid space at the rear of Luigi's Italian Trattoria. Franky's brothers' trap with no escape.

The battered rear door of the restaurant opened a crack, followed by the sharp jab of Anthony's finger into Franky's shoulder. Then a fat, greasy face poked through the door's opening. The balding head, backlit from the kitchen, swiveled, checking all directions of the alley. The nervous man bumbled into the dark corridor. Much movement with minimal progress. Pathetic.

Anthony shoved Franky from behind the dumpster. He staggered forward. The force of the push propelled Franky to within a few feet of the frantic figure. The doomed man's knees buckled and smacked to the hard asphalt. A woeful moan echoed against the filthy brick walls. Sounds bubbled unintelligibly from the cowering mound. Words so full of spit they sounded underwater. Pleas of mercy most likely. Better that Franky couldn't understand.

The huge, ugly pistol seemed to levitate out of Franky's pocket. He aimed the Magnum at the middle of the man's forehead. The victim's eyes looked bovine, a cow ready for slaughter—a sacrificial calf. A giggle escaped Franky's lips. He tried to swallow. He was losing control. Sweat somehow formed despite the crackling cold.

The weight of the alien object in his hand brought him back to the stinking alley. His finger gripped the trigger, squeezing. Nothing happened. Seconds passed, time creeping towards eternity. He couldn't do it. The fact slammed Franky with the finality of judgment day.

Then the crushing grip of Anthony's hand. Franky's finger forced against the trigger. The shocking explosion of the .357 with its blinding flash. Warm fluid soaked Franky's crotch.

"Once more." Anthony's harsh, guttural voice floated disembodied out of the void. "For insurance."

Steam rose between Franky's legs. The smell of his urine mixed with the thick odor of death and waste. His hold on the gun tightened. He pulled off another round into the inert body on the unforgiving concrete. This time, to Franky's surprise, he had no problem. He had disconnected.

TWO

Ten miles from the Texaco station, Matthew checked his rearview mirror. Nothing except a gathering storm to the west, chasing him across the plains. And a growing, frightening awareness. He had again overreacted, bringing him close, too close, to murder and a new set of nightmares. Over what? Two rude country bumpkins pumping gas in the middle of nowhere?

An uncontrollable and unwelcome tide of anxiety swept through him. No rhythm, just the erratic gravitational pull from an irrational, evil Asian moon.

Murder in Viet Nam had been part of the job description. No accountability in war, no penalty. Hell, killing had become an acceptable and expected response, mandatory for survival, rewarded with continued life. He swallowed an acid taste, the burning sensation sinking to his gut.

If he didn't get his act together soon, he'd end up in jail. He had to leave the haunting images behind. That goddamn shrink had warned him, "If I see your ass again, it's over." The other Army doctors had told him time would heal his wounds, diminish his dreams. Well, how much time? And what had just happened was no dream. Jesus, he was shaking now, big time.

Towns named Dunn's Glen, Mote, and Deeth did little to fill the welcome absence of humanity. Neither did the barely perceptible climb over the 5,100-foot Galgonda Summit or the drop into the Pumpernickel Valley leading to Elko. Who the hell had named these places? Drugs or alcohol must have played a part. Still, the empty highway and open spaces calmed Matthew.

Downtown Elko. He slowed. Available hookers not more than two blocks from the main drag. Could he still perform? A whore would have to overlook his embarrassing scars. Perhaps even pretend he was normal. Or would even she recoil from his ugly body? Laugh at his possible impotence? He accelerated out of town, loving the freedom of driving.

Imprisoned in a hospital bed, submerged in agony, he had often wondered if he would ever again experience the freedom and ecstasy of high speed. Choices. Control. And here he was. Too nervous and superstitious to allow complete acceptance of his realized dream.

He hoped he was headed towards something better. A simplistic ideal. He wanted to be a whole man again, to look in the mirror without flinching. Not a man who traded honor and integrity for survival. Who had only questions. Despite the sensual pleasure of speed, the calming Nevada badlands, and crystal-clean air, he knew self-respect lay at the end of a long and possibly infinite journey.

Matthew felt like a fugitive in his own country. He had been trapped, forced to fight, engulfed in a disintegration of moral standards by stupid, self-serving politicians and chicken-shit generals. He no longer asked himself, Why me?

But was he a danger to society? Evidently. He understood his anger, sadness, and loss of self-respect. They could be internalized. But the rage and his hard-earned ability to wreak havoc even in his weakened and damaged condition was what frightened him. How easily he had failed the simplest of tests back at the gas station. What would happen at the next test?

A Nevada Highway Patrol sedan, heading west, flew past. Apprehension swept through him as he watched the car shrink towards Elko. No reason to be concerned, speeding not a problem. But had Mutt and Jeff made a call to the state police? If so, the passing cop would have little trouble identifying his silver-blue rocket ship.

Matthew glued his eyes to the rearview mirror. Did he see the flash of a red light? The Corvette jumped to 125. The demand of high speed cleansed his mind for a moment. Matthew now had to focus on staying on the blacktop.

The hamlet of Wells, Nevada, rushed into view. Decision time. Fly straight down U.S. 40 to Salt Lake or turn north to Twin Falls as planned. His heart pounded. Adrenaline flowed from an inexhaustible pool. He may be flawed and dangerous, but he'd paid too high a price to end up in a cowboy jail this soon. And the horror of a return to Letterman loomed as great as any nightmare from Viet Nam.

Easy choice. Ninety percent of the traffic would head on to Utah. Matthew braked as hard as he could without screeching. He didn't see a soul in Wells. He made a semicivilized left turn at the deserted crossroad and blasted towards Idaho. Matthew kept his eyes on the road.

Wells disappeared as he clung tight to a sweeping curve on the narrow road. Maybe he had slipped his sports car unnoticed through town. He glanced as often as possible for the telltale red flash of a pursuing patrol car. Didn't matter. He was now committed to a rapid advance north.

THREE

Franky fumbled with the crumpled material at the bottom of the metal bucket. An uncontrollable desperation drove him to destroy last night's soiled garments. A fire flamed three feet away in the impractical miniscule fireplace. Gasoline fumes induced growing nausea. His senses revolted at memories of the disgusting alley, his reaction accentuated by the absence of sleep. His blood had turned to sludge. Things had gone to hell overnight, literally.

Anthony had dropped him at the small two-story brownstone in Jersey he shared with his mother and demanded the gun. Said he'd dispose of the weapon. You didn't argue with Anthony. Now his brothers would have a priceless piece of blackmail to chain Franky to their dangerous, idiotic plans.

He squeezed excess flammable liquid from his dress shirt, the remaining garment, then tossed the tight ball into the flames. Everything he'd worn last night now flared brightly in the miniature pyre. Except for the expensive camel-hair coat. There were limits.

He'd had to wait in bed until his mother left. Now he'd be late for work. He had watched through his bedroom window as his mother's slight figure, wrapped in her ugly gray coat and ridiculous pink wool hat, drifted into an unforgiving morning and her daily Confessional. Pity muted his anger. Pity, and not empathy. He knew the difference. Now the old questions: Did he feel obligated to care for her? For how long? Forever?

* * *

Sarah slipped out the door, bounced down the steps, and hit the sidewalk in a slow jog. The wintry blast off Lake Michigan had filtered unimpeded to her crumbling neighborhood. She trotted into the wind, down the deserted streets. No gradual awakening or warm-up at 5:30 A.M. Immediate entry into exercise forced the flow of blood into her sore legs and grateful lungs. Wednesday was Day Three of her five-day run week, always the toughest.

Her footsteps slapped flat on the cement in the comforting quiet of the early morning. Her thin-soled, men's Adidas required thick, wool socks to fill the excess width. Couldn't someone make a decent woman's running shoe? That would be the day.

Hat, mittens, and sweats hid her tight body from the occasional stare of one of the City's perpetual garbage collectors. Some still waved, others ignored her presence as they would a destitute, homeless soul on permanent Night Patrol. That served Sarah's purposes just fine. She'd attempted an afternoon/evening running routine and been harassed into crack-of-dawn peacefulness. The change had transformed the loneliness of her life at that hour into a temporary, comforting solitude during the calm morning runs. If only an equally easy solution existed for dealing with the ham-handed advances of her son-of-a-bitch boss.

She trudged down Lemon Street, following her usual route. The darkness of winter signaled the imminent reward for months of sweat and pain: Ski season, a return to Jackson Hole. Her pace quickened at the thought of her scheduled two-week passage to paradise at the end of February. She would be one flatlander who came to the mountains ready for the physical challenge.

She turned right on Rush Street. Steam from her breath was now visible, not stripped from her lips by the wind's harsh, head-on gusts. She nodded to the skinny banker pictured on the tattered poster advertising the Chicago Trust.

The faded, torn image always reminded her of Bruce Cohan. He had run cross-country for Loyola and provided indirect inspiration for her running career. She had run with him out of desperation. Anything for a date. He'd turned out to be gay. But she'd kept running through college, never looking back. She'd been viewed as a freak even then.

The corner of Rush and Detroit appeared out of the gloom. The three-mile halfway mark so soon? She performed her usual pirouette around the thick lamppost and headed home. Strange how the same distance expanded and contracted, depending on her mood.

Traffic picked up. She accelerated through the awakening city, cruising with the wind at her back. Comments from curious, early-morning commuters became more common. Intervals of speed had to suffice to simulate the extra effort of hills or the stadium steps of her earlier running routines.

A piercing wolf whistle bounced off her back. She considered turning around. One look at her large red nose and long chin framed by her homely knit ski cap would shut him up. Just like the Mad Magazine cartoon picturing the rear view of a voluptuous blond, who turned to present a mirror-shattering ugliness of buckteeth, pimples and crossed eyes. At least she wasn't that bad. And next week she'd be picking up her vacation tickets to Jackson Hole, where even she would be a star.

FOUR

Matthew stepped out of the plywood cell numbered four at the Homestead Motel halfway between Twin Falls and Pocatello. Last night, visibility had disappeared with the swirling snow and onset of evening. The low-slung, cracker-box motel had been as welcome as the Ritz in the blinding blizzard.

His previous night's workout had generated enough body heat to risk a quick shower before bed. Quick was the operative word. The hot water couldn't have lasted more than three minutes. Still Matthew showered every night. He had to. Each night's shower took him another step from war and fear. Weeks of sweat and filth, sleeping in slime and mud, never caring to even scrape the crap off his hands had generated a reaction that necessitated cleanliness. One night without a shower and he might wake up back in Hell.

Matthew crunched through several feet of new snow toward the unnamed coffee shop next door. The early morning sun's brilliant reflection magnified a world gone stark white. Life was too bright, too sharp, with no place to hide, no comfort zone. He could only stagger until his eyes focused. He pushed through the well-worn door of the blunt, flat bungalow that had to be a relative of the Homestead Motel and stepped into a swirl of warmth and breakfast smells. A definite improvement.

He ordered bacon, eggs, potatoes, and toast with lots of coffee from a cheerful, petite lady. She twirled around the tight space, handling the entire operation of cooking and serving the several small tables and stools. A clanging bell on the door kept up a nerve-jangling notification of each customer's entry and exit.

A large, unshaven farmer plunked his ample rear end on an adjacent stool, passing over two vacant ones further to the left. Why so close? Proximity fueled unease, even anger. Rage again stirred, and again out of proportion to the event. Matthew rose to relocate as his order arrived. So he sat back down and ignored the man, as well as a two-hundred-and-fifty-pound mass could be ignored.

The quality of the food was a pleasant surprise. He inhaled his breakfast, having missed dinner last night. Then, to the obvious delight of the cook, he doubled down on a duplicate order. Sitting on the unsupported perch of the hard stool intensified the pain. But his hunger and pleasure in breakfast, at least for the moment, masked the eternal discomfort, even with the proximity of his unwelcome neighbor.

Matthew had tracked the concept of pain levels through weeks and months. The First Level proved most terrifying. Immersed in wave after wave of maximum agony, he had cried out for peace. Even begged for instant death. Only the appearance of Dr. John Nordman, a newly minted surgeon serving his military time perfecting his trade at Letterman Hospital in San Francisco, had saved him. And there'd been no shortage of on-the-job material for the good doctor. Letterman was the primary depository of the carnage that was Viet Nam. Dr. Nordman had helped pull Matthew to the next level.

That Second Level of pain defined the point where life could be considered an equal option to death. He became a prisoner to the songs on the radios of his companions-in-suffering. Music he couldn't turn off marked the passage of time. The repetition—Janis, Jimmy and "Hey, Jude"—would now precipitate violence. But hope had showed up.

The second breakfast order arrived. Matthew plowed into his bacon and eggs. Once again the pleasure of eating sidetracked his discomfort. Too soon his plate emptied, his mind jerked back to pain.

Level Three had featured agonizing rehab, a return of sanity, iron discipline and a fierce, angry determination. But guilt, doubt, and bitterness also accompanied Level Three. Through all the misery, a plan developed. Head for the mountains, far away from the jungles and rice paddies. Once again Dr. Nordman came to the rescue, arranging a place to stay in Wyoming with his brother, Jim.

The actual absence of all pain seemed as improbable as Joe Namath and the upstart New York Jets winning next week's Super Bowl. He tipped off the stool, his movement rousing the hulk beside him. They both rose and moved in awkward concert to the register. The woman handed Matthew his bill first, ignoring the farmer. Matthew paid.

"Take care, young man." The lady's sweet voice and smile caught Matthew by surprise.

"Thanks," he said, and meant it.

Back outside, Matthew walked to his Corvette, cleared the snow off the windows, unlocked the door and started the engine. A good sign. The Corvette belonged in snow like a bear in the city. Enough powder had been moved around in the small parking lot to allow Matthew to slip-slide out to the highway.

Only two hundred miles to Jackson Hole, but today's road was as changed as the day. Yesterday's solid, stable ribbon of asphalt had become a treacherous surface of snow and black ice, dangers often invisible on the roadway. The piercing sun, accentuated by the one hundred percent, blue-bird sky, brought nothing but a headache. Now, on a snow-covered Idaho highway, his father's gift of fantasy wheels felt as unstable as Matthew's self-respect.

His lovely Corvette, the vessel that had sped him to a different world on a straight secure path, now became an accident waiting to happen. He crept down the highway, acknowledging insecurity under his tires, building his speed to sixty and tentatively holding it. He left Pocatello. Braille his operative driving technique. Like many things in Matthew's life, something positive had turned treacherous and evil.

Then his rearview mirror filled with a startling, huge, black truck. A gigantic black grill to be more precise. A painful, flashing surge of electric energy almost jerked him off the road. The surprise appearance of the massive machine had the same effect as an unexpected mortar.

And the goddamn truck pulled out to pass him.

Big tires kicked up chunks of snow and ice that assaulted his windshield as the black monster pulled in front of him after an effortless pass. How could anyone handle the deadly conditions of this road at such high speeds? The chemical surge in Matthew's body turned to anger. He instinctively accelerated. Wrong move. The car's rear end began swinging. The fiberglass body whipped from one side of the road to the other like a huge pendulum, fishtailing out of control. The car smashed against the right snowbank, a thick, white veil of moisture sweeping across the windshield, the blinding powder thick and impervious. Just like the damn tule fog he'd left behind—a solid, chilling mist rising from the rich valley earth of Northern California.

An overpowering memory. A desperate, twilight-zone dash through smothering, low-hanging fog and rush-hour traffic, his father clutching at his heart on the seat beside Matthew. The gigantic, white El Dorado had rocked and swayed like an overpowered whale, taking them to the hospital in time. His dad too tough to die. Had the Corvette been a gift of thanks?

The car represented his only positive connection to the past. Was it about to be destroyed? The snapping motion of the car cleared the blanket of snow from the windshield. Matthew clung to the wheel, reducing his speed, pumping a little gas to maintain some traction. The wide arcs lessened, and Matthew regained control. Control. He swallowed hard. Yet another reminder of how close to the edge he traveled.

Where the hell was that son-of-a-bitch truck? The black pickup was half a mile down the road and pulling away. The image seared into Matthew's mind: Large and black with oversized tires, an easy-to-identify green-and-yellow Wyoming license plate with its distinctive cowboy and bucking bronco, and gun rack with rifle in the cab's rear window. Maybe a Ford or Chevy, but definitely customized.

The bastard had almost killed him, then was gone. No way Matthew's pretty little plaything was going to catch him. Or her. Only an empty, disconcerting feeling remained, reinforced by a residue of unused adrenaline. How quickly things changed.

FIVE

Franky wedged himself into the cushions in the far corner of the over-stuffed sofa. Heavy burgundy velvet drapes framed two sets of windows, the glass covered with exterior black metal security grilles. His father's large office reminded Franky of a stage set from a gothic production of *Hamlet* or *Antigone*.

Two nights without sleep supplied a numbing anesthetic against the barrage of questions, fears, and doubts of last night's hit. But he couldn't shake the smell of his own piss, steaming into his nostrils. The nightmare image of a terrified, sweat-sheened face merged with exhaustion. Never had he expected to participate in the family business at this level.

Franky rubbed his hands together. He glanced at the heavy furniture surrounding Dominick Fiorini's uncharacteristic nod to frivolous expenditures, a massive, ornate Louis XIV desk. The broad, clean surface floated in the office, an aircraft carrier filling a fish pond. Franky never felt comfortable in the family's nerve center and occasional bunker.

The lacquered door burst open to an avalanche of noise and motion. Big brother Sal led the charge, followed by his other mutant, massive sibling, Marco. Then came Roberto, the consigliore, and the two capos, Thomas and Gino. "Consigliore" and "capo," the terms ridiculous imitations for the wannabe Mafia gang. Franky gave his best imitation of invisibility. All of them ignored him—invisible must be working.

Sal pounded around the room. Marco orbited the heir apparent in clumsy, tight circles, an outsized moon to Sal's angry planet. Roberto sat in counterpoint to the threatened chaos. The two thugs, Thomas and Gino, also sat still. Their tight expressions reflected nervousness, probably at the brothers' reckless lack of control.

What a breakdown in genetic lineage between the crafty, emotionless father and his two older sons. And Franky carried those fake mobsters on his shoulders. His intelligence and education provided them an avenue to escape the gutter. They in turn ridiculed their savior. He was at the mercy of violent men who had no clue. Goddamn animals.

"'Bout time you got your skinny ass back here," Sal said, acknowledging Franky.

What crap. Franky burrowed deeper into the couch. At first he'd wondered why Sal had demanded an early return from a well-earned, ten-day vacation in Colorado. Quick checks revealed no operational problems in the three companies he controlled. Maybe Sal was just flexing his new-found power. Unfortunately, the jerk had to be obeyed, the consequences of defiance terminal.

"Finally get a job for you," Sal continued, "and you're a thousand miles away."

Two thousand, you geographically ignorant ape. But that was where the danger lay. Sal was far from stupid. He possessed an unpredictable intelligence hidden behind a vicious surface. The inability to predict Sal's reactions left Franky perpetually frightened and defensive. Probably Sal's intention.

The older brother swiveled and caught Franky in a malevolent glare. Franky froze. How much of last night's details had Anthony shared? Based on Sal's continued disrespectful attitude towards Franky, Sal knew everything.

"Why the hell," Sal's voice boomed, "do you go to the freezing, fuckin' Rockies in the middle of winter? You want snow? Go to Central Park. If you didn't have shit for brains, ya'd head to Florida or the Caribbean."

Franky kept his stare neutral and passive, taking in Sal's dense, dark eyebrows protruding like awnings over the black stones serving as eyes. The two of them, Sal and Marco, though different heights, would always be recognized as siblings, sharing Neanderthal features and thick bodies. Little resemblance to Franky or their old man. Must be the mothers. His skinny and meek, theirs loud and robust. And ugly. No wonder Pops screwed around back in the days he could still get it up.

"Cat got your tongue, Franky?" Sal prodded.

Sal looked civilized in black turtleneck, gray flannel pants, and blue blazer, a respectable fashion plate. Hell, Franky had taught him how to dress. But the smooth veneer mocked the true man. One step from the jungle. Death and destruction only a comment away. How Franky wished he could physically respond to his brother's taunts. Crush the asshole before it was too late.

Franky still cringed at their failed attempt to carve out a small drug distribution territory. Sal, this accident-waiting-to-happen, controlled and endangered Franky's life. And the bastard had now coerced him into murder.

"Let's get down to business," Roberto said.

Sal landed on the front corner of the antique desk, conspicuously avoiding Dominick Fiorini's empty chair, emphasizing the unsettled, uncomfortable atmosphere of the stuffy chamber. Marco took the cue and leaned back against the wall next to the mortuary-inspired drapes.

"Sal, if I may proceed?" Roberto nodded with respect at the wild animal perched on the edge of the Louis XIV.

"Sure," Sal answered.

"Franky," Roberto said, "thanks for returning so promptly."

Unlike the brothers, Roberto openly respected Franky's business expertise. Sal gave him no credit for tripling cash flow in only five and a half years. Franky appreciated the business manager for his backing, but he kept his thanks silent. Undue attention meant destruction if Sal felt threatened.

"Come on, Roberto," Sal fired back. "The little college boy don't do shit around here of any importance. He's got all the time in the world."

Why'd the guy hide his own almost three years at Florida State? Maybe he'd really spent that time in the Florida State Penitentiary.

"There are a number of issues we need to address," Roberto continued. He gave another acquiescent nod to Sal. His handsome, well-proportioned features stood in stark contrast to Sal and Marco.

Roberto reviewed the various operational activities in subdued, precise words, covering everything from murder and mayhem to money management. The report, perfunctorily laid out, was a prelude to more important news. The meeting followed the familiar format of a family conference, another attempt at imitating the real deal. The less said about last night the better. Franky tried to block out his nightmare, dreaming of powder and pussy left behind in Aspen. A change in Roberto's tone regained Franky's attention.

"Dominick's latest appeal will be heard the first of February. I don't like the government's preliminary moves that the judge allowed. We've been unable to discredit the evidence illegally presented by our unknown turncoat. Your father is not happy in Leavenworth."

Franky, as well as Roberto, had been shocked when the government had pounced on the elder Fiorini. Their operation was small potatoes. Why pick on the little guy with many more obvious and prestigious targets available?

"That motherfucker's gonna die," Marco growled, pushing off the wall. "We gotta find him. Make an example."

"Well, we may be making some progress." Roberto's voice somehow remained calm, overpowering the riptide of emotion from Sal and Marco. "The Feds have a new system to hide individuals in danger, those foolish souls who have cooperated with the government. It's called the Witness Protection Program. Our friend appears to be one of their first customers."

"How are we going to find him?" Franky's first contribution of the evening. "We've got no grease."

"Don't worry, little man," Marco threatened. "We're gonna find that bastard and rip him to shreds."

"The program's new," Roberto continued. "We've received an offer of assistance from an interested party with far more resources than ours. Even they are having trouble piercing the shield of secrecy. But we'll soon be successful."

"Not soon enough." Sal pounded the thousand-dollar-desk like a cheap drum. "That pecker-head's makin' us look like wimps. I wanta cut his nuts off."

Sal could deliver on his promise if given the opportunity. No one in their truncated world of crime crossed Sal and lived. And they didn't die well either. But who was this interested party? What the hell had Franky gotten himself into with his headstrong return to his roots?

SIX

Matthew swerved into the small turnout at the summit of the 8,500-foot Teton Pass and stared straight down into what had been advertised as the wide-open spaces of Jackson Hole. Where was the view? His escape had turned into a circle. He'd left the San Francisco Bay Area engulfed in a depressing blanket of fog. He'd worked his way through the Sierras and across Donner Summit in low-hanging, snow-blowing winter clouds. Now a murky gray sea of fog filled the valley. Frustration generated anger, which in turn produced pain. His muscles knotted and spasmed. This was bullshit. He wasn't going down there.

The light vibration from the engine lulled him further from action. But spectacular vistas and peaks rimmed the fog-shrouded Hole, a tantalizing temptation to journey down into the unknown. He couldn't sit here at the top of the Teton Pass much longer.

The steep road down promised little comfort. He glanced up at the mighty avalanche chutes to his left, the Twin and Shovel Slides, frightening forces of nature that had scoured the mountainside clean of all vegetation. The edge of the even more murderous Glory Slide beckoned a short distance below the summit. How could this route be open to traffic? But where else could he go? He had no other plan.

Matthew reached the valley floor at Wilson. The Stagecoach Bar stood out from the few buildings that comprised the small town. Matthew parked the car at the side of the road and again experienced the misery of unwrapping himself from the Corvette to remove his tire chains.

Jackson Hole cold slammed him. His lungs froze in mid-breath. The lining of his nose contracted. His eyes watered, but no moisture survived to reach his cheeks. His lightweight clothes were as worthless as tissue paper. Frigid shock folded him right back into the car. The hell with the chains. Inevitably the links would break, wreaking havoc on the fiberglass wheel wells of his car. They could mangle the car all they wanted. He didn't give a damn.

Looking north up the valley, he picked out images of the Teton Range, emerging from what turned out to be only a thin layer of low-lying clouds. Some consolation, if he didn't feel like an emotional rag doll. Still, even at this angle, the mystic peaks stood out against the murky sky.

*   *   *

The car crunched the short distance to the road that led to Moose and the ski resort at Teton Village. He made the left turn and eased towards mountains that rose out of the flat valley haze like the city of Oz. An irregular border of barren aspens and frozen fir trees lined the way. Little other traffic distracted him. He focused on the view ahead and almost missed the large moose with its calf chewing branches ten feet from the road.

Matthew turned left down a plowed driveway across the street from a deserted KOA Campground, halfway to Teton Village. The small road opened up into a rectangular parking lot one hundred yards from the highway and across a snow-filled creek.

The Grand View Lodge sat at the end of the flat area, two stories, constructed of thick lodge-pole pine, gleaming even in the gathering gloom. A small, ancient log cabin squatted on the side of the lot nearest to the highway, close to the corner of the lodge. The structure, weathered to a dark brown, stood in stark contrast to the clean light wood of the newly completed Grand View.

Matthew put on his gloves and ski hat for the short walk to the large, varnished front door. A feminine hand-painted sign by the doorbell invited a visitor to ring the bell and step inside. Matthew followed the instructions and entered. A hallway of polished planks greeted him.

Matthew moved down the hall towards an inviting open space. A large woman appeared. She waited in the two-story-high living room. Light from a bank of floor-to-ceiling picture windows cascaded over her head and shoulders. Matthew snatched off his hat and stared at the goddess. This had to be Jim's wife, Julia Nordman.

Her huge breasts dominated his vision. Matthew raised his eyes with great difficulty to a beautiful face so unreal it lacked life. Flawless creamy skin stretched over a broad forehead and high cheekbones. Her luscious, full lips could swallow a man, yet were proportional to her impressive head. Long, thick blond hair draped below her shoulders. Ice-blue eyes held light but little depth. They were the disconcerting element in an otherwise perfect picture. Her eyes broke his trance. He took the last several steps into the living room.

"Matthew Green?" A slight smile changed little of the overpowering effect of her face.

"Yes," Matthew answered, extending his hand and grasping hers. Calluses and rough skin evidenced ungoddesslike work. "What a beautiful place."

Large, comfortable furniture and sturdy log tables filled the room. An iron buck stove stood in front of an interior wall of river rock, masterfully fitted to minimize grout lines. A glass-enclosed porch with plants and hot tub paralleled the large windows.

Magazines on the log tables lay in tight, measured formation. Stone-cold river rock overpowered the space. Every surface shone, immaculate, every piece of furniture positioned at perfect angles. But the staged setting chilled the room. Even dust motes fled to the perimeters.

"It's wonderful to have a guest, Matthew. You're the first one since Christmas week. Even though you'll be renting our old cabin, I hope you'll have meals with us." Julia swept her hand over a spotless end table. "Our prime booking period is in the summer. I'm afraid the winters will be very quiet. Lonely." Her voice became wistful, her smile lightly touching her incredible features. "A bed-and-breakfast needs guests."

Her words, empty of expression, left Matthew uneasy. Her unnerving beauty made him conscious of his sexual inadequacies. Why couldn't she be a fat, homely hostess, a surrogate mother? He had enough confusion and gaps. And he definitely was in no mood to chit chat.

"I appreciate your offer," he answered. "Would you mind showing me the cabin?"

Julia slipped on a coat the size of a sleeping bag. She led Matthew into the two-car garage attached to the kitchen, then out a side door that opened close to the old one-room cabin. Julia hesitated at the cabin door, her eyes resting on the Corvette.

"What a gorgeous little car," she said.

An unexpected look of sadness tinted the smooth features of her face. Her disconnected speech and movements distanced the effect of her beauty, making her both more approachable and yet projecting a melancholy aura. Then she pushed her way through the unlocked entry. Matthew shook his head, not sure what to make of his gorgeous, spacey landlady.

Matthew didn't know what he'd expected from his new home, but the warmth generated by a baseboard heater on the far wall was a relief. A single bed, narrow chest of drawers, small table, two wooden chairs, and stove with two burners and an oven filled the tight space. A large rock fireplace took up one wall. An alcove held a toilet, skinny shower, and vanity that doubled as a kitchen sink. Hard to believe that Julia and her husband, Jim, had lived here for almost two years. Matthew would have loved to see Julia cram her outsized body into the miniature shower.

"Please call me if you need anything at all."

Julia's soft monotone promised less than her words. Was her understated offer sincere? How could he function around such a spectral distraction?

* * *

Alone but content, Matthew unloaded the car. It didn't take long. He had brought little: A portable stereo, medium-size box of albums, one suitcase with toiletries, and basic clothes. A new life required leaving the past one behind.

He had also left his old boots and skis. The boards wouldn't have fit in the car anyway. His first move would be to buy warmer clothes, the weather being nonnegotiable. On his last trip to the Corvette, he picked up a small cardboard box his mother had begged him to take on his journey. In ten minutes he distributed his meager possessions and set up his stereo.

He turned to the battered box, hesitant to open the brown flaps. What the hell, better now than later. Four large manila envelopes labeled "Early Years," "Skylake Camp," "High School" and "College/Military" sat on top of some framed diplomas and wooden plaques. Matthew fingered through the envelopes, curious about their contents.

For over an hour Matthew explored the life of someone who had become a stranger. A newspaper clipping dated January 7, 1945. World War II on all fronts, but the end in sight. An auspicious day to be born? The first four chapters of a book, *Trip to Mars*, primitive long hand on graying lined paper, dated 1955. Fifteen small pages, then nothing. Characters abandoned, waiting for gas on the moon.

Report cards and SAT scores—unimpressive. Pictures of a boy evolving from a small child with huge, distorting glasses to a handsome smiling face on a ski trip to Aspen during college. A photo in Boot Camp, still the shadow of a boy lingers.

The lure of the bed fed his fatigue, tried to seduce him away from his discoveries. But nightmare monsters lurked beneath unconsciousness. He fought to keep his eyes open, turning back to the contents of the envelopes.

Many letters. Childlike scrawling from summer camp, bragging, and asking for cookies. Letters from college, well-written. Send money. Then a letter from Boot Camp, "I have been ordered to write… things aren't as bad as I thought, but damn near." More letters, but the messages too close to the pain.

Matthew could go no farther. He couldn't relate to the memories of this other person. Privileged and protected. Interesting, but he felt no emotional connection. Matthew lay down on his new bed and hoped without conviction for no dreams, unable to resist the pull of exhaustion.

An album by the Byrds filled the small space with the ambiguous words of "Turn, Turn, Turn." He'd lived through the seasons of killing, mourning, hate, and war. He awaited the promise of "peace, I swear it's not too late."

SEVEN

The night was stone black. Chaos erupted on all sides. Matthew rolled on the jungle floor grasping for his rifle, ready to fire. But his M16 was gone. That made no sense. He and his weapon were inseparable, gun cradled or strapped to his body when moving, eating, sleeping, shitting.

Automatic weapons, mortars and grenades rocked the clearing. The roar of battle intensified. He thrashed in the wet dirt and slippery brush for his rifle. Bullets and smoke filled the air. Moist earth and liquids drenched his body. Rain? Sweat? Blood?

Where was his patrol? Where was Bull? How could he be alone? Moments ago they had been together in the protection of their wheel, the six of them back to back. And Bull would never leave his side. He followed Matthew like a faithful mastiff.

Matthew panicked, accelerating his spastic search for his weapon. Still no rifle. He grabbed for his .45. Shit, he had lost that too. Impossible. Despair flamed as bright as the brilliant bursts of the fire fight surrounding him.

Grenades were his last hope. He ripped one from his web belt, jerked the pin and lofted it blindly into the dense, putrid foliage. Nothing. A dud. He grabbed another, same result. Then another, until there were no more. Worthless, fucking worthless. He clamped his hands over his face. Tears of frustration carved crevices through his filth-encrusted cheeks.

The crashing of bodies in the underbrush closed within feet of Matthew's position. Rage. Defeat. Nothing to fight with. Alone. His patrol must be dead. All of them gone. The battle reached a deafening crescendo.

A huge explosion of light tossed him into the thick air. He landed on his back, swallowed by pain. Matthew opened his eyes to greet death.

*　*　*

The light of the ceiling fixture blazed in his face. Matthew lay on his back on the floor's thin carpet by the single bed. Sweat soaked his too-light clothing. His body throbbed. His heart raced. Still a chill crept through him. And a large figure stood framed in the doorway.

"Matthew, you all right?" the man asked. A soft, tentative voice incongruous with the size of the body.

Matthew lay still, stunned. Nightmares weren't new. Still, he was unprepared for their violent effect on his system. He would never be prepared.

"I was getting wood by the garage. You were screaming, swearing." The voice was firmer, but not yet committed. "I'm Jim Nordman."

Matthew couldn't respond, but his inaction seemed to give the larger man more confidence.

"Can I help you up?" Jim asked.

"I'm okay," Matthew answered, his voice hoarse.

Matthew felt vulnerable on the floor, like a turtle on its back. He rolled onto his knees and struggled to his feet. He stood for several minutes in the middle of the room, putting himself back into the present. His clothes hung too loose and large on his gaunt, six-foot body. Jim remained awkwardly by the door.

"That baseboard heater," Jim said, "only gets you part warm in this weather. You need a fire. The wood's right outside the door. Take all you want."

Emotion and pain swirled in complex patterns, eyes unable to focus. Matthew still couldn't formulate a rational or civil response. The vivid scars on his face throbbed with his embarrassment. Matthew felt wounded, angry, dangerous, sad, vulnerable. He needed rest and peace.

"You hungry?" Jim asked.

"Yeah." The answer came before the realization that Jim might accompany him.

"How about you put some more clothes on and we go get some pizza?" Jim was now confident enough to step into the room and close the door behind him.

"What time is it?"

"7:35," Jim said, checking his watch. "You don't have a clock or a watch?"

"No."

Matthew took a good look at his landlord. A big man. Taller than his wife. Built solid but not bulky, despite the layers of clothing. Nordic face with high cheekbones. Tan, wind-blown face without blemishes. Straight, light-brown hair. He could have been Julia's brother except for the gray eyes that, unlike Julia's, were full of life.

"You'll like the crowd at the Calico. Pizza's good. It's the only decent pizza in Jackson Hole. A lot of ski patrollers and lift operators hang out there. I'm sure you'll want to meet them."

"Thanks for the invitation," Matthew said. "But I've got to work out first."

"You kidding?"

No, he wasn't. The last thing Matthew wanted was pizza with a bunch of strangers. He picked up a silver metal bar with large rubber suction cups on the ends. Maybe this would put off the man.

"What the hell's that?" Jim asked.

"It's my portable pull-up bar." Matthew walked to the bathroom alcove and twisted and extended the length of the chrome bar in the door frame.

"You don't need that thing." A smile appeared on Jim's face. "Come into the garage. Your clothes look wet. You want to change first?"

"These'll do." Matthew felt the lure of a possible work-out room overcome his desire for solitude.

"When you go outside," Jim said, "hold your breath. It's only a few feet. The cold won't register."

Matthew filled his lungs as instructed and followed Jim out of the cabin. He crossed the fifteen feet to the garage door holding his breath. The strategy, to his amazement, worked. He exhaled and looked around.

A large, rough-hewn bench sat against one wall, an array of professional-looking tools hung above. In the front section of the heated two-car garage Jim had set up a small gym with pull-up bar, rack for several sets of dumbbells, carpeted incline bench for sit-ups and a large Everlast body bag hanging from a reinforced hook in the ceiling. Matthew checked out the dumbbells, well-worn pairs of forty, thirty and twenty pounds as well as brand-new fifteens, tens, and fives.

Matthew began a sequence of pullups. First, a set of three, then four, five, swearing with disappointment at a failed attempt at six. Matthew reversed the sets, a minute in between each—five, four, three. He continued sets of pushups, situps and then chinups for the next half hour. Jim busied himself, first sharpening the edges, then waxing an old pair of scratched black metal skis, probably Head Standards.

"Hey, man, you got to take it easy," Jim said from the work bench.

"Two days ago I maxed out at seven pullups. Now I can't do six."

"Matthew, a couple of things you got to remember. One, you're at 6,000 feet today. Two days ago you were at sea level. Two, you need to get your lungs in shape and adjust to the cold. Three, you can't work out the same way every day. You've got to let your body rest, even if you're not banged up." Jim became more animated as he warmed up to the subject. "If you're interested in the weights, I can help you with a program. Plus I got a great rope-ladder setup outside when it warms up. It's great for mountain climbing. Why don't you get cleaned up and we'll go over to the Calico?"

Jim headed inside the lodge without waiting for an answer. When the door closed, Matthew let out a long, jagged sigh. His normal routine produced a steady stream of moans, groans and appropriate phrases as he battled pain and the too-slow response of his body. The foul language could be excused, but the moans and groans evidenced weakness. Jim wouldn't witness that.

EIGHT

Matthew took the three steps up to the entrance of the wood-framed Calico. Jim paused just inside the arch. The door swung open, propelled by four young children, parents close behind. Jesus, not a noisy, rug-rat-infested restaurant. But warm, moist air swept over Matthew. The contrast from the night's relentless chill startled him with a thick, comforting embrace.

A partition divided the restaurant into two parts. One side functioned as a family pizza parlor, the other a bar. Uncleared tables evidenced the recent departure of several groups of patrons on the restaurant side. The smell of pizza, solid and pungent, created an immediate need for food. Matthew's stomach contracted in anticipation, but Jim headed for the barroom.

The larger side, big only by comparison, buzzed and rocked with laughter and action. A counter with six wood stools took up the far wall. A full-size pool table, battered and frayed, proudly squatted in the center. Small round tables surrounded the green felt. The occupants, loud and boisterous, comfortable and secure, dressed like an assortment of rummage-sale models. A dart game occupied one section, a great shot countered by a misplaced missile bouncing off the wall threatening anyone close. The Calico bar appeared to be a male domain.

A discordant chorus of curses, comments, and greetings welcomed Jim. Everyone knew Jim—Jungle Jim—glad to see him. Matthew drifted in the wake of his landlord's acceptance, uncomfortable and anxious with all the activity.

"Let's get my table," Jim said, pointing to an unoccupied spot.

Jim's possessive choice of words confirmed Matthew's suspicion.

Everyone maintained their defined territorial space of table and seat. Good odds their spots were also permanent in the never-ending games of pool or darts. Jim took the narrow, high-backed chair against the wall, leaving two others, one facing the wood paneling, the other angled towards the back, away from the front door. Matthew stood, rotating his body, shuffling his feet. The sense of continuity and eternal order left Matthew feeling the odd man out.

"Have a seat," Jim called out over the din of activity. "John, give us a large special."

The order was directed to a sweet-looking, smiling, round-faced man behind the counter.

"Done," came the reply.

Matthew kept shifting, facing the front door or the center of the room. Hunger chewed at him, but the random movement in the bar unsettled him. The friendly good humor of the Calico couldn't cover his insecurity in a crowd, his need to keep vigilant.

"Hey, Matthew," Jim said. "I'll get some beers. Sit anywhere you want."

Jim got up, and Matthew pounced on his vacant chair, all the movement now before him. He felt a return of control and stability with his back covered. Maybe, just maybe, his fears might be misplaced. Then images of barrooms in Nam pricked his consciousness. He didn't give a damn how paranoid he was perceived.

He glimpsed unsettling characteristics common to both the Calico and the saloons of Nam, similarities that ebbed and flowed. Nicknames, crowded camaraderie, loud noise, the malty smell of beer, dirty haze, and the sweet odor of pot floating in the air.

Differences also existed, some comforting, some disconcerting. The faces at the Calico lacked the ethnic mix of Nam. Here everyone was white under deep tans and sunburns, with layered clothes testifying to freezing temperatures visible out the windows. And then too, unlike Southeast Asia, there was an absence of tension and the all-pervading fear, the forced hysterical laughter, and the emotional and dangerous overreactions.

But it sure as hell wasn't Kansas either. Drugs were evident in eyes as well as atmosphere. Also, the denizens of the Calico provided an encyclopedic assortment of beards, sideburns and moustaches with long hair displayed in everything from braids to buns. How had this group of young, healthy 1A studs escaped the war? Or had some served and survived whole? What were their stories?

Pushing themselves on the mountain didn't mean much compared to being pressured in Nam. How would they react under fire, with blood on their hands and in their soul? He couldn't ask. Yet questions persisted. These swaggering, loud-mouths were boys masquerading as men. He knew men. Fought and died with them. Contempt might be too strong an emotion, but lack of respect kept his lips sealed.

Only two names stuck. Jungle Jim and Mouse, the oldest of the Calico crowd, who sat at the end of the bar. Rat or Rodent would have been more appropriate. He had a large, sharp pointed nose that pulled his cheeks and protruding buck teeth forward. Tufts of hair sprouted from his ears, and probably his nose if Matthew wanted to get close enough to check it out. The rest were faces without names.

In the war many died or were carried out in their first weeks. Survive a while, and a name would register. Nicknames were earned by action or inaction, luck or mistakes, features or hometowns. Nam taught him to pick and choose who he could depend on. He would bide his time here in Jackson Hole before accepting the intimacy of friendship.

* * *

Jim made the rounds in the crowded room, then returned with two Buds and a smoking pizza loaded with a combination of ingredients Matthew felt best left undefined. He inhaled, as advertised by a sign on the front door, a "Decent Pizza at a Decent Price." Decent was an understatement, and Matthew acknowledged a degree of contentment as at least his stomach grew peaceful.

Jim sat at his table with Matthew, now crowded with two of Jim's ski patrol friends. Their names hadn't registered with Matthew. "Hi" and "Howdy" were the extent of his conversational contributions. He listened as stories, jokes, and lies spun around him.

"Here's what can get you in deep shit here in Jackson Hole." Jim's comment caught Matthew's interest. "Number one problem, moose. You come across a moose when you're on foot or skis, just turn and move on. You see a moose with a calf, haul butt. March and April they're nasty as hell, hungry, and bugs are bitin' the crap out of 'em. You meet 'em then . . . well, just kiss your ass good-by. They're dumb, mean, and unpredictable."

"You hear," one of the locals asked, "about the moose that attacked old Calvin's snowplow south of town? The son of a bitch kept charging the blade. Calvin just scooped it up and dumped that nasty sack of bones on the side of the road."

"Number two," Jim continued. "Cops. Especially where drugs are involved."

"They're just like moose," a tall, skinny kid with mutton chops and hair below his shoulders said, bringing an explosion of laughter. "Dumb, mean, and unpredictable."

"The cops here are redneck reactionaries," Jim persisted. "Possession, and that means one stinking little roach, brings a minimum of two years and up to a $5,000 fine. You can drive blind drunk over a little old lady, and they'll tell you to go home and sleep it off. But if you're dealing, you're dead. And they sure as hell haven't warmed up to skiers yet."

Jim dipped his head forward and lowered his voice a notch. Matthew caught himself leaning towards the man.

"Number three, the White Dragon."

A shift of intensity registered in the group. Matthew wondered if the White Dragon was the drug of choice for these children, cocaine, hallucinogens or some new concoction he'd never heard of. Who knew what strange element had become popular since he'd left for Asia?

"If you're gonna ski here in Jackson Hole," Jim looked straight at Matthew, "whether on a powder day at the resort or an out-of-bounds trip any day, you got to know how to survive an avalanche. And knowing how is no guarantee you'll live, just gives you better odds."

Matthew listened, then drifted off. He'd never heard avalanches referred to as the "White Dragon." He considered Jim's warning, but the dangers of nature had been displaced in Matthew's mind by his first-hand experience with man-made disasters. But the muted respect of the assembled group of wild men impressed him.

NINE

Sarah hesitated outside her grimy four-story apartment building. Another miserable, wind-chilled evening. She entered the musty, cloying atmosphere of the tiny shared vestibule and trudged up three flights of stairs. Wouldn't you think there'd be more of a secondary benefit to a thirty-mile-a-week running habit? But her mother's unpleasant presence hovered at the end of this slow climb. Psychological weight training at its most efficient.

Sarah worked her way through the four locks and deadbolts that protected their drab two-bedroom apartment. But from the ravages of what? She sighed. No rapist or thief in their right mind would dare face Thelma Ross. Her mother's aggressive, antagonistic aura protected her from personal contact as effectively as an advertised case of leprosy.

"Where have you been?" The question crashed upon Sarah as she moved through the fortress door.

"Good evening, Mother," Sarah said, reminded again of the value of working several overtime evenings each week.

"Why can't you get home at a decent hour? You know how much I worry about you."

As usual, Sarah thought, her mother ignored the often late-night demands of Thelma's own career downtown.

"I'm going to have a drink," Sarah said, dropping her purse and coat by the door. "Care to join me?" She knew the answer.

"You drink too much. Way too much. I'm the one who could use something to relax me, but I don't need the disgusting escape of alcohol."

You should knock down a few shots, Mom, Sarah thought for the hundredth time. She moved to the cupboard containing the few bottles

Thelma permitted: Smirnoff, Jack Daniels, and an aging, decorative decanter of kosher Manishewitz Concord Grape Wine. Sarah filled a chipped glass with ice and a double dose of vodka.

"Honey, that's too big a drink."

Her mother made a ritual reach for Sarah's cocktail. Sarah dodged the hand and collapsed into her chair of choice, a hard-backed rocker. Its range of movement created critical space between her and her mother.

"I don't know why the Lord chose to burden me with so much suffering." Thelma's scrawny hands fluttered for dramatic emphasis.

Thelma bitched and moaned about life's injustices. She covered a lot of sins in a few short minutes, a tribute to her years of practice while ignoring her massive contributions to her own miseries. Sarah sat a prisoner, still in the same damn place her whole life. When would she break the cord of love, duty, and her own insecurity?

Could the term "love" accurately describe Sarah's complex and difficult relationship with her mother? Thelma's unrelenting testaments of concern for her daughter couldn't be dismissed. Her mother's feeling towards Sarah was as close to love as the older woman would ever experience. And she had spent her life trying to please Thelma. Had she ever?

"You know," Thelma said, inserting an added tone of injury. "I hope and pray you don't become as selfish as your sister. Seems no one has any consideration for all the sacrifices I've made for my two ungrateful daughters."

Sarah looked up from a professional inspection of her vodka on ice. At seventeen, Helen had married a young premed student at Northwestern. Against all odds they appeared to be living happily ever after in Portland, Oregon, a location as far west as possible from Chicago and Thelma. Helen, buxom, brilliant, and brave, must have inherited undisclosed characteristics from her father.

"She never calls anymore," her mother complained. "She sucked me dry and discarded me, just like your father."

Oh, boy. Not yet Spring Training, and Mother was going to hit for the cycle: Sarah's inconsiderate failures, Helen's selfish escape, now her father's ancient desertion, and, soon to come, the cruel bondage of Thelma's workplace. Sarah stifled a sigh, thinking of all the places she'd rather be.

"Mom," Sarah begged, wondering why she wasted the words. "Don't start in on poor, departed Dad."

"Your father deserted me before you turned two." The request did indeed fall on deaf ears. "He didn't even leave a forwarding address."

Sarah had neither the energy nor will to point out the obvious. Thelma had cut the cord to all connection to her husband and his family. She was the one who had trashed every picture and reference to him. No doubt his New York relatives had cooperated, more than happy to trade a potential relationship with Sarah and Helen for freedom from a lifetime sentence of verbal torture. And who knew how long until the little girls morphed into nasty witches like their mother?

Enough. Sarah had to escape. She bolted from her rocking chair during a pause in Thelma's tragic performance. She pleaded fatigue and the need for a bath. Sarah wanted to plead insanity.

* * *

The energy level of the bar picked up as the night progressed, but Matthew faded. Jim didn't look too perky either. How the rest of the crowd kept reaching new highs could be answered only by chemicals. After a while nothing connected with Matthew until he heard the high-pitched squeak of the Mouse.

"You don't know what a bed-and-breakfast is? Listen. You screw all night, then they serve you breakfast in bed. And, with Julia performing the duties, old Jungle Jim can kick back and play all day."

The Mouse's drunken, shrieking laughter poked out above the clamor and good humor of the bar like a lone burnt tree after a bombing run. The decibel level descended. Matthew waited for Jim to destroy the Mouse like an angry cat. But Jim just looked with sleepy eyes at the unwitting jerk and flipped him off. The bar tuned back up to high. Matthew shook his head.

"Hey, man," one of the patrollers said to Matthew. "You wanta go outside and smoke some shit?"

The offer astonished him, his acceptance by Jim's buddies inconsistent with his brief experiences in the Bay Area. He had watched Viet Vets shunned or abused, never offered kindness or respect, let alone a joint. One of the attractions of the wilderness of Wyoming was the hope of blending unnoticed into his surroundings, or had he already blown that opportunity?

"No, thanks. I don't smoke."

"No," the young mountain man said, "I mean go outside and take down some pot, grass, you know, weed."

"Yeah, I do know. No, thanks."

"What?" Jim looked incredulous. "You spent nine and a half months in Viet Nam, and you don't get high?"

"How the hell do you know where I've been?"

Rage flared and Matthew's face burned with an uncomfortable heat. What facts did this guy have? This was an invasion of his private cache of personal facts.

"My brother told me," Jungle Jim said, embarrassment evident on his face.

"Maybe." Matthew's fingers strangled his beer bottle, tempted to smack Jim in the head with the glass container. "But your brother would never lay that information out in front of strangers."

So much for cover. But no one seemed to care. The two ski patrollers moved outside, searching for added perspective. Matthew's whitecaps of rage calmed. The exchange turned out to be a nonevent. He shifted on the stool and studied the remains of his beer.

*   *   *

Steam rose and softened the view of the shabby bathtub fixtures and stained walls of the bathroom. The denser the air became, the further Sarah drifted from the clutches of her mother. Until the bathroom door burst open. Jesus. Thelma's scraggly image filled the room.

"I forgot to tell you," Thelma said, "what happened at work today."

Sarah gave a futile attempt at a submarine defense, but her mother could talk much longer than Sarah could hold her breath.

"Damn, Mom, can't I have at least some privacy?" Sarah regretted her words before she even saw the stricken expression on her mother's hawklike face. She took several steps backwards, a sour twist to her lips.

"Fine," Thelma said. "Forgive me for interrupting your privacy."

"I'm sorry, Mother."

And she was sorry. Her response wasn't worth the toll, and it ignored her mother's undeniable concern and efforts towards Sarah's well-being. But she knew she would pay a price for her apology. Green light for Thelma. She picked up right where she had left off.

"They forced a new assistant buyer on me, Charmane Flowers. She's a

Negro." Thelma's indignation floated in the moisture-laden air. "It's a tragedy. Marshall Fields is headed for disaster. To think what great jobs I got for you and your sister. I wouldn't even let you girls work there today."

Great jobs? What a joke. Sarah and Helen had worked long hours after class and on most holidays during high school, paying their dues in the warehouse until rising to the exalted position of sales clerks making the fabulous sum of $2.25 an hour.

"Do you know how hard I've had to toil for you and your ungrateful sister?"

Bubbles and vapor distorted the image of the overwrought Thelma. An appropriate vision for her mother's schizoid personality. Sarah giggled. How could the same person be both an energetic, efficient buyer and the shrewish Thelma who exited the impressive revolving doors of the department store? That discovery had been enough to convince Helen of her mother's insanity.

"You don't remember. You were too young. Lord, the hours I slaved for twenty years," her mother puffed with pride. "It's a miracle I made it all the way from clerk to Head Buyer of women's sportswear."

If Sarah only had the nerve or energy to respond truthfully to her mother's complaints. To tell Thelma that, despite her sincere struggles, she'd proven a far better employee than wife or mother. How much longer could Sarah bite her tongue? How long could Sarah put up with this pathetic woman and not end up exactly like her? Life in Jackson Hole wouldn't be like this.

* * *

Two men took the patrollers' place, closing around Matthew's and Jim's small table. Conversation flavored with bullshit picked up again. Matthew wanted out, longing for the little cavelike cabin that promised peace and solace. A large, angular lift operator, hairless by genetics, directed a comment at Matthew.

"Sorry, what'd you say?" Matthew said.

"That POW, Major Rowe, whatta you think of him?" the hairless wonder demanded, leaning aggressively towards Matthew.

"Nothing."

But Matthew did have thoughts about Rowe. The officer had been imprisoned in Nam for five years. Turned out to be a total pain in the ass for his captors. Finally got loose and back to safety. Now the hard-ass Major had signed up for another tour to use what he called his "intimate knowledge of the enemy." Guy was crazy as far as Matthew could tell. Why hadn't the VC just snuffed him and been done with the problem? The Army and the media, led by *Time Magazine*, jumped on the story of Major Rowe, a true hero in a heroless war.

"*. . all kinds of officers (a yearning nation's blue eyed pride),*" Matthew mumbled.

"What the hell does that mean?" Mr. Hairless said. The stranger's Hitler-shaped moustache matched his aggressive Nazi-like arrogance. This guy fit the profile of the civilian pricks Matthew expected. "Rowe's tough as nails. More like him and we wouldn't be gettin' our asses kicked. Don't you agree?"

Internal heat built lavalike. He couldn't explode, lose control his first night. Memories of the gas station capped his flaring temper. Nam was the last thing he wanted to talk about. He needed to be left alone. He sat on his hands, offering temporary vulnerability as a distraction to a violent urge to crush his tormentor.

"Ain't you got anything to say?"

"I've got no desire to talk about it. Why don't you move on to something else or shut up?"

Seven or eight locals gathered for the show. The obnoxious one acted ready to fight, but his eyes reflected a different attitude when trapped in Matthew's hard glare. Jim moved between them. Matthew slipped off his chair and headed for the door. Jim followed.

"Where you goin', tough guy? You know it's a free country. I can talk about anything I want."

The man turned to his companions. Matthew noticed in the reflection off the glass window that several nodded in agreement. Matthew heard a parting comment above the clamor of the Calico as he left the bar.

"What an asshole."

Look who's talking, Matthew thought.

TEN

The Corvette had become questionable transportation between the altitude, snow and freezing temperatures. When the car did start, disasters lurked at every corner. Simple turns and cautious braking created complex spins and slides into ditches. Matthew had to dump the car. As little as six inches of snow would grasp the frame. The wheels would spin uselessly. A fly trapped in a spider-web.

"Go into town," Jim directed. "Take your Vette to Wesley Crow at the Blackfoot Garage. Let me call ahead to make sure Wesley isn't skiing."

Jim's conversation with Wesley Crow took a while, Jim probably warning Mr. Crow that a loose cannon was approaching. Then snow on the road made the drive to the town of Jackson a white-knuckle affair. But Matthew had learned a little about instability and made the trip without mishap.

An Amoco gas station, two islands and a tidy office, sat in front of the Blackfoot Garage. The large, new building filled the space behind the service station. A smaller, older structure appeared attached to one side of the impressive garage. Matthew parked in one of the spaces between the gas station and the Blackfoot. Black-painted block letters topped the closed double doors advertising a quality operation.

Matthew performed his slow unraveling out of the Corvette's white leather bucket seat. The gripping cold chilled but didn't dominate his senses as it had his first several days in Jackson Hole. He walked to a small man-door next to the large drive-in doubles and stepped into a world of clamor and action.

Country Western music competed with the clanging sounds of men and tools. Large blowers kept the temperature at a livable level. Temporary guests, both trucks and cars, occupied six of the eight work bays. Five mechanics in work-worn, black overalls hovered around, over and under their patients. The floor was immaculate despite the frenetic activity.

A tall, well-set-up man progressed with smooth, efficient movements from bay to bay. Shoulder-length black hair, a combination of Geronimo and Prince Valiant, emphasized high pronounced cheekbones, dark chestnut skin, all or part Indian. Blackfoot? Must be Wesley.

The man glanced up and acknowledged his visitor with a wave. He glided forward, stopped for several moments at a late model Ford Torino, leaned under the hood in conversation with a dirty, stubby little mechanic. Then he was on the move again, finally reaching Matthew at the front door.

"You must be Matthew Green." A comforting, resonant voice welcomed Matthew. A broad, stained hand extended to him. Deep, dark eyes smiled. "Glad you safely made it to town."

Wesley looked to be in his thirties, but ageless, appearing almost elegant in black overalls much cleaner than his employees. The man projected calm understanding, as if experienced in soothing unbroken horses and wild animals. Matthew's usual suspicion and intuitive mistrust took a half step back.

"Jungle Jim said you was lookin' to trade. I'm a trader. He told me to fix you up with somethin' practical. I'm a fixer. He also told me to be careful." Wesley's calm voice didn't quite cover up the spark of humor that lurked under the surface. "And I'm a careful man. Let's see if we can't do some business. But first, let me look at your hot little Stingray. There ain't a hell of a lot of 'em in this part of the country."

Matthew followed Wesley outside. The Indian circled the Corvette, a toneless whistle slipping through his lips.

"Seems a little dinged up," Wesley said. He ran his large hands over dents and scratches on the passenger side. "Cute. Not too practical for the winter. Great for the summer though. You know, I seen this car somewhere."

"Probably in a ditch." Matthew hadn't forgotten his near-death experience between Pocatello and Jackson Hole.

Wesley popped the hood and inspected the still warm engine crackling in protest against the brittle air. He eased the hood shut, then wedged himself into the driver's seat, dry shifting through the gears. Wesley nodded his approval and led Matthew back into the larger garage.

The Indian stopped at an old Jeep Wagoneer. The battered and forlorn car squatted in the last work bay. Charred engine parts lay scattered on the cement floor by the raised hood.

"Have you met our European contingent of ski instructors?" Wesley asked.

"No. Not yet."

"This is—or I should say was—their borrowed transportation. Jonesy, who'd let those boys use this here poor truck, called me two weeks ago, 'My engine's on fire!'"

Intense activity surrounded Matthew. He studied the Indian, the paradox of this smiling, pleasant man spinning out this rambling tale and running such a tight ship.

"Well, I popped the hood and that motor was fried. Here it is right on the floor. Those morons never put a drop of oil in the engine in three years. The instructors said they only had to fill it with gas. Never apologized to Jonesy. Didn't donate one nickel. He was so pissed he kicked 'em out of his cabin. They still don't understand."

"So what?" Matthew said. Where the hell was this conversation headed?

"So here's the deal," Wesley continued. "I'm rebuilding this here engine. Replacin' the hoses, fixin' the electrical, make it work pretty good. It'll take a couple of weeks. But, with a little work, this Jeep'll run fine if you occasionally put oil in the damn thing. I'll store your Vette. You pay me $100 a month, and I'll also keep the Jeep workin'. I got a truck out back you can use till the Jeep's ready."

"How do I know you'll guarantee the Jeep?"

Wesley's smile disappeared like a fast-moving cloud blanking the sun. His eyes hardened, full lips a tight, straight line. A different Wesley Crow stood quiet and tense.

"I'm tellin' you I will."

Matthew looked around the clean, efficient garage. Busy mechanics. Wesley as immobile as a drugstore Indian. No vacillation. An absolute. No gray here. A mistake to question this man's words. Wesley said it, that was enough. Matthew felt his mouth twist into a rare smile.

"A deal," Matthew said and shook hands. The cloud passed. Wesley softened, his face relaxing. "Show me my temporary transportation."

Wesley led Matthew out the back door. Several trucks filled the parking lot, an old Chevy sedan, and two John Deere tractors, one looking more like an antique than a working piece of equipment. Wesley pointed to a fifteen-year-old Ford pickup with more shades of green than the jungle.

"It's ugly, but it'll work 'til I get the Jeep fixed up. Got snow tires. Solid on these roads. Won't be as much fun as your Corvette." Even Wesley's sarcasm had a soft edge.

Loud clanging noises emanated from the older shed.

"What's in the other building?"

"That's for heavy machines. Workin' on a thresher and a big Harvester." The light in Wesley's eyes sparkled, adding colors to the deep, dark brown. White teeth gleamed as his grin took over his nut-brown face. "I guess I could show ya."

Wesley moved to the rear door and opened it. The sight of a huge man, black untrimmed beard, wild hair, and a big belly and butt filling out filthy overalls greeted Matthew. He pounded and swore at a large, rusted yellow machine.

"This is Gilbert. We don't like to let him out much." Wesley laughed as he accepted the bird from the wild-eyed mechanic.

Then Matthew's attention shifted elsewhere. At the front door of the building stood a hulking black pickup truck raised on huge tires, with a gun rack and no manufacturer's identification. He moved to his left for a confirming view of the truck's Wyoming license plates. His head swelled with heat.

"Who owns the truck?" Matthew tried to control the angry tremor in his voice.

Wesley held his palms out. His eyes attempted innocence and failed. A giggle blossomed into full-throated laughter.

"That's where I seen that little Corvette. 'Tween Rexburg and Jackson."

"You almost killed me, you son of a bitch." Matthew's fists clenched.

Gilbert made a quick move from the side of the yellow tractor. The giant gripped a wrench in a ham-sized hand. He took another step towards Matthew and Wesley. The man could do major damage with either fist or tool, and Matthew kept track of him. The huge man reminded Matthew of Bull. Sadness flickered at the edge of his rage.

"You were goin' mighty slow," the Indian said. "I nearly ran up your ass. You're lucky I passed in time."

Matthew tried to squeeze intensity into more vivid outrage. But Wesley's humor and smile extinguished what should have been uncontrollable emotion at being blown off the highway. Matthew just couldn't generate the appropriate fury and aggression. He could only shake his head, smiling despite himself for the second time that day.

"You been in the military?" Wesley asked.

"Yeah."

"Me, too. Korea. Mostly the twenty-first infantry regiment. There at the beginning. First got jumped and pounded. Then kicked ass. Then got our butts kicked. And, wouldn't ya know it? A hundred thousand dead bodies later, we end up in the same damn place we started. Sound a little like where you been?"

"Rangers, 173rd. Mainly recon. Dirtier and more worthless than Korea," Matthew said, surprised at what he had revealed.

"Let me buy a veteran lunch." Wesley's laughter had slid back into a smile. "'Less you're in a hurry."

"Time I got."

"Let me just make a quick swing through my garage. Make sure everyone's on track."

Matthew nodded his assent. Wesley's quick swing took half an hour.

ELEVEN

Wesley directed Matthew to the Log Cabin Coffee Shop. He followed the Indian into the cluttered restaurant, whirling with lunchtime action. Wesley greeted everyone, customers, waitresses, busboys. Matthew settled at a table in the rear.

"Been skiin' yet?" Wesley asked.

"Not yet."

"Jim said you been here a week. The snow's great. What you been waitin' for?"

Wesley questioned with a mellow tone of voice and warm smile. He didn't seem to be asking out of idle curiosity. No comparison between Jim's thoughtless comments and the Indian's kindness. He was taken off guard by the speed of his developing interest in and comfort with the older man.

"I've been checking out my body parts," Matthew said. "Making sure everything's working well enough to ski."

"Well, you figure it out yet?"

"Maybe," Matthew answered. "I'm giving it a try in the next day or two."

"What kind a injuries you dealin' with?"

This question brought a hardening of Matthew's jaw and a strong desire to retreat from the room. Unwelcome memories clouded his vision, distorting the objects on the table.

"Later," Matthew responded.

"You're a college boy, ain't ya?"

"U.C.L.A."

"How'd a sharp young man like you end up in Viet Nam?"

Smoke turned to fire. Anger. Pain. Even confusion. The Indian was walking through a minefield, setting off alarms. But Matthew didn't want to blow off Wesley. He enjoyed his company. He needed a connection with someone.

"As a sophomore I registered for the Coast Guard Reserves. There was over a two-year wait list. The timing would be perfect. Graduate. Get in the safety of the Reserves. We were all scared to death of going to Viet Nam back in the spring of 1964. I was into reading and history. Naive about many things. But I knew the dangers of being a grunt in combat. Some redneck asshole ordering me to charge up some worthless hill to die for no good reason."

I will not kiss your fucking flag . . . Words from the poem invaded his focus. Matthew rubbed his forehead. The habit attracted unwanted attention. He had to learn to control his wandering fingers.

"I was extending my stay in college into an allowed fifth year, having the time of my life, when my name came up. Coast Guard called me, and I went to Oakland for the physical."

A heavy-set, pasty-faced waitress appeared. Wesley smiled at her, prompting a broad grin full of irregular teeth. She wrote down their order, still smiling. He'd made her day.

"Then everything went to hell," Matthew continued after she left. "This arrogant jerk Coast Guard doctor rejects me because my record shows I had asthma as a kid. I hadn't been bothered for years, but this dick looks down his nose and says, 'Absolutely not.' But he said the Army would be happy to overlook it. I called the guy an asshole and a few other choice adjectives. That clinched it. The Coast Guard threw my butt out the door, prime 1A draft bait."

The waitress returned with drinks, ignoring other customers. Matthew used the break to gather his thoughts. He hadn't talked this much for a long time, amazed at his willingness as the words rolled out.

"Next day I went to talk to the Army recruiter. It was busy. The guys he was talking to would have trouble licking an envelope. I asked the sergeant if I could buy him a couple of beers after his duty hours. Wanted to check out my options outside the recruiting office without all those idiots hanging around. Buying those beers and the tequila shooters that came with them was the dumbest thing I've done in my life. And I've done some real stupid things."

Wesley kept quiet. Matthew felt encouraged. He experienced an unusual desire to travel through at least a few difficult moments from his past.

"He convinced me that the worst plan would be getting drafted, a ticket to death in Nam. I should enlist and have choices. First choice would be to become the aggressor, not the poor shithead draftee who was the helpless victim. Learn to fight, to kill, to survive, become a warrior, be in control. We staggered back to his office sometime during that night. I signed. I still don't believe I did it."

Several men entered, nodded at Wesley and bumped their way to a nearby table. Matthew measured them for potential eavesdropping. Dropped his voice a notch when he continued.

"Once in, I was so pissed off, so angry, I channeled everything into my training. Got accepted to Ranger School. Survived. Became the fighting, killing machine they wanted. And I still didn't have much control. Just dog meat thrown to the wolves."

Wesley's large fingers arranged his silverware into a sequence of orderly formations. An uncomfortable silence followed.

"Somehow," Wesley said, "I don't think I'm getting the whole story."

Matthew felt a little better, a slight lessening of pressure, not as over-burdened. But the "whole story" was more than he cared to deal with.

"That's plenty for now," Matthew said. "I've got a question. Are you a Blackfoot or a Crow Indian?"

"Half Blackfoot. My daddy taught school over in Idaho at the reservation. I was visitin' there when we met on the road." Wesley's grin lit their corner of the restaurant. "He met my mother, married her and moved over here to Jackson. Still teaches school at Wilson. Lives south of town off 89 on a small workin' ranch. That's where I grew up."

"How'd you end up running a big operation like the Blackfoot?" If Wesley was going to get personal, Matthew had no problem doing the same.

"You mean, how'd a dumbass, half-breed, Korean vet, farm boy end up with a business like the Blackfoot?" Wesley flashed his big grin, white teeth shining in his dark face. A large hand waved off Matthew's attempt to clarify. "After high school I enlisted to get the G.I. Bill benefits. Couldn't afford college otherwise. Got more than I bargained for in Korea. But I made it home."

The waitress returned with their lunch. Matthew accepted his turkey sandwich platter with both hands as she, eyes glued to Wesley, almost missed the table with his plate. She placed Wesley's greasy cheeseburger before him, a pink glow blossoming on her face, bringing life to her lumpy features.

"After the war, I went to the University of Wyoming. All through high school I'd been workin' on cars, trucks, any kind of equipment. Got pretty good at it. Worked full time during college at a big garage operation in Laramie. Put away a little cash. Moved to Jackson Hole and became a partner in a little two-man shop with a mean old son of a bitch, Leroy Elbert."

Wesley's delivery wasn't bragging. Rather that of a proud man who had accomplished much. Matthew was impressed.

"He died several years ago and left me his interest in the business. I moved out to the old tractor barn where Gilbert's locked up. Learned how to work with my boys. Troubleshootin' allowed me to hire a few more. Saved and borrowed enough to put up the new building. Bought me a house in town with a view of the mountains. I'm even a member of the Jackson Hole Rotary. Now I'm an All-American Capitalist Pig."

Matthew laughed out loud.

"You livin' in Jim's old cabin for the winter?" Wesley asked.

"Yeah. I've paid rent until the first of April."

"Well, don't get stuck out there. You need to get to town now and then. Meet some local folks. Good music. Good times. I'll show you around. Get your body parts headed in the right direction. I'll be happy to carve some turns on the Mountain with ya."

Matthew took in a deep breath. Wesley provided the first reassuring confirmation that escaping to Jackson Hole had been the correct move.

TWELVE

Franky sat in his favorite corner of the couch. Midnight. His father's office looked no different at night than day with the heavy curtains drawn and cigar smoke filling the room like a smoggy afternoon in L.A. Franky'd go nuts if he had to attend any more midnight meetings.

He had a 7 A.M. appointment tomorrow. Hell, he had a 7, an 8, a 10, and right on through the day. Franky worked his ass off, up every morning at 5. He had earned every goddamn penny, every opportunity with hard work, total focus and the resultant loneliness. His primitive, privileged half-brothers probably went to bed at 5.

Anger melded with fatigue. Franky fought to stay focused on safety. Cracks were appearing in the organization's façade. The brothers provided no direction. Their refusal to follow the suggestions and plans of Roberto and Franky created credibility gaps in the Fiorini family. His father's extended absence had become dangerous. Questions were creeping into various business negotiations where before there had been complete cooperation.

It didn't help that Sal and Marco despised Franky, considered him a pussy pencil pusher, deserving no respect. Nothing had changed even after he'd made his bones in the stinking alley of Little Italy. He had stumbled into this mess over five years ago, first just along for the ride, now a prisoner of circumstance.

"What about Mr. Fiorini's appeal?" Georgio, Sal's assistant enforcer, asked, breaking the temporary silence.

Encouraging. The man's concern mirrored Franky's. Georgio had also watched the brothers' brutal antics antagonize their own men as well as the anxious jackals of the competition. Those hungry bastards must be licking their chops watching Sal's heavy-handed mistakes. His older brother had to have some convoluted, ulterior agenda unknown to either Franky or Roberto. Sal might be an animal, but he was definitely no idiot.

"We got somethin' better," Sal boomed. "We just got a lead on the prick snitch."

"That why we're here in the middle of the night?" Franky's sarcastic question stunned him. Frightened him.

"Well, well, baby brother." Sal's voice had an edge that fueled instant regret. "I'm real sorry you're missin' your beauty sleep."

"Let's get down to business." Roberto's mantra attempted order. "Thanks to our associates, we've finally cracked the Fed's Witness Protection Program. Unfortunately, a crack is all we have. But we're closing in on where this guy is hiding out."

"And guess what, Franky?" Sal cut in on Roberto. "You're gonna get a shot at trackin' him down."

Franky's heartbeat shot off the chart. What the hell was going on? Sal, for once, played coy, and Roberto let the cat play with the mouse. Franky hadn't a clue. Was he being set up? And, if so, why?

"We got an opportunity for you that you just can't pass up," Sal said, eyes narrow behind the veil of Cuban smoke. His smile made Franky wish he were anywhere but this office. "Ya wanna be a big man, Shorty? Ya want respect? You been wigglin' into our family since your dumb-ass return. The only time you ever showed any balls was walkin' into D and F Construction demandin' answers from Pop. Well, it's time you put up or shut up."

Answers, give him answers. Franky's heart continued to race.

"You payin' attention, professor?" Sal continued. "We think we've traced the fink to Jackson Hole, Wyoming, wherever the hell that is. Word is there's a place to ski, and our bastard informer's hidin' there. You're the big time skier, and you don't do shit around here. This job's made for ya, Franky."

How could he leave? Demands of the businesses had mushroomed out of control. Who would run things in his absence? He looked at Roberto, the only man in the room who knew or appreciated Franky's expanding value.

"Franky," Roberto said, walking across the room. "It'll take another few weeks to confirm the location and then line up the proper backup. You'll have time to put our business affairs in order. I'll cover where necessary. We'll work out a plan before you head west."

His calm voice answered Franky's unspoken concerns, but fell short of the reality of his workload. And, as Sal had so kindly pointed out, there was no choice in the matter.

"The trip could take a couple of weeks," Roberto said. "All you have to do is find the guy and let the local muscle do their thing."

Could fate be knocking? Franky's brain spun overtime. The perfect opportunity to gain his brothers' respect? He knew his first—and only— hit had been tainted. Grab the breaks or they'd pass him by. Nailing this asshole could be the ticket to the top, or at least a higher level of security. Who knew how long his father would be locked up or how long before his brothers blew everything he'd worked for?

But this whole plan could also be a charade. Sal's perfect opportunity to forever dump Franky in the wilderness. Still, Wyoming looked a hell of a lot safer right now than New York with these demented bozos in charge.

*   *   *

Matthew pulled into the parking lot of Teton Village. A two-story building with a large clock tower stood in the center. A flight of wooden stairs climbed to the second floor where a small pipe matrix for crowd control fed into the tram entrance. No line. Thick cables began at the Tram departure point, continued upward, and disappeared from view well short of the Tram's final destination, four thousand vertical feet above the valley floor.

How many endless nights and sweltering days in that hellhole of Asia had he dreamt of this moment? Nerves, adrenaline, excitement, doubts, hopes, all swirled through him as he traced the Tram's wires up the steep mountain from the base of the Jackson Hole Ski Resort. Well, here he stood—reality check.

The bottom floor of the Clock Tower housed several ticket windows, offices and, hopefully, restrooms. A cafeteria door welcomed skiers near the top of the stairs, before the Tram. Nothing else? Such a modest welcome to the largest, longest, steepest, and deepest ski mountain in North America?

Superstition had kept him from visiting the mountain until he was ready to risk an attempt at skiing. Now the ski area seemed as vacant as the barren Idaho towns of Dillon or Victor. Perhaps the resort was closed? East, back across the empty valley, the far ridge top outlined the profile of the Sleeping Indian. How appropriate. He checked the Clock Tower, 9:35. Then he noticed movement behind one of the ticket windows. Minimal assurance that life did exist.

A chairlift could be seen to the right. Actually two. The first beginner chair rose only a few hundred feet off the base of the resort. A second more impressive one climbed a small peak, its top visible several thousand feet above. Behind the lift's crest, the shoulders of the Teton peaks promised a shot of the Grand, lurking just out of sight. Matthew's acid test lay on the slopes of that Apres Vous chairlift. When would he generate the confidence required to meet the challenge of the Tram's 4,000-foot vertical drop?

He leaned against the old green pickup and struggled into his new, stiff Heinke ski boots, resigned to the inevitable destruction of his feet. Too bad. Blisters and jungle sores had finally healed, his feet now one of the few pain-free zones on his battered body. Matthew, with hat, goggles, and gloves, pried his new Head 360s from the truck bed. He clumped over the frozen lot, up the snow-covered path towards the ticket booths and to the lone being behind a window. The bundled refugee, protected by the glass, chattered away at the prospect of a living, breathing customer.

Matthew put his $12 down for a one-day chairlift pass. He attached the ticket to his ski pants as a large, young black Lab loped up. The excited ball of dark fur jumped and wiggled. The dog acted as happy to see a warm body as the ticket agent. Matthew struggled to remain erect. The bottom of the hill was not where he wanted to experience his first fall.

Matthew walked to the corner of the tram building, looking around to make sure no one noticed him—no problem. He dropped his skis and poles and, with an awkward movement, went to his knees. The young Lab's ecstasy was apparent, tongue and tail leading the attack. Matthew welcomed the attention. Then he had trouble regaining his feet, fighting off the dog's vigorous friendship on the slippery snow, ruefully aware he could be overpowered by a puppy.

He trudged up the slight rise towards the first chairlift. Teewinot. Weird name. The dog followed, making numerous assaults on Matthew's legs, but failed to take him off his feet. The Lab lost interest and charged back down the hill.

"That's progress," he said.

Jim had convinced Matthew to cross-country ski in the wide-open meadows near the Grand View. The flat, spacious openness had provided beautiful views, no bushes or trees to attract moose and an opportunity to develop strength and stamina. The results were evident as he walked to the lift.

Matthew put on his skis, secured the safety straps, and replaced his gloves. His legs quivered with nervous anticipation. He poled to the loading area. No one in sight other than the lift operator.

"Hey, man, how you doin'?" Another grateful employee.

"Okay," Matthew said, then nodded, not trusting the emotion in his voice.

He sat down on the slow-moving chair, the freezing seat occupying his immediate attention. After a short ride, the chair dumped Matthew at the top. The real test, the Apres Vous lift, sat 150 yards away. Matthew skied the flat connecting trail towards the second chairlift, experimenting with the edges of his new skis. Still no problem. The lonely lift operator smiled a greeting, and Matthew moved up the mountain, past the point of no return.

A spectacular view of the major Teton peaks opened up to his right. The quiet was crushing, broken only by the hum of the chairlift's cables and brief metallic clatter as chairs passed through the steel wheels of the support towers. Matthew's attention shifted to the snow below him. Occasional tracks cut through the deep powder. The main way down, the route packed by skiers, had to be over the ridge to his left.

Nerve-generated heat coursed through his body. What if he couldn't make it down? If the pain of skiing crippled him? Where would he go? What would he do? He had no backup plan. The hard-ass sergeants in Ranger School would not approve: "You gotta have a back door, grunt."

He was forced off the chair at the top of the Apres Vous lift. Still no skiers around. Where the hell was everyone? A small patrol hut was visible, though half-buried in a snowbank. Two pairs of skis stuck upright outside the shack's door. Proof of some human presence. A blue-lettered sign labeled the ski run "Upper Werner." The name had to memorialize the late, great Buddy Werner, U.S. Olympic star, snuffed several years before in a Colorado avalanche while on a fashion photo shoot.

"Great. How's that for a sign from above?"

The color blue indicated an intermediate way down, as compared to the threat of black, experts only, or green, pussies welcome. The hell with it. Matthew pushed off, the snow soft but firm enough for the slow, wide turns he carved. His new skis reacted as he unweighted from turn to turn. Matthew exaggerated his body movements as he moved from large, wide arcs to shorter and tighter turns—legs moving up and down, shoulders rotating, skis edging securely into the hill.

The movements and sensations of skiing on the easy hard pack brought back familiar technique as if the last two skiless years had never existed. A tidal wave of relief washed away his concentration. This would be a piece of cake. Then he almost crashed, thrashing to maintain his balance. Ugly but effective.

Matthew picked up speed. Heat from his efforts fogged the view through his goggles. The absence of air brought an end to the run. Panting, light-headed, Matthew screamed to the brittle, blue sky. No one there to hear his cry, to recognize his orgasmic explosion of emotion.

"Screw the backup plan, Sir. I'm going to make it."

Matthew trembled on the side of Werner's run. Yes, his side throbbed, his left thigh muscles popped and quivered, the scar tissue on his back communicated burning defiance. But only sharp pains from his new ski boots registered as a new problem.

Matthew's confidence soared. He made two more successful trips down Apres Vous. And, just like the old days, thoughts drifted to the Tram. Why stay at his comfort level? Why, indeed. Push it. Matthew skied down to the Clock Tower. Still deserted. Not even his new buddy, the Lab, to greet him. He purchased a single Tram ticket for $1.

* * *

Matthew clamored up the stairs to the tram entrance. No one in front of him. He handed his ticket to a familiar figure. Matthew recognized the happy blue eyes, perpetually crinkled at the corners. He had met TJ several times at the Calico. The man-child, bundled against the chill, stood with long hair hidden, a neck gaiter covering his face up to his nose. TJ acted as close to a flower child as the rugged country allowed, and, thankfully, without the judgmental accusations of the San Francisco Bay Area breed.

"Man, you finally made it to the Mountain. That's great." Effusive, sincere greetings were TJ's trademark. "You goin' up alone?" Concern crept into TJ's voice.

"No big deal." Matthew's own cocky reply sounded strange. "Only way to go is down."

"Yeah, but there's ways down you don't want to take. It's a huge, scary mountain, even if you know it."

Matthew shrugged and made his way to the metal-grate platform as the Tram approached from above. Two skiers and a ski patroller, all strangers, stomped aboard when the doors opened.

"Shebang," TJ called out to the patroller, "give my buddy, Matthew, a tour down the mountain."

"Can't," Shebang answered, abrupt and tight. "I'm on duty at the top for the next hour. I'll point out a few of the sights on the way up."

Doors slammed. The Tram crept out, cleared the platform and picked up speed. The two skiers, the patroller, Matthew and a tram operator filled a car built to hold fifty. Shebang remained silent until the Tram had risen over a thousand feet.

"First trip up in the Box?" Not a lot of interest or energy in Shebang's question. Definitely not the PR type.

"Yeah."

"You got a clue what you're doin'?"

"I got a clue," Matthew said and turned away.

Long, wide, steep ridges and gullies draped the lower third of the mountain to the south, back towards the Grand View and Wilson. Under the cables of the Tram and to the north, numerous trails cut through the dense pines, the Apres Vous lift visible and then the Tetons poking above the lower mountains. The terrain outside the tram windows expanded exponentially.

"Over there," Shebang pointed to the long, open faces of the south, "are the Hobacks and, closer to us, the Colter Ridges. Hot skiing if you can handle crud and powder."

The Tram continued climbing. At around the two-thirds point, Matthew looked beneath the moving car into long, steep chutes, bordered with rocks and trees.

"Some of the best stuff you can't see. They're over the ridge to your left, the Alta Chutes, Central Chute and Cheyenne Woods. Look to your right." Shebang's voice picked up some life, as if spectacular beauty had squeezed out previous boredom. "It's all there, man. Great chutes, Expert and Downhill. Sweet bowls, the Cirque and the Headwall."

Rock formations became more dramatic, hundred-foot sheer stone faces dropping into open glades. The last leg revealed magnificent views back down into the valley, across the flats to broad, rounded mountains. To the north, the mighty Tetons rose to almost 14,000 feet and, to the south, Cody Peak and Bowl, a huge pyramid-shaped mountain sliced in half.

"Now, if you really got balls," Shebang said, directing Matthew's attention to the unavoidable spectacle of steep, jagged cliffs out the Tram's glass windows, "you can jump into Corbet's Couloir." A narrow, bottle-necked chute carved a precarious path between massive cliffs before it flared into a steep bowl. "There's a rope you can use to drop down over the edge, about fifteen feet if you only got one ball. But diving in separates the men from the boys."

"More likely separates your soul from your body." Matthew had trouble imagining a jump into that death chute. "You'd hit the snow at twenty miles an hour and accelerate from there."

"Exactly." Shebang's smile lacked good will. "See ya, bud. We're at the top."

The Tram slowed for its entry to the top platform. Matthew scrambled out the sliding door. Everything silent, eerie. Massive peaks north and south. Immense spaces. And most ironic, he'd dreamed of being in this exact spot.

But what the hell was he doing up here?

THIRTEEN

Sarah floated out the door of Paradise Travel. Even the jarring, frenetic activity of Michigan Avenue couldn't interrupt the lightness of her attitude. She gripped the envelope, then raised it to her full lips for a kiss before placing her Jackson Hole vacation papers into her purse. She turned right and made her way the block and a half through lunch-hour congestion to the massive doors of the marble mausoleum and her employer, Gold, Smith, Knudsen and Harrington.

But nothing could spoil this day. Just weeks until her return to Wyoming. Thoughts of men, skiing, men, partying, and more men filled her mind as she rose in the elevator to a job others envied. If they only knew what she had to put up with. And she had the talents, the qualifications. College graduate. One year of law school. Now a skilled legal secretary in a high-priced, high-pressure Miracle Mile law firm. Fifteen hundred a month plus benefits. And a doctorate in self-defense resulting from the unsolicited sexual pawing of senior partner Irving Knudsen, tall, debonair, and persistent.

Knudsen had welcomed her, a young, fatherless and rather unsophisticated graduate into the comforting embrace of the firm. Her boss's mentoring led to increased skills and responsibilities. Then, within a year, arms turned offensive, hands groped. Sarah with her homely self-image found Knudsen's attraction to her hard to believe.

"You Know Who needs to see you immediately," Abigail, the company receptionist, offered as though she'd swallowed a rancid piece of meat. Her eyes held moist sympathy.

You Know Who could ruin her day. Sarah threw her purse on her desk, hung up her coat on the brass hat rack, and snatched a pad and pen. She moved down the plush, plum-colored carpet, her footsteps muted. A flash of anger whipped through her. She hesitated at the polished double doors, took a deep breath, then knocked. The muffled answer to enter came before she had finished striking the solid wood.

"Ah, Sarah." Mr. Knudsen's nasal greeting washed Wyoming out of her consciousness.

He opened the door for her. Sarah took several nervous steps forward, glancing over her shoulder. This slimeball must have something on his mind. He never got off his ass, let alone opened a door for her.

Perspiration and intensity patterned Knudsen's long, foxlike face. Sarah's suspicions deepened. The arrogant attorney could be accused of many sins, but he rarely lost his cool. She stepped to the middle of Knudsen's magnificent corner office on the twenty-eighth floor of the Midwest Mutual Life Insurance Building.

He moved towards his chair, gesturing at a stack of legal files perched on the edge of his expansive desk. Her discomfort increased as she slid to a spot beside him. The different perspective highlighted the reflection of the gray lake and winter slate-blue sky blending together off the glass frame of the expensive, utterly ugly, original Kaminski oil stuck on Knudsen's priceless rosewood paneling.

Knudsen cleared his throat, his hesitation and confusion further disorienting Sarah.

"You must understand," he finally began, "how important you've become to both the firm and to me."

"I do the best I can, Mr. Knudsen. What's the—"

"You have ignored or rejected my attempts to express my attraction to you." His hyperventilating chest heaved, threatening a coronary Sarah wished would come at this moment. "It's time for a more direct approach. Sarah, I offer you a belated holiday blow-job bonus."

Knudsen rose and pressed her back against the floor-to-ceiling windows, three hundred feet above Lake Shore Drive. His outstretched arms cut off several of Sarah's desperate attempts at escape. He towered well over six feet and weighed more than two hundred pounds. Yet his exposed erection, peeking out from his open zipper, barely cleared the palm of his sweaty hand as he thrust towards her. She considered her options. None looked good.

"Five hundred dollars if you'll suck me off. Of course, at that price, you'll have to swallow."

Sarah's nerve-racked emotions exploded. She let go with a hammering roundhouse punch. Fury and despair injected strength into her slender, clenched right hand. Her fist cracked into the man's patrician jaw.

His head snapped back. The blow and shocked surprise drove Knudsen several stumbling steps backwards. And then he fell. The back of his head smacked the edge of his desk, making a sickening sound. His butt bounced once on the carpet, and he sat still in a sitting position, long legs angled askew.

Sarah screamed, but the sound of her voice seemed muted and far away. She sprinted to the door, shouting for Abigail. The receptionist met Sarah's rush down the hall. Sarah grabbed her and wheeled back to Knudsen's office.

"What's wrong?" Abigail gasped. "What's the matter?"

Sarah didn't answer, just led Abigail into the office and to the attorney's limp figure.

"Holy Mother of God," Abigail cried. "He's dead."

Knudsen no longer looked cool and debonair. In fact, his shriveled cock hung out of his pants like a wilted banana peel. Then his eyes fluttered open. Sarah stifled a hysterical laugh. Abigail kept gaping from Knudsen to Sarah. The man's moan came as a relief.

"Don't forget this picture, Abigail," Sarah said, indicating the embarrassing organ.

"No way," Abigail said.

"Do you need a doctor, Mr. Knudsen?" Abigail asked.

A slow shake of his head and bright red face served as the answer. He appeared much shorter and rather foolish sitting on his ass. A startled expression turned sheepish as he gazed up at Sarah and Abigail. This could be Sarah's last day at Gold, Smith, Knudsen and Harrington, but she had leverage now. And she planned to take full advantage of it.

* * *

Matthew's skis were on. The two tram passengers had disappeared. Rendezvous Bowl sat wide-open to his right. He traversed across the top of the bowl, following tracks cut earlier that morning until he reached the middle of Rendezvous. One quick turn and he stopped. The two other skiers had already reached the bottom of the bowl. They looked insignificant against the vast valley floor stretching far below.

The unfamiliar warmth of the sun registered on his face. Snow had fallen for three days, skies clearing yesterday at noon. The mountain had been skied out only to a limited extent. Miles of untracked powder beckoned, still available late in the morning. The top section of Rendezvous Bowl had been packed down by earlier skiers, much easier to handle. As the bowl opened up near its middle, the friendlier, skied-out sections diminished. And the higher temperatures brought bad news—the snow pack would lose its crystal-dry lightness, to be replaced with moisture that would add a dense, grabbing stickiness to the snow's texture. Matthew felt sandwiched between excitement and intimidation.

When he rotated his tips downhill, gravity took over. The first series of turns were easy and solid. The bowl dropped with enough vertical descent to generate plenty of involuntary speed. He struggled with increasing amounts of thicker, chopped-up powder. His turns became jerky. He worked harder, his breathing irregular, his wounded body parts communicating their lack of cooperation.

Matthew stopped a quarter of the way down the bowl, gasping in ragged breaths, searching for oxygen in the thin air at 10,000 feet. His thigh throbbed. His side ached. His arm's frantic attempts to maintain balance had strained and stretched the scar tissue of his shoulder. No surprises. But when he looked down the remaining three-fourths of Rendezvous Bowl, he had a growing awareness of the snow's increasing density and the absence of packed turns.

Matthew again pointed his skis down, made one turn, struggled through another and flew out of control. He'd developed more speed than he could handle and instinctively leaned back for perceived balance and safety. The sudden eruption of pain in his thigh served as a catapult. Matthew bailed out, throwing his body to the side, crashing into the deep, chunky powder. His body stuck on impact. This time tears of pain fogged the portion of his goggles not packed with snow.

The size and scope of Jackson Hole hit him like an avalanche. The questions he'd asked, answered, and discarded on his easy runs down Apres Vous reappeared. The excruciating agony in his thigh frightened him the most.

This could be a serious control problem. Sitting back on skis was a time-honored defensive position. Leaning back was ugly and provided no future, but the technique served as an invaluable tool to check unwanted speed and offer a desperate skier a last-second escape hatch. Getting down this monster of a mountain with the growing grip of wet crud and without that option turned Matthew's doubts to fear. But he had no alternatives.

Matthew crashed and burned his way through the bowl. His frequent losses of balance resulted in nasty, body-twisting headers into the mountainside. Then he missed the Laramie Traverse pointed out by Shebang on the ride up, a long and winding snow-cat-packed trail that would have led him safely to the security of the Village. Instead, he found himself at the top of the Central Chute, which dropped into Cheyenne Bowl, Cheyenne Gully, and who knew what other calamities.

The drop down the chute provided a moment's relief. Steep and narrow, with less powder and crud. The vertical drop of Central returned Matthew to his element. He had grown up skiing the hard-packed cliffs and chutes of Squaw Valley's KT22 and Headwall. He'd made trips during college to Aspen, the new and overrated Park City, and magical Alta. He had broken an ankle in Sun Valley. Those resorts had runs packed out by skiers and snow cats long before noon. Finally something that provided a degree of confidence.

He hopped to the bottom of the chute. He surveyed the limitless terrain. No skiers anywhere in sight. Jackson Hole had to be at least twice as big as any resort he'd visited. And no one to ask directions. Well, as he'd arrogantly told TJ, only way to go was down.

The relative flats of Cheyenne Gully brought no mercy. Matthew's skis sank into the dense snow, tracking in directions of their own choosing. He had no steep hill to help initiate a turn, no rhythm, no safety valve in sitting back. He headed in directions he didn't desire, diving into the snow when hitting trees became imminent. His disastrous trip worsened. He eventually popped out of the gully and began the long, wide-open descent of Sublette Ridge. Pain and fatigue blended into a swirl of misery equal to the nightmares of Nam, lacking only the pure fear of death.

FOURTEEN

Matthew was hammered, humiliated, humbled. But he was off the mountain, resting and with no new injuries. At least nothing registered as abnormal amidst the usual and expected aches and pains. That was the good news, but he had to gain strength if he was to survive the real Jackson Hole.

His trip to the bottom of the mountain had blended into a semicomatose sequence of one mindless step after another. Or, in this case, one uncontrolled crash after another. Survival became a byproduct without conscious recognition. And to think, his own free will had placed him in such a miserable situation.

The bench of a picnic table on the cafeteria deck beckoned. He collapsed, wondering the time, too tired to turn around and look up at the Clock Tower. His new buddy, the young black Lab, supplied a wet welcome, working overtime on Matthew's face.

"Cody likes you." Shebang appeared at the edge of the deck. "Course he likes anything breathing. Even me."

Matthew nudged Cody and his hyperactive tongue away from his face. Cody accepted the rejection and turned his attentions on Shebang. The patroller grabbed the puppy with both hands, flipping him on his back. Shebang scratched the Lab's exposed belly. Cody's rear legs flailed the air like a demented bicyclist.

"But he can be a pain in the ass." Shebang's words were inconsistent with the affection he showered on the puppy. "I don't have a place to keep him during the days. If I tie him up, he barks nonstop. He loves roaming round the Village. Don't cause no trouble. But the new asshole Mountain Manager's threatening to kick out all the dogs and fine the owners. Doesn't want this high-class resort cluttered up with dog shit. Like it's so crowded you couldn't step around it. If he's got a hard-on for dogs, he should go after the nasty packs terrorizing downtown Jackson."

"You'd think management would welcome anything giving this desolate place a little life," Matthew said. Executives acted no different than officers, both a pain in the ass. "He's a great dog."

"Yeah, I do love him. But he pisses me off sometimes. I just got a real bad temper."

Shebang's square head and blocky body radiated aggressive, even angry, energy. He ripped at his safety straps and kicked off his skis. Then he reached down, grabbed his metal Fischers with a jerk, just missing his dog's head.

"That how you got your name?" Matthew had to ask.

"'Fraid so." Shebang leaned forward as he spoke to Matthew. The patroller's mouth, hard and straight, gave few clues. "Looks like you made it down okay."

Shebang took his skis and headed for the Tram.

"Okay's a relative term," Matthew said to Shebang's back. No wonder Teton Village lacked skiers, if this guy reflected the resort's approach to customer service.

Matthew groaned, picking up his new Heads, and stumbled around the cafeteria to the parking lot. He'd had enough. He was beat. Cody escorted him to his truck, then trotted away. Matthew struggled to get his boots off, then eased himself behind the wheel.

The Clock Tower was now visible out his windshield—12:21. An hour and a half to pay his dues on the tram run. Pretty pathetic. He needed rest. And he needed some lessons.

*   *   *

Two vehicles stood in the parking area in front of the garage back at the Grand View Lodge. Wesley's unmistakable black monster pickup faced Matthew's modest one-room cabin. The truck looked ready to devour the small structure. A large, new brown Wagoneer sat next to Wesley's. It still had the dealer's cardboard license: "Salt Lake Motors, Utah's 4-Wheel Headquarters."

Matthew stepped towards the quiet comfort of his cabin, hesitated, then succumbed to the lure of Wesley and his laughter. He entered the front door of the lodge and limped down the hallway into the bright sunlit living room. Wesley, Jim, and another man sat at the dining room table, papers, maps and blueprints littering the large surface.

"Well, well." Wesley's smile overwhelmed the day's dazzling sunshine. "Looks like you finally made it to the mountain."

"Looks to me," Jim said, "like a case of hit and run."

"Hey, you were supposed to call me to ski with you." Wesley's mouth puckered as if sucking a lemon, but his eyes sparkled as if he enjoyed the taste.

"It was ugly," Matthew confessed. "I did you a favor by not ruining your morning."

"Well, other than looking chewed up by a snowplow, how was it?" Wesley's voice shifted into concern.

"I survived. I was okay on the hard pack. The one chute I hit wasn't too bad either. But I died in the crud. Never struggled so long and so hard. Biggest problem, I can't lean back . . . " Matthew let his words trail off. No reason to dwell any further on his weakness.

"That's fine." Jim got up and motioned Matthew over to the table. "To ski this stuff, you've got to be on top of your skis. Not sitting back is gonna force you to handle Jackson Hole the right way."

"Yeah," Matthew admitted, "but sometimes you've got to bail backwards to save your ass. At least the weather's getting nice."

"You ski alone?" Jim asked.

Matthew nodded.

"The way to get better quick," Jim said, "is to ski with guys better than you."

Wesley seconded the comment.

"Before I ski with anyone decent," Matthew said, "I've got to take some lessons. These conditions are completely different from anything I've skied before. At least skied voluntarily."

Julia floated into the kitchen like an awe-inspiring, oversized nymph. Matthew noticed, so did Wesley and the unintroduced guest. Eyes followed her movements until she turned and acknowledged their stares with a slight smile and nod. Only Jim ignored her, focusing on the papers spread over the table. He pulled Matthew back into conversation.

"You know who could help you?" Jim said. "Kurt Sidon is one of the only Americans working full-time as an instructor. 'Full-time' is the joke. The little ski bunnies and flatlanders jump on the studly European instructors. It's bullshit. They barely speak English. Arrogant jerks. Kurt's usually the last to pick up clients, but he's good. Got a way of connecting verbally. Translates technique to your individual needs. Uses good imagery."

"Imagery?" Wesley chuckled. "Why, Jungle Jim, I had no idea there was a literary side to that Mountain Man personality."

"Screw you." Jim flipped him off. "Kurt's got lots of down time. You could work a deal with him since you're pretty flexible. When he strikes out, you could fill in at a discount. Call him at the ski school. He's probably available now."

"No way. I'm trashed. I'll check in with him tomorrow."

The third man continued to sit quietly at the table. Medium-length dark brown hair framed a face of dark olive complexion, the features of which didn't quite match up. Nice manners. Patient. Who was he?

"This here's David Moore," Jim said, making the belated introduction.

David stood as Matthew moved over to shake hands. The new man was several inches shorter than Matthew's six feet, had a medium-firm grip and a crooked smile. Matthew took in the large, long nose, small mouth, tiny, strangely misshapen ears, and the mismatched cheekbones, one slightly swollen, the other partially indented.

"It's a pleasure," David said.

His soft voice sounded sincere, almost sweet, inconsistent with his disjointed features. The total effect was that of a good-looking man who'd been in an accident. Enough of the original promise remained to present a not-too-unpleasant picture.

"Dave's a financier," Jim said. "He's staked a number of us. I built him a nice log home over on Fish Creek, north of Wilson, when he moved here two years ago. He's helped Wesley with his garage expansion and me with the Grand View."

"We're looking to buy two hundred acres of Morgan's Circle C Ranch." Wesley pointed to a map of the Jackson Hole valley. "The old man told me he's willin' to sell acreage between the Wilson highway and Snake River. All flat, great views of the Tetons, river frontage. Dave puts up the money. I get the zonin' changed to residential with my outstandin' and upright connections with the County Planners. And Jim builds the houses. We break it into four- or five-acre parcels and go slow."

"Slow seems to be the operative word in all of Teton County," Matthew said.

"Hey, man. One day this place is gonna be big time," Wesley said, poking at the map. "Right now we're goin' through some growin' pains, but Jackson Hole's beautiful and the mountain's bitchin'."

"Bitchin' or a bitch?" The immediate investment future of Jackson Hole, Wyoming, didn't look that promising to Matthew.

"Once word gets out," Jim said, "Jackson Hole'll be as hot as Aspen or Sun Valley, it'll be a boomtown. Houses, hotels, condos, restaurants, bars, more lifts at Teton Village. We got history as well as scenery and wild animals. The place'll be packed during ski season and summertime."

"Be careful what you wish for," Matthew said, recalling aggravating crowds at most ski resorts. "I'm going to shower and take a nap while you three take over the world. Nice to meet you, David."

FIFTEEN

Matthew looked out the window at the imposing shadow of the brand-new Grand View Lodge. A pond, creek, and several rows of leafless aspens sat between the cabin and the highway. Snowplows would awaken Matthew at night. But unlike the panicky, sweaty nightmares that jerked him out of sleep, the roar of the engine and clanking of the tire chains confirmed the safety of the present. Everything he valued fit into his dark cocoon—clothes, books, records and turntable. No radio, and sure as hell no TV.

Traffic's album "John Barlycorn" blasted through the small room. He felt secure, calm and in control after surviving his first day on the mountain. The echoing words from "Freedom Rider" rattled in his head. Something about hope.

Low flames glowed a deep orange, heating the tight space. Matthew completed his stretching and sat clad in only a t-shirt and long-john bottoms, despite the thirty below temperature outside. Little to look at sitting at his table, except the driveway and lit opening of the lodge's master bedroom.

The master bedroom. Something had changed. The old shadow beyond the bedroom drapes was gone. A small piece of furniture, perhaps a coatrack, had blocked the view through the window when he had first moved in. Then Matthew saw movement. The fabric curtain parted.

Julia looked out towards the driveway. She was topless—and maybe bottomless—absently caressing her massive breasts, fingers lingering on large nipples. Matthew watched, then remembered to breathe. Waves of emotion and heat swirled through his battered body. Over six months without any sexual feeling or desire, six months without an erection.

Instead, he'd endured the embarrassing fear of being sexually damaged or impotent. But as he sat staring at the outline of Julia's exposed ample breasts, life came to what he had feared had become a vestigial organ.

And tears. His tears. Another dormant function of his body. Not the tears of rage in battle. Not the tears of anger and bitterness in the hospital. Rather a soft, comfortable wetness that evidenced some form of humanity. Matthew focused on the moisture on his face. What human emotions must these tears represent? He touched himself, and his eyes flowed unchecked.

Did Julia know he often sat there in the evening, lights out? She had backed away from sight, but not from his memory as he remained hard. What would happen when a woman caressed his body? Would a warning help? "Rough road ahead." Making love in the dark might hide the visuals, but not the sensations of touch. He pulled his shirt off. Shivered. The fire had lost some of its intensity.

His head wounds, coming only six weeks into his Viet Nam tour, had been the easiest to deal with. He had poked his head out of a filthy drainage ditch, then a soundless explosion had consumed him in a vibrating vortex. He had regained a degree of consciousness in the chopper. Bodies surrounded him, some dead, some wounded, all covered in blood. He had fit right in, had moved, touching his head, feeling the sticky fluid, attracting the attention of one of the medics. A quick needle, and even pain had subsided. The only clear thought: Cool, I'm going home. "Hey, man, a little skin and blood is all," the grungy medic had said. "We'll get your sorry ass back on the line in a week."

Seven days later he had rejoined his unit, a small hole in his face and an ugly scar from his forehead to the top of his head. Now he fingered the old wound in the dark. The once deep furrow had begun to fill in. The mirror would continue to provide more lasting evidence of the experience.

He reached over his shoulder and traced as much of the large piece of scar tissue disfiguring his upper back as he could touch. This was the one that still brought out the rage. Napalm. U.S. of A. napalm, delivered to the wrong address by Matthew's own Air Force. Still no ticket home.

The third time had been the charm. But at a terrible price. Life changed forever. He felt the still tender scars on his left side, unable to tell the difference between the ragged entries of shrapnel from the extensive slices by the surgeons when they removed his shredded kidney. He didn't bother to extend his journey to the red, ridged damage of his thigh, covered by his long johns.

Now, how would this work? Maybe a set of instructions with a map? Look, Ma'am, you can touch my right side, but stay away from my left thigh. Your lips are welcome below my nose, and you can whisper in my ear. Just don't run your fingers through my hair. Please study this map before we turn off the lights.

"Hope springs eternal or something like that," Matthew said out loud, hoping tonight for different dreams with beautiful, creamy breasts.

SIXTEEN

Man, he was starving. The taxi, Franky's one daily luxury, had dropped him at his Jersey apartment at eight, an hour and a half later than usual. That son of bitch Ian Murphy, the new union rep, created more grief than the tax man.

"Dinner's a little cold," his mother said at her normal church-mouse volume. "You didn't tell me how late you'd be."

Franky ignored her and shoveled a forkful of pasta into his mouth. What was this shit? Tasted like sawdust in an old leather pouch. Resin-bag ravioli.

"Jesus. You gotta be the only Italian woman in the world who can't cook."

Her injured look, as usual, generated regret. The poor thing had no redeeming qualities, but her love was the only constant in Franky's life. That alone was worth protecting. He had to be more patient with her.

The real source of his anger was Murphy. Only two months on the job and he was demanding an additional ten per cent kickback. Labor costs already cut the biggest chunk out of D and F's profit margin. This asshole didn't realize how far out of line his demands took him. Didn't he know not to fuck with Franky?

A pounding on the door interrupted Franky's thoughts. Not a knock, but blows just short of blasting the front door off its hinges. His mother's wild-eyed glances jerked from Franky to the vibrating door. She jumped to her feet, made a full, frightened circle, then ran to the increasing racket in the entryway.

"Who is it?" she asked, her voice as fragile as blue-veined china.

"Just open the door, please."

Jesus Christ. Sal. What in the hell would bring him to Jersey from his Manhattan cave? All remnants of hunger disappeared like a mouse in a hole. The door blew open, and Sal and Marco barged in.

Sal led the charge that ended abruptly when the older brother realized the momentum of their entrance had bounced Franky's mother against the wall.

"I'm so sorry to interrupt your meal," Sal said, astonishing Franky with his unexpected shift to courtesy. "We've got a crisis that requires immediate attention."

He swept over to the table and glared at Franky, jerking a thumb towards the front door. Sal's consideration did not extend to Franky. Franky's anger flared at both his and his mother's treatment, then sputtered, doused by a wave of all-encompassing fear. Franky grabbed his coat and followed Sal out the door without hesitation into the freezing winter weather. What the hell was going on?

"You still got your car?" Sal asked outside on the porch.

"Ah, uh." Franky had an old Nova in the garage, but he hadn't started the rusted heap in days.

"It's a simple question, Franky." Sal's voice rose in irritation, a bad sign. "For a college boy, you're mighty damn slow with the answers."

"I don't know if it'll start," Franky whined. "Can't we use yours?"

Sal directed primitive, flaring eyes towards Franky.

"Get the fuckin' car."

Franky headed to the apartment's four-car garage. He gave a prayer of thanks when he found the keys in his pocket. He struggled to unlock the padlocked door, then stumbled to his lime-green sedan. Sal snatched the keys and pointed to the back seat.

"Marco's driving."

Franky groped his way into the rear, fear growing exponentially. Would they kill him? Why? What had he done? How could he save himself?

The Nova coughed, then turned over. Franky didn't know whether to thank God or hope the puny engine would die. Marco accelerated out of the garage, jamming on the brakes when he hit the street. Franky slid to the floor. He scrambled back onto the slippery vinyl. Marco bounced down the darkened street, Sal riding shotgun without a look back at Franky.

Franky rode helpless, a prisoner, no options, no weapons, no escape.

This must be what the German Jews had felt in the hands of the Gestapo. He bit down on his lip. Tasted blood. Refused to moan. Fought back tears. Might as well go out like a man. At least he hadn't peed his pants.

Franky looked beyond the cell of the back seat as they rumbled through the Lincoln Tunnel to downtown. If his brothers were going to kill him, why head back into the city? Wasn't he worth more alive than dead? Sal was smart enough to analyze a profit and loss statement. He must know where the swelling cash flow came from. But a small voice in his head, close to hysterical, kept refuting logic—his brothers didn't always react in a rational manner.

"Whatta you think, Franky?" Sal directed a look towards Franky. "Good thing they dumped McGuire and hired Holtzman? They been kicking ass since trading for DeBusschere."

What were the morons talking about now? Basketball? The Knicks? Who gave a shit?

"Goddamn Golden Era for New York." Marco's voice had the same threatening tone as his brother's. "Need a few white boys to keep those niggers, Frazier and Reed, in line."

Franky's lips remained sealed. Was this what these guys talked about at a funeral?

"First the Jets win the Super Bowl. Now the Knicks can go all the way," Sal hummed, almost happy.

"Yeah," Marco said. "And it's only a matter of time before the Yankees get their act together again. Whatta you think, Franky, ain't that great?"

They're playing with me, Franky realized. Lull him into comfort, then blow his brains out. Fear reached new levels, his body aching, heartbeat hammering in his ears.

"Franky," Sal said, "I'm talking to you." This time the older brother lifted his body, turning to face Franky. "Look, little man, nothing's gonna happen to you if you do what I say. I promise on my mother's breast, and that covers some territory."

His laughter echoed through the Nova, drowning out the sound but not the vibration of Franky's heart. Marco jerked the car to a halt. Franky had no clue where they were within the empty caverns of the city.

"Stay here," Sal warned.

Doors slammed, and Franky slumped against the window. Should he run? Nowhere to go. He remained paralyzed, frigid air filtering back into the car. Time passed. Franky sat. Finally, movement in the shadows. Sal and Marco returning to torment their victim.

This time Sal pushed into the back seat with Franky, crushing him further into the corner. The large man filled the small space as the car again rocketed down the deserted streets. He flipped an object to Franky, who instinctively grabbed it. A heavy gun. He shifted his grip from barrel to the grip, reacting to the warmth of the steel. A .357 Magnum. The same weapon Franky had used in the alley? Sal snatched the pistol back with gloved hands.

"Anthony's dependable," Sal said, "but not too smart. Forgot you was wearing gloves. I ain't quite as low on the evolutionary ladder as him. Can't depend only on ballistics to convict a man. Not a problem now."

Again laughter barraged Franky's eardrums. Marco lurched to a stop, and Sal headed to the front seat, pausing to lean back towards Franky.

"You should thank us, bro." Sal's leer brought a spinning nausea to Franky. "We just took care of the biggest pain in your ass. You'll be dealing with a new, more cooperative union rep now."

Son of a bitch. A bitter sense of relief surfaced. No reason to eliminate him now. His fingerprints covered a pistol that had killed at least two men. A flash of admiration lit the darkness in his soul. Pretty slick for a couple of dumb pricks.

Fear drifted to controllable limits. Fierce hatred filled the vacuum. Franky ignored the brothers' conversation as they reentered Jersey. To think he'd moved out of Manhattan to avoid family pressures. He'd have to travel a hell of a lot further for any safety from these two psychopaths.

Marco headed the Nova into its space. Sal opened the rear door and yanked Franky out.

"Get your momma to cover your ass," Sal directed. "We was never here, and you never left home. You gotta realize you'll be the prime suspect now that Murphy's disappeared. You had every reason to kill the prick. Punk was a pig."

"Not sure Mother will lie," Franky said. "She'd consider it a sin."

"Tell that bitch she better cooperate," Sal flared, menace reflecting despite the dim light. "She can go to confession and cleanse her whoring soul. Had plenty of practice."

SEVENTEEN

Nothing had changed at the nearly empty parking lot in Teton Village. Clear skies, but colder temperatures even now at 10:30 in the morning. Matthew had no illusions about the task at hand. His quads throbbed, the wound that took his left kidney ached and an impressive bruise flowered red, black, and blue on his right hip, planted by his ski-pole handle sometime, somewhere during yesterday's chaotic, crashing journey down the tram run. Still the absence of any new serious injuries encouraged him.

Then Matthew surprised himself. He walked past the lonely ticket window and into the resort offices to purchase a season pass. The impulsive move was like the reappearance of an old high school buddy, the companion or accomplice who pushed and prodded you into your most exciting adventures. The same one who goaded you over the edge into deep trouble. Perhaps even the inner voice that had convinced him to enlist and sign up with the Rangers.

Hadn't Matthew left this questionable friend in the jungles and rice paddies of Viet Nam? No way to know for sure yet. At this point, he'd welcome any temptation that would shake him loose from his disturbing past, expand his horizons. But most important, he had no other plan, nothing else that would provide the focus to free him from the nightmares. So he bought the pass. Charged the $200 to his credit card. And felt good, regardless of the taint of the decision as compulsive or impulsive.

Matthew entered the small building that housed the Jackson Hole Ski School, the tiny lobby as empty as the resort. A bell on the counter summoned an overweight, sunburned, wind-blown blonde of indeterminate age and about as feminine as an old pack mule. She walked to the desk with an expression that could have been a smile.

"Help ya?" Her twang matched her creased skin.

"I've got a lesson with Kurt. Do I meet him here?"

"Got a lift ticket?"

Matthew showed her his pass.

"Just wait. He'll be here in a few minutes."

Slam, bang, thank you, Ma'am, and she went back through the door to the back offices. Probably weeks behind on her paperwork.

A large, framed shot on the lobby wall pictured Pepi Steigler, Ski School Director and 1964 Olympic gold medalist from Austria. The photo captured the intensity of his eyes, the determination of hard mouth and jaw. Impressive, but where was the patience and understanding, requirements for a teacher of students way over their heads in the wilds of Jackson Hole?

Matthew checked out the twelve smaller pictures of instructors, a handsome group—Hans, Walter, Franz, Gunther, Eric, Peter. And Kurt, indistinguishable from the Europeans, with long dark hair, piercing brown eyes, a weird small nose, reminding Matthew of a UCLA cheer leader's nose job. Kurt offered the foreign teachers' same condescending smile for the camera. A serious face. Not necessarily a happy one.

Then Kurt, in the flesh, stepped into the lobby from outside. The photo had captured the man but left out a layer of history etched on his face.

"I'm your instructor, Kurt Sidon." The instructor shook hands in businesslike fashion. "You ready? What's your pleasure? Tram or chair?"

"Tram."

Matthew figured things couldn't get any worse than yesterday. And the instructor would know the best ways down, Matthew hoped, as they walked the short distance to the Tram.

"I'll watch you ski, get an idea where you need help," Kurt said and pointed out the tram window. "We'll head down Rendezvous Bowl, now that it's skied out and easier to handle, and cross the Laramie Traverse."

"I'd like to catch at least one steeper chute," Matthew said.

Kurt looked somewhat dubious, but agreed to Matthew's request, choosing the Tower Three Chute. Matthew skied, thrashed and crashed once. But he did have his positive moments, especially in the steeps.

At the bottom of Tower Three Chute the instructor asked, "How often do you want lessons?"

"Everyday."

"You've got that kind of time and money?"

"That kind, yes."

"All right," Kurt said. "I'll fit you in at the same low rate of $8 an hour for three or four days a week, two-hour shots, if you stay flexible. Lessons that often may be too much. You've got a ways to go."

* * *

Sarah glanced at Abigail for the twentieth time. The secretary returned the same smile and vigorous nod. Sarah had practiced her routine with Abigail during lunch. But, now, back in the office, the plan seemed less plausible.

"Sarah," Abigail said. "Do it now."

Sarah took a deep breath. Her sweaty palms matched the trembling of her hands. Maybe she should just forget this hair-brained scheme. Then Abigail spoke into her intercom.

"Mr. Knudsen, Sarah has some papers that need your immediate review."

"You bitch," Sarah's squeaked. Abigail smiled as Knudsen consented.

"Honey, you got the cards. I'm here to back you up. Move your cute little butt."

Sarah snatched an empty folder, filled it with several case studies and began the long walk to her boss' office. She dared not look back at Abigail. Instead, she focused on her outrage with Knudsen's transformation from a father figure to a sex-starved bastard. She knocked.

"What do you have, Sarah?"

Sarah entered, keeping her eyes on the blue-gray winter sky outside the huge picture window. She sat in the leather armchair before his desk, folding her hands in a tight ball on top of the file. No question he had been shaken up by his blow-job-bonus fiasco. He'd kept their required exchanges to a minimum, devoid of the usual sexual innuendos and gestures.

"Mr. Knudsen," Sarah said, "I haven't been feeling well for several weeks. I'm nervous, my stomach's constantly upset, can't sleep, and I'm having trouble concentrating at work."

"Have you seen a doctor?"

"No. I don't really know what to tell my doctor."

His eyes reflected instant recognition at where the conversation was headed. His impressive jaw tightened.

"What can I do to help?" he said, his hands working overtime, twirling the gold Cross pen he always used.

Sarah had expected an angry response, an immediate rejection of her concerns and ejection from the room. But Abigail had been right. Knudsen grew more tense as the silence lengthened.

"Sarah, you're a very critical part of our practice." Knudsen gathered himself, sat up straighter. "There's something I have to confess. While I have apologized for my clumsy advances, I haven't properly expressed how much I care for you, both as an employee and a woman. I hope we can overcome the silly games we've played and get back to business."

We. What an asshole. Anger drove Sarah beyond her fears and any consideration of her boss' lame comments.

"I would do anything to help you through any difficulties." He sounded sincere, but trust was no longer in the picture. "Why don't you take some time off?"

"My vacation starts in three weeks. I already have plans. If I take time off, I'll jeopardize – "

"No. No. Not at all." Her boss smiled, sweeping off the thin sheen of sweat blossoming on his high forehead. "Nothing is more important than your health."

"What about the Dumas bankruptcy?"

"Damn, I forgot about that." Worry warped the fine features of his face. "Trial's set for next Wednesday, isn't it?"

"Yes, sir."

"How much longer will it take for you to prepare?"

"Normally, three or four days, but I can't seem to focus. It might take the full week."

"What if you do the best you can in the next couple of days and we use Margaret to finish up? You could take a leave of absence and add it to your vacation."

"Paid leave?"

"Absolutely."

Abigail, I love you. Sarah sat as long as possible, pretending to consider the offer, patience as difficult as holding her breath under water. Should she give her boss another chance?

"Okay, Mr. Knudsen," Sarah said. "I'll do my best under the circumstances."

EIGHTEEN

Matthew's confidence soared with his improved technique. He now felt comfortable skiing and hanging in with a core group made up of Wesley, Jim, TJ, and David. The instructor expressed himself as advertised: Tight, simple imagery. He had connected well with Matthew, teaching him big-mountain skiing and providing insight into Jackson Hole and the men who skied it.

"Forget all that shoulder rotation bullshit," the instructor explained, as his stable head and chest belied the compression of the bumps of Paint Brush. "Ski like you're driving a car. Keep your hands in front of you at all times, your shoulders facing down the hill. Use your legs as pistons. Your upper body stays quiet.

"Your thigh injury keeps you from sitting back?" Kurt said when Matthew complained. "Good. Use the pain as a governor, like a car with the carburetor rigged so you can't go over 65. Whenever you feel the pain, you're back too far. Be conscious of your hands and lean forward until you're back on top of your skis.

"There's a sweet spot where you always want your weight." The instructor demonstrated, standing upright on top of his skis. "It's right under your boots. Feel the pressure on the balls of your feet, never your heels.

"Always look ahead. Pick a line, at least four or five turns ahead all the time. When you're tree skiing," he said, leading a tight path through the firs and pines above the Mushrooms, "never look directly at the trees or you'll meet them up close and personal. Pick a path through them.

"Your double-pole-plant method in the steeps is good," he complimented Matthew after a rapid descent down the Expert Chutes. "Both hands are forward, shoulders squared. Just build a more secure, balanced platform with your skis before each turn.

"Watch the Europeans. I know I'm good, particularly in the steeps. But I'm like the local high school football star. They're pros, N.F.L. All Stars. They're also pretty decent guys, despite what Jim says. They're shy and uncomfortable out here in Wyoming. Give them a chance, and you'll like and respect them a lot more.

"The ski patrol is the wildest, craziest group of fuck-ups ever assembled in one resort. Half of them are on drugs, the other half drunk. But even in their altered states, they know and respect this mountain. The head of the patrol, Billy Simpson, is probably the only straight one of the bunch. And they make him pay for that."

At the beginning of the third week Matthew realized that Kurt never talked about himself. Kurt would have the occasional beer at the Mangy Moose or the Alpen Haus after a day on the mountain, but he avoided the social scene. That was just fine with Matthew. He had no desire to share his clouded past. Mutual silence was a gift of comfort. Matthew had all the social contact he needed with Wesley and the calm presence of David. Jim took up too much space already. Still, a ski instructor should exhibit a few more social skills than the taciturn Kurt if he wanted to build a clientele. Maybe that was the reason he had so many open slots.

February
1969

NINETEEN

Matthew drove into the Calico's parking lot, the old Jeep bouncing over the rutted snow pack. Snow had fallen in various amounts for eleven straight days. Tomorrow promised no break in the streak. He jammed on the brakes and pulled to the right to adjust the direction of the Jeep's headlights.

His high beams lit up a dented, bruised VW convertible of many shades and indeterminate color. The top was down despite the below-zero evening air. The car and the falling snow resembled a Christmas scene for a stoned hippie—the inside of a crystal ball with the flakes flying when shaken.

Matthew parked and walked by the strange, out-of-season Bug. Snow filled the car, except for a space carved out for the driver. A thin new layer of light powder filtered over the exposed seat. The convertible top had been ripped from the car, the metal hinges attached to the frame twisted and mangled. Hell, the VW made his old Jeep look respectable.

Thursday night, seven-thirty, all was well at the Calico. Matthew made his way over to a table inhabited by TJ and a strange, short young man. TJ's long hair and shit-eating grin looked conservative compared to the wild man vibrating on the stool next to him.

"Matthew, my man." TJ's smile widened beyond the physically possible. "Meet my good buddy, Abraham. Call him Abe and he'll kill you."

A full natural flowed into an additional foot-long length of growth flaring over Abraham's shoulders. His huge, round hazel eyes reflected passion, excitement—and heavy drugs. The boy resembled an electrocuted lion. His grip, as he grabbed Matthew's hand, left much more than just a firm impression.

"Abraham's back from a temporary gig down in Alta. He patrols here from the middle of February until the season ends first of April. Things actually get a little busy in Jackson Hole in March when the cold lightens up a little." TJ's smile partnered with a giggle. He'd find humor in a dead cat. "If Abraham's too long a name, you can call him Ace."

Large features sculpted Ace's dark face, further distorting his strange image as he stood to his full height of five and a half feet. A thick, wide body provided practical support for his outsized head—a maniacal prophet from an unholy land. The energy of the two men-children brought a smile to Matthew's lips.

A pile of soaked, still steaming ski equipment—gloves, hat, neck gaiter, facemask, goggles—cluttered the table. Matthew cleared a small space, wiping away a wet puddle of melted snow.

"Careful. That's my drivin' gear," Ace said. "It gets a little chilly in my machine. Heat doesn't work at all."

"What happened to the top of your car?"

"Well, I bought my little baby in Salt Lake." Quick, choppy words exploded out of his large mouth in deep, tense tones. This boy was wired to the gills. "The damn top had so many holes in it, I had to drive with hat, gloves, goggles and even a facemask. Plus, the noise of the air whistling through the torn canvas drove me nuts."

"Bet that was a short drive," Matthew said.

"Funny," Ace said, not the least bit offended. "There's a small park at the mouth of Little Cottonwood Canyon. Got a cute rock arch you can walk over. I measured the height. Took the old ragtop half down, sticking straight up in the air. Snow wasn't too deep in the gully below the arch. Got a hundred yard run and went under the bridge at forty miles an hour. Just cleared the windshield. Man, it ripped the top clean off."

"Clean?" Matthew remembered the jagged metal on the sides of the VW.

"The seats were all soggy and stinkin'," Ace continued, pride evident in his staccato delivery. "I let the snow pile up and freeze the suckers—no smell. First, though, I drilled holes in the floor so when the snow melts it'll drain. That idea came from my engineering background."

"What engineering background?" TJ snorted.

"Let me ask you something." Matthew imagined Ace flying along the road with top down, hat and goggles. He hadn't smiled this much in years. "Cops ever stop you for impersonating a hallucination?"

Ace howled, looking over at TJ, jerking a hand at Matthew with obvious approval. Laughter seemed to be one of the few things that could stop Ace from talking. But he and TJ could be sidetracked for only so long.

"In the summer, though," Ace said, "a convertible's great. Even if it stinks a little."

"Yeah, I've got a convertible myself," Matthew offered. "At least your VW handles okay in the snow. My Corvette's not worth a damn. If the road's straight and dry, great. But the Vette can't corner, and it's got too much torque for the snow."

"I'd love a Corvette." Ace looked out of the Calico's window to the parking lot. "I don't see it out there."

"Well, Ace, it happens to be pitch black and snowing outside. And the parking lot's on the other side of the building," Matthew said, pointing through the civilized half of the Calico in a directional gesture wasted on Ace. "Besides, the car's at Wesley's garage 'til the spring. Hell, if I had to pick one of the two cars for the winter, I think I'd rather have your Beetle. I've been closer to death driving that Corvette than when I was in Nam."

Damn. Matthew hadn't meant to let that piece of information slip out. He squirmed in his seat against the wall. Sure enough, his comment opened the wrong door.

"You were in Nam?" Ace leaned closer. "I thought so. You got the look."

"Yeah. You?" Matthew asked, knowing the answer.

"Are you kiddin'? I'm 4 fucking F."

"How'd you pull that off?" Matthew popped the question he longed to ask all of these crazy, healthy ski bums.

"You hear all about those guys drinking, doing coke, sipping soy sauce all night to screw up their blood pressure. Well, I just cut to the chase, man. The morning of my physical I dropped acid. It wasn't close. I started laughing, couldn't stop. They pulled their come-back-tomorrow-son on me. No problem. Another fat tab of acid and I was more screwed up than the first day."

"And they let you off?"

"Sure." Ace's smile was almost angelic. "Said I had a bad attitude. Psychologically unfit. No shit. Man, I hate war."

"*. . . a conscientious object-or . . .*"

"Yeah. Something like that," Ace agreed.

"Sure's a hell of a lot simpler than what Shebang did," TJ volunteered.

"Probably bit the recruiter," Ace said. "Gave him rabies."

"Shebang and his brother, Luther, went hunting out of season. They went up into Granite Canyon and searched till they found a mountain sheep. Shot it. Lugged it all the way out of the back country and tied it to the front bumper of Shebang's old Ford. Drove from Jackson Hole thirty-five miles down to Alpine, and then all the way back to Moose before a ranger finally busted them."

"So," Matthew said. "What am I missing?"

"It's a felony to shoot sheep out of season," TJ explained. "And you know what? The army won't take felons. Three months in jail beat the hell out of the draft."

So this was the way out for some of the locals. Interesting. Their escapes from the draft generated little anger or bitterness, just sadness at the events of his life. Fate. Matthew had been a fool.

"Ace wants to go to town with us to the Million Dollar Cowboy Bar," TJ said. "Couple of locals working the mountain were raving about a new band, the Rhythm Wranglers." He turned to Ace. "Plus, Wesley's been giving Matthew static for sitting on his parochial ass—those were Wesley's words—and to get his butt into town and check it out. Wesley promised to meet us after ten."

"Fine with me," Matthew said.

"Great," TJ said and smiled. "The more the safer."

Matthew was dubious of any safety these two wild men would provide, but he was getting stale. He'd been working out and skiing for weeks. He needed some kind of new action. Many fruitless evenings alone in the dark of his cabin, hoping for a reappearance of Julia at the window, had not helped. Some live music, a little diversion, sounded like a good move.

TWENTY

Matthew followed the two boys across the empty street and into the Silver Dollar. They would hit the mellower, cheaper bar until Wesley showed up at ten at the Cowboy. Broad bands of hot pink, lime-green, and light-blue neon tubing on the ceiling traced the bar's L-shaped curve. Tables were full. Compared to the Calico, the place was jumping.

Matthew and TJ found stools. Ace stood, twitching. Matthew leaned onto a bar top inlaid with over two thousand silver dollars, back when a dollar was worth a hell of a lot more than today. Unfinished wood-paneled walls held the history of Jackson Hole: Photos and paintings, animal heads, snowshoes and several green-and-yellow Wyoming license plates.

The mix of patrons leaned towards town folk and businessmen more than redneck mechanics and cowboys. With one exception. Some good old boys filled a table in the opposite corner, next to a small stage set up for a guitarist. Matthew's antenna was up and functioning, stimulated by the crowd and activity. He tracked the cowboys in the full-length mirror behind the bar as they hooted and banged the table, occasionally pointing at the three new arrivals. After a few minutes, Matthew's beer arrived, and the three of them attempted to avoid the locals' attention, succeeding like three painted whores in church. One of the cowboys got up, glanced his way, then sauntered out the door to the street.

The guitarist came back from his break, picked up his guitar, and began his set. To Matthew's dismay, the singer played classic country-and-western twang. The musician's cattle died, ranch got foreclosed, wife left, horse broke a leg, and he ran over his dog. The music left no reason for Matthew to listen. No reason for the old cowboy to keep singing either.

"The Rhythm Wranglers better be further from the grave than this poor son of a bitch," Ace said. "Look, before we storm the Cowboy, let's smoke some shit in the Square."

"A very good idea, Ace." TJ was always ready.

"It's not quite ten," Matthew said. "Let's just hang out here for another few minutes. I don't think we want to make our grand entrance at the Cowboy Bar until Wesley shows up."

"No way," Ace said. "This half-dead guitarist belongs at a funeral, his own." He moved from foot to foot, swinging his arms, but going nowhere. "I'm overamped, man. I need to calm down with some smoke."

"Overamped is a goddamn understatement," TJ said. "I'm fed up being bruised by Ace's flying body parts. Come on, Matthew, you never been to the Town Square. It's a block from here, right across the street from the Cowboy. We'll have a doobie right in the middle. No one in their right mind'll be out there freezing their ass off tonight."

TJ and Ace pulled Matthew out of the Silver Dollar and moved him the short block to the Square. Matthew jerked to a stop at the entrance. A huge pile of elk antlers arched over the path into the Square. The jumbled mass of bleached horns brought disturbing images of wasted bodies and bones—battlefields, killing grounds, burnt villages, concentration camps. His body heat rocketed, perspiration popping out on his forehead and armpits despite the zero-degree temperature and light snow drifting down from the black sky. Matthew tried to regulate his breathing, to overcome the light-headedness and random flashes of anguish and horror.

"Man, you okay?" Ace hovered next to Matthew, following Matthew's eyes to the arch. "There's one of these antler arches at each corner of the Square. You don't think they're pretty cool?"

Matthew's mouth was stone dry. He nodded an indeterminate answer. TJ reached out to Matthew's shoulder. Matthew jerked away.

"They're picked up off the ground," TJ said. "They fall off the elk every year."

Ace and TJ struggled towards the empty, unlit center of the one-block square, shaking their heads. Matthew followed with short, twisted glances above his head.

New snow made progress shaky. He caught up to TJ and Ace in the center of the large X formed by the four entry paths. Matthew could barely make out the four arches. The men were hidden from the street. But the

Cowboy Bar's garish neon sign of a bucking bronco with cowboy throbbed in living color through the leafless aspens of the Square. The huge sign seemed dropped from outer space. Just like his two friends shuffling next to him in the darkness of the park.

"Man, it's nasty out here." Ace pulled out the fixings to hand-roll a number.

"How you gonna put that together with it snowing and blowing?"

"TJ," Ace answered, his teeth visible in the dark. "I can roll one of these on a chairlift in a blizzard." He held aloft a bent, wet but tight joint. "Practice makes perfect."

Ace lit up, inhaling like a vacuum cleaner. He handed the number to TJ, who imitated Ace's Hoover impression. Matthew declined. Even in the dark Matthew caught Ace's astonished look. When TJ handed the joint back to Ace, Matthew knew they had company. Safe to say, unwanted guests.

Matthew's senses reacted. Survival instincts took command. Slice and dice the sounds. Work through the layers. Know each little squeak. Wait for the one that don't belong—then blow the bastard away. Lessons taught in Ranger School, perfected in action. Flunk, you die.

"We got trouble," Matthew said in a low, soft voice.

"What you talkin' about?" TJ was too stoned to worry.

"What'll we do?" Ace, even chemically enhanced, reacted quicker to the changing dynamics.

"Close in tight behind me, both of you." A command. Matthew's voice was steel, hard, tight. "Stay on my butt. Move when I do. When I go, you go. Once we clear the Square, we're going straight to the Jeep."

"Optimistic, buddy," Ace said. "Do we run or walk?"

"If you're tucked next to my ass like I told you, you'll know, won't you?" Matthew's words bit through the wet cold. These two would never be confused with battle-hardened veterans.

"How many you think?" TJ's voice quivered, head rotating as he belatedly responded to noises, flitting shadows.

"Seven or eight. Maybe more. Some on each path. Stay close."

"Well, well," slurred taunts came from the darkness. "Looks like we got ourselves some dirty little long-haired hippies."

"Come on out, you motherfuckers." Ace's voice blasted into the thin air. "Show us your ugly faces so we can kick your equally ugly asses."

"Great, Ace," Matthew whispered. "You're probably scaring the crap out of them. They're probably going to hightail it back to the Saloon."

"You punks are breakin' the law." The rasping comment didn't convey concern with legal implications. "Smokin' that nasty shit out in our beautiful Square. Pollutin' our lovely community. We're gonna have to educate you boys. Give you a little spankin'."

"Hey, ya pig farmers—" Ace started up again.

"Ace, shut up." Matthew grabbed Ace's shoulder. "It's best if they think we're afraid."

"Goddamn it, I am afraid."

"Good," Matthew said. "We're just going to stand here back to back, ready to move, unless either of you happens to have an M16 on you."

"A spankin' and a haircut." The threat from the disembodied voice produced enough scattered laughter to let Matthew know they were indeed in deep trouble.

"Let's go," Matthew said.

Matthew led the huddle of three back up the path they had entered. Activity was evident on all sides. Soft chuckles grew into growls. A large cowboy, made bigger by his hat, appeared from the darkness, blocking their exit. Another figure stood behind him. Matthew sensed the other rednecks stumbling in for the kill.

Matthew moved in a swift, direct line at the big cowboy. Movements, thoughts, and sounds receded into the familiar slow motion of battle. Four steps took Matthew's little group right up to the talker.

Matthew used the momentum of the last step to drive his right hand, shaped like a tight claw, into the large cowboy's throat. The man's head flew back, hat flying, gagging. The man windmilled his arms searching for balance. Matthew lifted himself into the air, landing a karate kick at a right angle to the cowboy's shin. The crack ricocheted through the park like a gunshot. The cowboy crashed to the snow-covered ground, crumpled in a heap. His gargled cry rose through the misty air.

Number Two had watched as his larger buddy was dispatched in seconds. His charge lacked steam, but too late to stop. Matthew met the fading rush. He folded into the cowboy's lanky body, fired two hard chops, one to the solar plexus and one to the ribs. The heavy clothes muted the blows to an extent, so Matthew pivoted and sent the cowboy slamming into the snow with an old-fashioned right cross to the temple.

Matthew's heavy breathing and the moans of the two shocked and injured cowboys filled the cold Square. Matthew felt pity for these drunken hicks. Their strength was perceived in numbers and fortified by alcohol. The last thing on their peabrains would be an attack by their trapped victims. Ego and bragging were lousy weapons. Even worse protection. Matthew, with Ace and TJ almost attached, moved down the path, his last glance up at the antler arch less troubled.

Matthew led the way across Cache Street to Broadway and the Jeep. He struggled to process the weird transition from fighting small, fearless gooks in the hot, steaming jungle to battling large, drunken cowboys in the freezing snow. Everything had moved too fast. The scene replayed itself, but in dense, humid foliage.

"Matthew, you're one scary dude," Ace said.

"Sorry," Matthew said as they scrambled into the car. "We'll have to do the Cowboy Bar another night."

TWENTY-ONE

Franky entered the door to the Stage Deli, the lunch-hour frenzy of raised voices and clanging dishes as noisy as traffic on Seventh Avenue. Why the hell had Roberto demanded a lunch meeting twenty blocks from the warehouse? Franky'd never catch up.

He searched for Roberto in the packed restaurant. There, at a table against the far wall, the dapper figure leaned forward. But he wasn't alone. Franky worked his way across the room. Who was the man sitting opposite Roberto?

The two men resembled each other, same style of dress, slender, handsome features, hair recently cut. But as Franky approached, catching the men's attention, he noticed a sharpness in the other missing in the dapper Roberto. The stranger rose with quick movements to meet Franky. His eyes had a hard edge, lips tight, his smile debatable.

"Meet Mr. Giacomo, a business associate of mine." Roberto's words came out more clipped than usual.

"A pleasure," the man said. Giacomo's handshake was hard and short, his look piercing.

Franky took a chair facing a signed photograph of some vaguely familiar actor. A waiter startled Franky with the speed of his arrival.

"Corned beef on rye," Franky said.

No time for a menu. Play it safe. This guy, Giacomo, didn't look too patient. Franky's nerves tightened, something that happened with increasing frequency since the incident in the alley. Why couldn't he control his emotions, get some decent sleep? The whole goddamn murder had been so unnecessary.

"Franky," Roberto said, without even a nod to small talk. "Mr. Giacomo is one of our prime suppliers. He's impressed with your progress. The construction business and our retail operation. I just told him about the fourth Treasure Chest location. He's particularly interested in the accounting system you've implemented to, ah, absorb the flow of merchandise and building materials we've been fortunate to obtain."

Mr. Giacomo remained silent, watchful, his gaze locked on Franky. The attention did nothing to dispel a growing uneasiness.

"You've been working your butt off." Roberto placed a hand on Franky's wrist.

"Thanks, Roberto, but—"

"And now all your work's headed down the toilet," Roberto continued. "Your brothers are jeopardizing the operation with their petty violence and lack of control."

"Petty?" Franky almost rose from his chair. Roberto had let them force him into a hit. The old man had wanted to keep him clean. Shield the business side. Keep producing steady cash flow. "You call what they've done the last few weeks petty?"

"I think I understand the problem," Giacomo said.

What did this guy know? Who the hell was he? Giacomo's entrance into the conversation shocked Franky. His survival instincts kicked in. Their food arrived as Franky's appetite vanished.

"No one expected your father to get nabbed," Giacomo said as he spread hot mustard on his pastrami. "The Feds never expected a gift-wrapped package of incriminating evidence. And you can't control Sal and Marco. Your father let them do their thing to keep them out of your hair."

"Those boys are dangerous," Roberto said. "Their marginal activities in enforcement, loan-sharking and gambling contribute less income than their combined I.Q.'s."

"Exactly," Giacomo agreed.

Franky waited for more. Giacomo focused on his sandwich. Nothing seemed to affect Giacomo's appetite. Franky's head spun. How had the Fiorini family's chicken-shit operation stayed connected with the flow of stolen goods and sweetheart union deals? And the stream hadn't stopped with his father's imprisonment. Was Giacomo the key to the big boys?

"We have more construction contracts than you can currently handle," Giacomo said, wiping his hands and mouth. "You've swallowed, or rather absorbed, a number of independent contractors. We want to encourage that."

Who the fuck was we? Franky's body generated a growing heat. Was this the connection? An entry to the big time?

"So what's this bullshit about sending me to Wyoming?" Franky blurted out, unable to contain himself. This guy knew everything anyway.

"We have a problem with what happened to your father," the stranger said. "An organization like yours has to provide better security. You blow it, shit flows back to us. That's not good."

Franky believed him. He glanced at his uneaten sandwich like an opportunity lost.

"This bullshit, as you call it, could be the luckiest break of your life," Giacomo said. "This business is far too valuable to let your brothers piss away."

Giacomo's voice was low. Franky leaned forward, interest overcoming suspicion.

"Roberto and I think you've got a great future, if Sal and Marco leave you alone. But you've got to clean up this unfinished business with the informer. That's why we're helping you with both problems."

Holy shit, was Giacomo going to take out those morons? Franky wanted his freedom, but he wasn't about to get suckered into more violence. He held up his hands and tipped back in his chair. Giacomo's smile looked like broken glass, sharp and fragmented.

"If you're out of town and in the dark," Roberto said, "you'll stay clean. In a position to continue doing what you're doing. And, if you're fortunate enough to flush out the informer, you'll also be a hero. Be ready to head west whenever we get things lined up. Oh, and use your old name, Pieri. The one you had before you hooked up with your father. Don't want to advertise your mission."

Once again, Franky felt the unseen hands of manipulation. Again a fucking puppet. But as Franky rose to leave, he felt a blue-steel chill— never underestimate Sal Fiorini.

TWENTY-TWO

Matthew's eyes opened. He couldn't have been asleep for very long. Last evening he'd crawled under the blankets at eleven-thirty in a useless attempt to sleep. The events of the Square hadn't seemed like much. Why had the action and excitement filled him with anxiety, anger and confusion? Why couldn't he find solace in the minimal human damage and give himself credit for not overreacting? Bull would have told him to waste the whole damn bunch.

Did he want to get out of his warm cocoon of a bed? His vision focused on the cabin window. Light flakes, rhythmless, swirling. Jesus. Twelve uninterrupted days of light, beautiful powder. Twelve straight days of skiing. He hadn't skied twelve days in a row in his entire life. And he'd never skied twelve days total in conditions this outrageous.

His joints were sore, his quads stringy and tight, his lower back begged for time off. A bruised left shoulder was a new entry to the physical litany. A lesson in physics: The mass of a frozen fir tree trunk will overpower the humble construction of a human shoulder at any speed.

Minimal warmth from the baseboard heater kept him under the covers. Physical fatigue also registered, but the emotional calm of a dreamless night seduced Matthew into immobility. Then again, one of the immutable laws of the mountain pricked at him: When it snows, you goes. The mantra stirred him from his delicious inertia.

A door slammed. Jim was up and about. Must be around seven. A kick at the cabin door.

"Powder day, boy. Better get moving if you want first tracks."

First tracks lasted all day at Jackson Hole. Still, Jim's words pulled

Matthew out of his unfamiliar reverie into the chilly embrace of the morning and the promise of another day floating through paradise.

* * *

Matthew huddled on the tram platform's metal grating. The usual cast of skiers gathered for the first run of the day looked like a group of frozen refugees, bundled and shuffling for warmth, about to struggle into a freight car. Steam from their breath created its own low-hanging cloud in the Arctic valley inversion. A few new arrivals stood out, their excitement muted by the mass of locals beaten down by twelve days of too much of a good thing. Hard to believe he harbored fleeting thoughts of sunny days sunk into the warm sands of Malibu Beach.

TJ shivered as he clipped lift tickets at the gate to the Tram and spread the news of last night's Affair in the Square. Eight twenty-five, five minutes before the first tram run. Billy Simpson, Ski Patrol Director, positioned near the door of the waiting Box, mumbled instructions to several subdued patrollers. Only Ace acted alert and fresh, first day back on the Mountain.

Ace's hair stuck out from his hat and gaiter. He used animated gestures as he pointed over at Matthew. A wired dog arousing a flock of sheep. A flicker of interest showed on patrollers' faces. They moved their heads in slow motion, checking out Matthew. Matthew's hopes for anonymity in Wyoming were now history. How high a price would he pay for his violent response in the gloom of the Town Square?

Wesley wormed his way through the passive crowd of skiers.

"Well, well, buddy," Wesley said, head to head with Matthew. "One broken leg with bruised larynx. One concussion. Both visiting the hospital. And you stood me up."

"Sorry, Wesley." Matthew's mouth moved inches from the Indian's muffled ear. "We got a little sidetracked."

"TJ and Ace'll get the word out quicker than Paul Revere hauling ass through the countryside." Wesley indicated Ace's patrol group with his chin.

"Paul Revere?" Matthew said, a smile hidden in his gaiter.

"You nailed a couple of local tough guys last night."

"Don't know how those boys built their reputation," Matthew said. "They fight like old ladies."

Wesley shook his head.

"It's Billy Simpson's birthday today." A voice, maybe Shebang's, rose above the silence of the platform.

Quiet indifference greeted the news. Then movement rippled in the crowd toward the patrollers by the tram door.

"Happy birthday," Shebang said and thrust something at Simpson, who reached out to grasp the object.

"Shit! Run!" Simpson screamed, holding up what looked to Matthew like a bottle with a ribbon. Simpson blasted through the stunned crowd, trying to exit the platform area. "Dynamite!"

Matthew took off his goggles to focus. Billy's hand held aloft three sticks of dynamite wrapped in a red ribbon and a lit fuse—a short one at that. What the hell was going on?

Billy screamed and stumbled along the arm of the platform. He flailed through the last few startled skiers and off the deck. Reaching the snow, Billy lofted the dynamite, then hit the ground. The gathered group of skiers followed his example, dropping to the metal grate—skis, poles flying. Matthew moved several steps to position the stationary Tram between him and Billy's birthday present.

Nothing happened.

"Billy." Shebang's hysterical laughter echoed in the air above the platform. "Watcha throwing your birthday present away for?"

Then, as if rehearsed, Shebang's black Lab galloped into view headed for Billy's rejected gift sticking in the snow. The excited dog snatched the dynamite in his jaws and lumbered through the snow back to the tram platform. Cody dodged the kneeling Billy Simpson and pranced along the arm of the platform. He headed towards Shebang, ten feet from Matthew and Wesley. The snuffed fuse was two-thirds burnt.

Shebang bent over in convulsions. Wesley, under several skis and a backpack, looked up. Cody hesitated in front of Shebang, then threaded his way around several fallen bodies and pieces of equipment to present his package to Matthew.

"You didn't seem too worried," Wesley said and scrambled to his feet. "Shebang's a maniac. Who knows what the hell he'd do."

"Even Shebang wouldn't blow up the Box and a platform full of people. He'd be out of a job."

Matthew smiled down at Cody. Then he dislodged the dynamite from the dog's soft mouth and pulled the fuse. It slipped out without resistance.

"No blasting cap," Matthew said. "Nothing would have happened."

"Couldn't Billy have just pulled out the fuse? It ain't like he don't deal with dynamite daily."

"I think he panicked," Matthew said. "And the package had been a gift from that psycho, Shebang."

Matthew looked over where Shebang held his sides in laughter. The renegade patroller then made his way through the crowd to the loading gate and past TJ. Escape was an appropriate plan. Billy Simpson, several years older on this birthday, held rage in his eyes, visible even through his goggles. He scrambled over and around the crowd of skiers. But Shebang had disappeared.

* * *

Matthew stood with Wesley on the small porch of the ski-school shack. A full day of skiing finished, the last two hours with the instructor, Kurt. Matthew felt worn out, but Wesley looked trashed.

"We've gone full circle, buddy," Wesley said. "I'm the one trying to hang with you on the mountain. I don't know if that's progress or not."

"Conditioning's just a function of more hours on the hill," Matthew answered. "Time with the instructor's what's really making the difference. And skiing's my day job, not yours."

"I've shot the whole day. I'll stay here in the Village if you'll have dinner with me."

"Absolutely. I'll even buy," Matthew offered. "If you got a change of clothes, we can run over to the Grand View and come back. I've got to shower."

"That'll work. Go to the Mangy Moose. They got a skier's dinner special for $2.75. Hell, I might go whole hog since you're buying and order the roast beef dinner for another 75 cents." Wesley performed a quick reverse. "You can afford it, can't ya?"

"I'll count my change to make sure."

"They're showing *The Maltese Falcon* after dinner," Wesley said. "I'll spring for that. Then we can cruise over to the Alpen Haus. When the boys party there, it gets real serious. We might have a good time."

"Like last night in the Square?" Some openings Matthew just couldn't pass up.

"I got another surprise for you," Wesley offered.

"I can't wait."

"Have to. For another week." Wesley looked smug.

"What's up?" Matthew depended on Wesley's straightforward approach to situations. Suspicion surfaced at his friend's unusual coyness.

"Damn few women in this town, wouldn't you say?" Wesley's guilty grin fueled dubious thoughts in Matthew.

"True."

"You do prefer women, don't ya?"

"No, Wesley, I'm into sheep."

"Well," Wesley said. "A good friend of mine is flying into Jackson Hole. Name's Sarah Ross. I think you'll enjoy her company."

Matthew's stomach twisted. Wesley worked too hard to draw Matthew into any kind of social situation. The very thought of dealing with a female relationship unsettled him.

"Sure, Wesley," Matthew said. "What's *The Maltese Falcon*? Any good? And don't give me that 'pity the poor white man' look. I've never seen the movie."

"It's a classic. Whoa, check this out."

Wesley pointed up the hill towards the maintenance building. Shebang held a leather safety strap attached to the grid of a large cage, dragging the metal box down the hill towards the parking lot. Cody, locked in the cage, seemed to be enjoying the ride. Shebang screamed and swore as he tugged the cage across the packed snow.

"That's Shebang," Wesley said. "A three-ring circus."

The cage slid into the back of Shebang's legs, knocking him into the snow. The crazy patroller regained his feet and jerked towards the parking lot. Cody bounced against the bars. Concern for the Lab swept through Matthew.

"Those bastards," Shebang sputtered. "Think they're locking up my dog. Fine me $50."

The cage, Cody, and Shebang crashed past the ski school hut onto the snow-packed lot, and over to Shebang's rusted truck. The volume intensified as Shebang pounded with a hammer at the lock. A crowbar worked better. Cody strolled out looking pleased with himself. Shebang kicked the metal cage into the middle of the road, promising to straighten out the Mountain Manager as he headed back to the maintenance shed. Cody followed at his heels.

"Is that guy an asshole?" Matthew asked. "Or just not playing with a full deck?"

"I've known Shebang his whole life. I'm still not sure," Wesley answered. "No doubt he can cause some damage. I don't know if he's evil or stupid. But you gotta keep your eyes on him. At least he ain't pure bad like Ty Corbin. That's one mean bastard you never want to meet. Let's get cleaned up. I'm already hungry, and it's only 4:30."

TWENTY-THREE

"Not a bad movie," Matthew said. He and Wesley crunched across the frozen road from the Mangy Moose to the bar at the Alpen Haus. "A little slow at times. Seemed like Bogart jumped to a lot of conclusions without many facts."

"How often do you get all the info you need to make a good decision?" Wesley moved fast through the cold night. "I gotta hand it to that Sam Spade. He never trusted that dame. Despite all the moves she put on him."

Did Matthew share a distrust of women, or did his insecurities demand distance?

Wesley climbed the exterior stairs to the balcony outside the bar and restaurant a few steps ahead of Matthew. The black Lab was there, tied to a pole up against the wooden railing. The dog barked a noisy greeting.

Matthew bent over, allowing the grateful puppy's tongue access to his face, then pulled away. Cody howled louder. The door from the bar banged open. Shebang stumbled out.

"Goddamn it, Cody, if you don't shut up, I'm gonna shoot your ass." An evil smile lit Shebang's face as he recognized Wesley and Matthew. "Hey, Matthew, I hear you're quite the dangerous hombre. Wasn't that a pretty cool birthday present for Billy?"

Shebang slurred his words and tripped over Cody, swearing. He kicked his dog in its sleek, black side.

"Take it easy, Shebang." Matthew moved towards the drunk.

"Oh, sorry." Shebang dropped to his knees and let Cody's large tongue work over his flushed features. "Look, Cody, you got to cut out the racket. The guests are complaining."

Shebang staggered to his feet and headed back inside. Matthew and Wesley followed into the warmth and chaos of the Alpen Haus. Matthew entered with caution. What did he expect, an ambush? He swallowed his unease, but still ready for an immediate exit if necessary.

Matthew recognized many of the patrollers, instructors, and lift operators, a diverse cultural collection. A few guests, mainly women, that most treasured commodity, drank and laughed to a Stones' album cranked high. Everyone welcomed Wesley. They acknowledged Matthew with more reserve. Several boys, soaking wet from a fully clothed dip in the nearby heated pool, surrounded a young girl, also wet, stripped down to bra and panties. Matthew looked to Wesley, who opened both arms wide and grinned.

"Welcome to the real Jackson Hole."

Glass shattered in accompaniment to the rock and roll. Shooters slammed, beer chasers an afterthought. Boisterous laughter competed with the music—a tie. Only 9:30 and the action seemed out of control. Matthew would have hated to be a paying guest in any of the rooms within a quarter mile of the Alpen Haus.

A rowdy group of old friends soon swallowed Wesley on the far side of the room. Matthew's nerves stretched. Too much erratic energy. Desperate attempts at having fun had been a constant element back in Southeast Asia, everyone trying with little success to dodge reality. These people grab-assed without a care. Time to split.

Matthew scanned the area for Wesley. An animated, arm-waving exchange between Shebang and an older man caught his attention. Shebang jerked away and stomped over to his backpack against the wall. He reached into the large red canvas bag and flung the contents onto the floor. Then Shebang's hand emerged with a large revolver. This idiot truly needed to be locked up.

Shebang stumbled over a couple making out in the middle of the carpet. He headed towards the door to the deck, large pistol much in evidence. Cody's unrelenting yelping resonated despite the din in the bar.

A bloodcurdling cry burst from Matthew's lips, an animal howl of warning and anger. He rushed for the deck. All other movement froze.

Shebang aimed the gun at the wagging Cody. The dog jumped with joy as Shebang pulled the trigger. Cody slammed back and crumpled against the deck railing.

The explosion of sound brought life to a nightmare. The village empty, nothing but smoke and shadows. The hot white vision of soldiers, his own men, having turned their ultimate frustration and hatred on the only living things they could punish. Chickens disintegrated into fluffs of wet feathers. Dogs split in half from the barrage of M16's. Two water buffalo, the wealth of the hamlet, brown eyes uncomprehending, died in a hail of fire. Matthew had been helpless.

Now he charged, screaming. The revolver swiveled into Matthew's face. The force of the rush drove him into Shebang and then against the balcony rail. Matthew grabbed the barrel, twisting the pistol out of Shebang's grasp. Then Shebang was gone, over the railing. Matthew stood stupidly with the gun's barrel pointed at his face.

He dropped the weapon and dove for the black Lab, piled in the corner. The entry wound in Cody's chest was obvious, blood flow moderate, no bubbles. Not dead yet. He grabbed a handful of snow and packed the snowball against the bullet hole. Wesley appeared.

"Get me napkins, towels," Matthew said. "Something for a bandage."

Matthew's hands moved along Cody's quivering back and discovered the exit hole. Hope. He slapped more snow on the second wound. Cody lay quiet, eyes fixed on Matthew. Wesley returned. Matthew made compression bandages with napkins and wrapped a cotton tablecloth around Cody's chest. He used a piece of wood lying on the deck to form a tourniquet. Then he waited.

"He gonna make it?" Wesley handed Matthew his gloves, parka, and hat.

Faces at the glass door and deck windows peered out, everyone silent. Matthew stared back. Would they just watch Shebang shoot his dog?

"Bullet went through his side. Missed his lungs. Any other vital organs hit he'd already be dead."

"Should we move him inside?" Wesley asked.

"No. Internal bleeding's the big danger now. The cold out here will keep the blood flow to a minimum." Matthew stroked the Lab. "We'll move him inside if he survives the next fifteen minutes. The cold's okay for a while, then it could push him further into shock."

Wesley got up, walked over to the revolver in the snow. Matthew watched him crack open the chamber of an old .32 six-shoot. Wesley put the remaining shells in his pocket, stepped on the snow wedged against the railing and peeked over the edge. Wesley shifted to Matthew's side, a smile breaking through the gloom of the moment.

"I'm sorry to say you didn't hurt Shebang."

"But it's a ten-foot drop onto hard-packed crud and driveway?"

"Nope, fell too far to the left. Five feet into soft snow. The Lord protects his children." A wry smile reflected off Wesley's lips. "Shame, ain't it?"

"Good thing he's a lousy shot." Matthew shivered as chill, stiffness, and reality worked their way through his body.

"Shebang's been shootin' things since he was born. He missed 'cause you distracted him."

Matthew recognized Wesley's attempt to comfort him, especially if the dog didn't make it. But Cody hung on, the Lab's breathing shallow, but regular. Matthew crouched by his side. The faces behind the glass faded one after another. Matthew estimated the passage of fifteen minutes as the last witness at the window drifted out of sight.

"Let's pull him inside. Got to be careful. Can't move him much further than off the deck. Wish I knew the internal damage."

"What'll you do with him when you get inside?" Wesley asked.

"Need to keep him quiet. I'll spend the night here with him."

Matthew went to his knees, Wesley following, then together slid Cody across the deck, minimizing any bumps or jerks. Matthew took extra care as they maneuvered him across the threshold of the restaurant. Not much of the party remained. Matthew leaned against the wall, Cody lying next to him. A balding man, friendly features, kind, patient eyes, walked over to Matthew. The same man who had argued earlier with Shebang.

"I'm Mel Jarrett. I own this place when it isn't being occupied by the skiing horde. Sorry about the dog. I told Shebang to leave with his mutt. This little sucker's been barking and howling on the deck since nightfall. Too many complaints."

"Mel, this is my buddy, Matthew," Wesley said. "He'd like to spend the night here with the dog."

"Here on the floor?"

"Yeah," Wesley said. "We're afraid to move him."

"No problem." Jarrett seemed relieved. "Can I bring you something to drink?"

"No, thanks," Matthew said. "Why do you let these guys trash your place?"

"If I call the sheriff, he'd just dial up the Mountain Manager," Jarrett said, resignation evident in his tired voice. "Manager'd say he can't run the ski hill without his crew, so the sheriff can't lock them up. The crew knows the score. They party till they drop. Only happens every other week, not like it's every night. They're not bad kids. One day they'll grow up. What do you think, Wesley? Think I can wait 'em out? Three or four years?"

"'Fraid they're gonna last a lot longer than you, Mel."

A chilling draft reached Matthew on the carpet. Shebang entered the restaurant, uncomfortable, sad-eyed. Matthew stiffened. Snow still clung to Shebang's hair and clothes. Wesley stepped closer to Matthew on the floor.

"Be careful, Matthew," Wesley said under his breath as Shebang made his way closer. "You humiliated and manhandled that crazy boy. You got an enemy for life. Remember, never turn your back on him."

Shebang slunk across the room to Matthew.

"I really blew it this time." Shebang appeared sincere, but Matthew didn't doubt Wesley's warning.

"I want to thank you, Shebang," Matthew said.

"Uh . . . whatta ya mean?" Shebang said.

"I've got a great dog now. And a safe place for him at the Grand View. If you haven't killed him."

"Man, that's good." Shebang's miserable expression would have generated sympathy in another setting with different facts. "I really feel like an asshole for shootin' Cody."

"You are an asshole, Shebang. I suggest you be more careful with the helpless and unarmed. Don't abuse them."

"Why?" Shebang stepped back, fists clenched, remorse disappearing.

"You'll lose your soul. If you still have one."

The words were wasted on Shebang, but Matthew felt their weight.

TWENTY-FOUR

Franky rode flight 580 from Denver to Jackson Hole. The famous Vomit Comet, named in honor of its turbulent route. This was Frontier's second attempt at reaching the fog-bound airport in Wyoming on February 12, Lincoln's birthday. Franky had been warned of the often-cancelled flight. The travel agent in New York had laid some bullshit on him about the absence of VAR equipment and the difficulty of winter landings in the small Jackson Hole Airport. Based on his fellow passengers, VAR stood for Various Assholes Returning.

Franky sat next to the aisle and preserved the empty window seat with scowls and grunts at any loser who came near, including the long-faced, skinny chick with the too-wide smile. Nice ass, but he could do better. He also rejected each of the stewardesses. The small blond with the pasted smile would be too dumb. The second golden-haired broad—why were over fifty per cent of stews blonde?—had fat legs and a big butt. The mousy brown hag looked like she'd been flying since the Wright brothers. The tall brunette had promise, but she ignored Franky's initial come-on. Piss on her.

A pudgy guy with a heavy coat and sweaty forehead bumped down the aisle. Something about him ripped Franky's confidence. The man in the alley? Calm down. That sucker was through traveling.

But reality griped his stomach producing an acid wash of discomfort. Yeah, it was a little weird. He was a college boy, hadn't exactly trained for murder. A ripple of regret traced its way down Franky's spine. The fat slob had been stealing from the family, hadn't he? Somebody had to put him away. Or was the victim some poor bastard who couldn't make

Sal's excessive loan-sharking payments? Didn't even matter now after his brother's latest frame job.

The voice of an irritated and fatigued woman overcame the loud hum of the aircraft. A mother battling with her young son. The boy's plaintive whine rose to meet his mother's increased volume. A "that's it" cry from the lady preceded the sound of a sharp slap. End of discussion.

Franky would have respected a firm hand in his childhood. But his weak-willed mother had accepted the role of slave. Of martyr. She had been filled with an unspoken guilt that had driven her four or five days a week to a reserved seat in the confessional booth at Saint Justin's. No style. No class. An embarrassment. The mother seated in front of him would have been a welcome substitute to the emotional cripple he supported in Jersey.

Women and respect, though, seemed to be oxymorons. It wasn't that he didn't want or enjoy women, but he'd never met one worthy of his full attention. Most were selfish, weak, or mindless. Yeah, he'd love to connect with some fine broad with both looks and brains. So far no chick had qualified, but there had to be someone out there.

"Excuse me, sir." The heavyset blond stewardess leaned over him. "Let me turn that overhead light on for you."

Her ample bosom brushed against Franky as she reached above his head. She took a few moments with the switch, Franky's shoulder forming a comfortable indentation in her breast.

"Isn't that better?"

Franky smiled an answer and turned back to his book. She was no babe, but he'd come a long way from the rejections of the stuck-up snobs of Dartmouth and Columbia. Ever since he had walked through the door of D and F Construction, things had looked up.

Family connections and acceptance into the business by his father had brought a welcome flow of women in all sizes and shapes—all willing. The comfort of cash flow hadn't hurt either. Problem was, the available ladies were all bimbos, more than happy to get laid and abused for money, gifts, and wild nights on the town by what they thought was a hotshot gangster. The fact that he was really small potatoes just confirmed the girls' ignorance.

Of course, the reckless search that had led to his father had also made his life a roller coaster the last six years. Hell, he had terminal whiplash from the crazy ups and downs. Doors that had mysteriously opened up also slammed shut in time to catch Franky in the back of the head.

*   *   *

Sarah's window seat provided a perfect breathtaking view upon Frontier's approach. Her lungs filled her taut body with what felt like carbonated oxygen. Light-headed, light-hearted. No place in the world she would rather be. A paradise she dreamed of every single day. Now four incredible weeks stretched before her. Twenty-eight days. Eight hundred and forty hours. She giggled, too giddy to compute the minutes.

Then, off the nose of the plane, the Grand Tetons appeared, jagged and magnificent in the crystal-blue heavens. The dramatic mountain range slid by her window. And as the jet vibrated towards the Jackson Hole landing strip, Sarah recognized Rendezvous Peak. The understated rock pile sat low on the shoulder of its soaring siblings. She picked out the dramatic ski runs climbing from Teton Village. They lived up to their reputation as the steepest, toughest in North America.

Jackson Hole was a man's mountain and Jackson Hole a cowboy town. No place for sweet, tender, well-mannered little girls. They went to Sun Valley or Aspen. But rugged Jackson Hole was the perfect place for her. Now, after another year of scraping and saving, she leaned forward, poised for her now-extended fantasy vacation in the womanless wilds of Wyoming. A land of beautiful, horny, hard-core skiers, mountain men, and cowboys.

Wesley Crow would be waiting, perhaps with TJ. They had taken her under their wings, gracious and protective, and then between their sheets. They had treated her with respect, kindness, and, when appropriate, passion. Even as she had moved back and forth between the arms of Wesley and TJ, she had felt like a priceless piece of art. Honored, not traded. When she feared her new friends would view her rapid passage from one suitor to the next as promiscuous, Wesley had swept aside her fears.

"Darlin'," he had said laughing, "you're just pickin' and choosin' from the buffet of life. And it's a full table here in Jackson Hole."

A huge smile tested the limits of her mouth. What a concept. Sex with men she could actually respect. She could even keep the lights on.

Sarah floated down the gangway. A strong, steady wind sweeping across the Hole dropped the freezing temperatures well below zero. She twirled in a circle on the tarmac, soaking up the atmosphere. As she completed the circle, a body blow almost knocked her off her feet. She dropped her purse and boot bag and struggled for balance.

"Sorry," a young man in a camel-hair coat apologized. "You stopped right in the middle of the runway."

He handed her the boot bag. She picked up her purse. Then the man made a beeline to the tiny terminal without another word.

*   *   *

Franky entered the building, looking for his hired guns among the group of greeters. He had been given sketchy descriptions, and they knew who he was. They'd better. Giacomo didn't seem to be a man to mess with. But no obvious candidates appeared

"Mr. Pieri?" A tall, rangy cowboy put his hand on Franky's arm. Franky jerked away. The use of his old name jolted him.

"Get your fuckin' hand off me."

Suspicion overcame confidence. Why was he really sent to this dump? Lack of control bit deep, leaving a slew of unsettled questions. Enough of this manipulation crap. No more surprises.

"I'm here to give you a lift," the cowboy said, unfazed.

"Bullshit. I'm here to meet two guys. And you aren't either of them."

"They didn't want to be seen in public with you at the airport." The thin man spoke in a soft, calm tone. "They got a place on the edge of town. Let's just get your stuff, and I'll take you to them."

Maybe Sal and Marco, not Roberto, were still pulling the strings. Who knew Giacomo's real motives? Franky sure as hell didn't want to be isolated with some complete stranger.

"You aren't taking me anywhere. I don't know your ass from a hole in the ground." Franky brushed past the towering, passive cowboy. "If you do know the two guys supposed to meet me here, tell them I have reservations downtown at the Wort Hotel."

The hick's face registered surprise. Franky enjoyed the moment.

*   *   *

Sarah burst through the glass door into the compact terminal. And right into Wesley's arms. Her eyes closed as she gripped his hard, lanky body. She kept squeezing. An irrational fear swept her. If she opened her eyes, would she be back in Chicago? Finally, she risked a peek. Oh, god. She really stood in Wyoming.

Wesley held her at arm's length. His broad grin had to be competing in brilliance with her own. A quick glance around the room sent pleasant chills coursing through her chest. People—men—checking her out. From overlooked in Chicago to looked over by every male in the airport in Jackson Hole.

Wesley pulled her back against his body. A perfect fit. Sarah felt his firm lips on her forehead. She tried to break away, a hopeless effort. Wesley hung tight.

"You look wonderful, Princess."

Wesley exuded a thick current of warmth and friendship. But where was the passionate, sexually charged kiss she had anticipated? Confusion and disappointment registered. Well, there was always TJ. Or, she could always just move on down an irresistible path of opportunity.

"I'm so glad to be back. You have no idea."

Wesley kept a physical connection to Sarah, touching and holding her as they waited for luggage and skis. He talked of TJ, Jim and Julia, David, Ace, Shebang, and the other characters she had met.

"There's a new boy moved to town," Wesley said as they climbed into his monster truck. "I want you to meet him."

Wesley packed so much expression into that simple statement that Sarah's attention snapped from her blissful reverie.

"I been givin' him the lay 'a the land. Got dinged up in Nam. But he's mostly healed."

Bingo. Things fell into place. Why Wesley hadn't even attempted to reconnect. She checked out his strong profile. You're so sweet . . . and transparent.

"My buddy, Matthew, is quite the cool dude."

Must be, if Wesley was willing to sacrifice time with her in this womanless town. She felt a strange surge of security, despite his unexpected reticence. She didn't need more than Wesley's friendship, and she felt little urgency to connect with his friend. Men filled every crack and crevice of this town. Damn near everyone of them licked their lips at her approach. Quite unlike the agony and insecurity of a one-shot blind date back home.

She listened, only half interested, as Wesley told her of Matthew

Green's trouble adjusting to civilian life. He mentioned severe wounds, physical and spiritual, the Viet Nam veteran struggled to overcome. He told her the story of Cody and Shebang, proof of Matthew's kindness and compassion. Glee lit his face as he described the Affair in the Square, an example of the man's strength and toughness.

Why did men feel the need to prove their macho side? Of course, she knew the answer. Sarah smiled in acknowledgement of its effect on her. Macho in the proper perspective made for an exciting evening.

"There may be just one little problem." The stumbling hesitation of the statement seemed out of place after Wesley's unbridled selling job.

"What's that?"

"I told you he's makin' good progress." Wesley looked uncomfortable. "But he's been shot up pretty bad."

"Yes?"

"Well." Wesley's chestnut complexion transformed to a bright red. "I'm not sure whether his wounds might limit his, ah, physical performance."

Sarah burst out laughing.

"Wesley, it would be a lot scarier if you intimately knew Matthew's sexual capabilities."

"True," Wesley said, relief washing the red on his face back to strong brown. "In a couple a days I'm takin' you to David's birthday party to reintroduce you to Jackson Hole's finest society. My good buddy'll be there."

Sarah settled into the truck's broad bench seat. She had four weeks. Matthew had to be interesting. He had Wesley's serious respect. Must be a damn good friend. Must be damn good reasons for Wesley to want to fix them up. And she was now curious.

TWENTY-FIVE

Describing this place as a hotel stretched Franky's imagination. The rock-hard frayed carpet felt like it had been painted to the floor, any cushioning effect a distant memory. The Goodwill would have rejected the dresser and battered end tables. And if this was a suite, he'd hate to hole up in a regular room in the Wort Hotel. The possibility that he might be here for weeks, maybe even a month, made it worse.

He picked up the ringing phone, relieved it worked.

"Franky Fiorini?" a toneless male voice asked.

"Who wants to know?" Franky, the hard ass. Let them know the ground rules. After all, wasn't this his operation? "And the name's Franky Pieri. Try not to blow my cover."

"Two business associates would like the honor of your company." The sarcasm caught Franky off balance.

"Come up."

Franky opened the door to two men who could have been refrigerator repairmen or insurance salesmen. Nondescript features, one medium height and weight, the other wider and taller. Both wore Levis' and plaid shirts underneath plain dark parkas, work boots, and lightweight driving gloves, still on. This last detail caused Franky to pause.

"You gonna let us in, or you want to see some ID?" the shorter one said, his tone as dead in person as over the phone.

Franky moved aside. The two men walked over to a table at the far side of the room. He studied the two men's movements, efficient, graceful. They sat down, backs to the wall.

"It would have been a hell of a lot easier if you'd just come with our man from the airport." The shorter one did the talking.

"Yeah, well, that isn't the way I liked it." Franky's discomfort cut into his patience.

"We gotta use common sense." The talker's dead eyes swept over Franky, irritation creeping into his flat delivery. "This is the last time we're coming to the hotel. The less we're seen together, the better. From now on you come to our place when we need to talk in person. Our cabin's at the end of Hansen Street. Makes your room here seem like a palace."

"Who the hell are you to give orders?"

"I'm John and my partner's called Hack. It's our job to make sure you leave Wyoming alive and clean. Word is you ain't had a lot of operational experience. We'll be doing all the heavy work."

"Bullshit. I didn't come all the way out here from New York to put up with crap from a couple of local yokels. Here's the deal—"

"No," John interrupted. "Here's the deal. You may be a big shot in New York. We piss you off on this job, then one day you can take us out. But we ain't concerned with the future, cuz if we don't take care of you and this hit, it's our ass in the immediate present. Our orders come straight from the Man. And for some reason that sure ain't clear to us, he wants to protect you, get you back to the big city safe and sound."

"So please work with us," Hack, the other partner said, with a gravel voice as lifeless as his partner's, except for his sarcasm. "Plus, we know what we're doing. We're good at it."

Franky backed off. He had no choice. But what was their whole program? And who was the Man?

"Okay, let's compare notes," Franky said, controlling his fear and anger. "This Witness Protection Program is brand-new. We spent big bucks trying to trace this slimy bastard. But we haven't been able to slide all our sources into place. All we've got for sure is that he's in Wyoming, in the Jackson Hole area."

"One of the reasons Hack and I are here is cuz we knew the informer's old man. Even worked with him till he got a little confused. When he screwed up, word came down to eliminate him. Just business till his son took it personal. Still can't figure out how an amateur like that boy could set up your father. But that's the trouble with you young punks. You can't separate business from personal."

"You know what this guy looks like?"

"Whatever he looked like probably ain't what he looks like now," John said. "We got pictures to show you, but he's had to have had plastic surgery to some extent—nose, eyes, hair, maybe even ears and cheek bones. They can do a lot with money. Height and weight might be the same, about 5'10", 165 pound, mid-thirties. Two and a half years ago, when he disappeared, the son of a bitch had dark brown hair and eyes. You know, the usual Dago."

"What's the 'usual Dago' look like, asshole?" Franky felt the heat building in his face.

"Dark, big nose, big mouth," Hack said. "Like you if you were five inches taller."

Franky took a step forward, then realized he had no place to go. The two men sat poker-faced, motionless and unconcerned.

"And he loves to ski, just like you," Hack finished.

These jerks were playing with him, trying to make him lose it, testing. Franky gave himself a moment to calm down.

"That's it?" Franky said. "Just go skiing and look for some thirty-five-year-old guy, 5'10", 165 pounds, who could look like anybody? We're paying you two?"

"Something else to consider," John said. "This kid wasn't some clean, lily-white choir boy. Didn't even know the punk existed. Turned out he handled his father's finances. And the father skimmed enough cash to fund several nifty operations in upstate New York. The guy we're looking for has assets. Knows how to compete in our business."

"Our job's to back you up," Hack said. "You're the advertised hot shot who can slip into the local ski scene and be sociable. A clean, educated stud like you should become King of the Hill in no time. And, you want the good news?"

"Maybe."

"This godforsaken town is empty. There ain't many people living here in Jackson Hole, especially in the winter. And there's damn few skiers. We drove out to Teton Village. Hard to believe that place stays in business."

"Well, thanks for all your research." Franky needed a drink. "I guess I'll shift into Plan B."

"And Plan B is, if you don't mind sharing your information?"

Franky smiled at his unwelcome partners. He didn't have too much faith they'd discover the fink. A long shot at best. He could cruise through the next few weeks with a half-ass effort. Ski. Enjoy himself. Then return to New York and his true worth, running the business back home, especially if Giacomo's promises to expand were true.

But, if he had to come this far west, screw up his daily responsibilities, then goddamn it, he'd make a legitimate search. Use his training from St. Albans prep school, Dartmouth and Columbia's business school. Show these goons the value of an education.

"Okay, here's Plan B."

Franky pulled a yellow pad from his briefcase and joined John and Hack at the battered table. He drew a line across the top and divided the space into five parts. Then he made another line down the page creating a right angle.

"We'll handle this problem," Franky said, "just like a case study from business school. I'm sure you're familiar with the analytical technique."

Franky's sarcasm matched his accomplices'. He searched their eyes for some flicker of comprehension. Not much.

"This top line is divided into all the ways you can discover who moved to Jackson Hole since our friend disappeared. Check the phone book, school enrollment, car registration, voting rolls, newspaper articles. Understand?"

Both men nodded. Neither seemed impressed.

"The other line will graph out probabilities. If someone new has made major purchases of property or equipment, purchased or opened a new business. The bigger the deal, the higher the probability he's our man. You can use the skinny John Wayne character that met me at the airport to help with some of the leg work."

"Naw," John said. "He's just a local gopher. Less he knows the better."

Franky continued to detail the exercise. Nothing John or Hack did encouraged Franky. These thugs were muscle only. He doubted they had ever attempted to implement an intelligent plan before. But they were all Franky had. He would squeeze as much benefit from them as possible. Even if his mission failed, Franky would show he'd made the effort.

"Yes, sir," Hack growled. "The value of a college education is clear now. This is a plan you couldn't have figured out without going to school. I feel much better."

"And I'll handle Plan A." Franky fought back a smirk after he'd finished. "Ski with the locals. Party with them. And find him."

"Just remember what's gonna happen if we screw up."

A chill flicked at the back of Franky's neck. Yes, he did. The smell of the alley floated unbidden into Franky's nostrils.

TWENTY-SIX

Cody had cooperated Saturday and Sunday, the days after the shooting. He had slept and rested on the throw rug covering Matthew's cabin floor, the damaged black body curled up by the roaring fireplace. Matthew had stayed close, feeding the hungry fire, coaxing small amounts of food and water into Cody. The Lab's rapid recovery was a revelation, especially juxtaposed against Matthew's own months of struggle.

Caring for Cody had a calming affect. The ability to provide comfort filled in some of his empty spaces. Perhaps he should use the G.I. Bill like Wesley had. Return to school and become a veterinarian. Nam had even provided some premed courses in treating blood and guts injuries. And animals were a hell of a lot easier to deal with than people.

Sunday morning the young dog had limped around the small room. Matthew had taken him outside for a painful piss and an abortive attempt at more solid relief. Monday the competition had moved in. Julia had spent half the day in the cabin with the Lab. Matthew maintained close supervision of her care for Cody, the calm of the previous days disturbed by her close physical presence. A fair trade? Matthew wasn't sure.

Now, Tuesday, the lovely lady had set up residence in the old cabin. Julia lay on the floor next to Cody. She gazed at the flames through half-closed lids, a far-away expression on her exquisite face. For the first time animation and happiness warmed Julia's ice-blue eyes.

But something felt wrong with the attention she lavished on the puppy. She ignored her duties in the Grand View, leaving Jim to pick up the pieces. Maybe she needed a child to fill her evident emptiness.

The familiar roar of an angry truck announced Wesley's arrival at the lodge. The cabin door burst open before the bang of Wesley's loud knock quit echoing. David Moore followed.

"Ah, the rumors of the mutt's revival are true." Wesley's eyes flashed from Matthew to Julia and back. The resulting smile reflected surprise, humor, and a nasty gleam. "Where's Jungle Jim?" Like Wesley cared.

"Busy catching up with honey-dos." Matthew offered a noncommittal grin in answer to Wesley's smirk. "Including shoveling the accumulation of thirteen straight days of snowfall off the roof, decks, and paths of this fine establishment. Normally, I'd be glad to help. But, after all, I've got the responsibility of a wounded dog."

David slipped over to the fire, Cody, and Julia. He stroked the Lab's head, then scratched behind his ears and under his chin. Julia's huge body, draped along Cody's back had to be a distraction, but David focused on Cody's half-closed, dark-brown orbs. Moisture collected in the corners of David's eyes.

"How could that bastard, Shebang, shoot this dog?" David's mismatched, irregular features didn't fare well under the distortion of a glowering frown, a Mr. Potato Head assembled by a three-year-old. "I've always considered that jerk a dangerous animal. Can't even be civil to that prick."

Matthew had never heard the soft-spoken, refined man use any kind of disparaging language. David always expressed himself in formal, courteous fashion whether in front of his wife and young daughter or skiing and drinking with friends.

"No problem," Wesley spoke up. "Ole Shebang's aware of your feelings, Dave, buddy. You ain't exactly subtle around him. And I don't think he's too partial to you. Matthew's probably not too high on his list either. Word is, Billy told the manager Shebang goes or he goes. Easy choice. Shebang's now fittin' skis and boots at Teton Sports. Village is so short of help Cody could get a job servin' drinks. Fact I heard they don't even bother changin' the sheets for new customers at the Alpen Haus, just slap on new pillow slips."

Jim appeared at the door. Matthew watched him absorb the sight of the crowded cabin with Julia fitted around Cody. The mountain man couldn't be happy with his temporary domestication. And could jealousy be a factor?

"Matthew," Jim said, "Kurt called to say he has a lesson slot from one to three today. He's booked for the rest of the week."

"Let's go," Wesley said. "Ya had your days off. Ya gotta jump back on the mountain, or you'll get soft. Cody looks like he's in good hands."

"Good hands?" Jim said with disgust. "Hell, he's surrounded by more tits and ass than I'll ever get again."

He wheeled out the door leaving a shocked Matthew. Julia didn't flinch, neither moving her body nor altering her expression.

"Go ahead, Matthew," Julia said from the floor. "I'm happy to care for Cody today. By tomorrow he'll be up and around. Won't need either of us."

Matthew shrugged, gathered his gear, and followed Wesley and David out the door. He turned at the threshold.

"Be good, Cody. I'll see you in a couple of hours."

Cody acknowledged his savior with only a slight twitch of an ear. The unappreciative dog was in ecstasy with Julia. He didn't give a damn about Matthew. Matthew experienced his own flash of jealousy, then the feeling evaporated. He laughed out loud. Matthew would have been as happy as Cody to be wrapped up by that woman.

* * *

The parking lot was packed. Matthew wedged his old Jeep Wagoneer into an illegal loading zone against the snowbank at the service entrance of the Alpen Haus. He put on his ski boots and walked the short distance to the ski-school hut, Wesley and David following. An actual line snaked through the tram matrix. Matthew had to dodge bodies slip-sliding on the packed snow. The crowds felt like a Saturday at Squaw Valley. Matthew led the way into the small ski-school building.

"I want an American." A short, dark young man spoke to Kurt with animated gestures and a loud voice. "Someone who speaks English. I don't want any goddamn fag Europeans."

Matthew heard the conversation, but his attention was drawn to Kurt's shaved head. A bristling G.I. butch replaced long, black hair.

"What the hell'd you do to yourself?" Wesley said.

Kurt put his hand to his bristling cut, smiling with a sheepish expression.

"Excuse me, sir," Kurt said to the short skier. "Matthew, this gentleman wants a lesson with a fine, upstanding American. What was your name?"

"Franky Pieri." His abrasive New York accent made Matthew question whether the man could communicate in English. "Can you fit me in or not?"

"Yes, but you're taking this boy's slot." The instructor sounded more courteous than Matthew thought the situation required. "I can get you three through the tram line without waiting, but this young man is paying for a private lesson in nondiscounted dollars."

"Kurt, who the hell shaved you?" Wesley asked.

"Well." Kurt sighed. "I guess you guys need an answer if we're going to move on. Two days ago I'm standing at the ski school meeting area. This kid points over at me and tells his buddy, 'Your lesson's with the groovy lookin' dude over there.' Second time this week some long-hair called me groovy. So I said the hell with it. I also generate too much heat skiing with my thick hair. More comfortable like this, okay?"

"Fine with me," Wesley said smiling. "You also don't have to worry about gettin' scalped. No self-respectin' Indian'd touch that homely head of yours now."

The instructor put his ski hat on, looking normal again, and led the way out the door to the first available tram. Matthew and his party of four cut to the front of the tramline, said howdy to TJ at the gate, and entered the Tram. The Box began the ascent to the top of Rendezvous Mountain.

The Box was packed, bodies crushed against each other. Matthew stood near Franky. This was not the place for anyone short. Franky reacted with violent motions, pushing and shoving at the skis, poles, and skiers who poked and pressed into his body. A large man with a Texas twang threatened to stomp Franky into the floor of the Tram if he moved one more inch. Impotent frustration registered in a nasty grimace.

This little turkey was a piece of work. Still, crammed in the middle, the Eastern asshole couldn't enjoy the spectacular view. What a difference from Matthew's first trip up the Tram over a month ago.

TWENTY-SEVEN

Franky was glad to be free from the crush of the Box. He rose from adjusting his bindings and ran a gloved hand down the new matching shiny navy blue parka and pants made of the current season's wet-look material. Brandnew Molitor cable boots sat on top of a sparkling pair of Hart Javelins. Except for the discomfort of his boots, he felt fantastic.

A wild-haired gremlin startled him, bounding in the deep snow around the corner of the small hut that housed the ski patrol. Where the hell did this freak come from? The strange apparition stomped over to Matthew and gave him a bear hug and a kiss on the cheek.

"You the action man." The crazy-looking boy laughed. "Congratulations on your new dog. I hear he's gonna make it. You should've wasted that son of a bitch. You know he hates soldiers, especially vets after takin' the chicken-shit way out."

Hard to believe this little homo wore the parka of the Jackson Hole Ski Patrol. Franky wrinkled his face in disgust, mouthing the word faggot, then caught an unsettling stare from Matthew. Fuck you, buddy. You're probably gay too.

"Franky," the instructor said, "let's get started."

"Why don't we ski with these guys?" Franky, fresh and dry, looked at the three locals. Might as well get started connecting, even if they all didn't seem to be playing with a full deck.

"Where'd you get the fine duds?" The Indian, Wesley, jumped in before the instructor could answer. Franky had to make the effort to keep the names straight if he was to ferret out the informer.

"Teton Sports. The damn place was busy as hell. Paid a guy an extra $10 to get everything mounted right away. Weird guy, weird name."

"Shebang?" Wesley asked.

"Yeah, something like that." Franky now felt conspicuous standing next to the grubby group. "Got the clothes on sale."

"I'll bet you did," the patroller said. "That slimy, wet-look material is real crap. I saw a tourist flying down the Alta Chutes on his back, picking up speed like a sled without brakes."

"I don't plan to fall much," Franky said. "I think I can handle myself on the mountain just fine."

"That ole Shebang's dangerous even selling equipment," Wesley said.

"He treated me all right," Franky said.

"This isn't exactly Shebang's fan club," the instructor said.

"Maybe you oughta ski with us," Wesley said. "You must be pretty good."

"Damn straight. Been skiing since college. Learned in New Hampshire. You ever been to Franconia Notch, Cranmore or Mount Sunapee?" Skiing had been the one pleasure Franky had allowed himself in Dartmouth. His only escape from loneliness. "If you can handle those icy narrow trails, this soft shit should be a piece of cake."

"Should be," Matthew said with a smile.

Franky looked over the immense terrain. Jackson Hole's runs bore little resemblance to the mellow cruisers six weeks ago on Ajax at Aspen or the friendly intermediate slopes of newly opened Snowmass. He wished he'd been able to check things out on the ride up the Tram.

"I think we should get warmed up first," Kurt said. "You said you'd be here at least a couple of weeks, let's not push it."

Was the instructor protecting Franky? Hell, he had paid full boat for lessons. Kurt would do what he told him to.

"You don't think I can ski with these guys?"

"Don't know," the instructor said. "Never seen you ski."

"We can start together," Wesley said. "And part company if we hit something too tough."

Franky's suspicion flared at the innocent look on Wesley's face. Franky ignored the cautionary tug.

"You're supposed to be a good instructor," Franky said to Kurt. "Instruct me if I need help."

"We'll just mosey on down a ways and jump into Corbet's," Wesley said.

"No way," Kurt cried out. "We'll head into the Bowl and catch you guys later."

"Wait a minute. We can at least check it out. I'm paying you, aren't I?"

"Yes, you are. But if you're going with them, you need to pay in advance."

"Don't give me that crap," Franky said. "Go ahead, hot shots. I'm right behind you."

Franky didn't like the way Wesley licked his lips before he headed down the far left ridge of Rendezvous Bowl. Maybe hanging with these guys wasn't such a good idea. A quick ten turns later, Wesley snapped to a stop at the edge of a snow-covered cliff.

"This here's Corbet's Couloir." Wesley grinned a welcome.

Below Franky a sheer fifteen-foot drop ended at the top of an impossibly steep, narrow chute. Rocky cliffs delineated the tight uncompromising walls of the Couloir. The precipitous drop fell for hundreds of feet as it plunged through a skinny bottleneck before flaring out into Tensleep Bowl far down the cliff face. Franky had never felt so small, dwarfed by the surrounding peaks, the gaping space below him, even the taller skiers grouped around him.

"Holy shit," Franky murmured. "How do you get in?"

"Jump or hang onto this rope to get you over the cliff face." The instructor pointed to a thick post embedded in the snow at his feet. "You go in parallel to the top, headed to the rocks on the right. The whole trick is to make that first turn. You make it, you're set up for three or four more tight, quick jump turns. Then it's just another steep Jackson Hole chute."

Franky flashed to a day when he'd traveled to the eastern edge of New Hampshire to ski Wildcat Mountain and its brandnew gondola. The raw beauty of the area had overwhelmed Franky's jaded attitude towards New England scenery. He'd taken a ride to Mt. Washington and a closer view of Tuckerman Ravine. Puckerman would be a better name for the frightening, elevator drop of the face. Franky had reappraised his abilities, not ready for that challenge.

"And if you don't make the first turn?" Franky asked.

"Kiss your ass good-bye," Matthew said.

Franky sidestepped back from the lip, overcome by a wave of vertigo.

This monster, especially at the top looking down, appeared worse than Tuckerman.

The scar-face one, Matthew, skied the few feet to the top of the cliff, gaining a little momentum, and launched into the thin air. Franky couldn't contain a loud gasp. Matthew landed hard into Corbet's. He compressed his body down, hands and shoulders twisted away from his ski tips, facing down the couloir. Then, before crashing into the rocky outcropping defining the chute, Matthew cranked a 180-degree turn. He edged so hard his shoulders scrapped the snow. He had no time to build a secure platform and whipped another 180, a little wild, then settled into a series of quick turns. Franky stared in amazement.

The Indian followed, stepping, rather than skiing off the top, to bleed some speed off his drop into the couloir. He made the critical turn with clean, effortless movements, not using as much body torque as Matthew, smooth jumps, body in perfect position. Wesley made the radical turns look easy.

David, the odd-looking one, went next. The stuck-up jerk had nodded to him once in the ski-school hut, hadn't said a word since. Ah, justice, Franky mused, happy to see David need the rope. The extra support didn't help. He slipped and scraped down the fifteen-foot sheer drop. When he let go of the rope, the back of his skis slipped too far below him. He almost recovered, but the rock wall came too soon. His panicked, flailing turn buried a ski tip and threw him forward over his skis. David performed a sequence of snapping somersaults, crashing down the center of Corbet's Couloir. The good news: No rocks in the middle.

Both of David's skis flew off. The straps kept the boards close to his body, two dangerous weapons capable of slicing through David's skin and clothing. The fall lasted only a few seconds, but David's flying, twisting body covered several hundred feet, until he stuck in deep snow at the bottom of the couloir as it opened into Tensleep Bowl.

Moments passed. Then movement. David raised his arms, flashed a peace sign, and began the arduous task of putting his skis back on in the clinging powder.

"You want to try?" Kurt asked, no sarcasm in his voice.

"Maybe later."

Much later. And how the hell was he going to connect with the locals if they all skied like this. Kurt better be the greatest instructor in the world.

TWENTY-EIGHT

Waitresses and two bartenders fought a losing battle, throwing food and beer at the Mangy Moose's screaming patrons. Franky flinched from the light pouring in from the windows on both sides of the restaurant/bar. Still, not a bad spot to wait for Shebang.

A balcony rimmed the large room on all four sides. Full-size Revolutionary-era flags hung on the railings—Betsy Ross's 1777 version, Bunker Hill, the Liberty Tree and even a nod to the jerk-off Texas skiers, a Confederate Battle Flag. The Moose vibrated with holiday action. Franky could really dig the craziness of this place.

Color movie posters plastered the exposed ceiling, grabbing his attention. Man, this had to be a collection of the biggest bombs in Hollywood history. He recognized a few: *Big Jake* with John Wayne and Richard Boone (who do you think is the bad guy?); Alan Ladd in *Duel of Champions*; *Black Spurs*, starring Rory Calhoun—*Every time he comes to town, someone's gonna die.*

Most he'd never heard of: *Zombies of the Mora Tai*; *Night of the Bloody Apes*; *Violent Roads*; *Guns at Batasi—Outnumbered, but never outfought.* One of the bright-colored ads had to be a Hollywood practical joke, *The Human Vapor*, not a single actor or actress brave enough to have their name on the poster. "Half Man, Half Beast, It Destroys, It Kills." *Presented on the Giant Screen, with Living Color and Stereophonic Sound.* Franky cracked up. Probably a movie about the kitchen here at the Mangy Moose.

Franky checked his watch. He'd been observing the scenery for twenty-five minutes. When the hell would the angry-eyed Jackson native show up? Maybe *The Human Vapors* told the story of the flakey Shebang.

He had connected with Shebang at Teton Sports and offered to buy him a drink. The ungrateful punk had held out for two. But Franky had to stay flexible. He needed information. So he waited alone at a table for two, distanced from the raucous bar. But he wouldn't be sitting on his ass much longer. Looked like this jerk would be as worthless as the Bruise Brothers, the new name that so perfectly fit Franky's accomplices.

Then Shebang blasted through the door as if connected to Franky by ESP. Another scary thought. He spied Franky and sped towards his table. Shebang braked half way, next to a chunky waitress, and grabbed her ass. She twirled, just missing his head with a tray of empties. Shebang snarled a laugh and continued to Franky.

"Sorry I'm late, man." He hit the chair with a thud. "This retail crap sucks. Only got a few minutes, then I gotta go back and help close. Equipment work out for you?"

"Yeah. Not bad," Franky said. "Went skiing with an instructor named Kurt Sidon. He introduced me to a half-breed named Wesley and two other hot shots, Matthew and David. Know any of them?"

"Surely do. But I need a drink." He stood up and yelled, "Hey, Pudge, how about a couple of Buds. I don't have all day. You said you'd buy me a couple, right?"

A sinking sensation gripped Franky's stomach. Jesus, this asshole was the guy he was depending on for connections?

"Kurt's a little weird," Shebang said. "Pretty much a loner. Knows his stuff."

Pudge, or whatever her name was, appeared within an instant with two bottles of Budweiser. Probably wanted to serve the maniac as fast as possible. Proved obnoxious worked.

At least Franky agreed with Shebang's quick comment about Kurt. The instructor had been cool. After Franky's initial shock at the top of Corbet's, Kurt had spent the afternoon working on the basics in Rendezvous Bowl and other saner runs. The instructor had understood Franky's intimidation and insecurity, and hadn't pushed him. Franky tipped him an extra $5.

But Kurt had provided little real information beyond skiing instruction, despite Franky's attempts to pump the man. The instructor said he was from Oregon, went to Utah State, made the ski team, been teaching in various resorts for ten years, lived in a small, two-room cabin near Wilson. Not much. Kurt also had little to say about the other characters they'd met. The total sum of worthwhile facts added up to very little.

"You really know how to choose your friends," Shebang said after gulping down the first bottle.

"Didn't say they were friends. Just happened to meet through Kurt. Ran into another freak at the top. Short, wire-haired faggot that's somehow on ski patrol."

"Ah, Ace," Shebang said through his second beer. "He's okay, just drugged out of his mind."

"What about the others?"

"You picked some pricks. Wesley ain't bad for an Indian, but Matthew and David are one-hundred percent-grade-A assholes. When I got time I'll tell you about them. Gotta go."

And Shebang was gone. No thank you. No see you later. Still, Franky felt an unexplainable affinity to the man. Must be the negative comments he had heard about Shebang on the mountain.

Franky had spent the majority of his life as an outcast. He'd been the butt of jokes and disdain all the way through prep school and college. He didn't consider himself a warm, fuzzy person. No flaming flower child. He could relate to the angry, intense Shebang. And his brief words confirmed Franky's opinions.

But Franky was surprised he liked the Indian. Maybe because he was only a half-breed. Wesley liked to talk, probably could be loosened up with a couple of drinks. After all, dumb-ass Indians couldn't hold their liquor.

Matthew seemed the opposite, unapproachable, uptight, and unpredictable. Franky doubted he'd get much out of that tight-lipped son of a bitch. He also didn't like that prissy pussy David. The arrogant ass said little, looked down his nose at Franky, and evidently had a hard-on for Shebang.

A noisy group waded into the bar. Four local losers and a girl, the normal odds in Jackson Hole. He recognized the slender, long-haired woman. The one from the plane whom he'd almost knocked on her cute ass heading into the terminal. The scroungy men were strangers, although one looked a little familiar.

The chick looked better than the other day, but definitely no beauty.

She glanced at him as the group worked through the crowd towards an empty table near him. Maybe she'd grow into a fox in a week or two, like ugly girls in a bar at closing time. Should he give her a thrill?

* * *

Life was great for Sarah. TJ hovered close, protecting his territory, supplying unrelenting service for three straight nights. She loved the attention almost as much as the sex. But a sticky situation had developed. Sarah wanted to expand her physical relationships. Unfortunately, many of the locals viewed her as TJ's girl.

Wesley had remained friendly but had maintained a different agenda. He wanted to introduce Sarah to his mystery man. Well, at least TJ provided convenience and pleasure as Wesley manipulated. Now Sarah succumbed to a gnawing feeling of lost opportunity. TJ didn't quite compare to her wild and wanton dreams. Sarah, awash in the glow of hungry stares, wished she had the confidence to freelance, give dreams a chance to come true.

She spotted the guy she'd bumped into at the airport. He sat alone near the far wall, slouched in his spindle-backed chair like James Dean. He hadn't grown since she'd first noticed him in Denver, but he did have dark good looks. And his wet-look fashion statement added a degree of class. Maybe he was lonely, something Sarah could relate to. She angled her group to the large table near him and chose a seat with a clear line of sight.

A warm rush washed through her as she caught him checking her out. She could make a casual move and greeting, include him in their conversation. What the hell? Rejection would be painless. An empty chair sat between Sarah's group and his table for two. Unlike his guarded, empty plane seat, the young man now seemed to invite her to his table's open spot. She screwed up her courage and moved to the vacant seat. She shot him a quick smile. His return grin seemed smug, all knowing, but no question he had directed the look at her.

"We keep running into each other," he said, New York advertised with every vowel. "Must be fate."

Sarah twisted towards the comment. The man's smirk almost turned her back around. But the word "fate" hit a chord. Fate sucked, but could the tide be turning? And he could be masking his own self-consciousness.

"Saw you on the flight, right?" Sarah cringed at her unimaginative response.

"Name's Franky. You live here?"

"No," Sarah said, proud to even be mistaken as a native. "But I'm here for a whole month. I'm Sarah Ross. Pleased to meet you." Each mention of the longer-than-dreamed-of vacation brought a pleasant glow of contentment. "How long are you here?"

"Couple weeks," Franky said. "Maybe longer. Got some business here. Plenty of time to ski too."

Sarah smiled to herself as he puffed up. An important guy, not some dumb tourist.

"Been to Jackson Hole before?" Sarah asked.

"Naw. Hit Aspen for ten days around Christmas. Lot more action there."

"More glitz in Sun Valley or Colorado, but less mountain."

"No kidding," Franky said, a shadow crossing his strong features. "No doubt about that. Where you staying?"

"Wort, downtown."

"Me too." Franky smiled. "Buy you a drink sometime?"

"Sure. I'll look forward to it."

Good start, Sarah thought, pleased with the attention from someone connected to the outside world, a place that offered her little consideration or comfort. And the contradictions in the man attracted her, a vulnerability hidden behind the tough surface. He had style and intensity. Interesting package. Certainly more potential than the simplistic TJ.

TWENTY-NINE

Phone calls had to be made from the Grand View. Matthew didn't mind. His visits to the lodge gave him the opportunity to view Julia. Watching was the operative activity with the beautiful, withdrawn goddess. Conversation occurred, but died like a match in the wind. Some vital ingredient missing, evidenced not just by her reticence, but also in a growing tension between her and Jim.

In the kitchen, the two-timing Cody stopped weaving in and out of Julia's long legs and crossed the room to greet Matthew. The dog showed rapid recovery with each passing day and had picked up the rhythm of life at the lodge—nights with Matthew, days fawned over by Julia and the guests of the bed and breakfast. A lapse in loyalty Matthew didn't appreciate. Bull would have died before compromising his loyalty.

Matthew dialed Wesley at the Blackfoot Garage.

"You hittin' the mountain today?" The usual orchestra of clanging metal and country music accompanied Wesley's greeting.

"Not till afternoon. Conditions suck. We need a couple of feet of new snow. These occasional two or three inches just create goddamn booby traps. It's like skiing down a giant washboard."

"Why don't you come into town? I'm havin' lunch with that nice honey I been tellin' you about."

"No, thanks." Matthew would dodge Wesley's female friend from Chicago as long as possible. And he had no desire to explain his ambiguous feelings about women, even to Wesley. "You're taking her to David's tonight, aren't you? I'll meet her then."

"Matthew," Wesley said, his selling tone wheedling through the phone lines. "Sarah's cool. Lotta energy, lotta fun. Hungry for lovin'. You're lucky I'm willin' to share her."

"What makes you think she's willing to be shared?"

Frightening how quickly his insecurities surfaced at the mere hint of a sexual challenge. Could he even get it up, feeling so self-conscious?

"Just make it to the party at David's house. You know where it is on Fish Creek?"

"Yes, Wesley, I know where it is. Been there with you. Several times."

"Know what time?" Mother Wesley working overtime.

"Yes, Wesley, I know what time."

"Don't go throwin' your back out in them nasty bumps." Wesley's musical voice was clear on the other end. "This girl needs someone in good shape. She's stayin' in town at the Wort. Likes bein' 'round the local color."

"The only man of color in Jackson Hole I know of is you—and you're only half red. I'll see you tonight." Matthew turned to Julia by the kitchen sink. "Do you know this girl Wesley's bugging me about?"

"Yes." Julia's answer was empty as usual.

"Julia." Matthew was exasperated with both his stone-cold landlady and Wesley. "Would you please share just a little more of your female insight?"

"She's a nice girl." A flicker of interest from Julia. "Full of life. Happy. A little too forward. Attractive, in a clean sort of way."

Wow, Matthew thought, a virtual dissertation from the Ice Queen.

*　*　*

Franky drove his rental Ford the five blocks from the Wort to the Bruise Brothers' clapboard shack on Hansen Street at the eastern edge of town. He'd made little progress. Plus snow conditions were the pits. But his pain-in-the-ass partners promised a major lead.

Franky huddled with the two men in the main room. Two portable floor heaters kept the dump habitable. A New York flophouse had more amenities than this shit hole. Franky's "suite" at the Wort, shabby though it seemed, provided more space and comfort.

"Making any progress, big shot?" John said.

John's lack of respect grated on Franky. Close proximity caused a claustrophobic tightening in Franky's stomach. The frayed dark drapes brought back memories of the family's unpleasant command center. And the Bruise Brothers weren't that far removed from Sal and Marco.

"We been here over a week, and all you've got's a tan," John added.

"Look, buddy," Franky sneered in response. "At least I been out there trying to dig something up. I'm connected with a group of locals that'll turn up a lead sooner or later."

"It better be sooner cuz word from back East is there's not gonna be much more later."

John's delivery came across hard. A note of doubt provided a sliver of relief. If these two had a different agenda than Franky, would they be worried at the lack of leads?

"You said you had information," Franky said. "What is it? Or were you bullshitting me?"

"Matter of fact, we do." John didn't sound too confident. "Searching the county records and title reports led us to five possibilities—people with the right general description who bought one or more pieces of property in the last two and a half years."

"You said you were gonna do a title search last week. What the hell took so long?"

"Look, Franky," Hack said, leaning forward, making the tight space smaller. "We needed a cover, so we said we were in the market to buy some property, investment stuff. Had to hook up with a local realtor and look at potential pieces."

"Only one lead makes any sense," John said. "In your living with the locals, you ever run across a guy named David Moore?"

"You've got to be kidding me." Franky snorted. "I know that jerk. He doesn't have the balls to walk in the dark, let alone set up my old man."

"Moore's the big mover and shaker in Jackson Hole," John said, leaning forward into the space Hack had just vacated. "First, July 1966, he bought a ten-acre parcel over on Fish Creek Road, up against the river. Built a house. We drove by it. Big. Impressive. Then in March of '67, he loaned enough money to a Wesley Crow on a commercial piece to control the first deed of trust, place called the Blackfoot Garage."

A thread of logic appeared with the addition of the half-breed's business. Franky became interested.

"Same kind of thing happened in November 1967," John continued.

"Got control of a piece on the Wilson-Moose road from a James and Julia Nordman. Think he did it financing this big new lodge, the Grand View. Checked that out too. Nice place. Called a bed-and-breakfast, whatever the hell that is."

"Finally," Hack said, "a couple weeks before we arrived, he bought a two-hundred-acre parcel between the same highway and the Snake River. Purchased the land from an old guy named Morgan. This jerk is making more deals than anyone else in the county."

David Moore. The asshole seemed to be a stuck-up lightweight. But the timing of David's appearance in Jackson Hole coincided with the disappearance of the stooge who had set up his father. Still, the more Franky pondered the image of the soft-spoken turkey, the less of a suspect David Moore seemed.

"You check him out back East?"

"Nothin'," John admitted. "But we're sure he changed his name. How's he compare to these pictures?"

John produced the folder of photographs. He shuffled through the small pile until he selected two of the clearest images of their target taken several years before.

"Moore's about 5'10", slender, dark hair and eyes," Franky said.

David fit the general description. Franky compared the black-and-white glossies with his visual impression of the man. David's face hardly resembled the pictures. His misshapen features were hard to categorize—different nose, ears and even bone structure. If he had paid for plastic surgery, he'd been ripped off.

"Naw, just don't think it's him," Franky said. "I'm telling you, he doesn't look Italian, and he's a wimp."

"We oughta search his house," Hack suggested without much conviction.

"Be my guest," Franky said.

These idiots were getting desperate. Franky relaxed. And they weren't out to kill him. Maybe more pressure squeezed the hit men than Franky. They didn't know his true value was running the business back East.

"Might do that." John stood, circled the small room, and came back to face Franky. "You telling us in a week and a half you've got no suspects?"

These guys weren't too happy. David was their only lead, and he thought it weak, if not worthless. Brains weren't the Bruise Brothers' greatest asset. But Franky wouldn't underestimate their ability to perform their more physical assignments.

"Franky." Hack's irritation turned to belligerence. "You don't like our idea, get another. There's only two thousand people in the whole town of Jackson Hole and four thousand in the entire goddamn county. They don't all ski. They ain't all males between the ages of thirty and forty. You could've talked to every single one of them in the time you been here."

"Sure, smart guy. Just walk up and ask every potential person on the mountain if he's hiding from the mob. I'm wondering if the bastard's even here in Jackson Hole."

"You know we got the information from reliable sources," John said.

"Yeah, who?" Franky said, once again wondering if he and his two bumbling accomplices were on the same assignment.

"Reliable enough for us to be sent here to find him." Hack didn't sound too comfortable either. "We'll search this guy Moore's house. You start working harder. Skiing and drinking ain't turned up much. Your old man won't be too impressed with your investigative techniques, especially with him sittin' in a jail cell."

Well, that comment showed how little they knew. The way things were shaping up back East, a jail cell might be the best place for his old man.

THIRTY

Very nice, Matthew thought, as he pulled into David Moore's driveway. The large log-cabin home, shaped in a fat L, took advantage of a curve in Fish Creek, more of a river than a humble creek. The kitchen, dining and living rooms occupied the short leg of the L, visible as he moved past them and a two-car garage to the circular driveway at the front door. Two stories of bedrooms filled up the longer, narrower portion of the house.

The entry opened into a wood-floored hallway similar to the Grand View's. Matthew approached a thin figure in the shadow of a large, potted ficus. The large, lush tree created a break between the one-story kitchen and the fifteen-foot clerestory height of the dining/living area—more similarities in design with the Grand View. David was in conversation with a chubby, blond man Matthew had never seen before.

"Happy birthday, David," Matthew said, closing on his friend from behind.

The man turned, but he wasn't David.

"Not my birthday," Kurt said. His hair, already growing back, looked better two weeks from the scalping. "But it's nice to see you off the mountain for a change. This is David's cousin from back east, Bobby Cetraro."

"Good evening," Bobby greeted Matthew, rather stiff and cool.

"You signed up for my inaugural Steep Class?" Kurt asked Matthew.

The Jackson Hole Ski School had been promoting a special one-week session on techniques for skiing steep and difficult terrain. Advertisements for Kurt's brainchild had been placed in Ski Magazine and sent to travel agencies specializing in ski packages.

"You can be the example of the 'after' for my 'before-and-after' comparisons."

"I'm already in and paid up," Matthew said. "How many skiers signed up so far?"

The $150-charge registered as no small commitment. And Matthew no longer needed the instruction. But he wanted to support his mountain mentor. The course also took advantage of some of Jackson Hole's best assets: Steep, long chutes and dramatic, expert runs.

"Over twenty, including your buddy David," Kurt said, displaying a rare expression of pleasure.

"Well, I'm ready," Matthew said.

*   *   *

Matthew moved into the living room. People gathered in small groups, neat and respectable in their Sunday best, quite a switch from the usual stoned, boisterous, hard-drinking Jackson Hole social gathering. He glimpsed Julia talking to several women in the kitchen, including a skinny, pleasant woman with washed-out blond hair and lively eyes that would be stunning with a little makeup. David's wife, Linda.

Whatever David's wife lacked in physical charm, she made up for with consideration, graciousness, and energy. She stepped away from the group of women, still talking over her shoulder as she pulled hors d'oeuvres from the oven. Linda whirled around the kitchen like a ballerina, filling trays, yanking glasses and plates from cupboards, all the time smiling at her guests. Solid was the word Matthew would use to describe her, despite the lightness of her step and spirit.

Six men stood in the center of David's large living room surrounding a slim girl in tight stretch pants and a vivid red sweater, her back to Matthew. Medium height in her after-ski boots, long, fine brown hair, tight butt. In fact, a very nice ass. Wesley and TJ seemed a little detached, but the others, including Jungle Jim, hovered close. Only anticipation of immediate availability could explain the brightness in the men's animated eyes.

"Matthew. Over here."

Wesley's cheerful greeting interrupted the competition. The girl turned. Large, long nose, fuller than necessary lips, just enough pimples and blemishes to mar otherwise attractive skin. Matthew flinched. But round hazel eyes sparkled, full of life. And, still, a dynamite body.

"I'm Sarah. Are you Matthew?"

"Yes, indeed." Wesley stepped into the exchange. "This is my good buddy I been tellin' you 'bout."

Matthew nodded, noncommittal. Her smiling energy caught his attention. The sound of the Midwest added depth to her voice. He glanced at the surrounding male faces, turned off by their almost drooling attentiveness. And why was Jim so interested with his wife only a few feet away?

Small talk and one-liners bounced around the group. Sarah's interest focused on him. Her expressive face looked attractive in motion, but strangely fragmented, almost homely, at rest. Matthew definitely wasn't ready for Wesley's setup.

Then David's cousin, Bobby, drifted into the group, as the conversation veered to sports.

"Looks like U.C.L.A.'s gonna kick ass again," Bobby said. "With that gorilla Alcindor, no one can touch them in the tourney."

"Didn't you go to U.C.L.A.?" TJ asked Matthew. "You ever watch them play?"

"Saw most home games. I left when Alcindor was a freshman. They beat the varsity that year."

"Exactly," Bobby stated. "Any school that got Big Lew would easily win all the time."

"It's not just talent," Matthew answered.

"Bullshit," Bobby said. "It's talent. Give me a seven-footer like Alcindor and I could be a great coach."

"Coaching and leadership are the reasons U.C.L.A. teams do so well," Matthew said. Support for his alma mater sounded strange as it left his mouth.

"Talent," Bobby repeated. "I went to Syracuse, and we'd be undefeated with Lew. U.C.L.A.'d be just another Pac Eight loser without him."

Why was Matthew arguing? Bobby acted like another loudmouthed New Yorker with all the answers. He looked at the soft-bodied man. Not only did Bobby appear unable to jump five inches, but his fat white hands would have trouble shooting a basketball against a wall, let alone through a hoop.

"You don't know what you're talking about," Matthew said. "In 1964 U.C.L.A. went 30-0 with nobody over 6'7". They had one star, a guard, Walt Hazzard. Next year they won the N.C.A.A. tournament again.

One star, a guard, Gail Goodrich. They beat your Eastern powerhouse, Princeton, with Bill Bradley. They won because they've got a great coach, John Wooden. And they'll win after Alcindor graduates because of Wooden's leadership."

"You can't give me any other concrete example of leadership," Bobby said, "being more important than talent."

Bobby hung on doggedly. But Matthew picked up the stranger's diminishing confidence. And a deep anger pushed him further than he had planned.

"The United States," Matthew said, overcoming his normal caution, "has more talent than the rest of the world combined. We've got the best planes, bombs, tanks, soldiers. But we've got weak leaders. A military more concerned with covering their asses than addressing the real problems. And our fine, new President Nixon's nothing but a crook who couldn't even get elected in California. . . . *our president threw the yellowsonofabitch into a dungeon, where he died . . .* "

The beat of the lines surfaced without conscious thought or intention. He couldn't shake the words, surprised that the lines of poetry escaped his lips like a sigh.

"Yeah," Wesley said, his laughter breaking the tension. "Instead of Nixon, you got a shitty actor, Ronny Reagan, for governor. Not much of an improvement."

Matthew used the change in moods to excuse himself. He moved toward several men by the large river-rock fireplace. He wouldn't be missed by Sarah's hungry admirers. And he'd had enough of this bullshit.

*   *   *

Sarah watched Matthew move away, something incomplete, a meal half-finished. How quickly things changed. It seemed just a moment since Wesley had welcomed Matthew into their group. She had turned and seen the man standing before her. Looked into his intense eyes and been shaken. Matthew looked lean and powerful. A large scar from his eyebrow to his hair line highlighted a face that reflected a world of depth and emotion—almost frightening. This man was a piece of work.

Her heart had beaten strong and rapid. Must have been the altitude. And the alcohol. Acclimatizing to the 6,000-foot elevation of Jackson Hole always took a while. But this Matthew took up some space. What a difference from the gathered throng, no transparent hunger or loud comments. Sarah had turned on all her charms.

Then an overweight, sloppy blond man had entered the conversation and started a heated argument, diverting Matthew's attention from her. Matthew had sliced up the newcomer. But, before she could reconnect, he had excused himself, saying he needed to congratulate the host on his birthday. A quick glance at Wesley confirmed his planned script breaking down.

What the hell? Sarah caught a glimpse of her image in the large plate glass window of David's spacious living room. Most of the available males circled her with rapt attention. Again she congratulated herself on her wonderful strategy. At odds of two- or three-hundred-to-one, she no longer played the role of the homely, lonely Jewish girl. Not only had she been the last to dance during the Snowball, but also the last to date. The last to make out. And the last to partake in the delicious sins of the flesh. She had turned the corner when she discovered Jackson Hole, Wyoming. Now a welcomed Princess, she was sought after and hungered over.

Conversation again washed around her like a warm bubble bath, restoring her confidence, filling the empty spaces never touched in Chicago. Sarah shifted her gaze back to her faithful following. She shook off her confusion and disappointment at Matthew's apparent disinterest. So much for first impressions. This man might just be too much to handle. The hell with him.

*   *   *

Matthew noticed the birthday boy, David, on his knees in the corner, attention riveted on his three-year-old daughter, oblivious to the activity around him. His little girl's bright smile reflected her delight. No competition for her father's affection. Matthew walked over to them.

"Happy birthday, David," Matthew said, this time to the right person. He dropped to the carpet, eye to eye with David and his daughter. "You having fun at your dad's party, Leslie?"

"Fine, thank you."

Leslie's voice squeaked, somewhat formal, shy, but unafraid. Matthew had little experience connecting with children. No practice. Still, tucked in the corner, he felt safe beyond Wesley's manipulations. And the child was kind of cute.

"Would you like to stay here?" Leslie offered. "With me and my daddy?"

Matthew didn't know how to respond.

"You've got the touch," David said, a broad smile contorting his irregular features. "Kids and animals like you. You must not be as tough as you act."

"I've been accused of much worse," Matthew said. "Thanks, Leslie. I'll stop by and visit you some time."

Matthew stood up and drifted out the French doors to an exterior wooded walkway paralleling the bedroom wing. He felt more comfortable in the frigid air, the muted murmuring of Fish Creek, vivid stars splattering the clear night sky.

Sarah interested him. But Matthew wasn't what he appeared to be. It wouldn't take her long to find out. Who would want to deal with all the crap he'd bring to a relationship?

A wistful desire to be normal drifted from him with the cloud of steam from his breath. He fought off the impulse to walk around the side of the house, jump in his car and return to the Grand View. He'd even have Cody to himself with Julia out of the picture for the evening. Matthew sighed, turned back towards the French doors. He'd have to trade the allure of a night as a hermit for the distasteful performance required by social obligation.

THIRTY-ONE

Matthew muscled his way through the heavy wood-and-glass doors of the Million Dollar Cowboy Bar. Mixed emotions tightened his gut. He'd yet to visit the infamous Cowboy and the hot band performing on stage. The Affair in the Square had caused one of several detours. Now he had serious doubts about this visit with Wesley, who was geared up for another matchmaking attempt with Sarah.

Big Bob Burlson, stationed to the left of the front doors with the usual scrawny wannabes, had bouncer duty. The Rhythm Wranglers and the cover charge of two dollars would begin in about thirty minutes. A motley assortment of mechanics and cowboys attacked the scarred green felt of four pool tables. The players included the team of Ace and David, shooting nine ball for a buck a game and getting their butts kicked. Three separate brass-trimmed bars lined the walls around the three levels of cocktail tables, the largest on the right with old polished saddles serving as bar stools.

Wall-size murals and paintings of western scenes pictured bucking broncos, cattle roping, lion hunting, and cowboys riding horses into a bar that may or may not have been the Cowboy. Shelves massed with sparkling bottles and glasses rose behind the bars. Stuffed wildlife and surreal-sized longhorns hung out on posts or walls and in glass display cases. Acres of cankerous, bulbous-shaped knotty pine made up the pillars and beams supporting the jumbled establishment.

Matthew edged his way over to Wesley, TJ, and Sarah. His gait held a slight limp, a gift from the rock-hard ski mountain. The Chicago Princess sat regally astride her saddle. He eased aboard the slippery vacant one to her left, sitting backwards for a better view of the bar's activities. And to cover his back.

The saloon jumped with increasing energy and action. A flood of patrons of various shapes and sizes streamed through the doors. The good, the bad, and the ugly were all present, heavy competition for the ugly. Matthew noticed a table against the wall inhabited by Shebang, Franky, and two lift operators, the bad. The good had to be somewhere. Wesley and TJ qualified, and probably the Princess.

"You lookin' a little weathered, good buddy," Wesley said.

"We need snow."

"I think we're in luck," TJ offered. "Wind's picking up. Weather service's promising a major dump. All the old local farts agree. They're rubbing their old, twitchy knees."

"This place is a zoo," Matthew said to Wesley. "More animals than Noah's ark. I'm surprised they let some of these wild things out of their cages."

"We're mighty tolerant here in Jackson Hole." Wesley reversed his position to face the lively performance with Matthew. He laughed and pointed out the group of misfits at Shebang's table. Wesley began a story about Shebang, then froze in mid-sentence.

"What's the matter?" Matthew asked.

"We got trouble," Wesley said, his voice tight. "You know what a grizzly bear can do to a peaceful day?"

Matthew put a concerned hand on his friend's shoulder. TJ leaned close to pick up Wesley's words.

"When you're not in grizzly country," he said, "you cruise comfortably through the countryside. You check out the birds and animals, the plants, the scenery. Nice and peaceful. Smoke a little grass. Pick your pace. Let your kids and dogs play where they want." Wesley reached around to the bar, grabbed his beer and chugged the remaining half before continuing. "But if there's grizzlies around, the game changes. You gotta always be lookin' for danger."

Wesley shifted, antsy on the saddle. He adjusted the buckle of his belt, then ran his fingers through his thick dark hair. Matthew had never seen Wesley react in such a troubled manner.

"All animals would rather leave you alone, except a crazy moose. But even them'll give you a chance to split. A grizzly'll attack you with no warnin'. For no reason other than you're in their territory. They're almost extinct cuz they're even nastier and more aggressive than man. No way to coexist. Well, a grizzly just entered the Cowboy Bar."

Matthew scanned the crowded bar. It didn't take long to recognize the cause of Wesley's concern. He stood just inside the entrance on the far side of the bar. He had no neck, his shoulders wide as a house. Over six-and-a-half feet tall, the monster made Burleson, the bouncer, look small.

"Jesus, Wesley, that guy's huge," Matthew said. Two or three days of stubble gave the man's face an evil look.

"That's the only man in the world I hate," Wesley said. "Ty Corbin. The son of a bitch's given me shit my whole life. Lives down in Alpine now. Comes to Jackson Hole now and then lookin' for trouble. Went to school with him. Always been a sadistic prick. No goddamn redeemin' qualities. Surprised someone ain't shot him. Probably not a big enough gun available."

"So what now?" Matthew said.

"He'll see us," Wesley said sadly. "And he will give us shit."

"Then let's just get the hell out of here."

"I'm sure he's already got us in his sights."

Wesley got off his saddle. Matthew followed, feeling more secure with both feet on the ground. Sure enough, the bear of a man, drunk and belligerent, plodded towards Wesley. As he got closer, his ugliness became clearer, small pig eyes and irregular teeth angled in a misshapen, thick-lipped mouth. The crowd parted like the Red Sea before the Israelites.

"My favorite wimpy half-breed," Corbin said and moved right into Wesley's face, towering over him, filling all the available space. "Now you know I just hate Injuns. Especially smart-ass punks that don't know their place. Think they're good as hard workin' white men."

Matthew shifted his grip on the bottle of his long-necked Bud. Red alert. Every fiber of his body tightened. Ty's breath reeked. Matthew focused on Corbin's narrowed gaze darting between Wesley and Matthew.

"... *Their passive prey did kick and curse* ..." The words bubbled unbidden to Matthew's lips. Then speaking more clearly, "You don't look too white to me. More like a shitty brown."

The speed of the man's movement caught Matthew off guard. Corbin's huge paw caught Matthew's throat and squeezed. The giant leered down at Matthew, keeping Wesley at bay with the threat of his other hand.

"So you're the little shit that picked on my buddies in the Square." Corbin now crowded over Matthew. "Payback time."

Matthew didn't know which would bring blackout first, the iron grip on his neck or the stench from the monster's mouth. But he knew through the growing haze of unconsciousness that any opportunity for action would be over within seconds. He swung his right hand, gripping his beer bottle like a club and aiming for the temple. But the distance created by Corbin's height and arm length shortened the arc of the bottle. The Bud smashed against the huge man's jaw. Damn.

A half-full bottle of beer to the face only loosened Corbin's death grip around Matthew's jugular. The bottle didn't even break. But air flowed back into Matthew's oxygen-starved system. Lights stabilized in his brain.

Matthew kicked hard, connecting with Corbin's groin. The loud grunt coincided with a complete release from Ty's meaty paw. The huge man bent over. Matthew came in hard and low with a karate kite to the solar plexus. Corbin's heavy clothing functioned as partial armor. But the combined kick and blow brought Corbin's massive head down low enough for the kill.

The stunned Goliath groaned, arms around his midsection, piggy eyes reflecting surprise and helplessness. Now you're at my level, Matthew thought as he coldly calculated options. Then, fingers curled, palm out, he stepped into Corbin, driving the heel of his hand towards the exposed, vulnerable nose, the angle now perfect to ram the cartilage into his brain.

Several thoughts flashed through Matthew's mind in mid-swing. First, Corbin's brain might be so small the bones of his nose would miss their intended target. The second thought came from some unfamiliar and unknown source, twisting the flight of his hand enough to prevent a deathblow.

The redirected hit flattened Corbin's nose onto the side of his face, blood spurting like an uncapped oil well. The big man toppled backwards, crashing to the hardwood floor. Matthew hesitated. Another decision. Don't bother killing the worthless bastard.

Arms grabbed Matthew from behind. He didn't resist. Two hundred party animals at the Cowboy Bar, but no sound. The bouncer and two deputies held onto Matthew. How the hell had they got there so fast?

Wesley still stood at one side. Matthew twisted and looked at the uniformed deputies, large enough to intimidate in most situations. They loosened their hold.

"Ty attracts a following whenever he hits town," Wesley said, nodding toward the immediate police presence.

Corbin moved on the floor, raised his head and shoulders. Two, then three, sidekicks struggled to lift him.

"Let him be," one of the deputies said. "We'll get an ambulance."

"Fuck the ambulance," the giant said, without much force.

Once upright, a few feet from Matthew, he shook off the helping hands. He staggered in a small circle, trying to wipe away the flow of blood pouring from what was left of his nose. He attempted weaving towards the door, his entourage falling into place behind him.

"You'll pay for this." A weak threat. Several deep, blood-choked breaths brought some energy to his words. "I'm gonna kill you one day."

Something clicked. Matthew broke away from the deputies' now loose grasp and attacked again. He clenched Corbin's coat and drove him back across the floor, tables, chairs, and cowboys flying in all directions. Matthew smashed Corbin through the wooden railing at the edge of the main bar level. Corbin landed with a sickening thud on his back, Matthew on top, forearm crushing Corbin's throat. He lowered his head, lips next to the red neck's ear.

"You won't do shit. I ever see you again, anywhere, I'll finish what you started. You deserve to die, asshole, and, believe me, next time I'll be happy to oblige."

A sharp, cold object pressed into the back of Matthew's head. The barrel of a large gun. Once again the grip of strong arms jerked Matthew off Corbin. Steel pinched his wrists behind his back, someone locking handcuffs as he reached his feet.

"Isn't this the same guy that nailed Tony and Gill in the Square a couple of weeks ago?" the larger of the two deputies asked anyone.

"Yeah," Wesley answered. "You'd think the local boys would leave him alone."

"Seems to attract trouble," the lanky, smaller deputy said, short black hair accentuating his large features.

"Well," Wesley said, "he sure as hell ain't lookin' for problems."

The larger officer, big belly, big shoulders, could have been Corbin's little brother. He leaned over the motionless figure on the dance floor.

"He's still alive," the officer said. "Hey, Ty, you want to file any charges?"

The sarcastic question received no answer from the fallen giant.

"Clarence, you're outta your mind," Wesley said. "I can see the headlines now: Poodle Arrested for Attack on German Shepherd."

"More like a pit bull than a poodle," Clarence said.

"Take the damn cuffs off," Wesley said. "You got a hundred witnesses saw Corbin grab this boy by the neck and then threaten to kill him. Hell, the marks are still there." Wesley pointed to Matthew's throat. "Corbin's the meanest son of a bitch in the state. You deputies follow him around the minute he steps into town. Fact is, you two are probably the entire police force in Jackson tonight. I didn't know you tailed him to protect the poor misunderstood child."

"Look, Wesley," Clarence said, glancing around and motioning in Matthew's direction. "This kid's gotta be a trained killer. If you're a boxer, your fists are registered weapons. You use them in a fight, you go to jail. Your buddy's a deadly weapon. He's going to jail."

"Clarence, you asshole," Wesley bellowed. "Your brain's a deadly weapon. Did he kill Ty? No. Could he have killed him? Yes. Has Ty ever killed anyone? Bet your ass he has. Take the goddamn cuffs off."

"He's going to jail," Clarence said, digging in. "I'm calling the sheriff. Let him decide. He's due back late this evening."

Matthew struggled for equilibrium. The raw adrenaline, the fear and anger, had the familiar feel of battle. But the reappearance of control, partial though it might have been, had deflected his normal response to danger and self-defense. Action, intuitively incomplete, fueled his confusion. Too late to finish the job on Corbin, choices had been made, but his instincts demanded more.

"I'll go with the cops, Wesley." Matthew felt Corbin's blood crusting on his face, knew he looked more victim than aggressor.

"Dammit, Clarence," Wesley said. "If you don't at least take his cuffs off and let me go with him to your nice new jail, I'm callin' Chauncy Lewis. That attorney'll eat your ass alive, sue the city for false arrest, and make fools outta ya. What a case. Two hundred witnesses'll say it was self defense."

"Call him anyway," a respectable-looking man called out. "Old Chauncey'll be pissed off if you don't give him a chance. He can't lose this one."

The two deputies traded uneasy glances. Clarence reached for the keys to the handcuffs.

"You come with us peacefullike if we take these off?"

"Yes, sir," Matthew said sounding much more composed and detached than he felt.

"I'm goin' with him," Wesley insisted.

"Okay," Clarence said. "You mess around, boy, it's obvious the only way to stop you is with a bullet."

The large man unlocked the cuffs, but kept a hand on his big .357 magnum.

"TJ," Wesley called out. "Can you and Ace get a ride back?"

Matthew glimpsed TJ with the Princess standing beside him, their mouths wide open.

THIRTY-TWO

The Rhythm Wranglers launched into their first set as Matthew was led out the door of the Cowboy Bar. The buzzing crowd turned their attention to the band. Sarah was not distracted by the music.

Her climaxlike rush faded. Not a sexual orgasm, moist and sensual, but an emotional and physical experience equally intense. Whatever the source, the drama had overpowered her. She sat limply in her saddle, heat of the moment receding.

A glance at TJ mirrored her own reaction—stunned. Now that was an expression she had never expected to see on the forever smiling TJ. She touched TJ's shoulder, and they pivoted back to the glossy bar top. Ace bounced away, unfazed. Sarah remained immobile, glad for TJ's presence.

"Why so surprised?" Sarah responded to TJ's dazed gaze into the mirror behind the bar. "I thought you'd witnessed Matthew in action in the Square?"

"Man, it was pitch-black. I'm still not sure what the hell happened that night. But this. This was broad daylight. He took down Ty Corbin."

"Broad daylight?" Sarah had to laugh.

"Well, I seen it clear this time. Slow mo. Far out."

Sarah's neck prickled from the presence of hungry suitors circling behind her. If TJ left, she'd be swamped by the assembled mass of single males. The tidal wave of hustlers might happen anyway. Sarah needed time, not male companionship, let alone sexual adventures. Was it her reaction to a macho man or the bloody violence that had swept her to such an incredible level of intensity? She tried to generate guilt at her excitement in Matthew's destruction of Corbin. But guilt wouldn't register. She had done nothing wrong.

So why did she feel so uneasy? What had moved her so passionately? Then the image of Irving Knudsen, flat on his ass, flashed before her. That event had created an impressive flow of adrenaline. But the pathetic, disgusting advances of her boss hadn't generated any sexual arousal. More relief and anger. Much different from tonight.

"Gotta hit the head," TJ said and bolted from his saddle before Sarah could restrain him.

She wanted out of the bar, preferably with an escort to deflect any advances. She didn't desire TJ or anyone else in bed. The swirl of stimulation from the events of the evening demanded sorting out. Matthew dominated her mind. His apparent lack of interest in her did nothing to mute the rush of questions.

Sarah picked out Shebang's table in the mirror, Franky's eyes glued on her. She hadn't appreciated Wesley's inclusion of Franky in the Indian's earlier derisive comments. She and Franky had never had their drink together. She'd run into him twice on the mountain, but both times she'd been surrounded by her usual legion of local talent. Now he caught her eye and smiled. But this wasn't the time either.

*   *   *

Scarface had kicked the crap out of the local gorilla. Franky was not impressed. Sal and Marco had exhibited equal street-fighting violence. Jackson Hole's resident bad boy must have an inflated reputation, or Matthew was even more dangerous than Franky gave him credit. Probably the former. Corbin appeared fat and out of shape. Still, Franky would watch himself around Matthew.

"Corbin must be getting old," Shebang commented. "I would've put big bucks on Ty against anything human. Maybe Matthew's an alien in drag."

Franky's attention moved to Sarah. Even from a distance she looked spaced. Her open lips glistened in the reflection of the small spotlights above the mirror. She looked great from the back, tucked tightly into the saddle. Hell, if violence got her off, how would she react to the hit in the alley? But the memory of that disaster brought a moment of discomfort. How would she respond to the smell of Franky pissing in his pants?

Well this was an opportunity to move on Sarah without her constant protection. She was plugged into a large group of Jackson Hole peasants, hard to approach. Shebang and his group of clowns hadn't provided any valuable information. No different than a bunch of gossipy New York Italians. Maybe he could squeeze valuable leads from Sarah. Better now than never. Franky stood and gave his best swagger crossing the crowded floor.

What was her attraction? Other than being one of the few babes in the county. Franky never chased women, he procured them with money and gangster status. Why was he willing to make a fool of himself? She had a lithe body. Not like the sloppy-curved bimbos he usually ended up with. And she radiated energy, sparks in her large, luminous eyes. Although, as he came nearer, the normal brightness seemed muted.

"I never bought you that drink I promised."

"Hello, Franky," Sarah said, twisting to meet his arrival. "Don't take this wrong, but I need to get out of here."

"Why don't I walk you back to the Wort. Buy you a drink at the Silver Dollar."

"I'll take the walk. How about a rain check on the drink?"

He held out his arm, hid his disappointment, and helped her off the saddle. Sarah glanced several times over her shoulder as she slipped towards the door with Franky. He enjoyed the looks and catcalls directed at them. He wished for the thousandth time to be another two or three inches taller. His shortness didn't inhibit a hard-ass stare at Burleson and his assistants at the entrance.

Wind and snow smacked his face as they turned the corner south on Broadway. A gust worked his hat loose, and he dropped Sarah's arm to keep from losing it.

"I appreciate you taking me to my room. I'm not much company tonight."

"No problem," Franky said.

Not the best time to put a move on. Might as well play the gentleman and live to try another day. He led her into the hotel and up to her room on the second floor, only a few doors from his own hole. The level of his frustration surprised him. She wasn't that hot a chick to begin with. Why did he feel like a rejected schoolboy?

"Thank you, Franky." Sarah fumbled with her key, opened the door and turned to Franky, her body blocking the threshold. "How about that drink tomorrow night? Maybe even something to eat?"

A flash of excitement embarrassed Franky, especially with the flush of warmth that had to color his face.

"Sure. I'll give you a call." Franky tried to cover his childlike gratitude. "After all, we're neighbors."

Sarah took Franky's hand and pulled him closer. He braked her with a stiff arm. He didn't need charity from this homely woman.

"You're very sweet," she said, then closed the door.

THIRTY-THREE

The deputies' beat-up Chevy sedan came to a stop. Matthew had found temporary solace in the car's back seat. He tried to distance himself from the violent events of the Cowboy Bar, but the surging adrenaline made a mockery of his attempts. Did he overreact to Corbin's assault? Should he have responded with even more deadly force? No answers.

Matthew stepped out onto the sidewalk. Even with limited light from the street lamp, the large, two-story building appeared new, filling the corner of King and Simpson. A cold, wet wind advertised a massive front due in from the South. About time Jackson Hole received the gift of fresh powder.

Wesley caught up to Matthew as they entered the lobby and started up the stairs to the second floor.

"What's the matter with the elevator?" Wesley asked as he trailed the trio.

"Don't want to wear it out," Clarence replied. "Might be the only one in town."

The procession, Matthew in the middle, made a right turn at the top of the stairwell and entered a reception area. A counter to the right stood empty, as did the desk behind it. Two sturdy reinforced doors, one to the left, one straight ahead, gaped open in an ominous welcome. Matthew, Wesley and the officers made the left turn, entering a compact, sparkling state-of-the-art slammer, still smelling of fresh paint.

The entry formed part of a rectangular racetrack that surrounded three cell pods of five, three and two individual small enclosures, each big enough for only a bunk and a toilet. The pods shared a common table for dining or social activity when the small cells were not individually locked, and assuming the assigned cell mates were not into mutual destruction. Matthew felt somewhat disappointed. Where was the old Western jail from Dodge City's TV series *Gunsmoke*?

"Take your pick," Clarence said. "You two can have free run of our hotel, unless someone else shows up needing a room."

"Hotel, my ass," Wesley said, checking out the austere accommodations. "Where the hell's the TV? The music? You could at least have picked up a couple of hookers for the evenin'."

Matthew drifted through the open spaces, Wesley's verbal jabs not registering through the questions roiling through Matthew. What did the old jail look like? This stark, sterile place had no history. Just an empty book, blank pages awaiting the entries of lives gone wrong.

"Sheriff's due back around midnight," Clarence said to Matthew. "I'll have to lock the entry doors. Ellis'll stick around."

"What if Ellis gets called out to save your ass?" Wesley asked.

"We'll worry about that later. Seems like most of this town's trouble's already here."

"We're honored to be at the top of Jackson Hole's Most Wanted List," Wesley said.

The comment forced a smile from Matthew. Wesley just hung in there, as faithful as Bull. Matthew wanted to provide his friend with a positive response, but the conversation seemed miles away, Matthew a distant observer.

"You don't have to stick around, Wesley," Clarence said. "Nothing's gonna happen to your buddy. Seems he can take care of himself just fine without your help."

"He's right," Matthew said, picking a bunk in the three-room pod, all connecting doors wide open.

"Naw." Wesley plopped down in a little cell across from Matthew in the same pod. "Never been in jail. New experience for me."

"You want anything," Ellis said, "there's an intercom on the wall by the entrance. I'll be in the dispatch office next door."

The two deputies left, locking both of the jail's entrance doors. Matthew leaned against the wall, unable to respond to Wesley's attempt at small talk. Wesley finally gave up and lapsed into quiet thoughtfulness. Matthew welcomed the silence that swallowed them.

Adrenaline still pumped in fitful spurts, all of Matthew's senses primed well after the fact. The energy would be wasted. Experience had taught him he wouldn't calm down for hours.

*　*　*

At first, Matthew felt comfortable and secure in the serenity and simplicity of the empty jail block, especially once Wesley shut up. He'd just sit and vibrate, hope the blank walls would leech out some of his excess energy. But soon the distractive benefit instilled by the night's action faded into the unforgiving stark cement.

Matthew glanced at Wesley. The older man's troubled gaze reflected Matthew's own uneasiness. He recognized the stubborn, silent vigil of the rebuffed Indian and couldn't suppress a quick smile.

Matthew could no longer sit still. He jumped off the cot and slammed his arm against the bars, the jarring pain his desired intention.

"What's the matter with you, boy?"

"I should have killed him," Matthew blurted out.

Wesley stood. Alarm registered on his chiseled features.

"I don't think he'll mess with you again," Wesley said.

"I had two clean shots. He's a worthless son of a bitch. A dangerous rabid dog."

"You kinda castrated him."

Matthew, Wesley close behind, paced through the open interior doors of the jail. Perspiration popped out on Matthew's forehead. Painful, disconcerting images streaked through him like low-voltage electric shocks. Unresolved flashbacks, fragments dangling with razor sharpness, whipped through his soul and conscience. A vision avoided, never confronted or discussed, leapt out of what had been a sealed container. A malevolent Jack-in-the-box.

Matthew whirled around into the trailing Wesley and grabbed his shirt. Sweat dampened his face. Wesley stood solid, concern and solicitude painted his face. The pressure building within Matthew demanded release. But he couldn't find it grasping Wesley's fabric. He let go.

"You want to talk about it?" Wesley asked in measured tones. A look of wisdom shadowed his strong features. Experience in handling similar demons?

"I don't need to talk." Matthew's voice echoed, unconvincing in the empty spaces. Then Matthew, in a soft, contrite murmur, contradicted himself. "But I've got to say certain things to someone. You're the only friend I have, Wesley."

Matthew moved back into the pod of cells. He wanted the words out clean, to only have to say them once. He sat at the small table. Wesley took his place on the other side.

"The powers that be, that is, the asshole General Staff," Matthew began. He took several deep breaths and forced himself onward. He described for Wesley how his Ranger units had been broken up. He'd been assigned to infantry platoons to train the grunts as LRRPS and point men. They were losing too many soldiers each week. No preparation, no motivation, too much fear. Matthew's platoon's Master Sergeant, a big red-headed, red-neck bastard from Mississippi, had a hard-on for the only black corporal in the unit, Jet. His buddies said Jet had been a boxer before the war, so fast and quick no one ever saw his punches coming.

The symmetry of the vertical bars, the absence of distraction encouraged Matthew.

"Red hated Jet. Baited and tormented him till one day Jet cracked. They squared off behind the barracks, Jet ready to fight even though he figured the Sergeant was setting him up. . . *'there is some shit I will not eat.'*"

Again the rhythmic flow of the poem popped forth without hesitation, neither comforting nor disconcerting. An irregular mantra defining Matthew's life.

"Jet played with him. Slowly beat the hell out of Red. That black brother kept the fight going, could have ended it any time he wanted. Red wouldn't give up. Kept getting pounded till he couldn't stand. Then he crawled at Jet, who'd lost any interest in mercy. Jet kicked the crap out of what was left of Red. As he lay there, Red managed to gasp out three words—'gonna kill you.'"

The dull hum of the jail's ventilation system was inconsistent with the memories of screaming taunts from vengeful soldiers.

"Jet's buddies, black and white, told him to finish the job. It would have been easy to put that nasty junkyard dog out of his misery. Jet sure as hell knew how. But he walked away."

Matthew shook his head. He fidgeted again, had to stand up, move around.

"Red stayed in the infirmary over a week. Never said a word to the docs, the lieutenant—no one—about the fight. I don't think anyone gave a damn. Three weeks later we're in action. I'm on point. Damn certain there's VC somewhere in front of us, waiting in ambush. Sure enough, I see movement. I hit the ground behind some fallen trees. No shots from Charlie. It's a good spot, I like it. I can even look through a break in the foliage to where I think they're hiding.

"SOP's to call in the quadrants fast and let the big guns blow them away. Behind me's Red. Jet and Henry, a poor moron from Kentucky we called Henry the Empty, are over to his left. The gooks hadn't fired, but they were there waiting."

Matthew licked his lips. A wet trickle down his spine transcended the present. His hands shook. He entered new territory of confession.

"Red had just re-upped for his third tour in Nam. He was a pro, but a sick prick. He knew the VC were holding their fire, hoping to trap us into moving forward. The radioman, back and to the right, was giving the coordinates to the arty boys. Just wait. Let the guns do the work. If there weren't any dinks, we waste a few taxpayer's dollars. But that butcher Red, he signaled Jet and Henry to move up. They must have suspected something."

. . . *being to all intents a corpse and wanting any rag* . . . Almost a sad melody now. Tears flowed in uneven rivulets down Matthew's cheeks, his face on fire, his stomach in knots.

"They hesitated. Red motioned again and pointed his rifle at them. They rose into a crouch, separated by a few feet, and took a couple of quick steps forward. I'd like to forget what happened next."

Wesley placed a comforting hand on Matthew's trembling forearm. Matthew didn't react. Maybe in appreciation. He didn't know.

"At least a full platoon of VC opened up. They cut Jet and Henry down. Artillery came crashing into Charlie's position before the two hit the ground. All Red had to do was wait—and he knew it. Noise and smoke everywhere in the forest as we returned fire. I pivoted around, Red fifteen feet from me. I blew the son of a bitch away. You can't tell the difference between a wound from an enemy's AK47 or our M16's when rounds have ripped through a body."

Matthew's emotional agitation climaxed. A degree of control seeped back.

"No one saw what happened. If they did, they never said a word."

Wesley looked at him with a strange mix of kindness, understanding and even satisfaction—almost an I-thought-so expression. What did it mean?

"If Jet had finished off Red, he and Empty might still be alive. Letting Red live cost Jet his life. The Sergeant was a bastard, but he served a function as a warrior. What value does Corbin have?"

Matthew slumped back into the hard metal chair bolted to the floor. A hollowness rang in his ears. His breathing approached normal.

"So," Wesley said, "you think you're evil? A killer? A unique individual who cracked under pressure?"

"I don't know what I think," Matthew said. "Red, Jet, and a hundred other nightmares are buried in my memory. I'm too afraid and disgusted to shine light on most of them."

"Fate—maybe God—made me your confessor." Wesley's voice slipped into a liturgical cadence, like a rabbi beginning a sermon. "War brings out the primitive. Every man will react at a base level when his survival's at stake. I told you I served in Korea. You know anything about that war?"

"No, not really," Matthew answered. "I've read a lot of history—Ancient and European history, Civil War, World War II, the Holocaust."

"Not many books about the Korean War," Wesley said. "A lot like Viet Nam, but Korea didn't generate any need for enlightenment or questionin' like Nam. We still followed orders then, not our conscience. Some felt guilty 'cause they missed the Big One. Not me. I was with the 8th Army, 24th Division, stationed with the occupation forces in Japan, a motor pool mechanic when South Korea got invaded. Talk about gettin' caught with your pants down."

Wesley shuddered. Matthew realized someone else dealt with nightmares. Still, had Korea presented the same moral dilemmas as Nam?

"Well, the shit hit the fan. The North Koreans blew through the South's army like my relatives slammed Custer at the Little Bighorn. They captured Seoul in a couple of days. MacArthur was in command. He threw any live American body he could into Korea—cooks, clerks, mechanics, and that included me."

Wesley spoke without much emotion. Matthew listened, watching, still somewhat disconnected. Another person's history lesson.

"The thing I remember most? The stench and the July heat. They used human waste for fertilizer on every plot of land. I still smell it today. Evil odors. Even here in the frozen, crystal air of Jackson Hole."

Matthew could relate to this. Some unknown event would open a door to an assault by smells that plagued him. Asia was indelibly stained on Matthew's memory, too. Another kindred connection tying him to Wesley. He focused on the Indian.

"The first of us to arrive in Pusan were patched into C Company of the 1st Battalion. One hundred and six of us, none with a minute of combat duty. We were under strength, inexperienced and poorly equipped with World War II leftovers. Thousands of North Koreans poured south with brand-new T34 Russian tanks. Firin' our 2.36 inch bazookas was like shootin' a grizzly with a pellet gun."

Disgust now crept into Wesley's delivery. The Indian's stoic expression wavered, his shoulders rolled forward. A gathering empathy filled Matthew. Concern shifted from his own personal struggles to his friend's.

"MacArthur, desperate, tried to buy time throwin' us into a hopeless fight. The South Koreans ran. We were outnumbered a hundred to one. We made contact with the enemy and quick as a snake strikes knew we were doomed. They slaughtered us. And our deaths didn't buy twenty minutes. Waves of those bastards came at us with tanks—our bazookas worthless, officers as panicked as us. Within those first few moments we'd taken fifty percent casualties, less than fifty able to run. Those of us capable, turned to bug out. One lieutenant started screamin' for us to stop, to fight. He waved a .45 at us—yellin' we'd only retreat over his dead body. A couple of us obliged. Shot him point-blank and hauled ass."

Different expressions played over his high cheek-boned face, but no regret. Could Wesley take such ruthless action? No way. One could smell evil. It had texture and depth. Wesley was not evil.

"I split. Got off the road, terrain full of ravines and rocks. Not too much vegetation for cover. I played Injun and laid low. Took me two full days to get beyond the North Korean advance. Hooked up with a larger group of the 21st Regiment—no better prepared than our original Company. But our carrier pilots had started doin' some damage, slowin' down the slant-eyed bastards."

A steely edge crept into Wesley's voice. Matthew reconsidered. Maybe his companion could wreak some significant damage if cornered or enraged.

"You know how many of C Company's hundred and six men made it back to our line? Six. And that's in the history books. Should we 'a stayed and fought an impossible battle? No way. Do I feel guilty? I feel lucky to be alive." Anger and belligerence painted a face Matthew had never seen before. "Should you have killed Red? Yeah, probably sooner. Should you have killed Corbin? No. He's a worthless piece of shit. You'll be out of here soon as Sheriff Olsen shows up. You kill Corbin, you could end up in prison. You did the right thing, lettin' him live. This ain't the war. We're in Jackson Hole, Wyoming, U.S.A."

"Wesley, Red's not even the worst thing that happened to me in that stinking arm pit of a war."

Wesley lifted his chin. Smoke swirled in the depth of his deep, brown eyes.

"You got more? I got more too."

A challenge? Matthew glimpsed an off-the-wall resemblance between the proud Indian and the pugnacious Red before his fight with Jet. Matthew wouldn't want to push this man too far. Couldn't think of anything worth fighting over.

"No more, Wesley. Not now."

The large jail door clanged open. Footsteps squeaked on the thick linoleum floor. A large man in his forties appeared, wearing an oversized black cowboy hat perched on an equally immense head. His belly bulged well beyond his broad, black tooled-leather holster belt. His bloated face surrounded large, dark active eyes.

"Howdy, Sheriff," Wesley said. He stood up and held his hard, brown hand out. Teton County Sheriff Eric Olsen grasped it with his own large fist.

"Wesley." The Sheriff's voice was cordial and deep, befitting the investment in his substantial stomach. "Thanks for not calling that damn attorney, Chauncey."

"You hear what happened?" Wesley asked. Olsen nodded yes. "Your deputy, Clarence, arrested this here boy for being a deadly weapon."

"Corbin ended up checking hisself into the hospital," the Sheriff said watching Matthew as he talked. "Said he tripped in the Cowboy Bar, landed on his face. You're a veteran, ain't ya?"

"Yes, sir." Matthew spoke with caution, encouraged by the Sheriff's understanding tone of voice.

"I fought in World War II," the Sheriff said. "Even got wounded on Iwo Jima. Of course we all got shot up in that mess. You get your face in Nam?"

"Yes, sir." Matthew's fingers jerked to the scar on his forehead.

"Sorry you had to spend a couple of hours in here. Nice jail, though, ain't it?" Sheriff Olsen smiled, a proud father scanning his immaculate cells. "We overreacted a bit. But you been making a name for yourself in a pretty short time."

"He didn't start any of those problems," Wesley said, once again stepping into the conversation.

"Wesley, you might be right," the Sheriff said. "Could be just coincidence. Problem is, no respectable lawman worth his salt believes in coincidences. You two can leave. Big storm's rolling in." Then he looked into Matthew's eyes. "Son, don't push your luck."

Sheriff Olsen turned with a ponderous movement. Matthew and Wesley followed his wide body out of the cell block. Olsen turned left towards the closed door of his office. Matthew and Wesley went right, through the reception area, down the stairs, out of the lobby, into hard-blowing snow.

"It's almost 1:30," Wesley said. "The road's gonna be a bitch. I live only a couple of blocks from here. Hansen Street. Why don't you spend the rest of the night at my place?"

THIRTY-FOUR

The sharp smell of fresh coffee pushed Matthew from a half sleep of indistinct images. His eyes traced the boundaries of a small room in a solid log cabin. A square little window admitted gray filtered light. Blowing snow added a pattern to an otherwise total whiteout beyond the glass. No clock. No clue to the time of day.

A wave of recollection flooded Matthew—the Cowboy Bar, fight with Corbin, jail time, partial catharsis, Wesley's home. And, for the second time in a month, no dreams. Matthew corrected himself. No nightmares.

He reached back to last night's fading memory of a fantastical drive in his blue Corvette, soaring like an F4 Tomcat on a strafing mission. But no gunfire, no noise, only eerie quiet. His trip had retraced his route across the high, empty plains of Nevada and Idaho, never quite touching the ground, often hundreds of feet above the road.

One vivid memory: The passage over the Snake River Canyon, not bothering to use the new Hanson Bridge. Matthew had anticipated a disastrous crash back to earth, his anxiety spoiling an otherwise exciting dream journey. The happy landing in Wesley's guest room provided a pleasant shock.

The previous night's adrenaline surge had evidently prepared the way for a painless, semiconscious passage through the early morning hours. Like the night following Matthew's Affair in the Square. But perhaps the real ticket to a restful night was sharing his past burdens with Wesley.

Matthew attempted to recapture the strange, blissful flight in his Corvette. Unlike normal nights with memories he couldn't shake for hours, last evening's dream dissipated like morning mist on a hot day, swallowed by the more welcome aroma of coffee.

The vibration of high-velocity gusts from the storm outside shook out the last remnants of sleep. He slipped out of bed, dressed, and walked into Wesley's tight but efficient, kitchen. Food and utensils crammed shelves and countertops. The small space reflected the same immaculate organization as Wesley's Blackfoot Garage.

The clock on the log wall jolted him with its report of 10:06 —three hours later than the day's usual start for Matthew.

"Ya must have slept good." Wesley's cheerful voice was an improvement on Jungle Jim's slamming wake-up calls at the Grand View. "I'd awoken you up earlier, but ain't nothin' gonna happen today. Snowed two and a half feet already. Can't see across the street. Storm's expected to stick around till tonight. Tram shut down. Wind blew the cable off Tower Three."

Wesley filled two mugs with hot coffee. Matthew stretched and sat down, sighing with relief at the simplicity and clarity of life in Jackson Hole. Things were black and white—easy to judge. Bad was Corbin; good, Wesley.

"I slept in myself," Wesley said. "Got up about nine. I gotta tell ya, buddy, when you come to town, you can really fill up an evenin' with interestin' activities."

"Seems to me every time I've come to town, it's been at your invitation."

"Want to take ya to a special place for breakfast," Wesley said. "Place called Dornan's in Moose. Know the owner. He'll throw together a fine meal for us."

"Moose is north past the airport, isn't it?" Matthew asked. "Why fight this storm when we can get something to eat in town at the Log Cabin?"

"Dornan's is special. You can mellow out. Put your thoughts straight. Got the most mystical view in all of Wyoming."

"You look outside lately?" Matthew said. "Can't see a damn thing."

"It'll be clear enough for us."

Matthew's hunger overcame any desire to rehash last night's wild times. Then, too, talk seemed redundant after the emotional interactions in jail. Wesley allowed the peace to persist while Matthew finished the coffee.

"All right, Wesley. Nothing else going on today. All the flatlanders shut off the mountain by this storm will be bored and hammered by early afternoon. Good day to work out, lay low, maybe hang out at the Calico."

"Great. We'll hit Dornan's, then I'll drive you back to your car near the Cowboy. Maybe I'll meet you later at the Calico."

Matthew coated up and headed out the front door. A blast of wind and snow greeted him. The storm might slow everything down for a day or two, but the huge dump would return the ski hill to its advertised perfection. A couple of days off would be a small price to pay for restoring great skiing conditions.

Wesley mounted his monster black truck and rolled the pickup out of the short driveway. Matthew's thoughts shifted from past dreams to future realities. Wesley's abrupt braking jerked him back into the present.

"That dumb son of a bitch," Wesley blurted out, peering through the murky gloom. "That guy almost took off my rear end."

Matthew made out the shadow of a car pulling next to the snow bank next door.

"I didn't know you had any neighbors," Matthew said.

"Yeah. 'Bout two or three weeks ago two out-of-town boys rented that clapboard shack. You can rent out a doghouse in Jackson Hole, housin's in such short supply. They'd be better off in a teepee than that piece of garbage."

A figure exited the car, leaning into the wind. A gust blew the short man's hat off. He made an impressive and successful dive to retrieve it.

"He look like that city slicker Franky?" Wesley asked as he started again into Hansen Street.

"Could be," Matthew answered.

The man scrambled to the front door of the small dilapidated building and pushed his way inside. Had to be Franky. The furtive movements couldn't hide the stubby body and impatience.

"There goes the neighborhood," Matthew said.

*   *   *

Matthew couldn't see a damn thing. This was nuts. Visibility varied from twenty feet to a quarter mile. But Wesley had been adamant about Dornan's. Blinding drifts swept across the two lanes, obliterating white lines and road shoulders. Didn't bother Wesley, but the crazy drive tested Matthew's nerves.

Wesley plowed his big, black pickup towards Dornan's at an insane seventy miles per hour. The vehicle flew by the airport cutoff. Wesley made a blind left ten miles later, then a quick right onto an even narrower lane. Several buildings appeared out of the gloom, among them a large wooden structure. Had to be Dornan's.

Wesley led the way through a wide, well-worn pine door. Matthew stopped four steps into a large, empty room. A gigantic, right-angled polished wood bar took up half the space. Multi-colored bottles—tools of the trade—sat in understated fashion on one long, low shelf paralleling a counter with a beautiful finish.

Huge wall-to-wall, counter-to-ceiling windows climbed above the work area. A swirling, gray mass of clouds filled the glass. The blankness brought back uncomfortable memories of tule fog and whiteouts. As Matthew watched, solid mist dissipated enough to allow a glimpse of the base of the Tetons, but nothing could be seen above a thousand feet. The Snake River, cold and lifeless, lay at the bottom of the valley floor. Matthew could only imagine the view on a clear day.

A tall, thin cowboy emerged from the kitchen. His scrawny neck supported a face with a bulbous nose displaying a red-vesseled road map of what could have been a major U.S. city. The click of high-heeled cowboy boots accompanied the man's progress to his anointed spot behind the bar.

"Hey, Wesley, where the hell ya been?" The man's delight at seeing Wesley was almost childlike.

"Howdy, Carl." Wesley held out his hand.

Dark, thick hair hung to the man's collar. His waxed handlebar moustache was so profuse and dense Matthew expected Carl's head to come crashing down off his shoulders from its weight. A long-sleeved, beaded buckskin shirt and new dark-blue Levi's sheathed his lanky body.

"This here's my good buddy, Matthew," Wesley said. "He's the reason I ain't been out here lately. Boy's high-maintenance and time-intensive."

"Pleased to meet ya."

Carl seemed sincere. He shook Matthew's hand. His elaborate handlebar stayed in the same place regardless of the man's movements.

Amazing the connections the Indian made with everyone he met. Matthew had spent his childhood with few friends and many books. He had been the proverbial loner growing up—a loser if one accepted the glass being half-empty. Wesley made the glass half-full, maybe more.

"Looks like normal business," Wesley said, surveying the vacant room. Fifteen to twenty unoccupied tables filled the balance of the space. "Slim pickin's without huntin' season. How 'bout fixin' us a nice breakfast."

"Sure. Be a few minutes." Carl beat a quick retreat from behind the fortresslike bar and into the kitchen.

Vague images in the window stimulated thoughts of control, or rather, frustrated efforts to achieve it. Matthew'd made progress since pumping bullets into the dead adobe building outside of Elko. Talk about melodramatic. The Affair in the Square represented a more important step forward. He could have taken out each and every one of those drunk, stumbling cowboy rednecks. Instead he'd created minimum havoc and gotten TJ and Ace out of trouble as quick as possible.

Then again, what would he have done to Shebang if the maniac had killed Cody? Anger welled. But hadn't he turned the corner of control when he allowed Corbin to live last night in the Cowboy Bar?

*   *   *

Matthew looked up from his plate and the remnants of Dornan's specialty, elk and eggs. Through the glass, clouds thinned as Wesley had promised. Indistinct ridges could now be seen across the valley. Now an outline of the jagged Tetons played a game of hide-and-seek. A few moments of clarity were followed by the solid wash of swirling mist, his internal struggle not much different than the muted views out the window.

"Okay, Wesley, what's on your mind?"

"Nothing," Wesley said, a large smile brightened the gray gloom penetrating from the outside. "Just time to relax. Get your mind straightened out like I promised. Things'll pick up soon enough. There is a piece of wisdom I'll pass on to ya."

"What's that," Matthew said, not sure he wanted to know.

"There's two ways you can look at the world. One—there are no miracles. Or the second—every day's a miracle."

"Who said that? Billy Graham or Walt Disney?"

"A wise old Jewish man named Albert Einstein. Ever heard of him?"

The Indian's grin still lit up the room, but no more words disturbed the cathedral quiet of the bar. Matthew felt a lifting of his soul. He felt good for the first time in many months, whatever the hell good meant. Could he be finally regaining some degree of control?

THIRTY-FIVE

The storm couldn't have come at a better time. Sarah closed her eyes and burrowed deeper into the blankets. Her body begged for rest from the nonstop skiing and partying. The bed's warmth and security exerted a gravitational pull strong enough to immobilize her. And, to her relief, no man in bed to force her into performance and decisions.

My, my. What a difference from her normal solitary situation in life. Happy to be alone? Only in the wonderful world of Wyoming. Then last night's images rushed into the peaceful void, flooding her with excitement, disturbing any attempt to drift back to sleep. Matthew's explosion into violence reverberated incongruously with Franky's concern and consideration.

Blood and booze had melded into an unsettling cocktail that aroused rather than calmed. Guilt at deserting TJ increased the discomfort of her thoughts, the rush of emotions too contradictory to catalogue. Everything that had happened the previous two weeks was alien to the life of a lonely working girl imprisoned in her mother's apartment. Too much action? No way.

Sarah swung her legs out of bed. Energy swept the cobwebs from her head and anesthetized the painful bruises discoloring her legs and the raw, red ski-boot damage decorating her feet and ankles. Ready to roll but no place to go. The gray curtain of the blizzard eliminated options. Ten A.M. and nothing to do but choose between breakfast now or lunch later.

Franky popped back into her mind. Strange man. Acted like an aggressive hard-ass. Hung out with the bad boys of Jackson Hole. Had the same horny desires as every man in town, but he'd respectfully accepted temporary rejection after an opening most men couldn't or wouldn't resist. There was an intelligence that shone through Franky's macho bullshit. And despite his loud noises, Sarah sensed the soul of a loner, just like her.

No comparison with Matthew. He was the unstable volcano of intensity that he appeared to be. Was the man always dangerous, or did he overreact to being cornered? The now familiar ripple of interest brought a shiver to Sarah. Well, she was tired of TJ, and Matthew was in jail. She owed Franky. Let's see where a couple of drinks would lead.

*   *   *

Too much pent-up energy made Matthew antsy. Time to pry his dog away from Julia and a lodge full of snowed-in guests. Matthew would reward Cody with a romp in the woods. Also, he needed the quick, aerobic burn of a thirty-minute trip on Jim's ancient pair of snowshoes.

The appearance of a large and not too friendly moose could complicate their trip outside into the surrounding forest and meadows. The black Lab was dumb enough to harass the local wildlife. A moose was no grizzly, but Cody would be in deep trouble if attacked by one. He'd carry a weapon, just in case.

Matthew cleaned his .45, slammed home the magazine and slipped the heavy semiautomatic into the holster of the webbed vest he'd picked up cheap at Jackson Hole's Army-Navy Surplus. Shooting a moose was illegal. Using a pistol on one qualified as stupid, if not suicidal. Matthew would count on the explosive sound of the .45 to sidetrack any potential threat. Being prepared the operative strategy.

The temperature hovered at a comfortable 25 degrees, but snow poured from the heavens. Erratic winds lowered the wind-chill factor to a more normal Jackson Hole cold. Cody came alive as Matthew put on several layers of clothing. Matthew headed across the Grand View's parking area heading west, away from the highway. An ecstatic Cody disappeared into indistinct woods.

Wind-blown snow reduced visibility even further. Matthew followed the remaining top third of a log fence sticking above the mounting white drifts. He realized his mistake when he reached the end of the fence line. Two more steps and he'd be adrift in a total whiteout.

Matthew remembered the unsettling sensation of skiing in these conditions. Vertigo and claustrophobia joined in a contradictory combination, creating an unpleasant dreamlike discomfort on the mountain—up and down interchangeable. Snowshoes might have provided a more stable foundation, but his sense of direction disappeared into the solid curtain of mist. A frightening familiarity between tule fog and the invisibility of the present once again swept through him.

Then Matthew heard Cody. But the wind fragmented his bark, the sound coming from different sides at the same time. Forget this hike. Five minutes into the walk and already time to bail.

"Cody, we're outta here," Matthew yelled, his own voice dissipating in the wailing winds.

He turned around, no easy task in the clumsy snowshoes. He shouted for Cody several more times. Frantic barking answered, the dog indiscernible though nearby. Then Matthew picked up a change in the sound of Cody's explosive yelps. Something was wrong.

The comforting trail of his tracks blurred with his erratic movements, screaming for his dog. His circle of confusion widened, points of reference gone, sight reduced to ten feet. He couldn't be lost a hundred yards from the Grand View.

Was that the crack of a rifle? He picked up a whiff of rancid, jungle foliage. Distant, disjointed cries worked through the thick haze as his panic built. He thrashed in a circle, heat building, sweat forming beneath his layered clothing. How could his body be on fire in a blizzard? Where was he? The last months couldn't have been a dream. He fought desperately for control.

Calm down. Stand still. Find the damn Lab first. Make some noise. Focus on the dog. Cody'll show up.

And show up he did.

Cody scrambled into view in front of Matthew. Then a huge shadow materialized on the Lab's heels. An enraged moose, steam pouring from its enlarged nostrils, charging. Matthew dove to the side. A solid object, Cody or the moose, smacked against his flying legs. Matthew stuck face first in the deep snow.

Barking and snorting, too close for comfort, fueled panic. Matthew contracted into a ball, waiting for the moose to crush his unprotected back. Cody howled nearby. Matthew rolled on his side and looked up. His vision filled with an enormous, brown, hairy butt. Matthew glimpsed the faint image of his frightened puppy through the animal's legs, crouched behind a broken birch tree. The moose lunged. Cody dodged. But the dog's short legs weren't about to keep him out of harm's way for long.

Matthew fumbled in his parka. He pulled off one of his gloves, then yanked the .45 out of its holster, fingered off the safety and held the large pistol towards the rear end of the pissed-off moose. Now what? The animal's back legs were only a foot from Matthew. One kick and he'd be history. Hell, he could shoot the moose in the ass and still be stomped to death. He needed some distance from the deadly hoofs.

Matthew struggled several feet to a skinny aspen, too thin for much protection. He stood, yelling into the wind and fired two shots into the air. The resulting loud discharge registered even through the howling storm.

His pathetic excuse for a plan worked. The moose whirled around, Cody took off, and Matthew wondered where to place the next few shots. With one more nod to wildlife conservation, he fired close to the startled animal's massive head. The bullet whistled by the incongruous, tiny ear. Rumor had it the brain of a moose was even smaller than its ear. But this specimen showed a degree of intelligence. It ambled away, long legs oblivious to the dense, clinging snow.

Cody had disappeared, no doubt back to the safety of the lodge. Matthew, still trembling, picked out the distant sound of a car horn. A pause in the blowing gale gave him a directional fix. Matthew hadn't been outside long, but he'd had all the aerobic exercise he needed.

THIRTY-SIX

Matthew shut the door behind him. A calm, secure workout in the Grand View garage seemed a much healthier activity than a stroll outside. This time Cody stuck to him like a Siamese twin. Matthew took off his sweatshirt; sweat pants to follow when he warmed up.

He began his stretches, attempting the faithful performance of his normal routine. But the image of a moose distracted him from the required calm focus. He performed perfunctorily. Still, he hadn't skied much in two days, and combined with his switch several weeks ago from daily workouts to alternating days, his body felt strong and rested.

The draining sequences incorporated ever-increasing sets of pull-ups, chin-ups, push-ups, sit-ups and weight work with Dumbbells. The routine had now expanded into a ninety-minute butt kicker. The added rest days gave his body the opportunity to consolidate strength and allow his wounds extra time to heal. Matthew had come a long way since early January. Now, the end of February, he approached a rock-solid two hundred pounds for the first time in his life. His new power provided a source of security, control, and, he admitted, pride.

He used the time in his small gym to think. When he drifted to uncomfortable issues, he picked up the pace, added to the reps and the weight. The range and scope of his life was expanding by the week. He could feel himself being drawn back into the complex world of the living. Outside pressures and events eroded his protective resolve to resist human relationships and commitments.

He reached his favorite part of his training—the body bag. First came the karate kicks, sets of ten, alternating legs. Karate chops and kites followed, the dense bag quivering with each blow. Sweat flew off his face and arms. Today his body hummed.

Matthew jabbed, the bag popped. He ramped up the power with sets of right and left crosses. The large hook attaching the bag to the ceiling squeaked in protest. Cody stirred, then moved to a doormat further from the action. Finally, uppercuts and full-on haymakers. Massive blows rained on a helpless bag that bounced and jerked with each crashing punch.

Matthew reveled in the ecstasy of power, the low level of pain, physical recovery close to complete. He roared at the defenseless leather container, imagining it held his personal frustrations and sins. The whole garage seemed to rock. He couldn't stop. Didn't want to. Strength flowed with the perspiration. Instant, simplistic gratification. Escape.

A yell registered from outside his world of release. Matthew turned to see Jim at the door to the lodge, his face a complex expression of awe.

"Man, the whole damn place is shaking. Julia's mother's porcelain clock just shattered on the floor." Jim stood half in, half out of the garage. "You're scaring the hell outta the guests."

Matthew stopped, unable to hold back a smile. "Sorry. Tell Julia I'll buy her a new clock."

His sweat pooled beneath the swaying leather bag.

"Next time, give us some notice." Jim tried to sound angry, but his handsome features reflected confusion. "You know, you're not the same guy who checked into this place two months ago."

* * *

The chick had balls, calling him for a date. Franky had been surprised when Sarah rang his room. But then, upon a moment's reflection, understandable. Treat them like a lady and they'll fall all over you. Hadn't had to use that strategy much, but it worked. He slung down his second double, plunking the glass on the silver- dollar-studded bar top. Always need a couple of quick ones to get in the right frame of mind.

Franky dropped from the stool, the distance to the floor amplified by the sharp jolt through his legs. He'd do anything for a couple of more inches. He thought Sarah had said she'd meet him in the bar. Maybe not. She was twenty minutes late. He'd give her room a ring. Don't know what the hell she could be doing with the ton of snow smothering Jackson Hole.

Then he saw her, swinging through the connecting door to the Wort, fielding greetings and stares like a prom queen riding the Homecoming float. Her broad smile squeezed out the imperfections of her features. She moved with an athletic grace the floozies back home could never imitate. An unexpected tug of pleasure jerked Franky's pulse to a higher level. She swept across the room to where he stood, grabbed his arm and settled on the stool he had just vacated.

"Sorry I'm late," she said. "Weird day without skiing. Lost track of the time."

Her smile demanded forgiveness. Granted.

"No problem."

Franky ordered drinks, double scotch and soda for him, double vodka on the rocks for her. This girl didn't mess around. He snatched their tumblers and led Sarah to a table against the wall under a large elk. Swirling lights and movements brought unsettling life to the glass eyes of the imperious animal.

"Thanks again for last night."

"Was nothing," Franky said.

"What kind of job do you have that allows you freedom to spend so much time here?"

Just the question Franky wanted to hear. Time to educate this chick. Let her know she'd just graduated up from Wyoming hicks.

"I run several businesses in Manhattan."

"Businesses plural?" Interest animated her long face.

"Yeah." Franky'd use a different come-on than his usual boastful approach. Be cool. Understate things; she'd fill in the blanks. "I'm president of a commercial construction company and a small chain of variety stores."

He sipped his scotch. Should have ordered Chivas instead of this poisonous well crap.

"Wow. I'm impressed."

Franky fought the swell in his chest. Tried to control the self-satisfied smile spreading across his face.

"Also run a wholesale distribution operation." He'd dance around the facts. Pick and choose.

"Where'd you go to college?" she asked.

This was too easy. Franky kept his answers short, but Sarah looked more dazzled with each passing comment. It took a while, but he finally began asking the questions. She was only a legal secretary. No dummy though. College graduate.

Franky pumped her for information about the local crowd she hung with. More drinks. More sharing of information, but he sensed they both circled around revelations of their inner feelings. And that was okay. He looked forward to investing more time in this babe. In fact, the absence of any enlightening facts didn't bother him at all.

*　*　*

Too much to drink. Again. Sarah slumped into Franky. No support there as she veered against the hallway wall. Her giggle was answered by a snort from Franky that may or may not have been a laugh. She liked him. For a short guy, he took up a lot of space. A little too full of himself, but for good reason. Cute. Successful. Entertaining.

Sarah bounced along the shabby corridor until she bumped into Franky's back at her room. Should she take this sweet little man to bed? She unlocked the door, pulling him with her, not bothering to answer her own question. Franky represented the real world. No rough country boy as desperate for sex as Sarah. A validation of her worth within the meat market of life outside Jackson Hole. It'd be like having sex with a star. Yeah, like James Dean. She couldn't control her laughter, until she glimpsed the look of insecurity on Franky's dark features.

"I might have had one too many," she apologized.

"Should I leave?"

Franky backed off. The questioning expression looked out of place on his normal, cocky face. He seemed confused. Tenderness flavored her hungry desire. She reached for him, kissing the first thing she connected with, his forehead, then collapsed onto the bed.

Come on, Franky. Get over it. Make love to me.

She picked at his clothing, clumsy in the shadowy room. It took a while to get undressed, but persistence paid off. She stroked his chest, shoulders and arms. His body was soft with thick hair covering most of his exposed skin. Not her first choice, but a break from the hard bodies she'd been loving. And there was nothing wrong with the large, hard cock rising from the thick patch between his legs.

THIRTY-SEVEN

Matthew awoke. He'd just left Jet, dying, dead. He'd leaned over the young-old soldier. Jet's face, filthy, but unmarked, had tried to smile up at Matthew.

"Help me, Sarge."

"Sure, Jet, you're gonna be okay." But Jet's face was the only part of his body undamaged.

"I got two letters in my shirt pocket. Mail 'em for me. I'm gonna be laid up for a while. Don't want no one to worry."

Matthew's glance confirmed a mass of bubbling gore, small bits of dark material. The work of a direct hit. A meat grinder couldn't have caused more damage. Still Jet talked, not realizing he had been overtaken by death, asked Matthew for a drink, to hold his hand, to not forget the letters.

"I know you'll take care of me, man."

"Sure, Jet. I'll take care of you." Matthew's tears rained unchecked onto Jet's face.

The ghoulish conversation wouldn't end. Jet wouldn't accept death. And Matthew wouldn't leave him. Matthew kept repeating, " . . . *Unless statistics lie he was more brave than me: more blond than you . . .*"

Matthew couldn't staunch his tears. Finally his own moisture had poured him into a relieved wakefulness. Tears soaked his pillow, mingling with the sweat of unrelenting nightmares, a cold wake-up call in the cabin's early-morning chill.

Matthew had cried almost every night since his view of the naked goddess, Julia. He welcomed the tears, an affirmation of humanity, a cleansing as critical as his daily shower. Both acts required for the healing process.

"Matthew." Jim's pounding on the door rang out in the thin air. "Get your ass out of bed. You looked outside yet?" Jim opened the cabin door, a rare breach of Matthew's privacy. "It's a perfect day. Let's hit it. Breakfast at the Moose. I'm leaving in thirty minutes, soon as I finish my morning chores." He wheeled from the door, slamming it behind him.

Matthew glanced out the window. An unbroken blanket of white spread before him, birth of a cloudless day, blue sky on the way, wind left behind. Matthew hurried, whipping through his early-morning routine. He dressed and headed out the door to meet up with Jim at Teton Village.

* * *

Excitement crackled across the tram platform. Matthew stood with the chosen, impatient few crammed onto the metal grille. Any more sparking energy would have threatened electrocution. Another hundred expectant souls swayed in line—locals and the occasional fortunate visitor in the know. The manic vibrations were a vivid reminder to Matthew of the joy and excitement of powder skiing. Each day different, an adventure, conditions changing in midrun. You never knew what to expect until that dive into the next turn.

Matthew chuckled as the loading area filled with victims of Powder Flu. This reoccurring disease struck after every major storm, decimating the workforce at the Village. The employee sick calls were slowed from reaching their destination only by busy signals. If you didn't have what you needed—equipment or food—forget it until afternoon.

Wesley and Jim stood next to Matthew. David was missing; the man just couldn't keep his priorities straight. TJ gave garbled instructions to a new hire at the entrance gate—no way he'd miss this beautiful bluebird day on the mountain.

Ace, Billy Simpson and two other patrollers, covered with snow, pounded onto the platform. Shit-eating grins framed their teeth, all that was visible of their bundled faces. They were fresh from the bomb run, preparing and checking the condition and safety of the snow pack.

"How'd it go on the pre-run?" Matthew asked.

"Oh, man, more like pre-ejaculation," Ace hollered, hopping up and down, a psycho rabbit who'd smoked too many carrots. "No one's been up there for two days. It's better than sex."

"Ace, you already drop a tab this mornin'?" Wesley asked.

"No, man. I'm clean."

"Ace," Wesley said, "you'd have to dry out for ten years before you'd even begin to flush out all the crap in your system."

"Load 'em up," Billy called out.

The first tram filled faster than a beer disappeared at the Mangy Moose. Matthew pushed in early and captured a treasured spot by a window. Doors shut. The Tram shuddered, hesitated, and then headed for heaven amidst the hooting and hollering of sixty packed bodies in a space meant for fifty.

The final foot of fallen snow had floated straight down, the wind having died early. A white blanket of sparkling flakes smothered every surface, from bent branches to the tops of lift towers. The rising sun's rays created tableaus of art before Matthew's eyes. He conjured up memories of earlier tram trips, savoring his personal progress through that perspective. If only his emotional and spiritual healing could be as linear and measurable.

The Box rose in a chaotic cascade of anticipation—a combustible container filled with loud, boisterous local skiers ready for action after two weeks of hard, icy, bumpy conditions and two days completely shut off the mountain. As the Tram neared the peak, the crowd quieted, a gathering of thoughts. The promise of powder prompted a religious reaction. Matthew respectfully shared the moment of reverence with his companions.

The spell shattered with the opening of the sliding tram doors. Every man for himself, Matthew in the middle, swearing and struggling down the metal stairs. Skis on, safety straps clipped. Goggles, gloves and gaiters in place. Matthew led Wesley, TJ, Jim and Ace off the top in the first wave.

"To the Hobacks," Jim shouted.

No one disagreed. Matthew angled into Rendezvous Bowl, each skier spreading out for his own individual untracked virgin line. Everything worked for Matthew—legs and lungs, balance and rhythm. He shot down the bowl. The deep, fresh powder a little dense but consistent. Conditions were reminiscent of Squaw Valley the moment after a storm and before the sun popped out to produce Sierra Cement.

Fat, thick rooster tails of snow cascaded into Matthew's face with each turn. Breathing became the biggest challenge. Gasp air as you unweighted at the top of your turn, hold your breath as you settled down into the bottomless trough. He had to snatch his gaiter below his mouth, the snow packed thick against the fabric. He accelerated nearing the bottom of the bowl. Build enough speed to coast across the flats until the Rendezvous Trail dipped down towards the entrance to the Hobacks. That paradise of vast open ridges spread over the bottom half of the mountain.

Matthew paused with his partners at the top of Nirvana.

"Twenty-second rule in force?" TJ asked.

The "twenty-second rule"—you crash, your buddies give you twenty seconds before they take off without you—too much to ask, too long to wait on the perfect day. The steep, untouched ridges of the Hobacks went forever, demanding the clarification of etiquette.

"Suspended." Matthew joined the chorus, then gathered oxygen into his lungs.

Large fir trees guarded vast slopes that flared out to the valley floor. Trees stooped under the load of powder, snowy sentinels stationed at the gates of total satisfaction. Each skier took off down the mountain screaming with joy, until plumes of white moisture choked their voices.

Matthew ripped down the steep ridges, floating without effort, in perfect position on top of his skis. Gravity and ecstasy combined to increase velocity. He flew down the mountain, blinded by almost solid spray. Too fast? An oxymoron left behind on the high plains of Nevada. Who needed food? Booze? Drugs? Sex? Matthew had found perfect conditions. Commit and you're bulletproof.

He felt himself unweight, sensed his rapid progress over an unexpected raised knoll. In the air, in trouble, he instinctively sat back, realizing he had crossed the line. His damaged thigh was now vulnerable to potential painful exposure. Matthew landed, rocketing down the steep drop below the knoll, body thrown backwards, almost parallel to his skis.

He waited for the excruciating agony of torn scar tissue. But no pain came, just the normal severe strain on his quads. He bounced forward, regaining his balance, shocked at his contorted recovery. And then, as Matthew continued his rapid descent, the significance of the event lit up like an exploding flare in the darkness. No physical limits. Free to test himself.

This could be a big mistake. Franky followed Sarah up the stairs to a tram line long enough to be worthy of a holiday weekend at Stowe. The deep powder of the recent blizzard generated even deeper concerns for Franky. He was a hardpack skier. This bottomless shit didn't play to his strengths. But Sarah had pounded on his door, demanded a ride and Franky's presence on the mountain.

"I still don't know why you aren't skiing with your buddies?" Franky said, flinching at the defensive note in his voice.

"Simple," Sarah said over her shoulder. "They won't wait for me when the conditions are this great. I can't keep up."

"What makes you think I can keep up with you?" Franky whined, ego be damned.

"Come on," she said, stopping at the end of the pipe matrix. "The only way to learn is to dive in."

Franky leaned against the freezing steel, uneasiness fading a bit. He looked cool, standing in line with his new equipment. And he had that most valuable of all resources beside him, a woman.

After last night he had had doubts about an encore of any kind. What a horny bitch. He'd come twice, the second one a minor miracle in his state of alcohol-induced inebriation. Sarah hadn't even warmed up. He'd bailed back to his own room, thankful to escape her limitless demands. He must have done something right for her to drag him skiing. Or did she only want a ride from town, since her buddies had dumped her?

The line shambled forward with the next tram load. The temperature tightened his sore joints. He needed more than two days rest to recover physically from weeks of skiing.

Sarah dragged her skis and poles closer to the ticket gate, gaining excitement as she worked closer to her ride to the top. She chattered non-stop, the words flowing by Franky without sticking. His stomach twisted in direct relation to Sarah's increasing energy. Next tram load would be theirs.

"Hey, Sarah." Wesley's unwelcome twang rang out in the dry air. "On the mountain a little late, ain't ya?"

Five steaming snowmen—Wesley, Jim, Matthew, TJ and Ace—scrambled into the lift line. Powder stuck to every surface of the men.

Franky watched with growing apprehension. They wouldn't join up with Sarah and him, would they? They shook like two-legged dogs. Wet snow flew from hats and gaiters. Thick white chunks stuck to parkas and pants. Franky thanked the unseen force that placed the locals several matrix sections from Sarah and him. But distance didn't deflect pointed stares and catcalls from the motley group.

Before further comments could be made, the procession to the loading platform began again. Franky and Sarah pushed through the turnstiles. Fragments of phrases from the competition drifted to him. Nothing he picked up sounded encouraging.

Sarah waved to them, then flowed with the surge into the waiting Box. The doors shut, and Franky's heart skipped several beats. This was a big mistake.

THIRTY-EIGHT

Franky was not having a good day. At least they'd made enough progress to be in Laramie Bowl. He had lost both skis, hat, and a pole. Another yard sale. For once Sarah hadn't stopped nearby.

Snow caked on the bottom of one of his boots. Now his foot didn't fit into his bindings. Franky tried to lift his leg high enough to scrape the snow off, lost his balance, and toppled over backwards. Four feet of dense powder engulfed him.

Finally, exhausted, he had his skis on. He worked his way down to the cat track with a series of the ugliest turns of an ugly day. A continuous stream of profanity shared his labored breathing, directed at every thing and anything that evolved into solid thought. Sarah, Shebang, the Bruise Brothers, the local jerks, his family, all received the same foul tribute.

Sarah waited on the narrow road below. Franky landed next to her with an ungainly thump. Impatience painted her face into an unattractive mask. Well, piss on her.

"Look," Franky gasped, "just head on down. I'll take my time."

"It's all right," she said. "You've got to commit to the hill. You're fighting every turn. Relax. Don't be afraid of a little speed, it'll make things easier."

"Fuck it," Franky snapped.

Sarah looked startled. "All you have to do is—"

"I said, fuck it. Get your ass out of here and leave me alone."

Sarah's expression traveled from surprise to anger to relief.

"You know the way down?"

"I'm not gonna tell you again. I don't like skiing in this deep crap. Get your ass out of here."

"Sure," Sarah said. "I'll see you around. Thanks for the ride this morning."

Franky answered with another burst of explicit anatomical description. If this bitch didn't get out of his sight, he was going to bury her. Humiliation added to his frustration. He regretted the lost opportunity to be with her, and probably the temper tantrum, but getting her ass away was better than having her witness further indignities.

*   *   *

Matthew and crew took over a picnic table on the cafeteria deck. He had logged eight orgasmic trips down the incredible bowls, chutes, and ridges of the Jackson Hole Resort. Not bad before noon, a record for Matthew. The quality of the conditions had kept physical effort to a minimum. The Clock Tower registered 12:30. He wanted more.

"How about we head out of bounds to Rock Springs?" Jim suggested.

"Yeah, OB. Well, you guys enjoy," Ace said. "Billy's gotta be looking for me. I'm on patrol duty."

"You're takin' care of us poor beginners," Wesley said. "We appreciate your help and guidance, Ace. Maybe we'll drop a note in the suggestion box about what an excellent employee you been."

"You can do that for me," Ace said, "if you find the goddamn box. Meantime, it's been swell. I'm outta here. Gotta cover my ass."

Ace rose and picked up his skis and poles. Matthew noticed the patroller seemed to be in no hurry.

"Ain't it a little warm for goin' OB?" TJ spoke up. "It snowed over four feet top of rock-solid hard pack. Perfect conditions for slides."

"Rock Springs has lots of southern faces," Jim said. "Sun would just be getting there now. That bastard, the White Dragon's still dozing."

"Amazing how fast the mountain's getting chopped up," Matthew said. "Hell of a lot of people compared to the last couple of months. Good thing most of the tourists aren't powder-hounds, or there'd be nothing left."

"Told ya," Wesley said. "In March weather gets better and the flat-landers show up. But they sure as hell ain't headin' for out of bounds and Rock Springs. Untouched."

"I don't know if we're opening OB," Ace said, still standing at the edge of the circle, skis on his shoulder.

Matthew grinned at Ace's reluctance to leave. Tough to go back to work with your partners headed for ecstasy.

"TJ's right," Ace said, "it's warmed up. I'll tell patrol I saw a group of guys headed over to the Springs case something happens."

"Don't say anything till we've started down," Jim warned. "I don't want Billy flying over there trying to stop us."

Matthew flashed on Billy's panicked exit from the platform with his birthday present. Billy paid a high price for being the only straight man on the mountain.

"No problem," Ace said. "Just wish I wasn't on duty."

"Come on, ya little turkey," Wesley taunted. "You been on duty all morning. What's another run?"

"Takes too long to get from the bottom of the Springs to the Tram."

"Well, heaven won't wait," Jim called out, moving to his skis.

Matthew's smile felt permanently plastered on his face. Matthew didn't care where they went; he just didn't want the day to end. A high tide of unqualified, unquestioned joy. Reality would return that night, but this, now, he accepted with open arms.

"Hey, Matthew," Wesley called out. "Quit smilin'. Think of your reputation."

A crow's harsh cry reverberated through the Village. The bird's shadow caught up with the giant dark scavenger on the Clock Tower. Glossy black feathers blocked the hour hand. An omen. Good or bad? Matthew laughed. Hell, his omens came wrapped in explosives.

* * *

This trip up the Tram, the view at the top of Rendezvous Peak, captured Matthew's attention. The Grand Tetons and the unbroken, white expanse of Jackson Hole's valley stretched all the way north to Yellowstone. Huge triangular Cody Peak beckoned them to the hidden treasures of Rock Springs, located just beyond the southern boundaries of the ski resort. The many runs that made up Jackson Hole surpassed Rock Springs in quality and diversity. But anything out of bounds added excitement and fresh terrain.

Matthew followed Jim's lead out of the Box, across the top of Rendezvous Bowl. He trusted Jungle Jim's years of experience in the mountains of Wyoming, even as he grew more uncomfortable with the man's apparent lack of character. Jungle Jim's relationship with Julia was so strange. And how come he lacked the discretion of his brother, the surgeon?

Matthew stopped as Jim reconnoitered. Below, shade still defined many of the short chutes and small open faces of Rock Springs Canyon. The snow would be cold and stable. But beyond the safety of the canyon, the large open Rock Springs Bowl sat seductively in the sun.

"Not a tough choice," Jim said, pointing over at the sparkling, unblemished surface. Matthew couldn't agree more.

"Been in the sun most of the morning," TJ commented. "Looks mighty good though. Shall we give it a shot?"

Jim answered by pushing forward, continuing the traverse across the first crease that defined the birth of Rock Springs Canyon. Matthew went next, bright sunshine suffusing his body with liquid warmth. A sky too blue to be real expanded Matthew's consciousness of space, beauty, and contentment. Control became an unnecessary dimension, saved for later.

Matthew stopped behind Jim at the side of a tantalizing, untouched expanse—steep, sensual Rock Springs Bowl. The free-floating promise below brought a pleasant flutter to Matthew's stomach.

"I'll go in first," Jim said, pushing off. "I'd allow ten to fifteen turns between us."

Rays of sun lit up crystals shrouding Jim's body as he swept from side to side down the exact center of the two-hundred-foot-wide bowl.

"Right down the middle," Wesley howled in disgust. "What a Powder Pig."

Matthew forced himself to wait for the proper safe distance between him and Jim before he dove in. It wasn't easy. Then Matthew skied across the face, well to the right of Jim's symmetrical tracks. Jim had skimmed a quarter of the way down when Matthew made his first tight rotation back towards the middle. He gauged the now shorter distance to the trees lining the right side of the open run.

Whump! The semimuffled sound of a gigantic concussion vibrated across the side of the mountain. Matthew compressed to a stop after only two turns. But the sinking sensation beneath his feet contradicted expected physics. Matthew moved when he should be stationary. Then he knew. The White Dragon.

Arms flailing, Matthew attempted to regain balance and ski off to the safety of the fir trees. Too late. A world gone horizontal and dark swallowed him. The avalanche picked up speed. Panic and fear extinguished a flash of anger at Jim's choice of runs. Then debris covered Matthew, and a crushing, intense weight drove him under.

He knew the slide rules. He focused solely on breathing. Unlike a battle, unlike a fight, time did not slow down. Just the opposite. He had options, but Matthew had been too slow to respond to the danger. He flashed through the checklist of survival.

Scream.

Too late. Besides, Wesley and TJ had to know where Matthew had headed, assuming they weren't victims also.

Drop all your gear.

Again, too late. His boots twisted out of his bindings, but the skis augured down into the heart of the cascading snow, still attached to his feet by the safety straps. Safety—the irony of that adjective wasn't lost on him, even in his desperate struggle to resurface. He did drop his poles. That freed his arms.

Swim towards the top.

Breaststroking, head downhill, Matthew popped to the top. He gasped, gulping air, slamming his mouth shut as he rotated back into the maelstrom. Everything went black. Keep moving your arms. Now both safety straps ripped from his boots and bindings. Back on top, tumbling to the right.

Matthew had to make it to the trees. Death lay buried at the bottom beneath the tons of wet snow. Keep swimming. Under again. A solid object crushed his butt, jerking Matthew to a tentative halt.

But the force of the slide ripped him from his precarious perch. Inverted and disoriented, Matthew sunk again under the overpowering density of the avalanche. He worked to roll his body, arms flailing, until he faced downhill again. His breaststroke evolved into a frantic, spastic, acid-freestyle. This time he grabbed a tree, hanging on with arms and legs.

Matthew flipped the lower part of his torso to the far side of the fir, out of the fatal grasp of the killer slide. He clung to the tree with strength only the fear of death could generate as the roar passed him by.

Numbing silence filled the space. Matthew hugged the tree. The rasping sound of his gasps competed with the retreating echoes of devastation rattling through Rock Springs. Then the screams of Wesley and TJ rippled through the solid mist and clouds hovering over the avalanche chute.

Wesley appeared from the backside. He must have skied above the fractured fissure of the bowl and down between the trees along the far side. Gratitude filled Matthew. Thanks that he was safe. Thanks that Wesley had avoided disaster.

"Holy shit," Wesley panted. "You're alive. You hurt bad?"

"No idea," Matthew said, now that air circulated through his system. "But until I know, I'm not letting go of this tree."

The Indian's face was drawn tight over his high cheekbones and tall forehead. His face reflected the horror of their near-death experience.

"Wesley, you look like a white man," Matthew said.

Wesley's expression reinforced the constant thought that had resonated through the frightening chaos. That had fueled Matthew's desperate struggle, had helped pull him to the surface. The words escaped his lips.

"I want to live."

He looked up at his friend, the moisture of tears indistinguishable from the wet snow packed in every orifice and crease of his battered body. His moving parts still functioned. Too early for the pain from the bruises and connective-tissue damage to register. The numbness would wear off too soon.

"Did Jim make it?" Matthew asked, voice trembling.

Wesley's face faded from pale to gray. The pupils of his dark eyes distended, creating anxious pools surrounded by white.

"I don't think so."

Matthew still hung tight to the tree, his bruised arm rigid in its grip. A wave of vertigo and despair for Jim swept through him. He looked to the bottom of Rock Springs Bowl. The small, frantic figure of TJ bounced on top of tons of snow and debris, the mess solidifying into cement. Death and destruction had piled twenty feet high in an unforgiving mass. Jim would be buried near the bottom.

"Jungle Jim's in the belly of the Dragon." Wesley's chiseled countenance crumbled with emotion. "Ain't no hope. Won't be able to dig him out till late spring."

Wesley pried Matthew off the fir and helped him struggle out of the tree line. Matthew stood dazed, holding onto Wesley, the sun filtering through the trees on this once perfect day. Matthew attempted one step and sunk to his waist in the deep powder. Wesley grabbed tighter, supporting Matthew, unlikely lovers during the last dance.

"It's gonna be a bitch gettin' down to the Village without your skis," Wesley said.

"I'll make it." Matthew nodded towards the wreckage at the base of the bowl. "If I start to whine, remind me of the alternative."

THIRTY-NINE

Franky stomped by the Wort's reception desk. The pleasure of skiing faded with his lack of progress. The desk clerk didn't even bother to nod in his direction. Franky understood the boy's lack of respect or recognition. Hell, he'd ignored the retarded kid's existence for three weeks. Another day in paradise.

He took the wide stairs to the second floor, passed under the huge stuffed moose head, down the frayed carpet of the narrow hallway to the dented door leading to his dilapidated suite. The phone rang as he entered the room. Maybe Sarah. She had kept her distance since his outburst on the mountain the other day, but perhaps she'd forgiven him. An emptiness echoed within Franky, a disappointment he couldn't understand. He snatched the receiver. Any news would be good news at this point.

"Hey, Franky, how ya doin'?"

Sal. Franky wished he'd missed this call.

"You okay?" Sal asked. Where was the normal boom of his half-brother's voice? "Wanted to check your progress. Haven't heard from you in weeks."

Sal didn't give a shit about Franky. Who the hell was this imposter?

"Franky, you there?"

The voice on the phone line held a noticeable tremor, almost a stutter. Had to be a trick, a phone tap by the Feds suckering Franky into an admission of his hunt for a protected witness.

"Franky, you there?"

"Yeah." Keep the answers simple. Give nothing away.

"Been a few changes." The disembodied sound in the receiver resembled Sal. "We've merged our operation. Roberto's dead."

"Merged? Roberto's what?"

Franky sank onto the hard, spindly desk chair. Who killed Roberto? Did someone find out about their plans and pull the trigger? Was Franky implicated?

"Franky, it's okay. Everything's gonna be fine. We play our cards right, could be in the chips."

"What are you talking about?"

"I don't know why Roberto bought it, but he's dead. And merged is the wrong word. Swallowed's more like it."

"Who swallowed us?"

"I ain't telling you over the phone," Sal said, a slight increase in the energy level of his delivery. Then he slid back to meek. "The Man said you'd know him. Wanted me to give you a couple of messages."

Giacomo? But why'd he rub out Roberto and not his brothers? Why didn't they eliminate everyone? Had Franky's expertise saved him? And what value did Sal and Marco hold? Had Giacomo directed Franky's hit in the alley? Or had his father ordered Franky's entrance to violent crime the way he manipulated everything else? That son of a bitch had always paid the bills and pulled the strings.

"He said it's real important that you have a successful trip. You got one more week, then get your ass back here, finished or not. They need you."

"You don't sound too good, Sal."

"I'm fine. And, Franky, please be careful."

Confusion melded with fear and suspicion. Sal hated him. Why the change of heart?

"Thanks for your concern."

"I mean it. Anything bad happens to you, me and Marco are history. That's straight from the Man. Your high-priced Denver help know the score. Franky, I'd get the informer if I were you."

The phone went dead.

Franky let the conversation swirl through his head. Far more questions than answers. If Franky was so valuable, why not pull him back to New York immediately? Nothing could be done sitting on his ass in Wyoming. Why did Giacomo care so much about the informer? But he didn't doubt Sal's clear message—find the sucker.

Who would have thought he'd be so overwhelmed by this kind of a complex challenge. He traced the convoluted path that placed him in such a dangerous and ambiguous predicament. His M.B.A. couldn't get him a decent job. His grades got him in the door, but accounting firms and financial institutions were controlled by Jews or Wasps. He needed connections, a father or other well-placed relative. At the time Franky had neither.

That frustration drove him to the search that discovered a father and a prominent place stuck in his family's semilegitimate operation. What an irony. He'd just been looking for a damn job. Now he was locked into a current of activities with no escape. And once again, events outside his control jerked and twisted him down a one-way path.

Shit. Now what? Giacomo's insistence on a successful mission raised the ante. The Mob, or whoever they were, couldn't have much confidence in Sal and Marco. Franky knew he was a babe in the woods when it came to the violent politics of underworld power plays. Who the hell could he trust? Not Sal. Not the Bruise Brothers or Giacomo. And their quarry could be a lot more dangerous than Franky had been led to believe, although David Moore didn't seem like much of a threat.

He smashed his fist on the desktop. The only thing that cracked was his fingers. Never had any goddamn control. Now he never would. Just a pawn, unless his business abilities could save him. That would take awhile. If he lived long enough.

Franky went to the closet and pulled out his suitcase. He dislodged a .38 detective's special and box of hollow-point shells from under the false bottom of his Samsonite luggage. The pistol had been presented by Roberto before he'd left for Jackson Hole. No registration number. Clean. Use the weapon only in case of an emergency.

Franky slipped bullets into the cylinder with clumsy fingers. He placed the gun in his parka pocket. The weight brought a small degree of that most elusive element, control. Roberto should have hung onto the weapon.

FORTY

Even the small dirty windows of the Stagecoach failed to block the late afternoon Teton brightness. Matthew's pathetic partners sat beside him in a ragged circle at the end of the solid wood bar. Matthew anchored one irregular spot perched on the last stool. Now he turned facing the wall. He felt a fuzzy pride in escaping early from the miserable, empty wake that David had hosted. David meant well, wanting to honor Jim, his friend and business partner.

Matthew was drunk, hammered. His companions in mourning slobbered over platitudes, highballs, and beer. The many cuts and bruises from his wild ride down the Rock Springs slide were now vague aches and pains suspended in a welcome pool of alcohol. Images ricocheted through the maze of his befuddled brain. Occasionally, a stream of identifiable impressions drifted into a logical pattern.

The room swayed, Matthew unable to focus. He did recognize his arrival at the peak of plastered pleasure. He nodded to the shadows performing a stumbling dance on the walls. The feeble glow of past experience flickered the message that he couldn't get much higher. Not on booze anyway. From peak to puke, a short trip. Enjoy the high ground. He giggled at his choice of clever words.

Several firm taps on Matthew's shoulder pried him from his drunken daydreams. Someone had lit a large doobie right at the bar. Matthew glanced around daring anyone to object to the presence of the lit joint, wishing for an opportunity to vent frustrations on some unsuspecting redneck. But the two drunks at the corner table couldn't have cared less. And the bartender, Herbie, exhibited a new tolerance—skiers tipped better than the dirt-poor locals who considered the Stagecoach their private temple.

What the hell. Matthew took a tentative puff, cauterizing the nodules of his lungs. The remembered routine flooded back from the past. For some in Nam, smoking eased the pain, fear or anger. For Matthew, the big fat numbers increased his paranoia. The smoke seared his system, bringing back the frightening loss of control that had always accompanied the ever-present weed.

Heading into combat stoned had seemed suicidal. He wanted every sense on full alert. Even hunkered down in a camp, in a defensive position, left you a sitting duck. All the skill, cunning, and expertise a soldier possessed should be used to survive. Better to be moving, become the aggressor. Smoking, the escape shit, at best provided a false sense of security. At worst you were vulnerable with dulled reactions. But there weren't any dangerous gooks within thousands of miles here.

He took another drag, a little deeper. Well, smoking grass did put a different spin on things. Matthew hung onto the bar stool with both hands, the joint clamped in his mouth, smoke curling in his face. The rapid movements of the Teton light show against the pine paneling became more than he could handle. Matthew turned back into the circle.

His friends all looked like hell. Black-bagged, red eyes. Drooping lips. Stooped in sadness. He focused on the only female, Princess Sarah. Mistake. She looked terrible. Her features required animation. In stationary sorrow her face resembled a death mask.

An image of Julia's mother floated unbidden before his clouded eyes, just as she had seemed to drift unwelcome to Jim's funeral. Big and broad as her beautiful, majestic daughter, Ellen possessed the same blond hair as Julia. Excess flesh surrounded her cold blue eyes, drowning high cheekbones in a round, smooth pink sea of fat. She had seemed to have chosen food to fill her needs. Matthew marveled that, even with all that insulation, no warmth emanated from her, an empty vessel. Could Julia be the same?

Matthew shook off someone's hand intent on retrieving the number, then sucked in a monster hit. Just to guarantee the absence of any lucid thought that might slip through his diminishing faculties. But he couldn't purge the strange disgust and anger generated during Jim's parody of a ceremony.

Jim's memorial service had been Matthew's first individual funeral since before Viet Nam. There, the military routine had dehumanized the wave of departed soldiers, stripping away any emotion or compassion. The absence of Jim's body, buried under tons of snow until May or June, added a similar hollowness to an event that lacked meaning and a human context. He almost toppled off the bar stool when he realized that his dead friends and fellow warriors far outnumbered the living.

"God's been busy lately," Sarah murmured.

The comment washed up against the shore of Matthew's consciousness.

"He has if he's a friggin' undertaker," Matthew spat out.

"Don't you believe in God?" Sarah asked. The sound of her voice came from far away.

"Are you kidding?"

"No, I'm not kidding." Sarah's indignation registered through the hazy space.

The very mention of a rational benevolent order brought Matthew a moment of undesired clarity. A light shudder acknowledged the Pavlovian reaction he had had to the sign of the cross during Jim's service at the stark, cold Trinity Church—his Jewish heritage deeply seated despite his adamant rejection of an intelligent, compassionate god. His discomfort became further fueled as he checked off bogus references to Jim's untimely demise. "He died doing what he loved most." "A sacrifice to the White Dragon." "Right place, wrong time." "A mountain man fortunate to die on the mountain." What crap. Jim's death served no purpose, as arbitrary and impersonal as stepping on a mine in the Asian mud.

"If there is a God, he's a cold son of a bitch," Matthew spat out.

"You don't believe that, Matthew, do you?"

Sarah sounded sure of herself, protected by her beliefs. Where did this woman get off with such confidence? God didn't shine his light so bright on her life. She had to travel from Chicago to Jackson Hole just to get laid.

"Oh, yes. I do." Matthew tried to stand, pointing at Sarah with a finger, his body shaking from rage as much as inebriation. "And if three thousand years of history aren't enough to prove it, consider just the last fifty."

"God gave man free will," Sarah replied. "Mankind has choices. People bring evil upon themselves."

Matthew gagged. He hated all the pious bullshit. "God's will." "Into the hands of the Lord." "God works in mysterious ways." No kidding. The Viet Nam military way might actually be best—bag and pack 'em, label and ship 'em . . . *Olaf (being to all intents a corpse . . .* Who needed this drawn out closure bullshit?

"Look, Princess," Matthew felt his rage-induced clarity fading, but he slurred on. "Either God created man or he didn't. If he did, and man brought all this misery on himself, then God did a lousy job. I got more respect for a good mechanic like Wesley. His damn cars don't run over their owners."

A flaming red flush from either anger or embarrassment flooded Sarah's face. Matthew searched for balance. But the conversation had turned incomprehensible. Better to bail. Matthew was no longer willing to put up with this ridiculous discussion, even stoned out of his gourd.

"I'm gone." Matthew stumbled towards the door.

"How the hell you think you're gettin' home?" Wesley asked.

"God'll take care of me," Matthew shot back over his shoulder. "Doesn't he look after babies, innocents, and drunks?"

The effort to look back knocked him off balance. He slammed into the doorjamb, apologized to the opening, and staggered into the parking lot.

For some reason the key to his cabin wouldn't fit in his Jeep's ignition. Matthew almost gave up, considered returning to the Stagecoach. But then he dropped his keys on the floorboard and, in picking them up, connected with the car key. He fired up the old Cherokee and fishtailed onto the road. How the hell would he make it back to the Grand View? The gathering dusk would do nothing to increase his odds. What a great chance for God to show he was an equal-opportunity savior.

FORTY-ONE

Franky walked the block to the Cowboy Bar. He sat at what had become his regular spot at the edge of the second level. Fear and frustration boiled within him, overriding his momentary fantasy of sitting like Wild Bill Hickock, back against a corner of the main level, pistol in his parka pocket. On second thought, didn't Wild Bill get taken out with a bullet in the back of his head?

Franky shifted in his seat, glancing over his shoulder just to make sure no one lurked against the wall. Nothing there except shadows. These hicks drifting around his table would be a little more respectful if they knew he packed a loaded .38. He gulped a short scotch and soda, leaned back in his chair, and again imagined himself a modern-day gunslinger.

"Hey, man. What's happening?" Shebang asked.

Franky was working on his third drink. Shebang and two cronies flopped next to him.

"You're looking a little lonely, Bud." Sarcasm laced Shebang's sympathetic words.

"Not much happening in this boring burg." Franky tried not to sound glad to see the three men.

Franky had encouraged Shebang and his buddies with liquor and bullshit. The local troublemaker had bragged about having dirt on everyone and everything in Jackson Hole. Franky'd listened to a lot of stories about a lot of people, but none led to any information about a potential suspect. Enlightenment from this group seemed a long shot.

"Got a party to go to," Shebang offered. "You can meet some new friends. Fact, it's not just a party but kind of an unofficial wake for old Jungle Jim."

"What happened to him?" For some perverse reason Franky pretended he didn't know. Since everyone was dicking with his mind, he might as well play their same stupid-ass game.

Shebang and the other two scroungy locals, Jerome and Mitchell, had first sat with their backs to the action. Now they twisted and squirmed, finally scraping their chairs to an angle giving them a more comfortable view of the bar. They seemed more excited than normal.

"Man, you live in a hole somewhere?" Shebang said. "You ain't heard about the Rock Springs avalanche the other day?"

"Yeah, I heard something about it."

"More than 'something' if you're Jim," Shebang said. "That boy's buried. Too bad the Dragon missed that dickhead, Matthew. Almost swallowed him too."

"I don't know," Franky said. "There's others on my list I'd rather see snuffed first. David Moore, for example."

"No way," Shebang said with feeling.

"I thought you hated the little prick too."

"I do." Shebang's voice drifted lower. "But he's the main supplier in the county."

"Supplier of what?" Franky watched Shebang's face turn incredulous.

"Jesus, Franky. David's the major supplier of fruits and vegetables in Teton County."

Shebang and his two partners laughed. Franky felt heat rise in his face.

"We gotta protect the flow of products into the Valley," Jerome said. His long skinny face, pockmarked and sunburned, reminded Franky of a six-foot pile of rusted metal. Not much smarter either.

"Drugs, my boy, drugs," Shebang said. "Dope and acid. Rumors have it David's got a Mexican connection for the smoke and a basement factory near Idaho Falls for the tabs."

The embarrassing heat of Franky's face transformed into a comforting glow warming him like a shot of Tequila Gold. Shebang occasionally knew what he was talking about. If this piece of information proved accurate, David had just become both a more probable and more vulnerable suspect. He tried to mute his excitement.

"You never laid this on me before," Franky said. His tone crept up the scale of injury.

"You never asked nothing about drugs—ever."

"We figured you was a drug virgin," Jerome said and giggled.

"You're always too uptight to be enjoying drugs," Shebang added.

"You sure about David?" Franky asked, twirling the ice in his empty scotch glass, wanting a refill. But the good-looking waitress wouldn't give him the time of day.

"I'm not positive," Shebang said. "But I'd bet a pair of skis and an ounce of good shit on it."

Jerome and Mitchell nodded their agreement.

"Come to the party. There's stuff coming down." Mitchell's first contribution of the evening came out in a lisp. "David never shows, but one of his delivery boys is expected to pay a visit."

"Yeah, come on." Shebang poked at Franky, an evil grin infecting his face. "Party's at the Jackson Hole Trailer Park."

"Might even get a piece of ass," Jerome said, looking like one.

Well, now, the break he was so desperate for might just have been presented by the source he had so carefully cultivated. Franky exercised excruciating self-control, hoping his newly energized attitude didn't show.

"Okay, I guess I'll give it a try."

"Trailer park's six or seven blocks from here towards the Elk Refuge," Shebang said, pushing the bar tab to Franky. "We'll pick up some booze. Drugs build up a powerful thirst."

Franky caught a sly wink Shebang gave his two homely companions as he motioned Franky to follow them.

*   *   *

The trailer park looked to Franky like a shabby whorehouse, standing seductively in a faded pool of light. Piles of crap and junk competed with an aged assortment of metal boxes imitating dwellings. Even in the muted luminescence, the garbage of life dominated the surface in dark shades of brown and green. Where was he, goddamn Brooklyn? An occasional bright color popped out of the refuse, representing a token nod to the lazy, low-life hippies in residence.

Blaring music, shouts and banging doors emanated from the back section of the park. Movement flickered through the shadows. Franky followed as his friends fought their way through the debris. They reached the center of activity, where smoking fires flamed in two ancient metal garbage cans enhancing the glimmering atmosphere. Figures like homeless refugees moved between trailers and fires. Music and laughter provided a consistency missing in the erratic illumination and the helter-skelter activity of the partygoers.

Franky accepted his ignorance concerning drugs. He'd gladly been gapped out of the revolution by ten years of hard drinking and desperate searching. What he saw now confirmed his choice. Best to keep a distance from these drugged-out losers. Still, it paid to act cool.

Shebang pulled Franky into a large, rusted sardine can. A plastic awning above the door sagged low enough to make even Franky duck his head. Inside, the heat and smell of packed, over-dressed bodies explained the constant movement back outside for fresh air. Franky felt submerged in the crammed interior, counting the minutes before he could resurface in the welcome chill of the night.

This scene required a higher level of alcohol than floated in Franky's blood stream. He broke for the exit as the Doors blasted "Light My Fire." In the clear frozen air, the multitude of musical selections from the four trailers lost their identity, grinding together in an unrecognizable medley sounding like broken glass in a garbage disposal.

Franky faced a jumbled group of party animals bundled in hats and gloves. Couldn't tell the girls from the boys, not that it mattered. Franky accepted a bottle thrust into his hand. He gulped a burning, fiery rotgut fluid masquerading as bourbon. He offered no words of thanks and tipped his head back for another death-defying swallow.

Inside, outside, Franky spun through the evening. Bedlam ruled. He would have felt out of place if anyone had noticed. Nobody did. He hung tight to his mission. He'd confirm David's role in this insanity. Maybe even question the delivery boy. But the odds of accomplishing either goal slipped down the probability scale with each passing minute. Franky lunged for Shebang as he appeared through the smoke of the garbage can fires.

"I don't see anyone shooting up," Franky whispered into his friend's ear.

"This ain't New York." Shebang's face reflected disbelief. "You don't shoot up dope or acid."

Franky fought his embarrassment, but the bulge of the revolver brought him unexpected comfort.

"Keep drinking. I told you the good stuff's on its way, compliments of your good buddy, David."

Franky's ignorance now bothered him. Something didn't compute, even factoring in all the craziness surrounding him. Didn't dope smell? Didn't acid freak people out, make them crawl around, climb trees, cry or laugh hysterically? Everyone here acted drunk on their ass. No different than any other New York bar on a Saturday night.

Back inside one of the immobile homes, Franky noticed a lonely, lime-colored lava lamp performing on a narrow windowsill. He had never seen one before but had heard of the lamp's hold on hallucinating hippies. The hypnotic movement of the lamp should be attracting more stoned attention, shouldn't it? But it surged, transforming from shape to free-form shape, unnoticed by the frenetic druggies. Pretty cool, though. Franky stood transfixed until Shebang yanked him outside once again.

FORTY-TWO

Matthew took a wild, swinging voyage through another dimension, somehow finding himself back at the cabin. He staggered to the door. The only remaining danger tonight would be falling on his ass. Darkness didn't register when blind drunk.

He tripped on the door's threshold. Cody greeted him in a crashing rush. Matthew collapsed on top of man's best friend, then hit the hard floor. His hands failed him as he attempted to resist the Lab's slobbering tongue. He crawled to the bathroom alcove, took forever to strip off his clothes and climb into the tiny shower closet. More water hit the floor than his body, even at point-blank range.

Matthew grabbed a towel, then dabbed at that part of his body he could see—damn little. It would have helped if he'd turned on the light. Too late. He lurched around the small room until he connected with his bed. The bed frame smacked him low. He collapsed forward, his head thudding against the log wall. Neither blow would be confused as a caress.

At least Matthew reached his objective. The bed. He worked hard to climb under the covers, the chill registering despite the excessive ingestion of alcohol-based antifreeze. Seemed the problem had something to do with gravity. No matter how hard Matthew tried, he couldn't lift the blankets over his now shivering, wet body while he lay on top of them. The solution eventually wormed its way through a closing curtain of consciousness. Roll off the bed to the floor, then climb under the covers. Good plan. It worked.

Matthew lay on his back, focused on the dim light reflecting through the log cabin's window. The light gained importance as everything else in the room moved. Matthew accepted the lateral movement. Spinning items presented a more serious set of problems. Cody, at the side of his evil magic mattress, licked Matthew's already moist face—probably needed to pee. No way, Cody. Nothing could induce Matthew to leave the security of his position. It was pretty damn impressive that he'd made it to bed.

The room settled into a stomach-churning swing set. Puke or pass out? Matthew prayed for the latter. Sure enough, he'd been wasting his time praying. Change of plans. Matthew dove for the front door, made it and fell on all fours to the left of the entrance.

The freezing cold snapped him alert. Then the turmoil inside his system caught up with the outside's momentary, chill-induced relief. Spasms racked his body. Bile, booze, and hors d'oeuvres deposited on the snow. A great picture for the Grand View's advertising brochure—a naked guest on his knees, puking his guts out in the parking lot.

Only the extreme cold convinced Matthew to move. He covered up the mess with snow and put a handful of cool, refreshing moisture in his mouth. Cody brushed by him headed for the trees. Matthew hoped another moose wouldn't get him.

Matthew stumbled back to bed. At least he wouldn't be sleeping in his own vomit. Or would he? The puke-or-pass-out dynamic reasserted itself. Time passed. Finally Matthew passed from unwanted consciousness into a welcome void.

* * *

Matthew opened his eyes to a huge figure filling up the cabin's doorframe. Oh, man, another nightmare? The pounding in his head and his blurry vision gave Matthew pause. Maybe this wasn't a vision, maybe it was real. His inability to move more than his arms meant he hadn't been passed out for long, assuming he wasn't dreaming.

Movement at the foot of the monster. Cody squeezed into the room, trotting over to Matthew. Couldn't be too much of a threat if Cody didn't react. But Matthew knew his nightmares and reality inextricably intertwined. His life hadn't been consistently real in months. Years. What should he do? Lying there helpless shouldn't have been an option. His first choice would have been his .45. But the pistol hung on the wall in its holster. Might as well be in California. And his body had atrophied into stone.

The bearlike figure moved from the doorway towards the bed. Light from the entrance backlit hair flowing over its head in soft waves. Ah, an angel—maybe there was a God. About time. Two steps closer and the massive mound knelt at the side of his bed. Julia? Recognition was as astonishing as if a hibernating bear had decided to finish the winter in the shelter of Matthew's cavelike cabin.

Matthew knew better than to buy any of this mirage. He waited groggy and queasy for the terrifying dream element to reassert itself. He could count on one hand the number of pleasant dreams he'd experienced the last few years. Hell, one finger. A feeble, internal alarm tried to rouse his paralyzed body. Well, he'd lived through the nightmares, even the worst ones. Though he had to admit, none of them had begun with such a benign prelude.

He felt a hand on top of the blankets. A profile view confirmed the identity of Julia. The raw, foul taste of bile and vomit combined with cottonmouth to keep his lips sealed. He was torn between a desire to touch the woman, determine her reality and solid substance, or lie still, allowing the bizarre dream to stay comforting and erotic. And if he touched her, would she mutate into a vicious, wicked fiend? Perhaps an accomplice of the White Dragon come to drag Matthew to Jungle Jim in Hell?

Then he felt Julia's cold, smooth hand slip under the covers. She found what Matthew hoped she was looking for. His surprise and state of drunken dehydration left him limp. But not for long. Julia pushed the covers to the side and leaned forward, her long hair a thick veil over Matthew's waist. Her soft, wet mouth brought instant erection—hell, she could bring back the dead as long as it wasn't Jim. What a great dream.

Julia threw the blankets off. The cabin door, still open, gave the shadows substance. Her bulky sleeping-bag-sized parka parted, and Matthew's breathing ceased. She mounted what her mouth had managed to awaken. Her massive breasts filled his vision. Matthew felt little contact, swimming in a love box as wide as her broad shoulders.

Sounds finally emerged from Julia. Urgency vied with frustration as she methodically rotated. Matthew sensed his hard cock floating insecure without the desired boundaries. Satisfaction rattled too loosely inside Julia's walls.

Matthew waited for the disappointment, the pain. It's all a fantasy—an unfulfilled climax, never coming. There had to be an unpleasant new phase of this charade yet to appear. One consistent with Matthew's true reality—never ending nightmares.

Matthew felt the emptiness fill. Julia placed two, then three fingers into the contact zone. Matthew sensed a growing tightness, moisture lubricating the connection. Julia's rocking motion picked up speed but lost consistent rhythm. In no time, far too little time for Matthew, Julia's bucking, thrashing movements became accompanied by screeching vocals. Her giant tits slapped back and forth, swinging like weapons, barely clearing Matthew's immobile face. The screams intensified, Matthew an awed spectator.

Then everything stopped. Julia paused a moment above Matthew, the shuddering within her body dying. She slumped forward on Matthew's chest, large breasts a strange, impersonal barrier between her and him. Without a word, a kiss or a tear, the ghost dismounted. She wrapped her parka around her oversized body and walked out of the cabin, considerately closing the door behind her.

Matthew lay like a hit-and-run victim. His hardon still standing, a vibrator Julia forgot to unplug. How long had she lay smothering Matthew? Long enough for him to spout a hundred bullshit lines. Long enough for him to explain a hundred thoughts. But evidently not long enough for Matthew to regain any degree of composure.

The experience sobered him. He only had questions. Why did she leave me unsatisfied? Was she drunk? Stoned? What or rather which of my shortcomings prevented any kind of communication? Was this a one-shot deal? The last question was the only one he could unequivocally answer.

Matthew's dreams of making love to Julia existed even before her bare-breasted appearance in her bedroom window. His erotic hunger often burned, consuming and disconcerting, not like his destructive dreams, but unsettling all the same. Now Matthew reached for the tendrils of a thought, slipping like smoke through the cracks of a closed door. Something he had once told Jim: "Be careful what you wish for."

FORTY-THREE

"Freeze!"

The command reverberated through the trailer park. Echoes came back from all directions, but with different twangs and volumes. Apparitions emerged from the shadows, large and bulky, enhanced by oversized cowboy hats, heavy coats and dangerous-looking shotguns.

Franky, sitting on a crate by one of the sputtering, sparking battered metal cans, whirled his head around the circle. Cops, twenty to thirty, badges now visible, surrounded the area. Panic engulfed him. He lurched to his feet. Shebang grabbed his belt and slammed him back down.

"Don't move, Franky," Shebang said, an odd sound in his voice—excited satisfaction—inconsistent with the apparent danger. "Be cool. This is gonna be a classic."

Everyone was frozen, many in awkward or ridiculous positions. Jerome on one leg, listed forward, resembling a rusted hood ornament from an old Packard. Snickers and laughter bubbled to the surface.

"Come on in, boys. Buy ya a beer?" a large, bearded lift operator offered.

Police had encircled the four trailers and common area. Cops stood as frozen as the posed revelers. The officers seemed confused at the lack of any resistance from the busted celebrants. The very appearance of the unwanted guests worried Franky, but the strange reaction of the ambushed crowd mesmerized him.

"We got pigs all the way from Pinedale," Shebang whispered. Then louder, "Hey, Sheriff, why don't you and Clarence get warm here by the fire?"

"Nobody move," Sheriff Olsen barked, though no one had yet moved a muscle.

Then several drunks in convoluted positions tipped over and lay laughing on the dirty, crushed snow. Several officers stomped to the trailer doors, flushing the occupants. Happy hippies stumbled out, failing to control giggles and snorts as they hit the ground next to their quivering comrades.

"This is a bust," Sheriff Olsen cried out, uncertainty coloring the command. "We got search warrants for these pigsties." He motioned towards the decrepit trailers. "You all stand up over here. We're gonna search every damn one of ya."

"No problem, Sheriff," Shebang said and stood. He stretched languidly. "We been waiting for ya. Thought ya'd never show up."

Hoots and laughter rose into the thin air. Franky's fingers brushed the barrel of the gun. Fear filled him. Now the unregistered .38 pistol in his pocket felt like an anvil dragging him down to jail. Where could he hide? His cover would be blown, the whole operation a disaster. Could he toss the gun? No way out. Sweat beaded his forehead despite the freezing chill of the night. But something sure as hell was going on, based on Shebang's calm, disrespectful attitude. What had he gotten himself into?

"Man, I ain't been this drunk in years," a voice from the dark said.

Confusion, concern, and anger fought for dominance on the sheriff's florid face. He pushed forward and grabbed Shebang by the coat, hauling him forward.

"We'll start with you, punk. Line up these worthless pot-heads."

Franky scrambled on the ground. Jesus, he was in deep shit. He positioned himself at the end of the line, hoping against hope that buying time would save his ass from the search.

Headlights from an ominous barred prison bus pulled closer to the circle. Some officers tore into the trailers, while others either guarded the perimeter or took part in the body searches.

"You mind if we sit in your nice warm bus while you're working?" Shebang asked after a rough examination by a tall, scrawny deputy with the proud uniform insignia of the Alpine police department, thirty-five miles south of Jackson.

"Don't you touch that bus," the sheriff roared in frustration. "You'll be in it soon enough."

A third of the way through the search, Franky realized something. No one had any drugs. He cursed Shebang for not sharing the charade with him. He was the only fool not a part of the setup.

"Nothin', Sheriff." A bulky cowboy cop, bushy mustache covering his mouth, stood in the doorway of one of the tin cans. "Not a goddamn seed or stem. They musta knowed we was coming."

The locals roared and cheered, kids suckering authority. Franky cringed, unable to share their glee. Now only four revelers remained to be body searched before Franky. He was screwed.

Two of the largest cops conducted the body check, while the sheriff loomed nearby. The sheriff's irritation turned to rage. The captive crowd also felt the shift in the lawman's mood. Dangerous. Everyone calmed down a notch.

Another trailer declared clean and pure.

"Fuck it," Sheriff Olsen spat out. He whirled in a tight arc, as if searching for any poor sucker dumb enough to provoke him. The noise dropped another level. Then, "Let's go."

A raucous cheer erupted, shattering the growing tension. Franky's knees buckled in relief. The cops moved towards the bus. Angry frustration painted their faces. They looked ready to nail anyone within striking distance with a well-placed elbow or forearm shiver. Franky eased into the shadows, saved, as the jeering, celebrating throng scrambled out of the way of the police retreat.

Within minutes the bus was loaded and backing out to the street. The instant the sinister vehicle merged into the darkness, total chaos erupted. Jumping, dancing, hysterical patrons of the reverse sting slapped hands, hugged and kissed. Then Franky recognized a pungent aroma. Grass wafted through the air.

"I've been part-time pokin' the sheriff's hot little dispatcher for a couple of years," Shebang confided to Franky. "Man, we've known about this chicken-shit bust for weeks." Shebang snatched a joint being passed around. "It's time to really party down now."

Franky could have killed Shebang for placing him in jeopardy. He slipped away, welcoming a calm walk back to the Wort. At least Shebang had provided a lead worth checking out, though he'd been unable to confirm David's role in the distribution of drugs in Jackson Hole. One more nail in that prick David's coffin? This possible breakthrough called for a trip to the Bruise Brothers first thing in the morning.

Franky stood inside the door of the crummy shack on Hansen Street, shaking with cold and anticipation. John's sprawl filled the shabby couch, while Hack sat at the scarred kitchen table.

"Glad to see you're still working, Franky," John said, his voice forever sarcastic.

"You search David's?" Franky asked, beyond the need for courtesy.

Success would have been more achievable if he hadn't been saddled with these two jokers. Soon as he got back to New York, they would pay for their disrespectful mouths and their clumsy lack of progress. He'd made up his mind—these two jerks were toast. How he would mete out their well-earned demise would occupy his thoughts until this job ended— regardless of the success or failure of the operation.

"Nope," John said. "Been someone at the house every time we checked. There's guests always hanging out there."

Excuses. No surprise there.

"I've got some information that even you can help with." Franky's tone betrayed his excitement. Be cool, he reminded himself. "Our suspect, David, may just be the number one drug dealer in Teton County."

"How'd you find that out?" John asked in a skeptical voice.

"I told you I had connections with the locals," Franky said, pride and disdain equally mixed. "My buddy, Shebang, thinks Moore's the main man. Gets lots of visitors. Got lots of cash. Shebang said he personally knows one of David's street-level pushers. Marijuana and acid are the drugs of choice, and they all come from one source."

"Who's Shebang?" John said, still sounding doubtful.

"Shebang's my man. He's plugged into all the shit happening in this one-horse town. He's real tight with both the Viet Nam vets with the bad habits and the local ski bums looking for kicks."

"How sure are you this Shebang's for real?" Hack asked.

"Look, assholes, check it out with Denver and New York. You're not exactly overworked, and the pressure's rising, as you know. Find out who's got distribution in Wyoming."

Hack and John exchanged glances. What was wrong with these guys? Any lead should be welcome at this point. Especially one adding probability to their one and only suspect. Or had their instructions changed?

Their reaction once again stoked Franky's insecurities about the hit men's true agenda.

"Okay, Franky, we'll run it by our people," John said as Franky moved to the door. "Don't you want to stay for breakfast? We got Corn Pops and corn beef hash."

Franky flipped off the Denver men. Their snide laughter followed him out the door. Franky didn't care. He wanted out of the claustrophobic rat hole. They were all running out of time.

Now, if only Franky could confirm David's drug connection, they could pull the trigger. Literally. Franky laughed into the frozen morning air. Then he jerked to a stop before climbing into his rental car. What the hell? It wouldn't really matter if David were the wrong guy, as long as they bumped off someone. Who'd prove they killed the wrong man? Certainly the real fink wouldn't. He'd think the mob had been fed a satisfactory victim. The pressure'd be off.

But an innocent person killed? Maybe for a second time? That sweating fat man in the alley, had he been guilty? But after last night, it didn't look like he'd have to worry about that probability with David.

March
1969

FORTY-FOUR

Monday, 9:30, a crisp, clear morning. Matthew joined the twenty skiers milling around the cafeteria deck. Rectangular redwood picnic tables and benches, stacked on top of each other, separated the anxious class from a constant buzz and flow of skiers and resort employees. The Tram hummed overhead, the usual freezing valley inversion absent today. The two instructors, Kurt and Hans, huddled on the edge, probably comparing notes and reviewing strategies after their first glimpse of the mismatched collection of classmates.

He wanted to opt out of Kurt's class. This first day back since the avalanche should be spent reasserting control on the mountain. The only way to overcome the terror of the Dragon was to attack. Standing here on the deck with his thumb up his ass wasn't what he needed.

Matthew checked out the array of assembled students. The questions on Kurt's rather pointed, homemade questionnaire must have meant different things to different people. The selection process probably didn't matter anyway—Kurt needed live bodies to fill up his pet project. And skiers' appearances often had little relationship to their abilities. Matthew had only to look in a mirror or consider the unstylish but practical apparel of the three other locals taking the Steep Class.

Suzy Higgens, tough as nails and homely as an old horse blanket, had skied with the boys since she could walk. She headed the fashion parade with a pair of faded and patched, vaguely navy, powder pants and a quilted parka, once red, now various shades of pink highlighted with dark, greasy streaks of unknown origin. Several long, loose threads floated from her coat serving as sad banners flopping in the wind.

The other two scroungy-looking boys were spending their first full season working in Jackson Hole. One had dropped out of junior college in upstate Michigan, the other was a displaced surfer from Southern California. They might have migrated from different parts of the country, but they shared the look of half-starved, scraggly-haired Salvation Army dependents. They'd get every penny of their $150 investment in Kurt's class back in spades.

The sound of bickering drew Matthew's gaze to a tall couple wearing expensive, matching Bogner outfits of royal blue and white. Fashionable, tight stretch pants spread over perfect long legs—no creases, no bagging. They had to be man and wife.

The lady looked and sounded Swedish—medium cut, light blond hair, fair, creamy skin just beginning to crinkle, high cheekbones and nicely shaped lips. She spewed a constant flow of snippy comments at her tall, dark, once good-looking mate. The man's nasal answers, fighting for space in the unending flow of words, left no doubt of his Canadian origins. Wrinkles, deeper than his wife's, creased his face like fissures. Were they cracks from the intense pressure of her constant cutting comments? This couple would look good in Kurt's magazine ads for next year, assuming the camera's shutter speed clicked fast enough to catch them with their mouths shut.

Two large, loud European men gave Matthew cause to pause. Matthew knew where they were from, their harsh, guttural comments sounding like B-movie bad guys. Also dressed for show, their aggressive body language caricatured the pushy, obnoxious German tourist. The Katzenjammer Twins.

They bonded with the Austrian Hans, ignoring the rest of the assembled class. Matthew admitted that his instant dislike and discomfort with the two men reflected an unbecoming prejudice. But the longer he observed them, the less desire he had towards tolerance.

David stood close to Matthew, interest lighting up his usual somber expression. When David had learned Franky had also signed up, he had threatened to walk, forfeiting his entry fee.

"You want me to spend a week listening to that pain in the butt?" David had said. "There's tortures I'd volunteer for just to avoid even an hour with that obnoxious jerk."

David had agreed to stay only after Matthew had promised not to split. Now David's current attitude of contagious excitement contrasted with his earlier reluctance at joining the class. Matthew smiled. His serious sidekick exhibited the enthusiasm of a schoolboy.

"Kurt's instilled unwarranted confidence in Franky," David whispered to Matthew as the New Yorker preened and puffed out his chest like an overdressed rooster. "The punk doesn't realize Kurt's been real careful and consistent in steering him towards the less challenging slopes and conditions. He shouldn't be babying that jerk. Last thing Franky needs is an overinflated belief in his skiing abilities."

Sarah emerged from the middle of a group of male classmates who had staked an early claim on her attentions. The knit cap emphasized her long nose and large lips. But her eyes sparkled, speaking of edgy, electric eagerness. She was still a star, even though she didn't look her best bundled in a ski hat.

A quick comparison with the Swedish competition confirmed Sarah also doing a damn fine job filling out her form-fitting black stretch pants. Matthew caught himself smiling at her anticipation and exuberance. He had grudgingly accepting Sarah's participation in the class. Now he acknowledged a somewhat sheepish pleasure. She handled the mountain well for someone who only skied several weeks a year. The Princess grew on him.

But was he even a viable candidate for her interests? He considered the uncomfortable, shredded image of their theological discussion at the Stagecoach. Details hid behind a veil of scotch and marijuana. Still, his core beliefs stood solid in his mind. An improvement in his delivery would not have compromised his principles. Now he found himself in a hole, buried behind fresh, courteous, and respectful competition. And even Franky was ahead of him, if he was to believe the rumor. Could Matthew overlook her poor choice in men? Maybe.

"Good morning, everyone," Kurt said. "My name is Kurt Sidon. This is my partner, Hans Gruner."

Kurt's strange, bobbed prom nose pointed at Hans and then returned to the small crowd. Hans, good choice for an assistant, Matthew thought. The handsome Austrian projected patient mountain manners and charm, unlike Pepi's other imported European bombers. Matthew had heard all the stories. Pepi's recruits were red-hot racers, teaching out of necessity, not choice.

Hans had once challenged Pepi for top billing on the Austrian National Ski Team leading up to the Olympic season of 1964. Then a crippling crash on Kitzbuhl's forbidding and unforgiving downhill course put an end to Hans' racing career. Pepi had gone on to win Olympic medals in Innsbruck, gold in the Slalom and bronze in the Giant Slalom, confirming his dominance as the world's greatest skier. Hans seemed happier as an instructor than Pepi, a retired racing god paying penance as a ski-school director.

"I'm going to give you a rundown on how we're going to operate this week, then answer any questions," Kurt said. Matthew shuffled his boots, anxious to get underway, but curious. "We're going to ski together this morning. Check out your strengths and weaknesses. Divide you into two groups. Hans and I will rotate between both. We've spent some time getting our terminology and lessons the same. Want to have a consistent curriculum."

"Hans doesn't know enough English to order lunch." Franky's comment, although offered without volume, lifted loud and clear in the clean air.

"Franky, I vant you wit me," Hans said with an exaggerated Austrian accent. "I teach you technique, humility . . . unt manners."

And probably run you off the first available cliff, Matthew hoped. Matthew looked at David, who had an "I told you so" grimace on his face. Kurt kept talking, ignoring the exchange. He explained the primary goal—improving current levels of ability in steep conditions. With so many different skiers, he assured the class that emphasis would be geared towards each individual.

"I'm going to pass out racing bibs with numbers. It'll make it easier to keep track of everyone until we know your names. It'll also get us through the lift lines faster." Kurt and Hans tossed red bibs with white numbers to the class members.

"Hey, I'm not wearing number thirteen."

Once again Franky spoke, cementing his identity as the preeminent class asshole. No mean feat with the competition in this group. David rolled his eyes.

"I'll take it, Franky," Matthew said, and threw his number four in exchange for Franky's bib. "So happens thirteen's my lucky number."

"Are we really going to get into some steep stuff?" The question came from the Santa Monica surfer.

"Absolutely," Kurt answered. "After all, you've all prepaid. We got your money." Nervous laughter trickled through the skiers. "But we don't want to lose anybody during our first class. Terrible PR. We're going to head up the Tram. Follow me."

Kurt herded Matthew and the others in his large group to the head of the tram line, accompanied by a rude ring of rowdy and crude catcalls from the peasant skiers in line. The instructor entered the next car first and positioned his charges in the front left quadrant to better point out the spectacular sights. Near the top, the Tram moved across the face of Corbet's Couloir, attracting the expected religious oohs and aahs.

"You've all heard about Corbet's," Kurt said. "This may be in some of your futures."

"Should be renamed Dave's Demise in honor of the way he crashed down that mother," Franky spoke out. "You've heard of yard sales where a poor sucker's ski equipment goes flying? Well, Dave's performance looked more like a terminal 'Going Out of Business Sale.'"

What was with the nasty edge to Franky's voice? Franky had been the one to make a U turn at his first visit to the top of the drop. David's fall had certainly been spectacular, but why would the crash bring ridicule from chicken-shit Franky?

"You ever been down it, Franky?" Matthew asked.

Franky looked uncomfortable, perhaps aware he had gone too far.

"Then shut up."

* * *

Light white clouds scurried across the high ridge that gave birth to the chutes dropping into Laramie Bowl. The fleeting movement of vaporous images kept changing the shape of the horizon, but the jagged cliff face looked permanent and impassive to Matthew.

"We're going to split up this afternoon after lunch." Kurt stood between the class and the bottom of several long, steep chutes. "This is an excellent spot to gain a little perspective as to what we hope to accomplish this week. There are basically two kinds of steep, with many degrees of vertical drop and obstacles in each category. What we have here are classic examples of both varieties."

Kurt pointed straight up with his ski pole. The runs above his head reached for the agate blue sky. But Matthew, suppressing a shudder at the memory of the White Dragon, knew there were more dangerous conditions than steep.

"This is the Alta One Chute. Wide open at the top as it drops from the ridge and Pepi's Run. It narrows down in the middle. But this terrain, steep as it is, allows a skier to almost stop after each turn. You can dig in with your edges, build a stable platform, and swing your heels into the next turn. You can jump or hop all the way down, using the technique to keep your speed and balance in check. Most chutes allow this style."

Predictable, dubious comments circulated through the class: "You must be kidding," "Nice for you to say," "Gotta make a call, I'm underinsured." Matthew listened and waited.

"The second type of steep," Kurt continued, "is conveniently located to the left, Alta Two."

A gnarly rock-and-tree-lined doglegged funnel began far above at the edge of a tree-shrouded cliff. Almost vertical sides squeezed the chute like an unforgiving vise. Not even the shortest of skis could be crammed lengthwise between the walls.

"Alta Two is what I call a Chute of Total Commitment." Kurt's eyes and round, stubby nose made contact with each and every student. "There's no way to turn your skis sideways along the entire length of this sweetheart. No stopping. If you go horizontal to the hill, you'll stick your tips or tails or both into the walls of the chute. Then it's crash and burn all the way to where we're standing. You really don't need that experience."

No one spoke or moved. The power of fear, the only force that could keep twenty observers quiet. Including Franky. And Matthew had his own concerns. He'd chosen to live. How would he now react to extreme risk. Easy to take chances when you didn't give a damn.

"To ski a chute like Alta Two, you've got to pick a line of short, quick turns, really just edge checks. A steady, tight rhythm will get you through, but you'll accelerate to a higher speed than most skiers feel comfortable. Same with Corbet's. When you jump into that monster, you're landing too fast to change your plans. This type of chute is the ultimate test. We'll see who's willing to go for a master's degree at the end of the course."

* * *

The full class clattered into the Mangy Moose for lunch, clumsy ski boots creating awkward progress towards four reserved tables. Sarah sat down at one of the rough log surfaces, pleasantly aware of her fellow male students scrambling for seats next to her. She rewarded the victors with smiles. She ignored Franky, whose early- morning comments had been way out of line. But her mind drifted elsewhere, wide open to a strong current of change.

The harried young waitress threw down menus and a pile of silverware and napkins. Short of help and short on patience, Sarah thought. She remembered the "Help Wanted" sign in uneven print plastered on the entrance to the restaurant/bar. The notice supported a growing conviction within her. Why slave long hours, fifty weeks a year for one brief period of bliss in wonderful Wyoming? Why not move to Jackson Hole?

Granted, the current job opportunities, confirmed by a recent check of the classified ads in *The Jackson Hole Daily Guide*, gave little hope for more than housekeeping or waitressing. But Wesley and David had encouraged her, assuring that in the late spring she could find something more consistent with her talents. She didn't need much. And a small rental trailer would limit any potential visits from undesired family.

The waitress returned. She slapped down the class's orders and wheeled away before anyone could determine if they needed anything else. This little bitch actually made Sarah's mother look pretty good. At least Thelma knew the value of a customer.

But why was she stuck with so many of Thelma's physical features? Was there no justice? What Thelma viewed as the patrician elegance of her elongated facial characteristics—long nose, sharp chin, large lips and high forehead—Sarah more accurately described as resembling a red-faced, stark-featured vulture, nowhere close to the majestic Roman eagle of her mother's imagination. The men at the lunch table might seem happy with her looks, but Sarah wasn't fooled. Their attentiveness had more to do with the economics of female supply and male demand.

So, could she place a thousand miles between her and her mother? Could she walk from her "great job?" The distance would be a relief. Sarah certainly had no doubts now in Teton Village. She'd go home with David tomorrow, accept his offer of dinner and discuss possible Jackson Hole opportunities.

FORTY-FIVE

Matthew stood with Kurt's group of ten at the top of Alta One. The class had toured a good portion of the mountain. Shadows lengthened, sunshine and visibility dissipated as the instructor increased the difficulty of the descents. This was their sixth and final tram run of the day. Everyone in Kurt's group had proven they deserved to be with the better skiers. Except for Franky.

What was the deal with this guy? Franky didn't belong with the advanced group. The fact that the prick paid full price for his lessons couldn't begin to compensate Kurt for all that aggravation. Where did Kurt find the patience to deal with this jerk? Maybe Kurt kept the New Yorker in his group to protect Franky from Hans's revenge. Too bad. Hadn't Kurt mentioned that everyone, including Franky, had prepaid?

The Katzenjammer Twins did belong with Kurt, much to Matthew's chagrin and disappointment. So did the two young immigrants from Michigan and Southern California—focused, serious, listening. The slick married-couple's inclusion could be considered marginal. She skied stiffly but used correct technique —the obvious beneficiary of many private lessons. Her Canadian husband hung on for dear life, strength substituting for talent.

Suzy's tuition might as well be a donation. She could ski well enough to serve as an instructor. Kurt rented his small cabin from her parents. Maybe Suzy wanted to help him pay the rent. Or perhaps she wanted to dispel the unkind rumor, which Matthew had heard several times, that an evening with a local heifer brought a higher probability of sexual rewards than time spent with the squat spinster. Sad really.

Then Matthew caught himself, not for the first time, wishing Suzy would trade places with Sarah in Hans's group. He would welcome Sarah's energy and interest. And . . . He couldn't quite fill in the blanks.

"As I pointed out earlier," Kurt said, "Alta One is very ski-able. It's wide. The snow's forgiving. No problem getting an edge, building a nice secure platform. As you look down, there's two routes."

Matthew doubted that a glance down the ominous face would add much reassurance. The bottom third folded into foreboding shadows underneath the dramatic angle of the diving slope.

"The right side, which is more open, is the main way down and the one we're using. To the left, as you can partially see, the alternative is much narrower and rockier."

A large rocky spine separated the two choices. Both razor-edged sides of the tight route were capable of ripping and tearing a human body. A more expensive price would be paid if momentum swept a skier over the granite shelf that made up the left side—a several-hundred-foot drop onto an exposed pile of brutal, unforgiving boulders. Great place to test your risk tolerance.

"We'll save that challenge for another day," Kurt added. "I'll ski to the ridge. Then, one at a time, I want you to make your way down to me. You can stop there or keep going to the bottom. Remember, stay in control. Don't ski on top of anybody."

Kurt made slow, stable turns, dropping down the steep face of Alta One to the dividing rocks. The two Germans, as usual, fired out from the pack first, despite Kurt's admonitions of one at a time.

One stopped next to Kurt. The other kept slugging down the chute, muscling his way, turn by aggressive turn, disappearing through the waist of Alta One. His compatriot seemed to realize he had erred in pausing, exposing possible weakness or lack of endurance. He turned and followed his twin's path down the steep face. The longer Matthew spent with the two Krauts, the more respect he developed for their skiing ability and the greater his dislike for their rude, pushy habits.

Then David skied to the instructor. He stopped out of the way, above the skinny alternate chute. Matthew followed and landed facing him. Together they turned up the hill to watch the next skier—Franky.

On his third turn, Franky jerked around without checking his speed or position. By the sixth turn his body hung back defensively like laundry blowing in a strong wind. He threw himself forward. Overcorrection drove his ski tips straight into the soft snow. His flailing body dumped headfirst over his skis, rocketing down Alta One towards the rocky spine on which Matthew and David stood.

The bundle rolled, bounced twice, and veered towards the natural indentation of the alternate route. Curses competed with the screech and clatter of equipment scraping the snow. Franky slid and twisted upside down and backwards, headed for a disaster he couldn't escape. Matthew moved back to avoid the inevitable crash.

Matthew flashed to the Rock Springs Bowl, the avalanche, the loss of all control. Empathy for Franky registered momentarily. Then he turned to David standing in a vulnerable perch at the chute's mouth. David watched Franky, paralyzed, a mouse hypnotized by a striking snake. Franky crunched into David, sweeping him off his feet.

Both men tumbled down the treacherous alternate chute. The figures careened down the narrow center like an out-of-control bobsled, miraculously avoiding the menacing, sharp rocks. Then they spit out through the narrow neck of the hazardous path and rolled to a stop near the surprised Katzenjammer Twins, who shrugged their mutual shoulders in disdain.

Kurt jerked into action. The instructor, facing the main run, skied towards the battered skiers. Matthew followed, choosing the narrow route. He slammed between the threatening rocks and arrived a moment ahead of Kurt. The crumpled bodies lay entwined in an unlikely embrace.

"You goddamn bastard." David's muffled voice came from the bottom of the pile.

The smothered sound of David's voice packed plenty of force. David couldn't be hurt too badly if anger dominated pain and shock. Matthew exhaled in relief.

The two men unraveled with spastic movements. Franky sat up, wide-eyed and gasping for breath. He looked like a giant cream puff, caked with snow, hat askew, goggles clogged with wet powder.

"You guys all right?" Kurt said, skis off, hovering over them.

"Yeah, I think so," Franky said, his answer meek.

"Not for long," David screamed. "Hey, wise guy. I'm going to pound you back to your New York roots."

David wormed out from under Franky, then pounced on top of him. Franky contracted into a fetal position. David's wild swinging punches, handicapped by the soft snow and thick ski gloves, smacked with limited damage on Franky's padded torso. But a few blows found their way through Franky's turtlelike defenses. One to the face cracked his goggles.

Kurt grabbed David and struggled to pull him off the passive Franky. He needed the leverage of the hill to separate the two. Finally, they released, and Kurt slid with David towards the bottom of Alta One. In the deepening flat light, David slid another twenty feet beyond Kurt.

"You'll pay for this," Franky shrieked with a venomous hiss. "You just sealed your fate, motherfucker."

Kurt, unencumbered by his skis, had popped back to a standing position. He whirled, looking back up at Franky, the instructor's face death-white. He took several awkward steps up the steep slope, both fists clenched.

"You're not talking to me, are you?"

Atta boy, Franky. The little turkey couldn't even keep his threats straight. How did this guy survive in the big city?

FORTY-SIX

Franky made a quick exit from the Steep Class. Where did David get off calling him a "wise guy?" His outrage burned deep and violent. He hated David.

Franky's hands shook with anger. Five attempts to make the key fit into the car-door lock. Boots, skis, and poles thrown into the rental Chevy. He slammed the door and trudged to the pay phone in the lobby of the Alpen Haus.

Franky had waited, felt it necessary to be sure. Gather all the facts. He'd leaned over backwards for that bastard. Enough. "Wise guy" was a mob term if there ever was one. That only added to the pile of evidence against David. If it looked like a skunk, acted like a skunk, and smelled like a skunk, then goddamn it, a skunk it was.

So this was how easy it was to cross the line. David's fate rested firmly in the finger of Franky's dialing hand. One phone call, one meeting, and Franky would achieve success, respect, satisfaction and revenge. Instant gratification. Why had he waited so long, David's guilt so damn obvious?

The Bruise Brothers didn't answer. Typical. When you needed them most, they couldn't be found. Franky finally had a job for them, their specialty. Kill the bastard.

Franky accelerated down the Moose-Wilson highway. Even at the end of a ski day only a few cars and old trucks shared the road. He swerved around a station wagon of skiers, locking his speedometer at a reckless seventy. He no longer enjoyed the absence of traffic. Hell, the noise, chaos, and crazy congestion of New York would be a welcome break from this desolate wilderness.

Wide-open country now bugged him. What did those old Dartmouth fossils call that condition? Agoraphobia? Time to move out of this barren, worthless wasteland. He passed a decrepit pickup on a curve. An oncoming car forced Franky back into their shared lane, almost driving the surprised farmer into the drainage ditch.

He reached the turn to Jackson Hole, made the left and hit seventy again, ignoring the posted 45-mile-per-hour limit. David thought he had it all—money, family, friends, respect, status. Yeah, Franky yearned for those too. But David had achieved them only through slimy, two-faced hypocrisy. And the ultimate irony? David's contribution to Franky's master plan. Not only had dear Dave put Franky's father out of the way, but his discovery and death would strengthen Franky's position in the new order.

First, Franky had to get those lazy, retarded Bruise Brothers on the phone. He tried again on the edge of town, the Amoco station in front of the Blackfoot Garage. Another little irony—order David's hit at his good buddy Wesley's station, a piece of property that David held title to. Still no answer. Franky felt tested.

He parked near the Wort and entered the Silver Dollar. An empty stool awaited him at the bar. Three scotches and three phone calls later Franky decided maybe the lines were out of order. He drove the short distance to the shack, darkness having descended. This should be one of the last times he'd have to go face-to-face with these hicks in their disgusting hole-in-the-wall.

A dim light shone behind the shabby curtains. Franky parked across the street in the deep shadows, ran over the uneven pavement of Hansen Street and up the dirty, snow-covered path to the front door. Those assholes had probably been here the whole time. Franky pounded hard on the door.

"Come in," a muffled voice came from inside.

Franky opened the scarred door and took a step. A huge arm came from behind and crushed his throat; another forearm of steel gripped his body, pining his limbs at his sides. Franky went limp, resistance useless. Before he could question what the hell had happened, powerful hands flung his body into the middle of the room, where he bounced onto the ragged couch.

"Damn, it's just little Franky." John's voice came from the semi-darkness.

"What's goin' on?" Franky's anger lay buried beneath fear and surprise.

"Not too smart, Franky." Hack's rasp came from above him. "You sneak up and bang on the door in the dark again without any warning and we might not be so gentle."

"Sorry, Franky." John's apology sounded sincere for once. Had Giacomo changed the dynamics? "We're getting a little stir-crazy."

"You dumb shits." Franky gathered himself. For the second time today he'd been pushed around. This was getting old. "I called five times. Where the hell you been?"

Neither of the two men answered.

"Well, the waiting's over," Franky said. He felt himself pumping back up as he savored his dominance over life and death. "David's the one. Take him out. Tomorrow after skiing."

"What happened?" John asked. "Why you sure now? We still got nothing on the local supplier."

"It's confirmed," Franky said. His fury with David flared, stoking his confidence. "He's the one."

"Okay, Franky." John's voice turned hard, serious. "We can do it tomorrow. Already got a plan, since he's been the only suspect. It'll be easy. No traffic on Fish Creek Road. We sure know the area. Been scoping out his house for a week, looking for an opportunity to break in. Your buddy Dave's gonna have an accident. End up in the river."

"With a bullet in his head," Hack added.

"Why a bullet?" Franky asked. "Can't you make it look like a car crash. You guys are supposed to be pros."

"Don't you want the proper message to get out?" John's voice had shed all traces of sarcasm or humor. Time for business.

"What do you mean?"

"We were told to make sure everyone knows it's a contract kill," John said. "You fuck with the organization, you pay."

Word did need to get out. Just that much more publicity for the prodigal son. Perfect.

"I want to put the bullet in that dick's head," Franky said.

His participation was out of the question. But the demand for vengeance sounded good out loud.

"No way," Hack said. "Don't be stupid. You got to stay clean, remember. If anything, you need a solid alibi. No one knows about John and me."

"You hope."

"We're sure," John said. "Unless someone's been following you and seen us."

"What about all the real estate you guys checked out?" Franky prodded. "Some agent'll remember two weirdoes like you."

"Naw," Hack said. "We did most of our business going through records at the Court House. Met a couple of clerks. Didn't do much talking with them."

"We'll see," Franky said. "What's your plan?"

"There's a good spot," John said, "a sharp curve where the river and the road are only a few feet apart. About a half mile from his house. Your class ends around 3:30, right? We saw David get home around 4:15 this afternoon."

"Yeah, I thought so," Franky spat out. "That stuck-up snob always heads home right away. Too good to drink with his classmates."

"After we do the job," John said, "we'll all get the hell outta Dodge."

"I can't leave until the class is over."

"Bullshit." Hack's voice picked up some energy. "We could be a hundred miles south of Jackson Hole by the time they pull his car out of the water."

"Go ahead and split," Franky offered. "Too many people know David's on my shit list." He wouldn't share today's humiliation at the bottom of Alta One. "If I leave unexpectedly, I'd become a prime suspect. Especially with a slug in his head, rather than appearing to be an accident."

"He's right," John said.

"But we can't leave until Franky does," Hack whined. "You know our orders."

"From now on we don't meet, don't talk. Franky, you don't know we exist." John's attitude had changed. He had become professional—tight, sharp, cold. "We'll be on the move after tomorrow. In an emergency—and it better be an emergency—call this number in Denver, 303-555-2669. Memorize it. Say 'I want an appointment,' period. Stay put at the Wort until you hear from us. We'll check in every two or three hours."

"Congratulations, Franky," Hack added, "you're gonna be a hero."

* * *

Sarah floated between the sheets of her bed in the Wort Hotel. A warm, sensual glow suffused her body from the rewarding combination of a successful first day in the Steep Class, two ice-cold beers at the Mangy Moose, and a long, hot bath. And still no good reason to return to her old life in Chicago. Tomorrow after class David would provide some direction.

How had she been so passive in the acceptance of her situation back home? She paid a high price for the security of a neurotic mother and shallow friendships. These now difficult-to-justify factors had chained her to an existence of minimal rewards. Inertia had sucked her into a comfort zone with no real comfort.

She pulled the blankets up to her chin. The queen-size bed floated in the oversized, threadbare room. The vast space in room 227 of the Wort Hotel, furnished with minimal furniture, created insecurity rather than any sense of spatial luxury. Too big and impersonal.

Her thoughts shifted to Chicago men. Her hands drifted under the covers, rubbing light circles on her hard, flat stomach. She deliberately avoided the embarrassing ridges of her rib cage, the least attractive part of what she had learned to be a sensual and serviceable body.

Her view of her assets had been supported by a pathetic parade of lonely losers, leftovers, and castoffs slightly more acceptable than Irving Knudsen only because they were polite and begged first. Sadly, the irregular stream of boys reminded her more of a collection of dance-card rejects than legitimate romances.

Were the men of Wyoming that different from the pale, pathetic selection in Chicago? Or was Sarah a different woman in the wide-open West where she could start fresh? The unquestioned advantage of being a valuable natural resource in short supply helped. Or was it a combination of all of the above?

Matthew's scarred face materialized before her eyes. Her hands rose, cupping small but full, firm breasts. Her large nipples hardened in anticipation of her finger's next destination. Why was he the only one resistant to her charms? What would it take to attract his attention?

Their disastrous exchange after Jim's funeral had at least shown promising intellectual depth and deep emotion missing in the visceral exchanges with her other eager subjects. She'd seen in him warmth and perhaps kindness. But he had also exploded into deadly violence at the Cowboy Bar. People were careful around Matthew.

Why, with the unlimited choices around her, did his resistance even matter? Why did she feel something missing? Her vacation into uninhibited sexual delights had taken a disturbing and unwelcome turn. His face kept showing up in strange and inconvenient places, at surprising and weird times. No desirable partner in three days. Matthew's presence had spoiled the purity and simplicity of her sexual desires.

Her fingers stroked the fine hair between her legs. Had she felt a softening in Matthew's attitude towards her at the beginning of the Steep Class? Perhaps he had been too drunk and stoned to remember their argument at the Stagecoach. She wished they had been in the same group in class, but she could focus better on skiing without him. Hans handled her with European grace. And the nine male students all showed varying degrees of interest. Also no Franky to bug her.

Changes vibrated throughout her. The wetness her fingers discovered spoke of her desire. She glanced out the window. Drifting snowflakes flickered in the streetlights. She tried to swallow her doubts, fire up her fading confidence. Well, no better time to capture Matthew's undivided attention than this evening.

FORTY-SEVEN

Matthew hesitated before entering the Cowboy Bar. Here we go again. Wesley had talked Matthew into showing up tonight. Probably another matchmaking venture with Sarah. At least this time he was up for it.

Matthew worked his way towards the Cowboy's main bar and its awkward saddle stools. His eyes adjusted to the semidarkness. Folklore held that the artwork behind the three separate bars had been a traveling artist's payoff of gambling debts from the Cowboy's wild and woolly past. Then he saw the back of the person he least wanted to meet.

Franky hung on to a saddle a third of the way down the long counter. He squirmed around towards Matthew, almost sliding to the floor. He used both hands to right himself on the saddle, looking lucky not to be thrown off. His short, stubby legs thrashed a full foot from the floor. His feet, encased in cute, fuzzy little after-ski boots, looked like raccoons had swallowed them up to his ankles.

No way Matthew would put up with that nasty little shit. He was out of there. The hell with Wesley. He wheeled in retreat.

"Hey, Matt," the short man slurred. "Get your butt over here so I can buy ya a drink."

Too late, and no one called him Matt. But next to Franky was the Chicago Princess. Oh, well. She had her back to Franky, holding court with a semicircle of five hungry, large wranglers. They ignored the obnoxious city slicker.

Matthew squeezed between Franky and the adjacent empty saddle to the bar. Maybe he could facilitate the punk's progress to the floor. He ordered a beer and pushed up against the loud mouth. But Franky hung on, his expression reflecting gratitude at having someone to talk to.

Matthew saw Sarah's watchful eyes in the mirror of the bar. Was she attempting to attract his attention? A smile crept across his lips, his expression startling when he saw his image reflected in the glass behind the neatly stacked bottles. Sarah winked once. He realized how happy he was to see her, encouraged that she snubbed Franky.

The local cowboys treated her with the utmost respect. Sarah, gracious as always, directed her large, luminous eyes and distinguished nose from subject to subject, smiling, nodding, and laughing in her loud, unladylike fashion. She always projected kindness, good humor, and consideration towards each and every suitor, no matter how lonely or pathetic their approach. Franky seemed to be the exception. She continued to ignore his struggle to look cool and stay upright in the saddle.

"What the hell's wrong with that chick?" Franky whined a little too loud as his head jerked in Sarah's direction. Even that minor motion forced him into a death struggle to stay seated on the slippery saddle. "She's the horniest broad in Wyoming, and I proved I could satisfy her. Man, she's lucky I even give a shit."

The evident animosity between Franky and Sarah was a pleasant surprise. The image of Sarah physically touching Franky had unsettled Matthew. Now, she gave a cold shoulder to Franky and his inflammatory comments. Maybe Franky's slurred remarks were sour grapes.

"She just keeps dicking around with these dumb-ass cowboys when I could screw her into ecstasy for the next week."

Matthew backed out of the tight space next to Franky and put an empty saddle between Franky and himself. Franky was so predictable— too loud, too drunk and, more important, totally lacking in common sense and basic concern for his own well-being. Couldn't Franky see the locals' interest had shifted from Sarah to the big-mouthed fool?

Perhaps Matthew should offer a little advice and warning. But why waste his time? Franky knew everything. Just ask him. Besides, the worst that could happen would be for the local gentlemen to beat the crap out of Franky. That could also be the best that could happen.

"These sex-starved local yokels would probably come before their cocks cleared their zippers," Franky continued. "They catch the clap and crabs on purpose for an excuse to play with themselves."

The closest cowboy threw a slow-motion roundhouse right. He caught Franky in the back of the head. The punch threw Franky forward into the bar, jerking him off his mount. His chest crunched on the edge of the bar top, interrupting his slide to the hardwood floor. Matthew remained motionless until the cowboy moved over to the crumpled Franky and drew his boot back for an additional punctuation of his displeasure.

"Hold it."

Matthew's voice stopped the foot in midair. The man paused on one narrow-heeled cowboy boot and appraised Matthew. The lanky wrangler perhaps remembered the story of a previous evening and stepped back, uncocking his leg. Matthew gave the tipsy cowboy credit for good balance.

"Thank you," Matthew said. "I know he's an asshole."

Matthew enjoyed and expected the cowboy's response. He felt more like a voyeur, not sensing any real danger. Still, his alarm system ratcheted up to medium-low. The mild flow of energy felt good.

Matthew turned to Sarah. An unmistakable flush colored her cheeks; her ample mouth was slightly open, the tip of her tongue visible, her eyes locked on Matthew. Then Franky was standing against the brass-trimmed rail with a snub-nosed .38 in his shaking hand. The little man's malevolent eyes added a degree of menace inconsistent with his twitching hand. Matthew surged to full alert. Franky had finally become the center of attention.

On cue Wesley sauntered up. "Anything happenin'?"

"Nothing yet," Matthew said. "But nice of you to come around. You're just in time to see the conclusion of Franky at the OK Corral."

The locals spread out in a large circle. None seemed too frightened. Franky's inability to keep the pistol steady had something to do with it. But Matthew was nervous, worried Franky might shoot somebody by accident.

"Franky," Wesley said, "the big, bad bouncer's on his way over here. Even in Wyoming, they throw you in jail for pullin' a gun in a bar."

Wesley eased up to Franky as he spoke. In a smooth quick motion, he grabbed the gun out of his hand. The startled New Yorker looked like someone had pulled down his pants.

"You're not doin' too good in the Cowboy Bar. How'd you think ya'd do in a cowboy jail? Scary thought, ain't it?" Wesley moved into the group of locals and handed the pistol to Sarah. "Hide it, honey. They don't frisk ladies in this part of the country."

Franky, in a rare intelligent move, used Wesley as a blocker, slid behind him, bumped off the approaching Burleson the Bouncer, and bolted for the door. Five big cowboys peeled out after him. Franky had a twenty-foot lead when he crashed through the double doors, knocking down two surprised patrons.

Matthew, with Wesley and Sarah right behind, scrambled towards the entrance. Matthew didn't want to miss this act. He followed the irate posse out the door onto the frozen street. Franky disappeared through one of the antler arches into the square, with five figures stumbling and sliding after him.

At least Franky's raccoon boots had ribbed rubber soles, giving him more traction than the boys in their leather-soled, high-heeled cowboy boots. Fear was also an excellent motivator. Franky'd need every advantage he could dig up. The men of Jackson Hole might not be too quick on the ice, but they wouldn't give up without a hell of an effort.

"They'll back off if he makes it to the Elk Refuge," Wesley said. "Get too much elk shit on their boots. Sorry I missed the early action, buddy." Wesley put his arm on Matthew's shoulders. "Let's go back inside. It's chilly out here. At least ten below."

Back at the bar, Matthew found himself face to face with the Princess. Sarah and Wesley mounted up on saddles, squeezing Matthew in the middle without quite enough space to avoid contact with at least one of the two surrounding bodies. Easy choice to lean against the Princess.

"What do you think is going to happen to the jerk?" Sarah asked, not sounding too concerned. "And what am I supposed to do with this gun in my parka?"

"I don't think any of us give a damn about Franky," Matthew said. "And you can give me the gun."

Sarah pulled the pistol out of her pocket, keeping her hand below the top of the saddle. She pressed it butt-first into Matthew's side. He reached down to take the .38 from her. She grabbed his hand.

"What are you going to do with it?" she asked.

"Keep the bullets. I can use them. Wipe the gun clean and drop it in the Snake on my way home."

"What do you want the bullets for?" she asked, her eyes inches from Matthew's.

"He oughta stick 'em up Franky's ass tomorrow in class." Wesley smiled. "Assumin' the boys don't string him up first."

FORTY-EIGHT

Loud voices and the banging of heavy front doors announced the return of the five swaggering buckaroos. They strutted their way over to Sarah. They again formed a respectful semicircle around the Princess. Body language, smiling red faces, and bloodshot eyes filled with laughter advertised the cowboys' cocky smugness.

"Well?" Wesley asked. "Where'd you leave the little dick-head?"

They ignored him, homing back on the Princess. Matthew sensed Wesley's displeasure with the lack of respect. Matthew had difficulty turning around, and as he did, Sarah wedged her knee into his crotch. But she too had to twist around to face her subjects, relinquishing her intimate position.

"Tell us what happened," she demanded with that smile the boys proved they would fight for.

Matthew did not appreciate the return of competition. But Sarah had to be a little turned off by the not too pretty sight and sound of a cowboy giggling, let alone five of them.

"Last we saw him," one said, "he was out east of Silver King, past the park. The little turkey could really run in those faggot booties. We heard the dogs. Sounded like they was real interested."

"What dogs?" Sarah asked.

Even Matthew knew what dogs. A wave of uneasiness passed through him.

"You know, the Jackson dogs," the largest of the cowboys said. "There's more dogs than people in this town. They lie in the streets blockin' traffic, bitin' people. Nasty things run down small dogs and cats."

"Real problem's when they run in packs at night," Wesley said. "Go from nuisances to threats. 'Specially to wild animals. When hungry wildlife grazes closer to town in the winter, the packs attack. They drive those poor animals into the deep snowbanks where it's easy to rip 'em to pieces. In January alone over twenty deer been found dead or dyin' on the outskirts of town."

"Not even three weeks ago," the large cowboy said. "A nasty pack nailed a young boy and his sister out walking their little terrier. Killed the mutt while he was still on the leash. Kids screamed and kicked at the pack, then one big dog jumped the boy. Only thing saved his ass was a passing farmer. Kid's got nerve damage, but he's alive."

"You think that city slicker's afraid of dogs?" A note of concern registered in Wesley's question.

"Hope so," the cowboy said, a smirk on his face. "Found another mutilated yearling couple of mornings ago close to where we chased that little prick."

"Don't tell me you care, Wesley?" Matthew said. "That pain in the ass is a dog."

"Yeah, but, Matthew, it's bad publicity for Jackson Hole if tourists start gettin' eaten by dogs. People already think the damn mountain's too steep, too cold and too hard to get to, accordin' to Pepi."

"With all due respect," one of the locals said, not sounding too respectful, "screw the tourists, especially the skiers. Ma'am, you and Wesley's buddy here might be the two exceptions."

"Gee, thanks." Sarah nodded at Wesley and Matthew. "We need to help Franky."

Matthew couldn't come up with any reason why he should leave the comfortable bar and stomp through the freezing evening. Did Sarah still care about Franky?

"Let's go before it's too late." Sarah pushed her way off the saddle and through the cowboys.

"I guess we can check it out," Wesley said. "I wouldn't feel right if those poor dogs came down with distemper chewing on old Franky."

Matthew realized there was a good reason to follow Sarah—he got her, and the Wyoming boys got dumped. He shrugged back into his parka and killed the last remnants of his beer.

"It's some kind a poetic justice," Wesley said as he headed towards the door. "You got Franky's little popgun, so you can shoot that boy if he's hasslin' the animals. We'll take my truck. It's right outside, and my buddy Matthew would rather be in it than followin' it."

Matthew flipped the bird to Wesley's lean back.

* * *

Franky's frantic cries could be heard amid vicious barks, snarls, and growls. The sounds echoed across a dark meadow. Matthew followed the uneven footprints for close to one hundred yards. Wesley had his truck gun, an old but well-oiled shotgun, to go with Franky's .38.

"Hey, Franky," Wesley called out.

"Help me!" Franky's hoarse scream emerged from a thicket of aspen not far away. "Please help me!"

"From the sound of those hounds, they're havin' a great time. Don't hurt them poor dogs, Franky. We're a-comin'." Wesley's voice excited the dogs even more. "Them mutts are thinkin' it's about time they got rewarded for cornerin' that weird little animal."

Franky stood in a clearing backed up against a clump of thick bushes, knee-deep in a snowbank, wearily swinging a four-foot branch. A group of eight or nine of Jackson's snapping residents surrounded him.

A giant dark Lab broke out of the circle and lunged towards Matthew. Wesley fired off a round in the air. The Lab stopped, but the pack continued unfazed.

"These are goddamn huntin' dogs, Matthew. They're all used to gunfire. They probably think they dun a good job. Let's charge 'em screamin'. I'll hang on to my second shot, but, Matthew, you pop a few rounds in the ground near 'um. Honey, you just scream like you're havin' some great lovin', and we'll go in together."

Matthew led the disorganized charge, screaming and shooting. Not much of an attempted rescue, rather a slow-motion stumble in the deep snow. It worked though. The dogs took off, howling good-bye.

Franky sunk into the snow. He'd been outside over thirty minutes without his coat. He had to be on empty.

"Come on, Franky," Wesley said. "You're safe now, boy. Follow us. We got my truck over yonder."

Franky was done moving for a while. Matthew and Wesley grabbed his shoulders and began the long haul back to the pickup. Sarah broke trail a little. But with Franky near comatose, the trip took some time. Then Wesley drove to the Wort Hotel.

"Let's dump him here in the lobby," Wesley said, looking worn out from their adventure on the edge of town.

"No, no, you can't do that." An agitated cry emerged from the mousey little hotel clerk behind the reception desk. "Here's his key. Please don't leave him here."

"What's the problem, boy?" Wesley argued. "He ain't dead, just a bit numb."

The nervous clerk scuttled from behind the counter and led them up to Franky's room. Wesley and Matthew threw Franky onto the mattress—a little too roughly. The frozen figure rolled off the other side of the bed, hitting the floor.

"I'll take these dead raccoons off his feet," Wesley said. "Then I think we've earned a drink."

Wesley jerked off Franky's booties, then wiped his wet hands on his pants.

"Help me get some blankets on him," Sarah said, ripping bedspread, blankets and sheets off the bed.

"Mother Sarah." Wesley laughed. "Always helpin' out the lonely losers."

Matthew didn't appreciate the humor.

FORTY-NINE

Sarah excused herself at the door to her room. She was in dire need of a detour.

"I'll meet you in the bar," she said, flashing Matthew what she hoped was an enigmatic smile. Keep all her options open.

Inside, she hurried across the wide expanse of her empty room to the bathroom. The drinks, nervous excitement, late-night exercise, and cold temperatures demanded a pee stop. She also felt relief. Saving Franky had taken care of any remote guilt or obligation. He had dug his own grave.

The mirror reflected a pleasant surprise. She turned her head, made a few silly faces, licked her lips and ended up in the same place—she'd never looked better.

"Mirror, mirror on the wall, is this really me? Let's check this out again. I'm looking like a hot item."

Her complexion had been sanded clean by days of sun, wind, and physical exertion. Not a zit in sight. Her eyes, which should have evidenced the fatigue of late nights and early mornings on the mountain, shone clear and bright. Hazel sparks highlighted the dominant dark brown, bringing additional life to her finest feature.

Ignore the nose and too long chin. Her wide mouth, aided by an application of lip gloss, looked dangerous, sensual—or ridiculously large. She shook her head, a useless entreaty for added body in her fine brown hair. She'd started the evening with the hint of a wave. Sarah's locks now hung straight to her shoulders. But tonight even her mousy mane threw off an added luster.

She brushed her teeth—god, if she could only get close enough for

Matthew to notice. Well, this was as good as it got. Take it or leave it. She crossed the fingers of her right hand as she opened the door. Before it closed, she doubled down, crossing the fingers of her left. You never knew.

* * *

The Silver Dollar had quieted down by the time Sarah entered. Ten o'clock on a Monday evening, half the stools and tables sat empty. She made her way to the bar where Wesley and Matthew huddled in conversation. She ordered her third vodka martini on the rocks. The confidence experienced in her room had fled by the time she reached the stool. Then Sarah's attention focused on Matthew, whose serious expression evolved into a question.

"What's that little putz doing with a loaded pistol?" Matthew asked.

"You think," Wesley said, "there might be more to our good buddy Franky than meets the eye?"

"And meets the ear," Sarah added. "He's smarter than he sounds or acts and maybe nastier. But I think he's just insecure."

Matthew pulled out Franky's confiscated .38. He inspected the weapon, running his fingers over the blue steel surface. The scar on his forehead became more defined as his features tightened. Sarah watched his mild curiosity condense into perplexed concern.

Desire and anxiety kept her shifting on the barstool. She longed for an opening—something leading to romance. She no longer gave a damn about Franky.

"I'll be a son of bitch," Matthew said. "The serial number's been filed off. Strange that Franky's carrying. A scarier thought, why is it clean?"

"Well," Wesley offered, "aren't all short, greasy, loud-mouthed Italians from New York gangsters?"

"Wesley," Sarah said, "that comment's beneath you."

"Yeah," Matthew agreed. "Pretty judgmental for a half-breed. But Franky's packing. Been here for around three weeks. Seems to have plenty of money. Here for at least another week if he plans to finish the Steep Class."

"He'll stay," Sarah said. "We wouldn't be so fortunate."

"If he's a member of the Mafia," Wesley said, "they just lost much of their murderous mystique."

"Unless he's acting dumb and obnoxious for some reason," Matthew said.

Sarah watched every movement of Matthew's face. Cool outward composure couldn't cover the subtle play of emotions below the surface. In the pink-and-lime fluorescent light, he looked younger, but he certainly didn't look vulnerable. A tenseness gripped her stomach. An aching need tested her patience and control.

"Well, we'll give ole Franky a little more consideration," Wesley said. "I'll be back in a minute."

Sarah smiled at Wesley's obvious exit. She felt light-headed, stripped of artifice by the events of the day. Hope soared as she recognized desire in Matthew's eyes locked on her.

"You look great," he said.

The words escaping Matthew's lips seemed to surprise him. Sarah felt equally overwhelmed. She made a slight tilt towards the large mirror behind the bar. Her flushed face, already alive and vibrant, took on an aura of joy that embarrassed Sarah with its transparency. He must notice the hunger and emotion she now radiated.

She placed her hand on Matthew's knee. He covered it with his own. An array of expressions—excitement, pain, longing, bewilderment—flooded his face. What incredible experiences would she have to live through to project such a kaleidoscope of feelings? Her senses surged. A charged shock jolted her thoughts into words.

"Matthew, let's go up to my room."

This time Matthew's face flushed, not easy, considering his deep copper tan. His controlled demeanor crumbled into confusion. Sarah was astonished at the transformation. But sensual currents flowed between them, and Matthew seemed to respond with passion, matching Sarah's anticipation.

"Sarah, you don't really know me," Matthew said.

"Yes, I do," she whispered, afraid another aggressive move might turn him off. "I can feel you. Your strength. Your power. Your goodness."

"Two out of three ain't bad." The birth of a smile shaped his features into softer lines.

Now or never.

Sarah slid off the stool. Her hand rotated under his grasp, capturing his wrist. Her heart pounded. Could he hear its loud thuds swelling in her ears? She drew him off his stool, pulling him towards the hotel lobby. Matthew's resistance felt feeble as she led him through the deserted hotel, gliding up the stairs.

They entered her large spartan room. At the foot of her queen-size bed she turned him around. Embraced him. Their lips met, hers hungry, his tentative. She held a marble statue. Matthew's upper body was almost too hard and muscular, lacking a warm, soft connection to reality.

They kissed again. Better. She forced her tongue against his teeth. Her kiss was answered, his outer shell dissolving. She paused for air, breaking the newly formed seal of their lips, snapping the spell. Mistake. Matthew stepped back, wedged against the bed. What was he thinking? Sarah didn't move. Trembling, she watched his face settle into an expression of confused self-consciousness.

"Ever make love to an alligator?" he stammered.

"What?" Sarah answered in an equally disjointed voice. "A few pigs, but no alligators. What are you talking about?"

"I've got some pretty gross souvenirs from Viet Nam."

A disconcerting thought swept Sarah. Finally, the man of my dreams—and he's impotent.

"Can you make love?"

"Probably, if you're still interested after checking out the damage."

"Take your shirt off."

Shirts would have been more appropriate. Matthew, with awkward movements, unbuttoned his flannel shirt. He took off his long-sleeved t-shirt. Then, like a nervous stripper on her first night, pulled off his long underwear top.

A red ridged, thick scar wrapped its ugly fingers around his left side below the rib cage. He twisted his upper body, exposing the burnt scar tissue branding the back of his shoulder. Puckered, pinkish-red flesh covered a large quadrant of his rock-hard torso. Matthew turned to face her. She saw anger—a challenge—in his dark eyes. What happened to the momentary vulnerability that had melted her heart?

"You look like an ancient Greek god." Sarah's words came out chant like. "After a terrible battle."

Matthew said nothing, just stared hard at Sarah. The layered muscles of his arms and shoulders tightened, creating even more definition.

Sarah's fumbling hands ripped at her clothes. Buttons popped. Zippers tore. And then there was nothing for her twitching fingers to do. She stood naked, exposed.

She prayed for any positive response from the specter before her. Her eyes swept the length of his body, pausing at the top of his pants. She saw no obvious bulge. Was he incapable of consummating the act she hungered for? She shook, committed, but unsure of the next step.

"Please," she whispered, meeting his troubled gaze.

No other word. How could her throat be so dry when moist passion coursed through her body?

Matthew sat on the end of the bed. Removed his boots, his Levi's, and, as his long johns appeared, so did evidence of his arousal. Sarah sighed. He removed his underwear, his hard cock framed by more cruel damage to his left thigh.

She stepped forward, closing the distance between them. The momentum forced Matthew backwards onto the bed. Sarah kissed him, all lips and tongue, while fingering the ravaged skin on his back. She still sensed restraint, but his arms encircled her, welcoming her into his private, protected space.

Sarah wanted a total, unquestioned response from Matthew. No holding back. No doubts. Overpower whatever inhibitions he had, physical and spiritual. She slid down, kissing and sucking his hot flesh. Her lips paused at the scars on his side, licking the ridges, accepting his imperfections.

She arrived at his erection, fondling, caressing. Her mouth massaged the stiff organ until she felt tightness, an explosion imminent. She lifted her head. Hands under her armpits effortlessly brought her back up to his level gaze. His hands, palms calloused, fingers gentle, traced the line of her jaw to her red, swollen lips. A veil lifted from his eyes, for the first time exposing pure pleasure. For all his strength, his touch was tentative. What an incredible contradiction.

Matthew rolled over on top of her. His gentleness, accented by the tremor in his fingers, transmitted through his shaking hands. He began his own passage of exploration over her body. She closed her eyes, moaned as he reached her breasts, nipples, flat, tight stomach, and then her thighs. She felt his growing excitement, his kisses and licks less smooth and controlled, more electric. Her first climactic orgasm shook her as his mouth reached the exposed gash of her inner lips. A loud, deep, primitive cry erupted from her.

Matthew hesitated. Sarah grabbed his head in both hands, yanked him towards her, jerking their bodies fully onto the bed. They swayed from side to side. Sarah poured herself over his body, liquid, molding to him. She pressed and arched herself to connect with as much skin as possible, enflamed by the transition from smooth, solid muscle to jagged, ridged scar tissue.

He fought to enter her. Succeeded. And Sarah soared from the Wort Hotel, Wyoming, the West, the gravity of earth, never to return to the old world.

* * *

Something besides the bone-chilling cold and dense, moisture-laden air inhabited the impenetrable tule fog, as it crept from Matthew's knees to his waist. A solid force chaining his feet to the ground. He couldn't find the courage to reach down, identify the source. Jungles, rice paddies and rolling, forested hills swirled before his eyes. No order. No continuity.

Then faces appeared. Passive portraits. Soldiers. Villagers. VC. The pictures drifted in and out of the landscape, hovering above the freezing ground fog. No one recognizable. The Vietnamese all looked the same. So did the American soldiers. Nothing really disturbing, except for the ominous anchoring of his legs within the opaque gray, groundcover. But Matthew understood an unidentifiable evil lurked below the layer of fog. This temporary calm was no preview of what lay in store for him. He knew. He'd been here before.

The foul presence had a name. If Matthew could only discover the name, he felt sure he could fight back. His horror mounted, despite the awareness he must be buried deep in a dream.

Expressions now appeared, painted on the portraits. Still-lifes, reflecting moments of sadness. Now despair. And Matthew waited for the unavoidable transformation into pain and terror. Predictable as the original peacefulness proved preposterous. The images gained movement. The faces contorted, raw wounds, slashes, ruptured skin wasted the sound-less features. The need to move grew, but Matthew couldn't even shift his weight.

Sounds. First distant. Then closer. Soon cries of anguish and anger rose from the lips of the disembodied heads. The volume increased, Matthew's ears ringing with pain. The terrifying masks drifted closer. Fear ratcheted higher and higher. An unseen monster snatched the heads down towards the dark fog at his feet.

Now Matthew recognized the faces rushing into the void. First, fellow fallen warriors—Tiger, Sleepy, Jet, Red, Bull. And now Jim? Matthew watched in growing anguish as his companions' images exploded. Their remains settled into the soulless fog. Innocents and enemies, eyes stamped with pain and suffering, followed in remorseless procession. Matthew cried in frustration and impotence.

Matthew knew he was trapped in a nightmare. Safe, if such a condition existed. But the knowledge brought no comfort. His sensations of pain, physical, mental or spiritual, couldn't be more real. Heat intensified around his exposed upper body, the fierce temperatures exaggerated by the contrast of the numbing chill of the tule fog. The hidden evil crushed his legs, sent vibrations to his frantic, desperate mind. A message. "You know me. Let me in or you will die."

"No. I don't know you."

Matthew's scream filled the room; echoes resonated as he jerked up from the bed. He saw Sarah next to him. Crouched on all fours. Trembling. Concern filled her huge, wide eyes.

"My God, Matthew. Was that a nightmare?" Her cool, tentative hand reached out and stroked his heaving shoulders, slick with sweat. "You've had these before?"

Matthew waited, willing his breathing back to regularity. The presence of dark forces faded. Minutes passed. The monstrous images hovered near their perpetual perch in the back rows of his consciousness.

"Almost every night." He could hear his voice reflect the complexities of his emotions—apology, embarrassment, even a tinge of sarcasm. "Hope you're not a light sleeper."

"You all right now?" Sarah looked so pure, innocent, naïve.

"Not a simple question. I told you earlier. You don't know me."

He had to move on. Shake off the terror. Find distractions. He turned to Sarah, the night's earlier delights pulling him back towards her, flushing the nightmare. Remembered sensations hardened into sexual desire, filling corners and crevices. He reached for her. She pulled him down beside her.

He stroked her slender body. Skin smooth and comforting to the touch. Nipples erect. His hand discovered additional life. He escaped into the demands of his body and the healing emotion of desire. He made love to her. The actual phrase "made love" emerged from deep in his chest—his heart? Their physical actions, slow and languorous, a far cry from earlier thrashing inflamed by desperate passion. They melded together, rhythmically rocking into mutual satisfaction and a slow-motion climax.

Matthew held her, Sarah's head on his chest. Soft sighs slipped from her lips. Her hands traced tender paths over the ridged damage of his satiated body.

"Do you need anything else?" Sarah asked.

Matthew felt her mouth moving on his skin. Light kisses surrounded her words, a question requiring no answer.

Matthew drifted back to his father's advice: "Find a woman who makes you stronger, not one of those conceited beauties that suck you dry." Sarah was a giver, not a taker. Who cared about the bullshit rumors or her previous escapades?

As wonderful and comforting though the moment felt, the nightmares had made their usual appearance like a bullet tearing through tissue. No simple fix for his sins. The more he thought, the brief flash of security succumbed to doubt. One night with the Princess of One-Night Stands had to be put in perspective. And how would she treat him if she knew the things he had done.

"I've got to get back to the Grand View."

"I don't know why you can't spend the rest of the night. It's already 2:30," Sarah said. "But whatever you need to do, Matthew."

"I'll see you in class tomorrow," he said.

His insecurity depressed him. He dressed, sat back down on the edge of the bed next to Sarah. Her lingering kiss and Mona Lisa smile almost sucked him right back into bed, but his past chased him out of her room.

"Thank you," he murmured.

FIFTY

Franky opened swollen eyes to a world turned upside down. Most of his discomfort could be attributed to a splitting hangover and the fact that he lay on the imitation carpet of the Wort Hotel. Slowly Franky pieced together the series of events that had left him a wreck on the floor of his hotel room. The memory of those pieces was not pleasant.

Trapped by the fucking dogs. Chased by a bunch of yahoos. Humiliated by that asshole half-breed Wesley. Snubbed by that bitch Sarah. Pushed around by the Bruise Brothers. Beaten by that dick David. And with the thought of dear Dave, the first positive ember of the day registered in his damaged psyche. Not much he could do right now about the rest of his tormentors, but David was history.

He struggled off the ground, dragging his blankets back onto the bed. The movement stimulated a new wave of nausea. He wrapped the bed coverings around his trembling body. He had forgotten to include Matthew in the list of the damned. He'd seen the winks and smiles exchanged between Scarface and Sarah.

Matthew was the reason he'd been discarded by that skinny bitch. How could he take all of those assholes down with David? Get the Bruise Brothers to blow up the Tram with all those pricks in it? Then deal with the hit men when he returned to New York. The fantasy brought some comfort. No dream sequence required for David. The real thing waited for him this afternoon on Fish Creek Road.

With David's death, Franky could return to building the family business into a powerful conglomerate. And if the last conversation with Sal was for real, he wouldn't have to put up with his brothers' bullshit anymore. Unless Giacomo was only halfway through whatever convoluted manipulations he was planning. But every scenario required business expertise, didn't it? No one else could run the businesses like Franky. Could they? So many unknowns. So little control.

Well, let's take one step at a time. Get up. Somehow overcome this monstrous hangover, the aches and pains, and the bruised ego. Maybe force down breakfast with a Bloody Mary. He had to get to the Steep Class. He needed an alibi.

*   *   *

Second day of class. Emphasis on steep technique. Body position. Edge control. Platform building. Little actual skiing. By noon Matthew wanted out. Only his promise to David kept him around for the afternoon session. That and lunch with Sarah.

Nervous anticipation. She had shown up late, just catching up to the class for the first tram run of the day. A smile, bright below her goggles, had warmed the chill air surrounding the two. Then the classmates split up at the top of Rendezvous Bowl, Matthew with Kurt, Sarah following Hans.

Sarah had time only to touch Matthew's arm as they hurried to gear up. Not much of an exchange to gauge their new relationship. Then Matthew had been forced to wait around all morning. He definitely felt uncomfortable, ambiguous. Losing his grip on independence and control—two prized possessions. He didn't like the feeling of vulnerability, the new, even partial dependency on someone else.

But his unequivocal desire for Sarah had changed the equation. Harder to protect himself. Was it worth it? More depth of feeling, a physical hunger that could thankfully be satisfied. Hell, he looked forward to the fact that he could perform. Sarah's acceptance of his damaged body lifted a dense layer of self-consciousness. Opened up the possibility of living a normal life, whatever normal meant.

The minute Sarah saw Matthew in the Moose at the break, she excused herself from her admirers. Matthew's confidence soared. He enjoyed the disappointment of Sarah's fan club. He relaxed, savoring the replay of the sensual memories of last night, now, hopefully, a preview of this evening. Sarah locked in on him, promising him a second evening—and more. They broke for class, and the afternoon session felt like a three-and-a-half-hour root canal appointment without Novocain.

Matthew kept a curious and suspicious eye on Franky, who maintained a consistent distance from David. The New York irritant never said a word to Matthew, just lay low. Surprising. Certainly out of character. His minimal interaction with his other classmates upset no one. But the clean .38 opened the door to a multitude of questions.

"You sticking around to have a beer?" David asked as he and Matthew gathered their ski equipment on the cafeteria deck at the end of the day.

"No," Matthew said. "Just waiting for Sarah. Want to check in with her before I work out. Mighty slow on the mountain today."

"Not for me," David said. "I've got to admit, I'm still learning even after all those hours with Kurt the last two years."

"You should buy him a drink of gratitude. Buy one for Sarah too. Keep her from the competition." Matthew made the statement sound light. He still wasn't sure of the depth of Sarah's feelings.

"Can't," David replied. "I really shouldn't even be skiing today. Something I've been working on for a long time is about to pop. Very important. And I forgot I promised to take Sarah home this afternoon for some career counseling."

"Anything I can help you with?" Matthew asked.

"Yes. Tell her I'll reschedule soon as I can." David smiled a weird grin, or maybe the look resulted from the misshapen configuration of his features. "I need to get home. Damn glad it's being resolved. You know, there's a lot of things you don't know about me."

That statement caught Matthew off guard. A curious glance at David confirmed his friend's seriousness. An air of confidence colored the expression on his strange face.

"Need new gloves, though," David said. "I'm going home soon as I pick out a pair at Teton Sports. See you tomorrow."

Matthew watched the incongruous figure of David clomp away, dressed in a new, stylish $200 outfit with shredded gloves and beat-up boots. What event could be so important to David?

Sarah finally appeared, sweeping down the flats, chased by her pack of hungry hounds. Jealousy surged within Matthew again but dissipated when Sarah, in a series of smooth motions, released her bindings and safety straps, dropped her poles, and took two steps onto the deck and into Matthew's arms. Her offered lips demanded immediate response. Matthew was happy to oblige.

"Let's head to bed," she whispered into his ear. No embarrassment evident, only transparent desire.

"Don't you have an appointment with David?"

"Damn." Sarah pulled away from their embrace. "I completely forgot, thanks to you."

"Well, he can't make it anyway," Matthew said. "He's caught up in some big deal. Look, I've got to work out."

"I'll give you a work out," she said.

"No. This class is too slow. I've got to maintain my program. Believe me, you'll enjoy my company much more if I do at least a short routine."

"You're a sick boy," she said, her surprise and displeasure evident.

"Look," Matthew said, "give your deprived classmates a break. Let them buy you a drink. I'll meet you at the Wort in two hours."

"What if one of my horny classmates sweeps me away?"

"You'd be responsible for his demise."

He wasn't serious about the comment, but her eyes opened wider, lips parted. Matthew grew uncomfortable with the strange effect his words had on Sarah.

"That's the nicest thing anyone's ever said to me," she murmured, her body again pressed against him.

He pried himself loose, walked to the parking lot, and jumped into his Jeep. The abused old Cherokee had been running poorly. No improvement in performance heading for the highway. He'd have to get the car to the Blackfoot Garage, soon. He traveled the short distance to the Grand View and turned into the driveway. David, several cars behind, honked and waved, then puttered down the road, traffic stacking up behind him.

Matthew changed into his sweat clothes and stepped from his cabin towards the garage. The thermometer on the Grand View's log wall registered a comfortable 24 degrees, reminding him of how complete an adjustment he had made to Jackson Hole and the weather. He took several deep breaths, the crisp air a physical and spiritual caress. Only fatigue, constant and oppressive, resisted progress.

The outside world seemed far away. The local paper was just that, local. World and national news rarely crept into print. Now and then a short story appeared about a Teton County soldier, killed, wounded or returning from Nam. The important news was the religiously reported results every Thursday on page six—the whole page—of the Jackson Hole bowling leagues.

The simplicity and space of Wyoming provided a healing environment. Everything shone clear and bright. Decisions uncomplicated, easier to make. Right and wrong now black or white.

Just because things appeared less complex, even one-dimensional, did not diminish their quality. No question the residents of Jackson Hole had their challenges and crises; life was just a matter of perspective. Well, he had no shortage of perspective. From spectacular natural beauty to deep, meaningful relationships, Wyoming was where he needed to be. And now a woman.

I'll be damned, he thought. I might just make it after all.

FIFTY-ONE

The dumbbells had never felt lighter. Matthew picked up speed with each sequence as he worked out in the Grand View's garage. A noise behind him made him turn. Julia stood in the frame of the connecting door to the lodge.

"Wesley's on the phone," she said. "He sounds upset."

As usual, Julia didn't. Space had thickened between them since the evening of Jim's funeral, adding a density to their mutual silence. The absence of any emotional response from Julia reinforced the unreality of the event. Maybe their sexual encounter had been a dream.

Matthew dropped the thirty-pound dumbbells and followed Julia to the kitchen and the telephone. She had never mentioned their dreamlike sexual encounter after Jim's funeral. Matthew sure as hell had no desire to bring it up. He wasn't even sure what had happened.

"Bad news, buddy." Wesley's voice quivered.

"What?" Matthew tasted bile rising in his throat.

"David's car's in the middle of Fish Creek, about a half mile from his house. Got both my tow trucks on the way. I'll meet you there."

"What about David?"

"Don't know. Police dispatch called. Said the rancher who reported the accident saw someone in the driver's seat. Creek's covering two-thirds of the car."

Matthew rushed by Julia to his cabin. A sick, heavy wave of emotion blew away his previous high. He threw on his ski pants and parka. Matthew spun out of the parking area and accelerated in fits and starts down the Moose-Wilson road. Focus on the light traffic. Try to control the flow of disastrous possibilities. An image of Sarah swept through his mind, his promise to meet her, but he pushed it aside.

He couldn't contain his concern. Still in the car in the freezing waters of Fish Creek put David in serious jeopardy. How long had it been since David honked on his way home? Thirty, thirty-five minutes. Ten minutes to David's from the Grand View even at his friend's little-old-lady rate of speed. If David was in the car, he'd die from hypothermia in no time. But what if he'd stopped for an errand? He could still be alive. Keep your head down and don't jump to conclusions. Matthew pushed harder on the gas pedal. His beat-up Cherokee struggled for speed.

He slid through the stop sign at the turn to the town of Jackson. He flew in the opposite direction, swallowing the mile to Wilson and Fish Creek Road. Behind him, in the distance, he picked up a brief vision of flashing red lights. He left Wilson, headed north towards David's. In moments he slammed on the brakes behind a Teton County Sheriff's sedan and two battered pickup trucks. He pulled the Jeep off the road into the snowbank and sprinted to the edge of the creek.

David's new Jeep Cherokee sat in the middle of Fish Creek, twenty feet from shore. Blue-black creek water parted unconcerned around the vehicle. The rippling energy of a river in early spring thaw brought a symphony of sound inconsistent with the specter of disaster.

A deputy and a cowboy fought the strong current as they wrestled with the car door. The door wedged open, and they scrambled to pull a figure out of the driver's seat. David's limp body hung suspended between the two unsteady men struggling in the freezing, swift-flowing water.

Matthew jumped off the bank. The shock of the freezing water shot up his spine, his body submerged to the waist. The two rescuers stumbled, their numb legs losing control. Matthew reached the men in seconds. They staggered to shore as Wesley's two tow trucks, with another sheriff's car in the lead, roared down the narrow passage. The wail of an ambulance sounded not far behind.

David had no need for an ambulance. The blue of his skin contrasted with the bright red blood and gore seeping from a massive wound in the side of his head. Matthew ignored the throbbing pain in his soaking wet legs. He leaned over his friend in disbelief. A gunshot wound. A familiar sight from the past, but now in the wrong place.

Wesley came up beside him. Sheriff Olson spouted orders nobody listened to, shouldering Matthew and Wesley out of the way. The ambulance crew, their vehicle trapped on the clogged roadway, ran to the huddled group. The driver and his assistant took one look at David and then offered help to the two dazed men who had helped pull David from his Jeep.

"This don't make sense," the sheriff said, his two deputies pushing forward to stand next to him. No one else said a word.

Matthew looked at the tire tracks in the snow on the road's shoulder. Small bushes lay crushed by the car's progress. No evidence of a skid sideways. David had driven straight off the road. No other way to get that far into the creek. And his friend shot in the head at point-blank range.

The brutal damage further distorted David's face. Matthew had to convince himself of David's identity. A series of similar faces from old battles swept through Matthew's memory. He'd seen many bodies dispatched in a similar cold-blooded manner at close range. His knees buckled.

Wesley and a deputy dragged him to the front seat of the nearest patrol car. The engine still ran, generating welcome heat. Wesley leaned in, cranked up the fan to maximum, rolled down the passenger window and shut the door. They left Matthew shaking, leaning out the open window, only a few feet from the body. He listened to their confused and empty comments.

"Wesley, you and David were buddies," Olsen began. "Hell, you was partners, right?"

"Yeah, we were." Wesley's voice came out low, subdued, sad.

"Who the hell would do this?" The sheriff's question could have been directed to the river as much as to Wesley.

"I got no idea."

"Ya know," Tommy Baker, one of the deputies, said. "I heard rumors that Mr. Moore might have been involved in some questionable activities."

"What are you talkin' about?" Wesley barked.

He wheeled on the tall, skinny man. The Indian's chiseled features took on a primitive cast, dangerous and enraged. Baker stepped back, slipped in the snow by the creek and almost toppled into the water. Sheriff Olsen grabbed him.

"Tommy, what rumors?" Olsen asked, both hands holding up his deputy.

"Just talk, Sheriff. You know. Bullshit in the bars. Nobody knows where Mr. Moore came from or how he got his money. So word spread—"

"Shut your mouth." The threat of violence radiated from Wesley's dark eyes.

"Look, Wesley." Sheriff Olsen stood between the two, facing Wesley. "This weren't no accident. Someone killed your friend. Blew off half his head and drove his car into the creek. That don't happen without a reason. We can't find out why without a motive or a suspect. If you got no clue, please shut up and let me ask the questions."

"I told you I don't know why." Wesley stared at the sheriff. "But David's a good, honest man. He comes from old money back East. He's an investor with a wife and kid."

"That don't mean diddly, Wesley, when someone's pumped lead into your head. What rumors, Tommy?"

"Well, I heard talk of drug distribution."

"You're nuts, Baker," Matthew called out from the car.

"Yeah, soldier boy?" Now Olsen turned towards Matthew. "Well, just whatta you think's the reason for this mess?"

"I'm not sure of the motive. But I can give you a prime suspect," Matthew said. "A little punk named Franky Pieri. Staying at the Wort."

"That's a pretty strong accusation," the sheriff said skeptically. "Seems to me that a number of your acquaintances have run into some bad luck. Maybe you're a suspect?"

"Franky's been hanging out in Jackson Hole for weeks," Matthew said, ignoring the sheriff's comment. "He's not your normal tourist. He and David don't like each other. I even heard Franky threaten him on the mountain yesterday." The sheriff looked interested. "Most important," Matthew continued, "Franky's been packing a loaded .38 with the serial number filed off."

"Where's the gun?" Olsen asked.

"It's back at the Grand View," Matthew said. "I was going to throw it in the Snake, but I kept it."

"This was no .38, Sheriff," one of the ambulance drivers said. "Too much damage."

"Hey, Sheriff," Wesley said. "I just thought of somethin' else. Matthew, you remember the mornin' after you was a guest of the sheriff in his new jail?"

"What are you talking about?" Matthew's mind felt sluggish.

"We was pretty sure we saw Franky goin' into that shack near my place on Hansen Street. Couple of out-of-towners been holed up in that dump for over three weeks. No idea what the hell they was up to. But, if Franky visited 'em, you can bet they was up to no good. I'd sure check them out, Sheriff."

"Let's go see Franky," Matthew said to Wesley. He opened the car door and stumbled out.

"You two ain't gonna do nothin'." The sheriff stepped into Matthew's face. "We're running this investigation by the book. You got information, give it to us. You get in the way, I'll throw your ass in jail. We'll give you your favorite room from last time."

"Someone's got to tell Linda," Wesley said to Matthew. "Probably should be us. We'll get you a pair of dry pants. I came in one of my trucks. You can give me a ride to town later. That is, if you're able to drive."

First there was the perfect day of skiing. Then the White Dragon had swallowed Jim. David cheerfully waving, then, minutes later, dead in the river. Rapid change. Every time things looked good, shit hit the fan. Was all change bad? Sarah? Maybe not all change. He wanted to crawl into her arms, escape, burrow into the warmth of her body. An incredible weariness settled over Matthew.

"Wesley, you drive."

FIFTY-TWO

Anger more than sadness spurred Matthew to join Wesley at a meeting with the sheriff. Thursday morning. Two days and zero progress discovering David's killer. The sheriff led past the secure doors guarding the entrance to the sparkling new Teton County Jail and around the reception desk. Matthew followed Wesley and Olsen's broad butt. A chill breeze licked at Matthew's legs. Tendrils of tule fog slipping under the locked door? The damn clouds again moving in on him.

Matthew felt Wesley's glance. That night in jail after the fight with Corbin had opened the gates to a confessional catharsis without conclusion. They'd danced around the subject several times since. Wesley hadn't pushed, mentioning only the necessity of "clearin' out the closet if you wanted redemption." Closet my ass, Matthew thought. More like a warehouse.

A big-bosomed girl sat at a desk by the door to the sheriff's office. Wesley nodded a "howdy" and flashed a smile at the young lady. Light brown hair, ratted into a massive tangle, surrounded her smooth oval face. She smiled back. No one could resist Wesley.

Small, alert blue eyes matched her cute pug nose and small pouting mouth. But Matthew had seen her several times with Shebang, enough evidence to eliminate her from any positive consideration. He gave her the briefest of greetings as he entered the sheriff's preserve.

"Sit down," the sheriff ordered.

The wall clock behind Olsen beeped as it hit 10 A.M.

"I'm meetin' with you boys outta courtesy."

"Bullshit," Wesley said. "You're talkin' to us cuz you ain't got much to go on. It's Thursday mornin'. David's 'accident' took place Tuesday."

"Whatever I share with you two is confidential." Olsen kept his voice cool in contrast to the pretty shade of pink that blossomed on his full face. "You're right. We ain't got much. You and your sidekick have given us the only leads we got. Problem is, they ain't led us very far."

"Well, what have you got?" Wesley asked.

"Someone put a .357 Magnum up to David's head and pulled the trigger. Powder burns indicate point blank-range. Blew half his head off. Died instantly. Found a large rock wedged against the gas pedal. No prints, no sign of a struggle, no nothin'. Coroner says he died twenty to thirty minutes before old Gabe noticed the car in Fish Creek."

"You don't give a damn if you solve David's murder," Matthew said in a voice that reflected more than disrespect.

He was close to exploding at Olsen's emotionless presentation of the information. The sheriff was a cold bastard. Just the facts, man. Matthew held onto calm for dear life.

"That's bullshit," the sheriff sputtered. "I do care. My reputation's at stake."

Matthew couldn't have said it better.

"Still no idea why?" Wesley interrupted.

"Nope," the sheriff said. "Sure as hell haven't found any evidence of a drug connection, though this does look like some kind of gangland killing."

"I'm telling you there is no drug connection," Matthew interrupted. "You call David's family back East?"

"Yep," Olsen said. "Yesterday morning. Talked to the police in Greenwich, Connecticut. Family's got big bucks. Reached the father later in the afternoon. At first, he made a lotta noise on the phone. Real indignant. Then sure recovered quick from any grief. Already talking about a funeral back East next week some time. We'll ship the body back." Olsen's pensive expression looked out of place on his florid features. "He ain't seen David or his family for over two years. Little strange. He was loud, but it sounded more for show than concern. But then he offered a $10,000 reward for the killer."

"So much for any drug connection," Matthew said.

"Not necessarily true," the sheriff said. "I been doing this long enough to know things ain't always what they appear."

"You're reachin'" Wesley said.

The sheriff would have made a poor poker player—not too subtle during interrogations. Bar fights, drug busts, stolen cars and cattle required minimal sophistication. Olsen depended on the force of authority and intimidation. Matthew doubted he'd spent much time exercising any advanced tools of investigation. He hoped the good sheriff possessed more intelligence than could be seen on his open face.

"What about Franky?" Matthew asked.

"Now that's an interesting subject. Unfortunately, despite your feelings, Franky's got an airtight alibi."

Franky had covered his ass in a most obvious manner. He'd been drinking with the Steep Class. Sarah had even sat at the same table with him in the Moose at the moment of David's murder. Frightening to think she'd been close to being in that Jeep.

"We know he didn't pull the trigger," Matthew said, "but that doesn't mean he's not involved."

"We did a check," Olsen said. "Got answers yesterday. I'll tell you what we discovered. Your buddy, Franky, appears to be quite the contradiction. Real name's Franky Fiorini. Born and raised in Long Island. Expensive prep school called St. Albans. Graduated from Dartmouth. M.B.A. from Columbia. The kicker? His old man's Dominick Fiorini, a minor gang figure currently vacationing in Leavenworth Prison. Franky's employed by D and F Construction Company. He's a Vice President. He's also an officer of two other companies. Hard worker, wouldn't you say?"

"Well, what else do you need?" Matthew jumped up. "I told you that slimy bastard was responsible."

"Sit down," the sheriff demanded. "Franky's got no record. Clean as a nun's butt. Nothing. Not even a traffic violation. Whatta you want me to arrest him for? Being an asshole?"

"Come on, Sheriff," Wesley said. "It's easy for the mob to fix things."

"You been watching too many movies, Wesley." The sheriff's face pinked once more. "He says he's embarrassed about what happened to his old man. Just wants to lay low and stay out of trouble."

"You questioned him?" Matthew asked.

"Of course," Olsen said. "He was real cooperative. A little snotty and arrogant. But his alibi and the absence of any incriminating facts keeps him pretty clean."

"Speaking of clean," Matthew said, "what about his .38?"

"Says it wasn't his pistol. Said you and him didn't get along. Felt you might be trying to set him up."

"Sure." Desperation pulled at Matthew as Olsen rejected each possible connection to Franky. "Daddy's a convicted crook. Franky's in the business. He's just here for an extended vacation. Carries a clean revolver to the Cowboy Bar. Threatens David. David's killed. No connection at all."

"Look, Matthew." The sheriff shifted his large bulk in his overworked swivel chair. "This country's legal system works good. No proof. No conviction."

"Right," Matthew said. ". . . *his well beloved colonel took erring Olaf soon in hand . . .*" He tried to keep his voice calm and civil, but he couldn't. "The legal system of this country allows us to slaughter innocent civilians in Viet Nam. Allows criminals to run roughshod over whatever they want. Let's—"

The sheriff raised both hands, palms out.

"Sheriff, I was there at the Cowboy," Wesley said. "I saw him with the pistol. So did at least six other witnesses. Can't you just pick him up and interview him again. This time beat the truth outta him?"

"Great idea." Matthew met Wesley's glance and confirmed the possibility of conducting their own interrogation if the sheriff refused.

"Not yet, boys." The sheriff's lack of condemnation gave Matthew the slim hope of official action. "David got it with a big Magnum, not a little .38. Couldn't lift any clear prints after you manhandled the weapon. Also tried to check out those two strangers you mentioned living near you, Wesley. They've skedaddled. Nothing in the house. Ain't been gone long neither. Rented McGraw's cabin for four weeks. Paid the old man cash up front. He saw them one time to exchange the key for the money. It was evening, they wore hats. McGraw didn't get a good look."

Matthew shot Wesley a frustrated look.

"Why don't you put out an APB or whatever the hell you call it?" Wesley said. "Them two strangers buggin' out right after David's murdered. Don't that make you wonder, Sheriff?

"I would if I had a clue as to what they looked like, other than big. Or if I knew what kind of vehicle they was driving, let alone a license plate number. Jesus Christ, Wesley, they was living almost next door to you. Can't you give us anything?"

"You know, there never was a car parked in front of their place." Wesley looked sheepish and unhappy. "Remember seein' a sedan parked further down Hansen. Maybe a Ford. They must'a had dealin's with somebody in town."

"I got Oliver and Clarence working downtown," Olsen said. "So far they ain't found anything of value."

"Well, we still got Franky," Matthew said, concentrating hard on the sheriff. "What happens if he leaves town?"

"You tell me," Sheriff Olsen said. "I got to have some reason to stop him. If I arrested every local boy or ski bum who threatened someone, I'd have to turn the entire new court house into a prison."

"What about chargin' Franky with assault with a deadly weapon in the Cowboy?" Wesley asked.

"How many local boys giving him trouble?"

"Five," Wesley answered.

"Five big cowboys against one little tourist." Sheriff Olsen came close to sneering. "You ever hear of self-defense?"

"Sheriff." Matthew's voice rose. "You know David's death was an execution. You know Franky's connected to illegal activities. You know two strangers that Franky was meeting split the moment David died. What else you need to grab that greasy slimeball?"

"Just a little thing called evidence." The sheriff heated up again, jowls jiggling. "I know David was your buddy. But you got to let us investigate in a proper manner. By the way, Wesley, I got the father's phone number. He wants you to call him. Now stay outta trouble and be patient."

Olsen's voice betrayed doubt and frustration along with his irritation. Matthew kept quiet, afraid of what the tone of his voice would divulge.

FIFTY-THREE

Matthew fidgeted at a table in the Log Cabin restaurant. Wesley had swung by the garage after their discouraging discussion with Sheriff Olsen. He wanted to check in with his mechanics and call David's father. He'd meet Matthew in a few minutes for a cup.

The coffee shop echoed with the sounds of banging pots and pans from the kitchen—breakfast cleanup. Only one other table was occupied, but Matthew still had trouble prying a mug of coffee from the same homely waitress who'd slobbered over Wesley during Matthew's first visit to the greasy spoon.

Memories of last night with Sarah came as a relief. They had still found the desire and hunger to make love, despite the shock and sadness of David's death. That is until, like an unwelcome third party, shadows haunting Matthew's conscience again inserted themselves, driving him back to another restless night at the Grand View.

The more he considered the last few days, the less doubt he had of Franky's connection. In Nam he had watched without emotion as Bull wasted no time forcing information from a frightened, beaten prisoner. They'd never considered coercion of the enemy torture. The intelligence they demanded had life and death implications. Necessity, not right or wrong, drove the Rangers to extract what they needed. And God help the tough, grizzled VC who didn't share at once. No time for extended questioning. Talk or die. The freezing chill of memories closed on Matthew's heart. Talk and die.

Shouldn't Franky be treated like the enemy? Five minutes with the little mobster would be all Matthew would need. Squeeze him. He'd squeal with minimal effort. The sheriff's interrogation didn't really qualify as questioning.

Wesley banged through the front door and moved to the table. Matthew's swirl of emotion cleared. Wesley's butt hardly hit the seat before the elusive waitress materialized at his elbow. Wesley had things on his mind. Still, he touched her arm with a kind greeting, then drove her to despair when he ordered only coffee.

"Just talked to David's father." Wesley squirmed in his chair. "No warmth. David was right—a very hard man."

"David wasn't exactly a slap-you-on-the-back, hail-be-merry kind of guy."

"True," Wesley said. "But this is gonna blow you away. The old man's the executor of David's will. You know our buddy financed my garage and the Grand View?"

"Yeah." No surprise to Matthew. From the first time he'd met David, he'd been impressed with his kindness and class.

"Well, David gifted the outstanding balance on the Blackfoot to me. Man, that's close to $200,000 bucks. And he willed the balance of the mortgage on the Grand View to Julia. That's another $150,000."

Wesley leaned back in the old wood-spindled seat, the look of awe in his face emphasized by the shrill creak of the chair's cracked legs.

"What about Linda and his daughter?" Matthew asked.

"I asked about that. Mr. Moore says not to worry. There's plenty left, although he sounded pretty cold towards Linda and the kid," Wesley continued. "Like the sheriff said, funeral's in a week or two back East. No one's comin' out here to be with poor Linda."

"She's got better friends in Jackson Hole," Matthew said. "But doesn't the wife usually choose where the funeral's going to be?"

"Not accordin' to David's will. Gives the old man control."

"Would a guy David's age have a detailed will?" Matthew asked.

"Maybe. If he was real organized and had lots of assets." Then Wesley brought his chair back down with a thump. "Or if he was worried about gettin' bumped off."

"Come on, Wesley. You don't think that deputy, Tommy Baker, knows what he's talking about. He'd confuse the milkman with a drug dealer. He's dumber than a tree stump."

"Matthew, somebody shot David." Thoughtfulness reflected in the dramatic angles of his face. "Sheriff's right. Had to be some motive for a hit like this."

"My gut—hell, your gut, too—says David was what he appeared to be," Matthew countered. "The old man sounded substantial, didn't he? What kind of crook wills big chunks of property to his friends? Although hard to believe David's face would be mistaken for someone else. He had unique features. You know how he ended up looking so strange?"

"He didn't end up that way," Wesley said. "He started that way. I guess I never told you much about Dave. Promised him I'd keep the info to myself. He popped out four weeks premature. Folks was vacationin' on their own private little island on the St. Lawrence River. Just a hired hand 'round when David's mom went into labor. Some complications. The two men panicked when the bleedin' got bad. Yanked poor Dave outta his mother, messin' up his head. Mother died, and the old man blamed David. Made sure David knew it too."

Didn't mess up David's heart. Or his integrity. Sad, no parent to recognize what a fine man he had become.

"David said he had something critical he was working on," Matthew said. "You know what it was? Maybe I'm wrong. Maybe David had some heavy shit coming down. Tried to get out of the way, but Franky and his boys took him out first."

"Naw," Wesley said. "David was fightin' his father over control of David's trust. Biggest chunk of the family money came from the grand-father. David wanted to invest part of the principal in real estate 'stead of only bonds and stocks like the original trust instructed. They duked it out for years. David told me last week the trustees were about to side with him against his old man."

"His old man sounds like a nasty son of a bitch," Matthew said. "I'd be proud to have a son with David's integrity."

"Should we take Franky out for a little interview?" Wesley asked, frustration simmering to a boil.

"We?" Matthew said, smiling for the first time. "An upstanding citizen like you? A member of the Jackson Hole Rotary?"

"The sheriff won't figure this out till the turn of the century."

"No doubt. You heard Olsen say the legal system works pretty good. What convoluted logic. Let's see. Scientists suspect the earth is round, but all the sheriff's visual evidence supports the theory that the earth is flat. Therefore, according to our experienced lawman, the earth must be flat."

Thousands of miles away in Viet Nam, suspicions equaled convictions, and conviction usually meant death. Hard to swallow the principle of innocent until proven guilty. That legal concept dissolved into worthless words when the system had more holes than a sieve as well as incompetent cops.

"Franky's a crook," Matthew continued. "Carries a gun, hates David, brings along two hit men. But since he was drinking beer at the Moose when David got it, he must be innocent."

But without substantiating evidence, Franky might get away with the crime. Despite Matthew's belief in his guilt. Still, could Matthew cross the line? Again? Take the law into his own hands? Let that bastard Franky go free? Or had the line ever been crossed? Was he still the same creature who had inhabited the jungles and rice paddies of Viet Nam? The same man who'd shot Red?

"Maybe Olsen's Franky's cousin," Wesley said. "Both sound like idiots but are actually sharper than they act or sound."

"Screw the sheriff. He won't get his proof. Let's go for justice."

But a cold chill again glazed his vision. David was dead. Matthew couldn't bring him back. What would killing Franky accomplish? Only confirm Matthew had been swept back to the dark side. This time he wouldn't have all the rationalizations and special justifications of war. Just vigilante justice—murder.

"Jesus, you all right?" Wesley asked.

"No."

Why were standards so different? Justice had been served in Nam regardless of questions. Hadn't it? But today doubt needed to be dealt with. Was he sure of Franky's guilt? Yes. Completely? In his heart he knew. In his tortured mind, though, indecision reigned.

"I'm telling you shit's happening," Matthew almost gasped. "And it's going to keep happening as long as Franky's around. It's time to get ready. I'm gearing up."

"What the hell does that mean?"

"I'm going to meet the class for lunch at the Moose," Matthew said. "See how Franky reacts to the offer of a reward from David's father. Pick up Sarah if she wants to cut the afternoon session."

"Fine. Then you and Sarah can meet me at Dornan's around two."

"You don't give up, do you, Wesley?"

"Dornan's a great place to think. We'll figure out a strategy to nail Franky. Could use some thinkin' time myself."

"We're out of time."

"Got to assume Friday'll be the last day he's in town," Wesley agreed. "Class'll be over, and he'll be gone. Give Olsen the rest of today. Then, for us, it's fish or cut bait. If we got to, we take things into our own hands."

"Right," Matthew said. "Maybe" would have been a more truthful answer. But he was no longer going to be unprepared.

FIFTY-FOUR

Franky smiled as he followed his classmates through the gate to the tram platform.

"How ya doing?" A shocked expression spread over TJ's face at the friendly greeting.

"Groovy," TJ responded after a hesitation long enough to stack up the line. Franky's grin broadened.

Franky floated into the Tram, nodding at the grizzled visage of the bundled tram operator. Never noticed the little dwarf before, Franky thought. He's even shorter than I am.

The Tram lifted the full load without effort. Franky positioned skis and arms to preserve precious space in the cattle car. The unweighted sensation now felt natural to Franky.

He caught Sarah's eyes on him, large and round. Her expression reminded Franky of TJ's surprise. She turned her head. Piss on her. The skinny bitch. A Princess in Wyoming. She wouldn't rate a glance compared to the available broads back home.

And he'd have the pick of the litter in New York when he arrived home Saturday night. The sly, conquering hero, home from the hills. His father avenged. Respect from every gang member, and more important, from Giacomo. That stone had killed so many birds Tuesday, it'd been more like a bomb.

A brisk wind from the southwest greeted Franky at the top of Rendezvous Mountain. Lacy white clouds chased each other like sheep through deep blue skies. Some weather coming in, but no serious snowfall predicted. Layers of abuse, anger and frustration peeled from his body, the crisp wind generating energy and excitement. Franky had never felt better in his life. He stood safe and free on top of the world.

Kurt guided the class into the bowl. Franky didn't care where they were headed. He turned with a lightness he'd been searching for since his first day at Jackson Hole. The importance of a positive skiing attitude apparent with the ease of his turns, his position secure on top of his skis. Franky could now embrace his last two days on this magnificent mountain.

Kurt led the abbreviated advanced group down Rendezvous, heading towards Cheyenne Woods and the promise of a tight tree run to test their new techniques. Franky tucked and raced past everyone on the flats of Cheyenne Trail, even those jerk-off Germans.

"I want you all to concentrate," Kurt said at the top of the Woods. "There's a lot of dense foliage and sneaky bumps . . ."

Franky ignored Kurt's offered instructions. David was dead. His dad had received partial retribution. Franky had accomplished his mission. Sarah would soon be a distant memory, as would the rest of her irritating crowd. And Franky was imprinted into the family's folklore. Monday he'd return to his stable of cash-cow businesses. Respect, the most elusive of necessities in carving out a power base, no longer absent from his resume.

Still, he needed to play dumb. Safety first. But today he could loosen up, enjoy himself, drop the role of tough-guy gangster. Be himself. The problem: Who the hell was he? What had he become? Could he separate the act from the actual?

*   *   *

Lunchtime at the Moose cut short a morning Franky wished would last forever. He ignored the table with Sarah and her sycophants—the big word popped up from the past, his vocabulary taking a beating from his five-year role as a bumbling mobster. No David and no Matthew made for a relaxing lunch break. The perfect pause after a perfect morning. The Canadian couple kept up their vaudeville routine. Franky wanted to stuff the Swedish bitch into a fuel drum and let her talk for eternity to the crabs at the bottom of the East River. But he chatted amiably about nothing with his tablemates.

Matthew entered the room, headed towards the two large tables occupied by the Steep Class. A shadow crossed Franky's festive celebration. The veteran moved with obvious purpose through the crowd. Fatigue etched Matthew's face, adding years beyond his age. The scars on his forehead seemed deeper and angrier than Franky remembered. Vaurnet sunglasses covered his eyes, lending an ominous feature to what Franky already considered a dangerous-looking face.

Matthew reached a spot next to Sarah, facing both tables.

"Anything new on David?" Sarah asked.

"Not much," Matthew said, his voice strained and louder than usual.

Matthew's loose-fitting ski pants seemed normal, but he wore a parka bulging with extra layers underneath. A lot of clothes if he was only here for lunch. Then Franky glimpsed canvas straps peaking out from under the parka.

Alarm turned Franky's discomfort into adrenaline-pumping wariness. What the hell was that tight-lipped, wigged-out, wonder boy doing here? Was Matthew watching him? The dark glasses shielded the direction of his gaze.

"A few interesting things happening," Matthew said. "David's funeral's going to be back East in the next week or two."

Franky knew Matthew suspected him of involvement in David's murder. Knew Franky had hated David. Knew about Franky's gun—even turned it in to the sheriff. Understandable that Matthew would put Franky at the head of the list of potential killers. Too bad Franky had a rock-solid alibi drinking beer with Matthew's snatch. Franky couldn't control a self-satisfied smile.

"David's father offered a $10,000 reward for the murderer." Matthew's voice rose above the clatter of the restaurant.

Father? The word ricocheted inside Franky's head. Fear struck Franky in the back like a knife blade, a numbing entry followed by an internal flash of pain confirming severe damage. His fingers acted independently, grabbing at his silverware, knuckles beyond white. Could David have been the wrong man?

Father. He had to check this out. How? His wobbly knees firmed up, ready to take off, but nowhere to go. How could he confirm Matthew's statement? Was it a trap? The hard-ass stood fierce, solid, a slight throb evident on his damaged forehead. Franky sensed Matthew's eyes boring into him from the cover of his Vaurnet's. Franky wanted out. But he couldn't leave the class and connect with the Bruise Brothers.

But why be so upset? What difference did it really make if David was the wrong person? But Franky knew. All the rationalizations in the world couldn't hide his descent into the animal world of Sal and Marco.

Questions leapt to his lips. But he couldn't ask them, didn't dare draw attention to any unusual interest in David's death. Why would he give a damn? Thank God he was sitting down.

He stifled a groan. He'd have to deal with those moron hit men again, assuming they had obeyed orders and hung around Jackson Hole. Jesus. Just the thought of those two deadly idiots made Franky sick. And putting up with them wouldn't even register within the avalanche of consequences if everyone discovered that they had taken out the wrong person.

He tried to shake off surging fear, to focus on his burnt burger and soggy fries. But he couldn't mute an echo of derision—his brothers leading a Bronx cheer. And if the fink wasn't David, then the guilty bastard was still out there. Laughing his butt off.

But then Matthew could be blowing smoke up his ass for effect. A sliver of hope wormed through Franky's apprehension. Matthew could be misinformed. If there really was a drug connection, or if Franky could determine a questionable source of David's money, or if David's father didn't really exist, everything could still turn out all right. Franky had heard that David's wife and daughter had moved in with friends in town. He'd contact the Denver men and they—or he, if necessary—would conduct the belated search of David's house.

FIFTY-FIVE

Sarah followed Matthew out of the Mangy Moose and into the packed parking lot. Wind whipped the temperature down into the teens. Sky dominated—a radiant sapphire, highlighted by stringy cirrus clouds thickening into a more substantial threat. Matthew looked haggard and irritable as he stood at the beat-up Cherokee. The bulky protrusions under his parka profiled a different person than Sarah knew.

"Aren't I even going to get a kiss for cutting class with you?" she asked.

No answer.

He opened the battered passenger door for her. She ignored the car and stepped into his arms, lips connecting. Nothing wrong there. Her arms encircled his body. The flush of warmth from their embrace chilled as several hard objects dug into her breast and stomach. She released her grip.

"What are you wearing? Feels like I'm hugging a hardware store."

Again no answer.

Anger and wounded pride welled within Sarah. Matthew's moods tested the depths of her love. Both of their passionate nights together had ended when he'd bolted. And for what reason? Now this.

"We're going to meet Wesley at Dornan's," Matthew said.

He planted a perfunctory kiss on her forehead and exerted light pressure to guide her into the front seat. Then he shut the door and walked around behind his Jeep to the driver's side.

"What's Dornan's?" she asked as he settled behind the wheel.

"I thought everyone knew about the place," Matthew answered. "It's a bar and restaurant in the town of Moose. North, past the airport, near the Teton Park entrance. Not much of a town, but it's home to one hell of a bar."

Matthew wrestled the Jeep out of the parking lot and headed south onto the highway leading back to Wilson and Jackson Hole. The bags under his eyes, visible below the rim of the Vaurnet's impenetrable yellow lenses, looked like bruises from a fistfight. But it was understandable. David's death had upset him. She needed to exercise patience.

"Aren't we driving the wrong way?"

"Have to go through Jackson to get there." He gripped the wheel with both hands. "Road north to Moose from Teton Village is closed during the winter."

Sarah's life had been turned upside down and backwards by this man. Now he had less to say than a truculent Chicago taxi driver. They passed the Grand View in silence, then made the left turn to Jackson Hole several minutes later. Nothing wrong with the old Cherokee's heater. She unzipped her parka, took off her gloves, and shook her brown hair loose from the imprisonment of her ski hat.

"How long to Moose?" she asked.

"Be there in fifteen minutes."

"Aren't you a little overdressed for driving?"

He glanced at her, then snapped his head back to the road, too quick to receive her offered smile. He loosened his coat, revealing the top half of his web belt. She reached over and pulled the parka open wider. Metal glinted. Armed. The sight of the large, ugly pistol strapped to his body brought surges of fear, anxiety and . . . excitement.

"Why do you have a gun?"

"Just got on what I wear when Cody and I go cross-country skiing. A couple of large, nasty moose hang around the Grand View. Cody hasn't figured out they aren't playmates. Slow learner. Like his master."

"I thought we were going to a bar, not for a walk in the woods." Nervous concern and curiosity worked on her emotional state from different extremes. She tried to stifle her next comment, but failed. "That's not the reason you have it on, is it?"

"Sure it is. You know what they say. They're dumb, mean and unpredictable."

"Moose?"

"Moose."

"You're the unpredictable one," she said.

Shivers coursed down Sarah's spine as she slumped back into her seat. He gave her another quick look. Surprise, then thoughtfulness, flashed across his features before he returned his attention to the drive.

Her adrenaline pumped as they cruised down an empty road in the wilds of Wyoming, man of her dreams by her side, shadow of danger hovering around them. But images of Bonnie and Clyde didn't fit with her future visions of herself and Matthew. She should be ashamed at the thrill she felt. And the sensation shared space with an unpleasant disquiet.

She could neither predict nor control Matthew's inner conflicts. Rational motives, she hoped, drove his dramatic mood swings from tender love to savage action. But the force of his feelings frightened her. What had she gotten herself into? She pushed questions away, but they went no further than the butt of his huge pistol poking out of its holster.

A large porcupine perched in the bare branches of a tall aspen by the side of the arrow straight road. Safe within itself, protected from all predators by its prickly coat of armor. The animal had a lot in common with Matthew.

The raw beauty around her finally provided escape. Incredible vistas north of town overcame any attempt at conversation. The flat white valley spread to the very feet of the majestic Grand Tetons. Jagged peaks climbed precipitously up over 7,000 feet from the level plain. The effect added to Sarah's dreamlike perception of events. Things would work out all right. They had to.

The Jeep turned left at the sign to Moose and the entrance to Grand Teton National Park. Another quick right headed them down a rough lane to a small group of weathered wooden buildings. Wesley was climbing out of his jet black custom pickup. He must have arrived just before them. He waited, and she hugged him. Then she led the way to a wide, well-worn pine door.

*   *   *

Matthew stepped into the familiar empty space of Dornan's, but the view out the huge windows had transformed into the most spectacular sight he'd ever seen. The murky vision of his first visit had been replaced by crystal clarity.

Five major gnarled peaks filled one entire ten by twenty foot pane of glass, featuring the massive Grand Teton itself, all 13,770 feet. Matthew drifted to a bar stool, his troubled mind seduced by the natural beauty. He looked down near the base of the windows to the now seductive Snake River winding among leafless aspens and mature, full pines—close enough to touch.

Carl again appeared and took his accustomed position behind the massive bar. He smiled a greeting to Wesley and Matthew.

"Howdy, Carl," Wesley said. "Thought I'd introduce you to my other new friend. This here's Sarah. She's from Chicago. Kinda on a shoppin' trip."

"Nice to meet you." Carl grabbed Sarah's hand, hanging on as long as possible.

"How about givin' us three beers and a little privacy. Don't seem to be any customers in need."

"Sure, Wesley," Carl said and snatched three long-necked Buds. "You all call if you need anything." Carl disappeared from the room.

"Whatta you think?" Wesley's question was directed over Sarah's shoulders at Matthew.

Matthew gazed out the windows. Beauty and clarity. What a difference from his previous storm-shrouded visit. The Grand's breathtaking partners stood in formation in unbroken display behind the solid glass wall of Dornan's. To the left, the Middle and the South Teton and Buck Mountain. To the right, Owen and Teewinot looking like Siamese twins. The blue sky now shared space with gathering high clouds. Wind whipped plumes of fine white vapor, turning the highest ridges into smoking volcanoes. The Snake in the broad plane of the Hole contrasted with the jagged and serrated edges of the ancient rock towers.

"It's incredible."

The zenith of the Grand soared above the flat valley—seven thousand feet in one gulp. This glacial formation had been here for eons. Matthew longed for the stability and permanence spread out before him, a futile dream, considering current events. Hell, he couldn't even predict what would happen tonight.

"Why don't you two relax, take off your coats?" Wesley said.

Wesley shucked off his heavy sheepskin rancher's coat. Sarah did the same. Matthew just sat and sipped his beer.

"Seems a bit thick in here," Wesley offered after several minutes of silence.

"Matthew's waiting for the start of World War III," Sarah said.

"Sarah, I don't like being surprised," Matthew said.

"My God, Matthew, how paranoid can you get?"

Her voice held a frantic blend of irritation and concern. Matthew knew how to prepare. He had experienced the opposite once. That had been enough. That mistake cost his squad their newest recruit, his throat slashed taking a crap. Great way to go. And if he'd paid attention to his intuition regarding Franky, David might still be alive.

"Sarah," Matthew started to explain, surprised he cared about the Princess enough to make the effort. "I'm not a complete psychotic. You think danger just cruises down the middle of the street and honks to let you know it's coming? Trouble shows up when you least expect it. Ask David."

"I don't believe you're for real," Sarah exclaimed. "Look around. See where we are? The most beautiful, awe-inspiring spot in the world. And it's empty. Only four cars are in the parking lot, and two of them are ours."

Matthew looked around the room. He took off his parka. He unfastened the web belt, heavy with his holstered .45 and the smaller .38 secured in a side pocket. He placed his coat on the adjacent stool and arranged the vest to allow unhindered access to the semi-automatic.

He stared at Sarah, opened his arms and bowed. Blood rushed through her animated features. He enjoyed her coloring. She was so sweet. So innocent. So inexperienced, even for a city girl. She visited the vast expanse of Jackson Hole and the Grand Tetons and thought she knew the concept of size. Well, this little spot in Wyoming was but a linen closet in the mansion of the world. Her concept of danger was equally out of proportion.

FIFTY-SIX

"How can you look at that mountain," Sarah said "and doubt there's a God?"

The comment startled him, coming from as far away as the distant peaks. Matthew recovered, then couldn't resist.

"What the hell does a mountain have to do with God? Man's the key player in this screwed-up world."

"How does man determine good from evil," Sarah said, "if there's no God or religious direction?"

Sarah certainly had to be respected for her uncompromising, blind faith. More likely she'd suffered no severe tests or challenges.

"What makes you think man has that ability?" Matthew checked his angry impatience, twisting his neck to relieve tension. He recalled his uncomfortable unraveling during their last theological discussion in the Stagecoach. "History proves organized religion is nothing but another power base. Doesn't matter if it's Roman gods used to justify the death of Christians or the Catholic Church working its coercion through the Inquisition. Man's inhumanity to man transcends all religions."

Matthew looked over Sarah's head at his friend on the nearby stool. Wesley had been quiet, out of character. How long could Wesley keep his thoughts bottled up? And did he agree or disagree with Sarah?

"Matthew, I'm not saying evil doesn't exist," Sarah said, "but man has accomplished wonderful things. There is great good in most of us . . ."

"You're right, Sarah." Wesley finally waded into the discussion. "Despite my father's part-time preaching, I'm more comfortable with the Indian Way. We all got our own personal Guardian Spirit."

"But, if everyone has his own Spirit," Sarah asked, "isn't everyone forced to make his own decisions on what's right and wrong?"

"We may all generate our own force of energy and life, but our circles intersect with each other. The centrifugal force creates energy that keeps man—and of course women, Sarah—from unravelin' into evil."

Matthew knew Wesley's highly developed intellect lurked close below the façade of his country-boy persona, but hearing a lucid discourse on God at Dornan's left Matthew stunned.

"I'll be damned, Wesley," Matthew said. "You're a shaman disguised as a mechanic. Western movies with dumb Indians will never be the same."

"My religion may be personal." Wesley's face showed no amusement with Matthew's sarcasm. "But when something threatens me or my people, you gotta fight back."

"If only all wars," Matthew said, "were good, clean, protect-my-home kind of affairs."

"Many are," Sarah said.

"Many aren't. Most are fought over economics hidden behind political or religious motives. Some completely unnecessary, becoming unmitigated disasters."

"Like Korea and Viet Nam," Wesley added.

"But there were—are—good reasons for both of them." Sarah refused to fold. "Communist aggression and domination certainly qualify as evils worth fighting."

Matthew looked at Sarah, took a deep breath, forced his lips together. He gnawed the inside of his mouth. Then the remorseless, chilling, tule fog made a soft, sinister entry, licking the hairs of his neck to attention.

"You don't have a clue, Sarah," Matthew said. "We're repeating history, just a little different configuration. Nam is an exercise in futility. The U. S. Army's slash-and-burn retreat, not unlike Russia drawing first Napoleon and then the Germans into a devastated environment, suckered into an insupportable chase. The difference in Viet Nam is we're running around in a goddamn circle. And our soldiers are poor fools who were too stupid or slow to dodge the draft—like me."

"Let's get us another beer," Wesley interrupted. He vaulted over the bar top, reached into the refrigerator and pulled out three more Buds.

"We'll be out of Viet Nam soon," Sarah said.

"Bullshit," Matthew said. The empty room seemed to mock his intensity. He tried blocking out the view, his thoughts wasted on such beauty. "We're going to get our ass kicked—sooner or later. This war is being spun by popular opinion and chicken-shit politicians, not strategy or tactics. The evil and horror that's born from this nightmare will come back to haunt this country."

"Matthew, it's not that bad," Sarah said.

She put a hand on his shoulder. Was her comment offered as calm comfort or to further her argument? He rejected both options, shrugging away from her touch.

"No, it is that bad," Matthew said. "That worthless war is turning soldiers into vicious animals, destroying their souls—my soul. I've done things I can't justify but have to live with. The United States has been reduced to the destructive and aggressive levels of a World War II Germany or Japan."

"At least we're not Nazis," Sarah exclaimed.

The blinding fog swept over him. Then a bright neon sign exploded into his vision, engulfing him in harsh, undesired light. An anonymous Berkeley hippie, haloed by moisture-laden vapor, carried a placard, an inflammatory statement he'd seen once before. The damning message— BURN IN HELL, NAPALM NAZIS OF NAM—had assaulted him from a television in one of the lounges in Letterman Hospital, provoked him into kicking the screen into powdered glass.

Matthew's visceral reaction faded. He struggled for some small spot of stable safety. He drifted back to the present—to the Grand Teton in his face, to Wesley and Sarah beside him. He returned to Dornan's, but a new, aggressive anger filled his empty spaces.

Matthew looked at his friends, could see their concern, their awareness of the impact of Sarah's statement. Well, he might look like death, but a sea of change surged through him. Why hadn't he dealt with this disturbing image before? Screw the longhaired sign holder. Let that prick deal with death and survival dumped on his head by some faceless politician. Matthew would pull all those images out and deal with them right now.

And with that decision, a strange detachment overcame his growing fury. The same feeling he had had in the heat of combat. Everything around him in slow motion, except Matthew, moving in real time.

The ultimate question finally lay before him. A simple question: Could an individual maintain his own personal integrity while caught in the middle of an externally imposed immoral force? An answer swelled within him.

"Sarah, let me tell you how close to Nazis our actions in Viet Nam bring us. Civilians are killed for inexcusable, bullshit reasons. Our military justifies crimes against humanity with the argument it's for the good of our country. When overextended and beaten, we lash out with frustrated atrocities. Persecute ethnic groups. Make unilateral attacks on foreign countries. Sound familiar?"

"What do you think you are, Matthew? A Jewish Nazi?" Sarah asked. "There are a few differences."

Finally, the one identifiable demon he had refused to acknowledge. Matthew's scar twitched and throbbed, sweat blossomed on his face and under his arms. Painful memories flooded the room. He had trouble controlling his facial expressions.

"No, I'm not. But I've been forced into Nazi-like actions."

He'd done terrible things. But he was different than a heartless, despicable Nazi. He could accept the truth. Could even live with the truth. Matthew felt amazed, relieved. The need to shine light on his worst nightmare forced open the door to his suppressed past. He had viewed the irony of his Ranger squad's final hour only through the acidlike prism of haunting dreams. Now was the time for clarity.

Sarah and Wesley leaned forward, deadly serious—judges, therapists, inquisitors? Dornan's sat vacant, unreal. The distractions of the mountains and river lost their hold on his concentration. Pain from the past ripped through him.

Wesley was the only person he considered trustworthy or capable of witnessing what he had so long hidden. And he'd be damned if he'd let Sarah trivialize or forgive his past acts without understanding the complexity of his conflicts. The tule fog ebbed and evaporated. Time to share the story he had refused to confront.

FIFTY-SEVEN

Matthew had let the men collapse onto the red earth in a half-assed wheel. Bull had moved forward to a slight rise overlooking the rolling terrain. Pedro had taken the left, Eric the right, KC watched the rear. Matthew huddled next to Snot and the radio.

The men sprawled under a grove of medium-size trees in desolate country at the base of the highlands. Heat ignored the shade. Weariness wore away caution. Bull's disapproval radiated from forty feet. Matthew caught the look, despite the mask of dirt and grime layering his corporal's features. Matthew agreed with Bull's unspoken thoughts.

"Sarge," Pedro whined, ten feet from Matthew, "if those cosmic command cock-suckers wanted recon twenty-five klicks from where we was operating, why the hell didn't they give us a lift in that new-fangled invention, the helicopter?"

"Noise, numb-nuts," Matthew replied.

"Precarious" had been the Captain's description to Matthew of the rapid and abundant infiltration of North Vietnamese regulars into the lightly defended Puc Tho region. Immediate recon required. Matthew was painfully aware of the shortage of qualified Rangers or LRRP patrols. But humping full-tilt boogey across open territory seemed no less "precarious" to Matthew.

"Just a groovy walk in the park," Eric said over the reluctant squawks of their now part-time radio.

"Sure," Snot agreed. "Even the deserted villages are deserted. Make you wonder?"

"Don't mean we ain't being watched," Pedro said.

"We're taking a twenty-minute break," Matthew said.

"Man," Snot said, after calling in their position. "I hate cruising in broad daylight. It ain't in our Ranger Handbook."

Weak laughter trickled around the loose-wheeled soldiers.

His men slumped in the embrace of exhaustion. A temporary escape from the sharp discomfort of heat, rash, pain, fatigue and fear. Matthew shook his head and stood to deflect the encroaching wave of disassociation. Weird. Both extremes—either baking heat or freezing cold—took one to the same place, the desire to fold into the fetal position and drift away.

"Sarge."

The hoarse call from Bull grabbed everyone's attention. The men flattened on the ground, Matthew dropping to one knee.

"I'll be damned," Bull said, alarm fading from his voice. "It's a little dink. Just kinda materialized on the trail."

Matthew felt the instant adrenaline surge peak, then retreat within the undertow of fatigue.

"Look fishy?" he asked Bull.

"Naw," Bull said. "Just a baby really. Don't know where it came from. About sixty, seventy feet in front of us."

The rise hid the child from sight. Only Bull had visual contact. What's a kid doing miles from a village? Where'd it come from? Faint alarms rung on the periphery of Matthew's mind.

"This one must come from a wealthy family," Bull called out. "First kid I ever saw didn't look half-starved. Kinda chunky. Even wearing an old uniform shirt."

Alone? Wearing a soldier's garment? Well fed? An electrifying connection shocked Matthew into action.

"Shoot him," he screamed. He swung his rifle to his shoulder. Frantic steps propelled him towards Bull. "Shoot, goddamn it,"

Matthew's panicked cry came out in a fragmented croak. Bull hesitated, glanced at Matthew's rapid approach. Eric and Pedro rolled to either side of the faint trail into partial cover.

Matthew, fifteen feet from Bull, saw the child. A boy. Five or six, maybe. Confusion, fear on the face now only forty feet away. Matthew saw fate unravel before his eyes.

"He's not a child. He's a walking bomb."

Matthew fired at the small figure. Missed. Kept firing. Bullets found their target in the small frame, which jerked in irregular spasms. Blood spurted as the child slammed off the trail. The short body seemed to disintegrate within the underbrush. Matthew hit the earth.

Nothing.

"You fuckin' animal," Bull roared. "You killed a child. You're crazy."

The huge man rose and started toward the small, shredded body in the brush.

"Stay down," Matthew ordered.

Bull ignored him. Matthew jumped to his feet.

"The kid's wired with explosives," Matthew yelled. "Bull, stop goddamn it, you're gonna – "

The eruption ripped through the quiet countryside. A vicious burst of shrapnel crushed Matthew to the ground. Ringing echoes reverberated within his head. Pain blossomed in his side, his thigh, his face.

Those worthless, two-faced, sub-human bastards. All of them. Wipe out all the Vietnamese. The peasants worse than the VC. The people hate us. Fear us. Know where they stand with the VC. Cooperate or die. Two can play that game.

He couldn't move. He opened his eyes. Only one functioned. With it, he saw enough. Bull ten feet away on his back. His eyes open. Vacant. Dead. What kind of bastards sent kids on suicide missions? A terrible smell rose from the hot dust surrounding Matthew. A stench he sensed oozing from his own body.

Bull gone. Now him? The hawks had been right—nuke all the sons of bitches back to the Stone Age. None of them worth saving. Agony survived even the avalanche of darkness. Crushed by pain. Was he dying too? For nothing? Matthew felt his life ebbing out to sea, his body beached in the sand. He had to hang onto the pain and the hate. Pain meant life. Peace was death.

FIFTY-EIGHT

Matthew looked down at the slick varnished surface of the bar. A troubled, drained face peered up from the mirrorlike finish. Not a pleasant image looking back at him. Anger welled as he acknowledged his battered features. A deep rage, a wound as deep and damaging as napalm or bullets, filled Matthew, preventing eye contact with either Wesley or Sarah.

"It took a long time for that hatred to fade away," Matthew said. "Long after they lifted me to the hospital ship. And if those feelings of hatred surfaced once, then I'm capable of hating like that again."

He turned his gaze to the windows of Dornan's, holding tight to a fury that relieved him of guilt and shame. Bull's face sat superimposed on the flanks of the Grand Teton. The Ranger wasn't smiling. If this confessional was to lead to peace of mind, then it would have to be a delayed reaction.

"That was eight months ago." Matthew let his hand wander across the bar's surface. "Feels like an eternity."

Matthew waited, hoping for understanding, if not exoneration. Sarah and Wesley kept silent. Anything to confirm or justify his actions? Anything at all? Maybe Wesley understood, but Sarah was overwhelmed by his personal catharsis. He knew, in the stillness of the bar, that only he could provide his own forgiveness.

"You had to kill the innocent," Sarah said in an unconvincing tone. The look on her face said something else.

"Maybe that time," Matthew said. "But you don't know the many other things I've done directly or indirectly to put blood on my hands. You don't have any concept of the chaos and terror of battle. I became a heartless murderer. At the moment of Bull's death I would have gladly pushed the button of total destruction. Annihilate the whole country—North and South."

"But you didn't," she said. "You're not a killer."

"There's no distinction. I've killed," Matthew snorted. "Many times."

"Well, I've seen you not kill," Sarah said. "I think I've seen you come close to the edge and pull back. Even when you could have rationalized a violent response."

Impressive that she'd noticed. He searched her face. Her expression flashed from hopefulness to despair and back again.

"In the Cowboy Bar," Sarah said. "That monstrous animal who grabbed you by the throat."

"She's right," Wesley said. "There was two times you had a clean shot at terminatin' that no good bastard Corbin."

"That's now," Matthew argued. "It's the past that defines the man."

"But there's only the present," she said. "We've all thought terrible things. Wished evil upon people who hurt us. Thoughts don't kill, actions do."

She stopped talking and looked down at her hands. Went a little too far, didn't you, Matthew thought. Her eyes returned to his face. Her serious concentration cemented her features into unattractive immobility. Only her long, shapely fingers moved, tracing the Budweiser label as if it held a message in Braille supporting her arguments.

"You can't change the past," she said. "You're not a Nazi. Shooting that child—horrible though it might be—was in self-defense. It was the child or you and your men. You had a responsibility to them. You saved everyone but Bull."

Matthew could hear the depth of Sarah's emotional intensity as she rationalized his actions.

"Matthew," Wesley cut in. "I hate to keep pointin' this out, but Viet Nam weren't no different from Korea or any other war for that matter. Remember what I told you in Olsen's jail? About three weeks after we bugged out, we're still fallin' back towards Pusan. Last thing blockin' the North Koreans is the Nakiong River. They'd already squeezed us into a tight-ass corner. I was stuck back into a new unit, C Company of the 21st Regiment."

Oh, no. Another Korean War story. He tried to give Wesley his full attention, but drifted away. Wesley must have noticed. Irritation crept into his voice. Matthew looked up to find Wesley's anger visible, with the tightening lines around his mouth and eyes signaling a demand, a challenge. Matthew forced himself to listen.

"We was told to make a last stand on the south side of the Nakiong. Fact that pompous ass MacArthur told us to 'stand or die.' The flow of poor, panicked refugees was cloggin' the bridge. They all dressed in filthy white pajamas, all lookin' the same. My platoon sat one position over from the exit of that bridge. All of a sudden fire came out of that pack of pathetic humanity. The group of our boys closest to the bridge started droppin'. We couldn't see who to shoot. Those soulless commies was usin' the peasants as human shields."

Wesley reached over the top of the bar and grabbed a bottle of scotch. He took an impressive hit and offered the green J&B container to Matthew. Matthew passed, but Sarah didn't. Matthew no longer had trouble focusing. Agitation and waves of emotion played across Wesley's sculptured features.

"We didn't have no choice," Wesley continued, but not before he took another quick drink. "It was them or us. We started firin' into the middle of that crowd of Koreans. Couldn't tell the good ones from the bad. Most jumped into the water, majority of them probably drowned. Some lay flat on the bridge. Enemy shootin' stopped for a few minutes. The ones in front that didn't get hit crawled across the last few feet. We watched 'em close, searchin' for any North Koreans. I gotta tell you, I don't like talkin' about that day."

Wesley became more troubled, took another hit of J&B. Matthew had never witnessed his friend knock down more than a few beers. No question as to the price Wesley paid dredging through the debris of his military disasters.

"After ten or fifteen minutes, they started crossin' again. Pressure from the other side forced those on the bridge to move. Shots came at us again. This time the army called in navy carrier pilots. They strafed that bridge, clearin' it. I'm sure some North Koreans got nailed, but nothin' compared to those helpless farmers runnin' for their lives."

Now Matthew took a swig. The burning liquid failed to ease his discomfort. Sarah had a vacant stare. Too much knowledge. No way to absorb it. Matthew had seen others with the same look. He wanted to reach out to her, comfort her. But this time Wesley needed the space.

"War puts you in a position too close to the line between humanity and inhumanity," Wesley said. "Who the hell you think has to do the protectin' and fightin'? It's the good men; the young, strong men who got to step up. And good men can do bad things. That don't make 'em evil. Matthew, you had to stand up and go to war. You had no choice."

"I wish that were true," Matthew said wistfully.

He reached in the back pocket of his ski pants for his wallet, then pulled a thin, narrow strip of paper from one of the compartments of the ragged leather billfold. He unfolded the dirty, creased paper and laid the remains of a poem on the bar top. Stains marked the words with infinite shades of misery. Sarah and Wesley leaned forward, eyes scanning the almost illegible lines.

"I think it was my sophomore year in high school," Matthew said. "In school we were studying poetry. I got interested in a strange dude, E. E. Cummings."

Shadows crept up the flanks of the Grand Tetons. The valley floor lost its sharp edge of color. Thick clouds muscled out what had now become a gray-blue sky. At least Bull's image had departed.

"This one poem connected with the inconsistencies between protecting one's self and waging a useless war for self-serving politicians or selfish businessmen's agendas. I cut out a copy and kept it in my wallet. The damning evidence is that for all those years through college, I had an alternative to getting drawn into Viet Nam right there in my pocket. But I didn't have the courage. I searched and planned for the easy way out—the Coast Guard Reserve. Safe and short. When that plan blew up in my face, I really screwed up."

So long ago. A swift and complete disintegration of his world.

"Back then, all us enlightened college boys wanted to bomb Viet Nam into oblivion. How were we—naïve as hell—to know that the Great Liberal Lyndon didn't have the balls to bomb where it would make a difference? We were doomed to fight a sham war with real victims."

"This paper's so messed up," Wesley complained, "I can't read this here poem."

"I got it memorized," Matthew replied. "Fact is, I can't get it out of my mind. The damn thing haunted me my whole tour in that hellhole. Still does. I'll recite it to you:

> *I sing of Olaf glad and big*
> *whose warmest heart recoiled at war:*
> *a conscientious object–or*
>
> *his wellbeloved colonel(trig*
> *westpointer most succinctly bred)*
> *took erring Olaf soon in hand;"*

The poem seemed to evaporate before registering in Sarah's overstimulated mind. Matthew changed the cadence of his voice, turned on his stool to face her, then continued:

> *"but – though an host of overjoyed*
> *noncoms(first knocking on the head*
> *him)do through icy waters roll*
> *that helplessness which others stroke*
> *with brushes recently employed*
> *anent this muddy toiletbowl,*
>
> *while kindred intellects evoke*
> *allegiance per blunt instruments—*
> *Olaf(being to all intents*
> *a corpse and wanting any rag*
> *upon what God unto him gave)*
> *responds, without getting annoyed*
> *'I will not kiss your fucking flag'"*

The Princess' eyes widened. That line sure as hell woke her up. Or was it the use of her favorite pastime out of context? Whatever, whether it registered or not, he had to finish.

> *"straightaway the silver bird looked grave*
> *(departing hurriedly to shave)*
> *but–though all kinds of officers*

(a yearning nation's blueeyed pride)
their passive prey did kick and curse
until for wear their clarion
voices and boots were much the worse,
and egged the firstclassprivates on
his rectum wickedly to tease
by means of skilfully applied
bayonets roasted hot with heat—
Olaf(upon what were once knees)
does almost ceaselessly repeat
'there is some shit I will not eat'"

Matthew's bitterness left a metallic taste in his mouth. Who or what was he most angry with?

"our president, being of which
assertions duly notified
threw the yellowsonofabitch
into a dungeon, where he died

Christ(of His mercy infinite)
I pray to see; and Olaf,too

preponderatingly because
unless statistics lie he was
more brave than me: more blond than you."

That was it. Matthew was finished. He folded the bedraggled slip of paper and stuck his wasted ticket to salvation back in his battered wallet. Had he connected? How many repetitions had been necessary for him to comprehend the message?

"That's a mighty fine poem," Wesley said. "But it wouldn'ta kept you from being drafted. Of course you coulda gone to Canada or jail. Now that woulda been interestin'—you in jail."

"I didn't have Olaf's courage."

"Seems to me," Wesley said, "you wouldn't have survived Nam without courage."

"Luck," Matthew insisted, not feeling all that fortunate.

The heavy wood front door banged solidly against the log wall. Matthew wheeled to his left, one hand yanking his parka off the adjacent stool. His right hand grasped the exposed butt of his .45. Half kneeling, safety off, Matthew faced the commotion.

A heavyset, middle-aged couple stumbled through the entrance and towards the tall bar and inviting view. The noise brought Carl out from hibernation in the kitchen. Matthew put down the gun and picked his coat off the floor, covering the pistol.

"Howdy, folks," Carl said.

He escorted the two to the far end of the bar, away from Wesley and his friends. They sat down, the woman having problems balancing on the high wooden stool. Carl took their orders. Matthew willed away the tremor in his right hand, adrenaline coursing through his body, again out of proportion to the event.

"My God, Matthew," Sarah said, white as virgin powder. "You're dangerous. You could have shot that poor couple."

"I think," Wesley said, "you might be exaggeratin' some, Sarah."

"Yeah, Sarah," Matthew said. "I'm really not a psycho killer, remember?"

He couldn't hide his disappointment with Sarah's emotional responses. But what could he expect? He had needed time. Months had passed, and only now was he ready to accept his actions and move on. And progress wasn't linear. He stumbled two steps forward, one step back. Regardless of the inconsistencies, he was finished beating himself up.

"No, I know you're not," Sarah said. Fatigue and desperation shaded her words. "Let's just go back to the Wort."

Simplicity for Sarah would be a crawl back into the cocoon of physical affection and comfort. Matthew recognized his own familiar desire for simplicity in her disoriented gestures. But he doubted there would be any immediate relief for her after today's revelations.

"You just don't get the picture," Matthew said.

"Making love to me won't make anything worse." Sarah's face flamed red. "It might even help heal you."

Matthew wanted her. But she was a child—pure, innocent and soft. She didn't understand Matthew's resistance. She needed to deal with her inner conflicts. Matthew couldn't blindly make love to Sarah, that would be a violation.

"Buddy," Wesley said after an uncomfortable silence. "I know it ain't easy. I'll show you how to work through this nasty shit. I can help you." The concern coloring Wesley's angled face backed up his words. "I want to help you."

"There's more – "

"Goddamn it," Wesley shouted. "You always got more. More trouble, more evil deeds, more nightmares. Well, so do I. So does damn near everybody. The only time there won't be more is when you're dead. Wasn't your fault. Quit feelin' so sorry for yourself. You gotta move on."

Wesley, his anchor, hadn't understood, had cut him loose. Had turned on him, just like Bull. Why, Wesley? Matthew clamped down on a surge of hurt. Didn't Wesley recognize that Matthew had overcome his self-pity? Had turned to anger for sustenance, to help move into the future? What the hell was he supposed to do to make Wesley understand? Frustration drove him towards the door.

"Good idea," Matthew stuttered. "I'm moving on. Wesley, do me a favor and give Sarah a ride."

"What about Franky?" Wesley called out.

Matthew glanced back. A glittery shine of tears showed in Sarah's huge, wounded eyes.

"I don't know. I'll talk to you guys later."

He needed air. He stumbled out, struggled into his web vest and then the parka. He had to escape their confused conclusions. Outside the wind had picked up.

But what about Franky? That little prick had taken out David no differently than the colonel and his Nazi officers killed Olaf. Matthew should just waste Franky and be done with it.

FIFTY-NINE

David's father. Franky lost his skiing edge. He crashed and burned in the steeps and tight trees. David's father still lived? He tried to put the situation into perspective. Nothing could implicate him. Right? And what about his soul? Shit, he'd worry about that later.

But if David was the wrong guy, his immediate future could sure as hell unravel. What would happen with Giacomo and Franky's opportunity to take the business to the big time? What were his options? Very few. But he spun through them, over and over, like a record needle stuck in a deep scratch.

Ironically, if he and the Bruise Brothers had just given up and headed out of Jackson Hole, Franky still would have the strength of cash flow behind him. His failure out West could be overlooked. His value to the mob was in the successful operation of the family's businesses—profits generated forgiveness. Any overall timetable to gain more control and security within the organization might be compromised. So what? He would have had plenty of time.

But not now.

Killing the wrong person, execution style, would bring an unwelcome spotlight. If David was, in fact, the wrong man. And if so, there'd be nowhere to hide or avoid the cascade of criticism that would crash onto his head. Would his half-ass brothers still be in a position to use this disaster to bludgeon Franky out of the circle of power? Physical retribution would be only one consequence. The compromise of influence with Giacomo and previous supporters would be the most damaging.

Somehow he had to salvage something from this frightening mess.

He had to have more information, proof to connect David to some activity that justified his elimination. Or at least confirm that David truly had a father and family money to support his investments in Jackson Hole. But Franky had little time. Tomorrow, Friday, would be the last day of class. His ticket on the Vomit Comet had Franky on his way home at 10:15 Saturday morning.

He excused himself from class and reached the parking lot around two o'clock. None of his classmates seemed upset at his early exit. Franky's mind continued a worthless whirl, evading his efforts to organize his crisis into a business case study. Lay out the facts and find a solution—the problem no different than any other operational challenge. Instead, fear and panic clogged his mind.

He hurried to his familiar pay phone at the Alpen Haus. What was the new number his hit-men partners had told him to memorize? He recalled the area code and prefix, but the last four digits eluded him. He had written the number down, against orders, and tucked the slip of paper into a compartment in his suitcase. He would have to wait for their return call at the hotel anyway. Might as well retreat to the Wort to send the message. What a bullshit system.

He sped back to town and his hotel room. He found the number and relayed the primitive code—"I want an appointment"—and sat. And stewed. His only real option had to be a search of David's house. The wife and daughter had moved in with friends in town. Probably didn't want to be alone, considering David had been murdered—the stupid Denver men making sure it would not be mistaken for an accident. Franky now concentrated on the house on Fish Creek, fixated on any potential answers to be found there. Time passed as sluggishly as rush-hour traffic in the Midtown Tunnel.

* * *

His asshole associates promised they'd return the call in two or three hours. Why wasn't he surprised when the phone rang just after three hours?

"You got a problem?" John's businesslike voice wasted no time on pleasantries.

"I need to see you."

"No way."

"You don't understand." Franky didn't care if desperation crept into his statement. He needed action, ego be damned. "David may have a father living back East."

Silence.

"Supposedly the old man offered a $10,000 reward for his son's killer," Franky said into the void. "We've got to check this out. Quietly. Can't get our people on it at the other end. Only way to save our ass is to find out what's really going on. There's got to be plenty of information at David's place."

"Whatta you mean 'our' ass?" John said. "We just followed your orders."

"Look, we need to meet and figure this out."

"It's a different gig now," John cut in. "There's been a homicide. The cops could be following you. You're suspicious-looking naturally. And you said people knew you didn't like David."

"No one's watching me."

"Really," John said.

"There's only a few cops in this hick town anyway."

"Only a few? You know where any of them are at this moment?"

"Of course not. I . . ."

"You're gonna have to let it be, tough guy." John didn't seem concerned if they'd snuffed the wrong man. "Be cool."

"I can't just sit on my ass. I've got to check it out."

"No, you don't," John insisted. "You're not sure it's David's father, and your good buddy could still have been in the drug business. The message's been delivered—don't fuck with the Mob."

"Jesus. We may have whacked an innocent guy. We're idiots. That could be the message."

A humming dial tone evidenced John's lack of qualms.

Franky was on his own. Still only one option. Search David's. When? If the cops were watching, which Franky doubted, they'd be more apt to follow him that night. In the morning he could gather his ski gear and appear to be heading to class—early. How would he maintain his sanity until then?

Franky flushed the Bruise Brothers' worthless phone number down the toilet and headed for the Silver Dollar Bar.

* * *

Matthew plunged down the highway, south to the town of Jackson, and then over to the Grand View. He drove fast, the speed incidental. Wesley's words occupied his mind. Why hadn't he understood? Sarah's confusion reflected her need to consider the consequences of any relationship with Matthew. He knew the inner conflict she must be dealing with even if she didn't. But why had Wesley been so upset?

The answer sat squarely before Matthew. Wesley had become disgusted with Matthew's excessive self-pity. And Matthew agreed. Matthew thought he'd made that clear to Wesley at Dornan's.

He wanted to follow Wesley's advice, to move on. He ached to bury the burdens and nightmares of the past. The last shameful event and the accompanying fear of Nazi association that had finally broken through his fortress of denial. Now, strange as it seemed, the threat to his continued progress didn't come from his Asian baggage but the events of today—David's unnecessary death and what the hell to do with Franky.

Sarah would depart on Saturday morning. What a disappointing way to end her vacation in paradise, stuck with that bastard on a plane from Jackson Hole to Denver. At least she was heading to Chicago. Franky would be returning to the jungles of New York. If Matthew hadn't unceremoniously dumped her on Wesley, he might have shared with her one of his few clear thoughts: One way or another, Franky would not be on that plane.

If justice was to be served, it wouldn't come within the rusty machinery of the local law. The system protected the prick. Matthew would have to step outside the morals of society, back into the darkness. But if he took out Franky, how would Matthew react to the next challenge that didn't fit neatly into the laws and due process of his country?

Cody bounded to the old Cherokee from the side of the lodge. The black Lab reenacted his well-practiced attack, the same one Matthew had had difficulty avoiding months ago by the Clock Tower. His four-legged charge was still difficult to evade. Matthew had gained strength and confidence since then, but so had young Cody. The Lab mirrored Matthew's physical progress. And now the same could be said about spiritual and psychological improvement. But his life would never be as simple as his dog's.

Inside his cabin, he put on his workout sweats. He overcame an unusual reluctance and stepped into the garage and the waiting equipment. He searched for motivation. He was out of excuses. Then he remembered an acceptable diversion. He veered into the lodge kitchen to check for messages. Maybe a reprieve or an apology from Wesley.

Julia drifted around the empty kitchen, her wooden clogs a hollow echo on the hardwood floor. The counters sparkled, every dish and utensil in its proper place. And still the statuesque blond traveled back and forth cleaning and dusting from one side of room to the other.

"Any calls?" Matthew asked.

"No," Julia said.

Her overripe beauty no longer affected Matthew. Wax fruit—all show and no go. Too bad. Only Sarah stirred Matthew's juices. But her inability to understand and the limitation of her life experiences dampened his desire.

"Some good news," she said. "The lodge is booked solid for the next two weeks."

Sadness passed through Matthew. The Grand View seemed vacant without Jim, full house or not. He needed to move on, to find a place without the traffic of the bed-and-breakfast. And without the uncomfortable, guilty memory of Jim and the haunting presence of Julia.

"Congratulations, Julia," Matthew said and moved towards the makeshift gym.

SIXTY

Matthew returned to his one-room home after the workout. He took his ritual shower. He set a stack of records on his turntable, starting with his brother's latest offering, a rock opera by a new English band. Tommy, the Pinball Wizard, bounced against the log walls but brought no energy to Matthew. He lay on the bed, immune to the raw chords of the Doors, Credence, and Steppenwolf. Iron Butterfly's "In-a-Gadda-Da-Vida" seemed appropriate—the perfect cut for pondering the imponderable, spending a lot of time getting nowhere.

He had so accepted his constant state of fatigue that when he lay down, the last thing he expected was sleep. But semiconsciousness ambushed him. He drifted in and out of a dark space full of ill-defined images and fragments of visions. Nightmares took shape, then dissipated before causing the usual pain. Matthew finally sat up. A freezing chill enveloped his body, but not from his despised enemy, the fog. He had failed to light a fire or turn up the baseboard heater.

Darkness ruled outside his small window. The cold required a response. And a frustrated restlessness took over. Might as well dress for action. Hope some plan would take shape. In addition to yesterday's ski pants, medium-weight parka, and the web belt and harness with its holstered .45 and pocketed .38, Matthew slipped a handful of shells for the large semiautomatic into an ammo pouch attached to his web vest, LBJ for short.

The acronym brought a smile to his face. The official name the abbreviation stood for escaped him. Not sure he had ever known. The two favored choices of the Rangers were Load Bearing Junk or a disrespectful allusion to the good president who'd placed this load of crap on the back of America's youth.

Matthew withdrew his six-inch Randall knife from its scarred sheath. The nasty-looking, serrated upper ridge of the jungle knife sparkled, deceptively festive in the limpid lamplight. First, the weapon was replaced in its scabbard, then taped, handle facing down, to the back of his vest. The memory of another item he hadn't used since the war sent him rustling through his bottom drawer to dig out his waterproof black-rubber wristwatch, and strap the alien band to his wrist.

Next, cotton mitten liners and heavier outer gloves. Then his knitted facemask that doubled as his ski hat, needing only to be pulled down when his face demanded protection from the wind chill. What time was it? And why the stubborn refusal to buy a clock? Cold fingers wound his retrieved timepiece. Let the watch at least practice ticking until he could set it properly. Still dark. Matthew pulled out the two pistols, cleaned them for the hundredth time, reloaded both, slipped on the safety of the .45 and put both of them back into their proper places on his web belt.

Action required a plan. A plan required information. He had neither. Indecision filled the vacuum. He finished gearing up, gathered his ski boots and left a confused Cody pacing the cabin floor.

Matthew twisted the key in the ignition of the Cherokee. Nothing. On the fifth try the engine turned over, still not starting. Matthew, for once, could wait. He had no specific place to go, and he didn't want the old machine to flood. After several more tries, success.

Matthew checked the Jeep's clock and finally connected with the rotation of the planet—5:10 A.M. First light was still an hour away. He set his wristwatch, gunned the Jeep, pulled onto the highway and began an aimless drive towards the crossroads. He directed the car on a slow cruise to Wilson and made a right onto Fish Creek Road. The road and ill-defined thoughts drew him to David's home. Wesley's Guardian Spirit providing direction?

He drifted past the driveway, brushing the back of his hand against the scars on his forehead. A turnout used by local snowmobilers allowed him to nestle the Jeep thirty or forty feet into a spot adjacent to Fish Creek, where the unloading of vehicles had created a packed space. The gloomy, dense shape of David's empty castle stood against a dark-gray sky.

He faced the circular driveway a hundred yards away, his car hidden behind a thicket of ghost-shaped, winter-anemic aspens. Matthew turned off his engine. The comforting roar of the fast-moving creek brought a welcome, temporary peace. Maybe he should buy a small parcel by a turbulent, flowing stream. Wesley could help him set up a teepee. Go back to nature for the summer months. Become a hippie.

But disturbing thoughts of Franky interfered with the calming rush of the river. He hated Franky. Did his prejudice disqualify his conclusions? The outside chance of Franky's possible innocence nibbled at his assumption of guilt. Wasn't that what the legal process was all about? Be patient, gather all the facts? Mete out justice after due consideration? Innocent until proven guilty?

He thought of David. His love of family. His generosity. How close David had come to freedom from his past. Images fueled the desire for precipitous action. But, goddamn it, he couldn't let himself get sucked in. He'd be no better than that New York hoodlum.

He looked out the windshield to the sky. The thickening, low-ceilinged, murky-gray cloud cover continued to delay the break of day. But no tule fog, imagined or real. Too close to the real weather conditions? Matthew would welcome a sign from above. If Wesley's Guardian Spirit had brought him this far, he sure as hell could use some additional guidance.

Time to do something. Maybe head for the Wort or Teton Village. He started the old engine, heater blowing welcome warmth and the clock registering 7:05. He felt a connection to the beat-up vehicle, both of them damaged and abused, both repaired and healed by Wesley. Only now, machine and man needed a tune up. Enough. No more self-pity. But Matthew capitulated to indecision. He turned off the motor. He'd wait another ten, maybe fifteen minutes.

Moments later the Guardian Spirit made a belated appearance. A rental Chevy crunched down David's driveway. The driver made the circle and backed the car to the front door. A small, bundled figure emerged from the driver's side, walked to the front door. Franky.

Matthew slid out of the car, on the move. He made rapid progress down the game trail. Large moose and smaller deer had done an effective job of breaking ground. Their prints created an easy pattern for Matthew to follow. He slipped into a slow jog, each foot aimed at an animal hoof print. He stumbled, fighting for balance every couple of steps—not smooth, but efficient.

One hundred yards to the edge of the house. Matthew had little concern for cover in the faint light, plus Franky had his back to the river as he forced the front door open. No one in the house for Franky to hurt, speed not an issue.

Habit and common sense jerked Matthew's head to the right, to the circular driveway, checking every few seconds for a possible change in the situation. He wasn't even winded when he reached the edge of the bedroom wing. All systems working just fine.

A wood deck created an L-shaped walkway that followed the line of the house. Large windows looked into three rooms on the bottom floor facing the river. Matthew crept along the wood planks. The river muted any creaks. He was focused, fatigue left behind in the Jeep.

Movement inside, halfway down the bedroom wing, caught Matthew's attention. Franky's invasion offered proof of his complicity in David's murder. Matthew yanked off his glove and pulled out his .45. He wrestled an overpowering urge to kill. Franky had showed minimal caution when he had switched on the ceiling fixture. David's office. The light highlighted walls cluttered with the collection of a good man's memories and accomplishments. The brightness reflected off the inside of the window making everything outside invisible. Thanks for the cover, Franky.

SIXTY-ONE

Franky surveyed David's office. Easy enough slipping out of town and breaking into the house. He'd been careful on the drive over. Someone following him would have been obvious in the minimal early-morning traffic.

Seven o'clock. Class started at 9:30. Last one. Kurt had promised a final exam for each student. Big deal. Still, he had to show up. Needed the alibi. He had up to an hour and a half to search. One large filing cabinet and the smaller five drawers of the desk could be examined in less than ninety minutes.

Franky hoped to discover several things. David's checkbook or books and the corresponding bank statements would provide the most information. Franky didn't expect to find entries labeled "drug receipts." But a number of deposits without corresponding check copies would be a pretty good indicator. The problem would be if there were multiple accounts. What if David laundered money through the Blackfoot Garage and the Grand View? Secondly, Franky wanted to confirm his biggest fear: Consistent deposits from David's father or some trust account.

He wasn't so unrealistic as to think he'd answer all his questions. But some information could help save his butt. And Franky knew how to sift through David's records. Hell, running businesses and turning dirty money into clean cash had proved to be Franky's ticket to the top.

The first drawer contained records of David's investments in the bed-and-breakfast, garage, and three separate real estate holdings. He shuffled through notes, property tax bills, title reports, and operating statements of the two businesses. The properties, parcels of raw land for future development, had only title documents—no mortgages, no bank statements. Conclusion number one: David had plenty of cash. He'd had no need for institutional financing.

The second drawer held personal documents—a copy of his will, personal papers, birth certificate, passport, and most important, tax returns. Same conclusion. David's tax filings appeared too simple. Interest income from notes to Wesley and Jim, investment income in only four figures. What generated all of the pious asshole's cash?

Franky glanced at his watch—7:55—then he tackled the third drawer. Jackpot. All David's bank statements back to January 1967—two years should be enough. Franky didn't care about checks, only deposits, which cut down the required investigation time.

Then big trouble. Heat surged to Franky's face, coursed through his body. A pile of deposit slips, each one with a copy of the deposited check stapled to its back. Franky's worst nightmare. Monthly deposits of $15,000 from the Sigmond Young Moore Trust, an account held at First Boston Bank. The thought registered in Franky's overheated mind that the amount of the reward—$10,000—seemed pretty damn small. David's old man must be a cheap bastard.

The sound of tires crunching snow and gravel brought a frightening message. A car in the driveway. Franky dropped the papers, drawer wide open and wheeled. Piles of statements littered the floor. He sprinted out of the office.

Get out, the terrified voice in his head roared. Leave. Run. Down the corridor to the entry hall and the front door. The polished wood slab swung open as Franky reached for the handle. A woman and small child stood on the doorstep. The woman's questioning look transformed to fear.

Franky tucked his chin to hide his face, threw his forearms in front of his head. Nail her in the jaw, that'll distract her. He smashed into the woman, smacking her not in the jaw—he didn't reach high enough—but hard in her chest. Franky, surprised by the soft connection with her breasts, still slammed her to the ground. The little girl hung tight to her mother's leg, toppling over with her. The woman's screams choked off as Franky trampled over both figures. His only thought was a frenzied need to escape. The two couldn't identify him knocked flat on their backs.

Keeping his head down, Franky jumped into his Chevy. The key in the ignition saved him from losing shaky seconds. He fired up his rental and fishtailed down the driveway. A panicked glance in the rearview mirror gave a partial vision of the lady and child huddled together in a pile on the threshold of the door.

He knew he shouldn't leave witnesses, but there was no way in hell he had the balls to eliminate them. If they identified him, his problems would really begin, then his careful alibi would be put to a severe test. A charge of breaking and entering sure as hell would prevent him from getting out of town.

Great fucking morning.

Stupid. What had he accomplished? His efforts confirmed his fate—deep shit. For once the Bruise Brothers had been right. Franky flew down the country lane. His ridiculous, inadequate fallback plan: Get to class and pretend nothing had happened.

*   *   *

Matthew floundered in the deep snow at the end of the house. The sound of an engine and spinning tires confirmed his mistake. He'd waited too long to make his move. His position on the deck had been perfect for observation, but it had left him too far from the front driveway and Franky's car. And Matthew had put his .45 back in its holster as he watched Franky search. The little man's bolt out the door caught him unprepared.

Matthew peeked around the corner of the bedroom wing. Linda and Leslie struggled to a sitting position. Matthew pulled his head back and turned towards the game trail and his Cherokee. Neither of the two seemed injured. He had no time to help them now. He needed freedom to move.

Son of a bitch. Son of a bitch. Son of a bitch. The phrase set a cadence as Matthew trotted down the irregular path beside Fish Creek. He'd really screwed up. He kept his head low, didn't want Linda to see another person running from her house.

Franky had temporarily escaped, but he had no place to hide. Matthew had to get to Teton Village before Franky met up with the class and disappeared on the mountain. If Franky didn't show up for class, call the sheriff and let him track the bastard down.

He could have ended the whole drama by waiting for Franky at the front door. He was furious with himself as he moved to the Jeep, pulling his outer gloves back on. Out of the jungle, Matthew wasn't worth a damn.

Movement jerked him to a stop. Damn! Good thing he'd kept low. New action in the driveway. Ten feet from his car, he spied two large men moving with menacing speed into the yard. One held a shotgun.

He whirled and struggled back to the house. Matthew wouldn't have recognized the two even if he'd been closer. But he sensed who they were—the strangers from Hansen Street headed for another execution. This time he had to move fast. He extended his stride, landing in his own random footprints or animal tracks. He powered down the game trail.

The men walked purposefully, now thirty feet from the empty doorway. Linda must have gone inside. Matthew had fifty yards to get to the deck. He peeled off his outer gloves again and dropped them in the snow. Fingers fumbled for the .45. He could fire a desperation shot. Get their attention. But he didn't like the odds—two to one and undergunned. They'd leave three dead bodies instead of two. No, he had to get close enough to have at least the chance at taking them out.

He reached the corner as the hit men made it to the door. Only seconds and he no longer had visual contact with his targets. They would waste no time on their mission. He found himself in battle-mode.

Matthew knew seconds could last forever. But did he have enough seconds? He focused on his breathing, ragged from the dash to the house. Every sensation connected pure and clear. A matrix of options, variables, angles and odds flashed by as he jumped onto the wooden deck. A glass-paneled French door beckoned at the end of the walkway.

Seven running steps away. No time for a plan. Attack and react.

Six steps. He pulled his knit ski cap down over his head, now a face-mask covering his exposed skin. Jim had built this house strong and solid. Matthew needed leverage, speed and strength.

Five. The .45 out, safety off, both hands around the thick butt.

Four. An anguished cry sliced through the walls of the closed-up house. A glimpse through a window. Two men with Linda and Leslie on the far side of the kitchen.

Three steps. Can't be late. Not again. Not this time. Please, God. The plea sounded strange as it flashed across his mind.

Two. Matthew cocked his pistol, checked his headlong sprint. Gathered himself. Needed height at the other side. His body coiled for added power and thrust.

The French door disintegrated into a thick cloud of shattered glass fragments and wood slivers, the solid mist like a Hoback headshot in deep powder. The men had their weapons aimed and pointed at the defenseless mother and daughter. They swiveled at the crash. Matthew saw the flash from the shotgun, felt the whizzing pellets around his body as he squeezed off the automatic shots—loud, jerking explosions.

He floated in the air firing all seven rounds before losing altitude and crashing to the floor. The large planter divider blocked his view, but shielded his body from the other room.

He slid, flipped around and dove back headlong through the debris of the shattered door to the end of the long wooden divider. He dropped the .45 as he scraped across the floor. Yanked out the .38, poised to pump out more shots as the crumpled forms of the two killers came into view.

Matthew fired off two bullets into the bulky bodies before he realized they weren't moving. He sprung to his feet, .38 in both hands. He edged closer to the men. The kitchen glistened with blood, gore, smashed appliances and kitchenware. The .45 had its expected effect.

Matthew stood there, twitching, fired up, ready to go, not prepared for the absolute silence. Then Linda started a hysterical howl. The daughter followed with her own high-pitched shriek.

He brushed the remnants of the shattered door off his clothes and gloved hands. The screams of the woman and girl became disconcerting. The danger was over. Why didn't they calm down? He moved towards them. The volume of their cries increased. They held each other in a helpless huddle against the wall. Matthew realized he still wore the facemask. He snatched it off and dropped the .38 into his vest pocket.

Linda's cries changed their tone from terror to a sobbing, tearful moan as she recognized Matthew. He went over to her. She hung onto him with one arm, still gripping her little girl with the other.

What the hell should he do now? He had to catch up with Franky. Didn't want the cops in his face trying to figure out what happened here. But he couldn't just walk out the door with two dead bodies on the floor. He couldn't expect Linda to sit quiet in this mess waiting for Matthew's okay to call the sheriff.

"Don't leave," Linda begged.

A strange absence of feeling overcame Matthew. Linda and Leslie were no different from thousands of Vietnamese civilian victims. He glanced at the broken door to the deck, an exit he desperately wanted to take.

"I'll drive you to the Grand View," Matthew said. "We'll take your car, but we've got to get going. Now. I've got some unfinished business. So does David."

* * *

Matthew dodged the drainage ditch at the entrance to the Grand View. Linda's new Cherokee broke into a four-wheel drift. The condensed ridge of snow thrown up by the snowplows arrested the slide. Linda and Leslie hung to each other in the back seat, whimpering. He had to get rid of them fast or forget any hope of catching up to Franky. The new Jeep rocketed recklessly into the parking lot of the lodge.

Energy pumped from a bottomless supply, his current condition no different from battle-stoked adrenaline. Matthew felt fully functional and alert, although he hadn't slept a total of eight solid hours during the last three nights. And the massive shoulder bruise earned during his crash landing on David's dining room floor registered only in the recesses of his mind.

But the unnatural sources of energy came with a downside. The most debilitating feature—nervous apprehension. Matthew had planned to grab Franky at David's with incriminating evidence of the mobster's complicity stuffed in his pockets. But Franky had panicked. His empty-handed flight left the "proof" scattered in David's office. And now Franky was on the loose. What if he had headed straight out of town? Had an escape route planned? Matthew prayed—why the hell did he even think thoughts like that?—for just a few minutes alone with Franky.

Matthew helped the two traumatized victims out of the Jeep and led them to his cabin. Cody made his riotous rush, then stopped short. Must have sensed Linda's and Leslie's crippled emotional state, for he licked the little girl's hand.

Matthew sprinted the few steps to the kitchen. Thankfully, Julia was still busy cleaning the breakfast dishes. He gave a brief version of what had occurred at David's and the condition of the two disturbed witnesses. For once, Julia's dispassionate character came in handy. She hurried, as much as Julia could hurry, out to Matthew's cabin. He jumped into Linda's Jeep.

Matthew reached the Village, swerving into the bus loading zone. He ran for the Tram and took the metal stairs three at a time. He bulled his way through the line of skiers in the Tram's pipe matrix.

"TJ, you seen Franky?" Matthew gasped.

"Sure," TJ said, his usual smile plastered on his face. "He took the Box with Kurt's class a couple of minutes ago."

"Shit."

Now what? He considered his alternatives. He should call the sheriff, but that move would sure as hell take Matthew out of the action. He had to get to Franky first. No way to track him on the hill, especially with the thick cloud cover. How could he locate Franky's car in the mass of rental vehicles filling the parking lot? Whatever happened to the empty days of January at Jackson Hole?

Best thing to do would be to sit tight at the bottom of the mountain. Somehow he'd find the patience to wait. Now, no burning desire to kill. He just wanted to make the prick talk. And he hoped the little coward would resist just enough to require a small portion of persuasion.

SIXTY-TWO

The Box began its ascent. Franky found himself wedged into a corner. Thick clouds swallowed the tram car. Great. No goddamn visibility. His classmates chattered away, ignoring the dense, gray blanket wrapping around the Tram. Why the hell head up into these miserable conditions? Jesus, the last thing he wanted to do was go skiing.

The weather had further deteriorated at the top. Franky fumbled with his bindings and safety straps. Not exactly the desired conditions to test new skills. Maybe they'd take off without him. He could take the well-marked trail all the way down; hang out in the cafeteria or the Moose until lunch. Pretend he'd lost them in the whiteout. No pretend about it. Only Kurt remained visible a few feet away.

"Franky, move it," Kurt hollered.

"Fuck you," Franky whispered under his breath.

The class must have taken off with Hans. Franky couldn't see any of them. Only Kurt, smacking his gloved hands together for warmth.

"Let's go, boy." The instructor seemed disgustingly cheerful. "The class'll be waiting at the top of Laramie Bowl. There's a gnarly chute I've been saving for the final exam."

Franky could stall no longer. Kurt pushed off; making slow, rounded turns in the flat light. Franky banged over unseen ridges and moguls, his technique reduced to a modified snowplow for stability. Franky made a series of turns. Kurt disappeared only ten feet ahead. But, as Franky stumbled down what he assumed to be the east side of Rendezvous Bowl, Kurt's form kept reemerging from the murky mist.

This was taking forever. Franky struggled to keep up with the instructor. Where the hell was the goddamn class? Why not make a right turn and lose Kurt with a traverse, as far as possible, across the bowl? But he now had no clue where he was on the vast mountain. Blinded like this, he could crash into a friggn' tree.

Franky caught up to the instructor for what seemed like the hundredth time. He worked ten times harder unable to distinguish a goddamn thing. Being bounced and thrown off balance required continuous extra effort. He reached exhaustion.

"Where the hell are we?" Franky whined. Wind whipped sheets of loose powder against his face, compounding both his misery and inability to see.

"We're here, Franky." Kurt pointed to an indistinct, narrow ledge of hard snow. "The run starts right around the shoulder of those rocks. The class should be waiting where the hill opens up."

Franky didn't like the looks of the skinny trail. Where was the opening into a chute or any possible spot where the rest of the class could be gathered?

"Forget it," Franky said. "I ain't going down there. I can't see shit."

"Goddamn it, Franky." Raw fury exploded from Kurt.

Franky was taken aback. The instructor had never, not once, either expressed a single syllable of foul language or lost his cool. And there had been many appropriate opportunities for both.

"I've worked with you, babied you, and covered your ass for weeks," Kurt continued, his frustration rising above the howling wind. "You don't want to finish up with the class? Fine. I'm done trying to help you out."

What the hell was the problem? Franky skied just as well as any of the other jerks in the class. And who cared if he didn't?

"Okay, man, take it easy."

Franky inched forward, Kurt behind him. The path of snow angled down a slight but measurable descent. He picked up momentum. His skis slid smoothly along what appeared more of a ledge than a ski run. Then Franky's skis ran out of snow. Only a sliver of space. The tight shelf faded into a rock wall. Franky felt the edges of his metal skis grind against solid stone. He made frantic grabs at the small, sharp ridges jutting from the cliff face.

What the fuck was going on? He couldn't go back. He flattened against the unforgiving surface, willing his body to stick against the sheer rock, to defy gravity. He couldn't hold on. A panicked look down showed nothing but an empty vortex of swirling gray air.

"Kurt," he screamed.

Knife-like edges of granite sliced through his gloves. The edges of his skis scraped, then slipped off the last small, invisible outcropping. He was going to fall. How far? He'd get banged up pretty good. Shit, he could die.

"Kurt!"

"What's the problem, Franky? Having a little trouble figuring what's going on? Sharp little mobster like you should have put the pieces together."

Franky turned his head back the way he'd come. His face pushed hard against the rock, gouged and bleeding from the rough surface. Franky glimpsed Kurt through the gloom, fear and pain. And then the horrifying realization. This was the man he'd been searching for.

"Gives me great pleasure to hand you over to the White Dragon." The instructor's voice came out of the mist. "At least you'll be buried in one piece. They never found my father's body."

"You don't understand," Franky screamed. "It wasn't personal. It was . . ."

Then Franky lost his grip. Wait. This couldn't be happening. Deadly spurs of the cliff tore at his flailing arms, legs and torso. He was going to die. His skis smacked a protruding band of rock. The jolt forced Franky's upper body to somersault over his feet. Franky free-fell into the yawning void. Terror and agony swallowed him.

SIXTY-THREE

Matthew camped between two cars in the first row of the parking lot. Tense pressure in his gut returned him to the jungle, where he'd spent hours crouched in ambush. He visualized the thick, oppressive, steaming atmosphere of Southeast Asia. The uncomfortable memories distracted him from the bone-chilling cold of the packed ice and snow in the lot. The dominant view of the Clock Tower stood as a constant reminder of the time. Minutes moved like sap down the trunk of a winter maple.

Then Kurt appeared, leading his charges to lunch. Matthew's heartbeat surged. Moment of truth, Franky. Matthew checked his gear—pistols loaded, knife in place. Seven skiers followed Kurt up the stairs to the second-story restaurant. But where was Franky?

Hans's group showed up a moment later. Sarah and her entourage. Still no Franky. Matthew's nerves stretched to the limit. If Franky didn't show, Matthew would have to notify Sheriff Olsen. He'd have to face not just the mess at David's, but also answer questions like why he'd waited so long to tell the authorities. But Franky had gone up the mountain, and Matthew still wanted first crack at the punk.

Of course the little killer could have evaded Matthew if he'd known he had been followed. That was it. Matthew ran up to the tram line, empty during lunch. Faithful TJ still stood on duty.

"TJ," Matthew said, "did Franky make any more trips up the Tram?"

"Nope. The class made only one run so far today."

"If you see Franky, get your ass over to me at the Alpen Haus."

"Man," TJ said, eyes open wider than usual. "I'm in charge here."

"Franky's responsible for David's murder." That would get TJ's cooperation. "Find me, TJ."

Matthew hurried down the tram platform's steps. He made his way up the stairs to the second floor and the door of the restaurant. He looked through the large glass window. Kurt and the class—still without Franky—gathered in a far corner.

Eric, one of the instructor's from Pepi's militia, moved past Matthew with two older students in tow.

"Eric," Matthew said, stopping the tall Austrian. "I've got to talk to Kurt. It's an emergency. I don't want anybody in his class to see me." Especially Sarah. Not the time nor place to deal with her yet. "Tell him I'm here at the door."

Eric hesitated, then agreed, entered, and worked his way across the crowded dinning room to Kurt. He whispered in the instructor's ear. Kurt nodded, stood up and excused himself, never looking towards Matthew. He traced Eric's route back to the front door and porch where Matthew waited.

"What's up?" Kurt asked.

He drew Matthew down the stairs and over to a grove of pines behind the Ski School hut. Why was Kurt heading for the trees?

"Where's Franky?"

"We lost him on the mountain."

An edginess in Kurt's tone, an abruptness in his movements set off alarms within Matthew.

"What the hell do you mean, lost him on the mountain?"

Matthew grabbed Kurt's shoulder. The instructor looked at Matthew's hand, clutching the material of his parka. The cold expression on Kurt's face registered despite Matthew's anxiety. Matthew released his grip.

"He's in your class." Matthew tried to control the desperation in his voice. "How could you lose him?"

"Conditions suck," Kurt said. "Visibility ten feet or less. One minute he's right behind me, then he disappeared."

"TJ never saw him going up the Tram again," Matthew said. "You guys only made one tram run all morning?"

"The class took its final. One at a time. We critiqued each other," Kurt said. "Plus, we waited for Franky, first at the top of Laramie Bowl, then later, on the trail above the Colter Ridges."

Something didn't connect. Matthew's mind flew from one possibility to another. Matthew remembered their first meeting, the layers of history etched onto Kurt's strange face. Was he helping Franky? Matthew was out of time. How long before he'd have to call the sheriff? He focused his attention on Kurt.

"Somehow that little prick got by me," Matthew said.

"Got by you?"

Kurt seemed attentive, acting strange, inconsistent with his usual calm, collected demeanor. Still, he was the last one to see Franky. Matthew had nothing to lose.

"Franky had something to do with David's murder," Matthew said. "I think he's connected to the mob. He brought a couple of hit men to town to do his dirty work."

"Those are mighty inflammatory charges," Kurt said, but he refused to meet Matthew's eyes. "What do the cops think?"

"They don't think very well. Franky's scheduled to leave Jackson Hole tomorrow. I saw him break into David's this morning and search his office. I want to know what he was up to."

"I'll bet," the instructor said. "Why do you think Franky wanted to kill David?"

"I don't know who Franky thought David was." Matthew's frustration grew. "I think he made a very bad mistake. Now all I can do is call Olsen and let that incompetent idiot put together a search. And he couldn't find a moose in the middle of the Cowboy Bar."

"You're sure Franky had David murdered?"

Contrary to his statement, Kurt's expression held no question. A sharp stab of insight prodded Matthew. Neither David nor Kurt had ever shared much of their past. Of course, Matthew hadn't been too forthcoming either. But maybe for different reasons.

"You know, I'm sorry about David." Kurt's eyes locked on his. "I never put two and two together."

"What do you mean?"

Kurt's irregular features reminded Matthew of David, only their noses differed, David's thick and crooked, Kurt's weirdly bobbed. Kurt and David even had the same color hair now that Kurt's had grown out from his military buzz cut. Same height and slight stature. Both in their middle thirties.

"Franky's not coming down off the mountain," Kurt said in a solemn tone, eyes lifeless. "Not until the snow melts. Been swallowed by the Dragon."

A whirl of questions gained substance and clarity. Matthew had a prescient sense of what Kurt would say next.

"Franky came to Jackson Hole looking for me," Kurt explained.

Matthew was stunned. Did Kurt know the mob suspected David? Had he let David take the hit? Had David died at the hands of random fate or had Kurt set him up? Too many questions, only one fact apparent: Kurt was dangerous.

"Why did Franky come looking for you?"

"You don't need to know," Kurt said.

White heat flared through Matthew. His body tightened, fists clenched in his thick gloves. His friend had been innocent of any involvement with Franky or the mob. Yet David had been murdered, and Kurt, this mysterious stranger, had been spared. Maybe Kurt had a hell of a lot more responsibility than he admitted.

"The Feds alerted me to his arrival days before he landed. Offered to move me. I told them I liked it here. Then they suggested I at least split for a couple of months." Kurt chuckled, the nasty sound appropriate in the gray of the day. "Said no again. February and March are my favorite months here. I had confidence in my cover. Had surgery on my face. Even cut my hair off the day Franky got to town, just in case. Seemed to work pretty good. Except for poor David."

"David's dead," Matthew said. "You're alive. You knew who Franky was and why he landed in Jackson Hole. You better explain. You'd better prove to me that you had nothing to do with David's death. Kurt, if you're involved, I'm taking you down."

"Look, Matthew." Kurt's voice turned conciliatory. He took a step backwards, body language confirming a man looking for a way out. "Knowing who I am and what I've done will put you in unnecessary jeopardy."

"Jeopardy is the least of my problems. Talk."

A strange look came over the instructor's troubled features. An unexpected sadness softened his face. He shuddered.

"The story's complicated." Kurt seemed deflated. "My father owned a medium-sized construction company on the Lower East Side of New

York. He survived by picking up the legitimate leftovers from D and F Construction, one of the Fiorini family's business fronts. He provided the real work, actual project building. He played the game, kissed the Fiorinis' asses and prospered."

Matthew watched Kurt's eyes, searching for lies or deceit. He stayed alert, unwilling to accept the story as it unfolded, unable to believe David's death a trivial quirk of fate—wrong place, wrong time.

"Dad's business grew. He took on more and more large jobs. About five years ago, Franky began running D and F. Franky changed the construction company from primarily a front to a real business. The family used D and F to wash money from their illegal operations. Bigger the company got, the more cash they could clean. The business side got very profitable, thanks to Franky's increased use of stolen material and equipment, sweetheart deals with the unions, building department bribes, you name it."

A chill worked its way into Matthew's system. Kurt's prom nose turned white from the cold. His eyes, usually lacking in warmth, burned with a brightness testifying truth.

"Franky started buying other construction companies. Buying's the wrong term. He stole honest operations. Paid chicken-shit prices. Anyone who argued either disappeared or got nothing. They ripped off my old man. He got pissed, but continued to play along. Franky used Dad's expertise. Gave him more responsibility and more space. Dad used the opening to gather evidence of bribery, theft and tax evasion against D and F. Mr. Fiorini was President, Franky VP."

Matthew smelled the ending. But, had Kurt known about David's mistaken identity?

"My old man collected a stack of documentation. When he had what he considered enough to nail D and F and, hopefully, everyone involved, he brought me into his confidence. I was managing a lodge in Stowe, Vermont. Dad turned my life upside down. I hadn't given a damn what the mob did until a week after my father had slipped me a duplicate package of his information. Had told me to hang onto it in case something happened to him. Well, the bastards must have discovered his plan. My old man disappeared. Two weeks later one of his construction crews found a hand in a pile of building materials on a job site. The police identified Dad's fingerprints."

Kurt's eyes lost their fire, his voice flattened.

"One hand. That's it. One hand was all the fucking Fiorinis wanted found. I turned over the evidence my father had given me. The Feds used it to nail the old man. There wasn't enough proof to indict Franky or his brothers. Seemed like plenty to me, but the family's lawyers did a number on justice. I had to testify and then split. Forever. The government's got this new program for stashing vulnerable witnesses. I became one of their first customers. I hit Jackson Hole after plastic surgery in December of '66."

The wind died down. Visibility improved, but the lack of clouds allowed frigid air to fill the void. Kurt swung his arms, shuffled his feet to stay warm. Matthew resisted the temptation to swing at Kurt's head.

"I swear," Kurt said, "I didn't think Franky was dumb enough to suspect David. I knew they didn't like each other, but . . . I gotta get back to the class."

"Wait."

"As I said." Kurt swiveled his gaze to Matthew. "You won't have to kill Franky. You're a soldier, a warrior. You can kill, but you're not a killer."

"Really?" If not a killer, what was he?

"I know." A melancholy tone crept into Kurt's voice. "I've become a killer."

Matthew let Kurt move around the small hut. Emotions flowed— anger, relief, sadness—but he felt no more sympathy for Kurt than for the hit men on the floor of David's home.

SIXTY-FOUR

Kurt disappeared around the edge of the Ski School hut. Matthew paused. No hurry now. He knew the craziness that awaited at David's once he called the good sheriff. His minions would be in a frenzy, a flock of frantic chickens. Might also be a couple of FBI agents, if Kurt's story was to be believed.

Did he believe the instructor? Mostly. Nothing changed the worthlessness of David's death, as pointless as the mangled bodies of his nightmares. And Franky's body would be found when the snow melted. About the same time as Jim. At least they knew Jungle Jim's temporary grave sat at the bottom of Rock Springs Bowl. Only Kurt knew where Franky rested. And who except Matthew would ever know what Kurt had done?

The day's chill poked at Matthew, no longer protected by free-flowing adrenaline. A disconcerting tug of logic wormed into his mind. Maybe he'd follow Kurt's father's lead: Write down what he knew about Franky and Kurt, notarize the statement, and stash it in a safe deposit box. He slow-paced toward the Moose and the pay phone, smacking his gloved hands in a fast-rock rhythm.

He'd give the cops an hour or two to rattle around before he drove to David's home. Wesley would be over there, cars to tow. He'd overlook his friend's confusion at Dornan's. He loved the man and Wesley was a gifted healer. Matthew wouldn't have made the progress he had without him. But the Indian had trouble letting go of his patients. Wesley was like a wife. Matthew would have to take the good with the bad.

And poor Sarah. That lady had been slammed. Well, he knew a thing or two about getting the crap kicked out of you. He wanted to help work her through her emotional conflicts. Hell, he wanted her, period.

The Steep Class would soon be over. Pure, frigid air bit deep. Skiers, equipment clacking, swirled around him. Matthew glanced at the Clock Tower. 1:15. Blue skies and no crows.